“KEPTI[illegible] HY ARE YOU AND DR. McCOY PART OF THIS OPERATION?” CHEKOV ASKED.

McCoy and Spock looked to Admiral Drake.

Drake looked uncomfortable. “This is an extremely difficult situation for me,” he said. “I have been conducting an internal investigation. A very discreet one. Attempting to ascertain the sympathies of various Starfleet officers in sensitive positions. Looking for at least one individual who is unquestionably connected to the conspiracy within Starfleet to start a war with the Klingon Empire.”

“And have you found someone?” Uhura asked.

Drake nodded gravely. “I have.”

Chekov couldn't stand the suspense. “Vell, who is it?”

Drake's answer struck Chekov like lightning.

“James T. Kirk,” the admiral said.

Books by William Shatner

TekWar
TekLords
TekLab
Tek Vengeance
Tek Secret
Tek Power
Tek Money
Believe *(with Michael Tobias)*
Star Trek Memories
Star Trek Movie Memories
The Ashes of Eden*
Man o' War
The Return*

*Published by POCKET BOOKS

STAR TREK®

THE ASHES OF EDEN

WILLIAM SHATNER

POCKET BOOKS
New York London Toronto Sydney Tokyo Singapore

POCKET BOOKS, a division of Simon & Schuster Inc.
1230 Avenue of the Americas, New York, NY 10020

This book is published by Pocket Books, a division of Simon & Schuster Inc., under exclusive license from Paramount Pictures.

ISBN: 0-671-52036-9

First Pocket Books paperback printing March 1996

10 9 8 7 6 5 4 3 2 1

Printed in the U.S.A.

So delicate—that's her.
So dignified—that's him.
Handsome, winsome, graceful—that's them.

Judy and Gar Reeves-Stevens

and

An inspiration to my perspiration,
My muse mused suffused.

ACKNOWLEDGMENTS

My thanks to these fine individuals
without whom this show would not have gone on:

Kevin Ryan
Richard Curtis
Carmen LaVia

STAR TREK®

THE ASHES OF EDEN

PROLOGUE

Seventy-eight years after history reported him dead, James T. Kirk's journey had come to an end.

He was going home.

For the final time.

On a mountain slope, far above the simple cairn of rocks that was Kirk's grave, a lone figure stood in meditative silence, a sentinel keeping faithful watch.

His elegant black robes shifted in the twilight breeze of Veridian III. Their intricate embroidery spelled out the timeless principles of logic in metallic threads and Vulcan script. Those principles shimmered in the dying light of sunset.

The sentinel's gaze remained fixed on the battered Starfleet emblem that rested on the grave. In his expression, there was no betrayal of emotion, until his meditations were at an end and proper decorum had been observed.

Then a single tear welled up in the corner of his eye.

Ambassador Spock didn't fight it.

That battle between his two halves—Vulcan and human—had been fought and won decades ago.

Three weeks before this day, Spock had never known of this planet's existence. Yet now he knew he would never be free of it.

For history now recorded that it was on this world that James T. Kirk had reappeared, only to die again.

Spock's second grieving for his friend was far, far worse than the first had ever been.

What logic could there be in that?

Far below Spock, the setting sun drew long shadows from the modest pile of rocks he watched over. In the air above those shadows, five points of light sparkled to life.

Spock looked on as the transporter beams resolved into five Starfleet officers.

One he knew—William Riker, late of the Starship Enterprise. *Elsewhere on this planet, that vessel's shattered wreckage was being dismantled and removed by a team of Starfleet engineers under Riker's command. In accordance with the Prime Directive, no trace of advanced technology could remain behind. Should the future inhabitants of Veridian III's sister planet land here, they would discover nothing. Not even Kirk's body.*

The four others with Riker formed the honor guard that would travel with Spock back to Earth, for Kirk's official interment. A hero's funeral.

For all that Kirk had meant to the Federation, that honor seemed trivial to Spock. Yet what more could be done to assuage the sorrow of those Kirk had touched when his spirit had fled?

Spock had passed through that last veil himself. But because of Kirk, he had returned.

"You would do the same for me," Kirk had told him, long ago on the summit of Mount Seleya, when Spock had been reborn.

Now the tear grew in Spock's eye because he knew he could not. Though against all logic, he desired nothing else.

At least, he knew, Kirk had not faced whatever lay beyond his moment of death unaware of its coming.

Spock knew his friend had confronted his fate and reconciled himself to it, in that time between Kirk's return from Khitomer and the launching of the new Enterprise *which had sealed his fate.*

Spock took comfort from that knowledge. He found it to be most logical.

On the horizon, Veridian set and the stars shone forth from the gathering dark. The day at last was done.

The honor guard waited at attention by the grave. If all proceeded according to schedule, at this moment, far overhead, a starship would be shifting orbits, preparing to lock her transporter on the remains beneath the stones.

There could be no Mount Seleya in Kirk's future. Logic, therefore, directed Spock to seek solace not in what might lie ahead, but in what had gone before.

The tear slipped down his cheek. Spock watched it fall to the dust of this world. Swallowed as if it had never existed.

Except in his memories.

So to his memories now he turned, to the final adventure and the revelations of those last days he had spent with his friend.

When the journey of James T. Kirk had been ending—

—but was not yet over . . .

ONE

☆

Kirk didn't look back to the past—he slammed into it running, diving, hitting the volcanic ash of Tycho IV shoulder first, rolling to cover by Ensign Galt behind a jagged boulder.

But the boulder hadn't been good cover for Galt. The ensign was dead. Skin blue-white. Body locked in a final contortion of pain.

Kirk faltered. He was twenty-four years old, a lieutenant three years out of the Academy. Ensign Galt had been only nineteen. On his first mission. He had looked up to Kirk, and Kirk hadn't protected him.

The communicator at Kirk's side chirped and reflexes took over, freeing him to act. He snapped it open.

"Kirk here."

"Where are those coordinates?"

It was Garrovick. Kirk's captain hadn't beamed back to the *Farragut* when he had had the chance, before the transporter coils had overloaded. He had stayed with the wounded. Waiting for the shuttlecraft. Still ten minutes away.

"Scanning now," Kirk said. He forced himself to his feet, exposing himself to whatever lay beyond the boulder. Whatever had attacked the *Farragut*. Whatever dwelt among the ashes of Tycho IV and was now picking off the *Farragut*'s crew, one by one.

Kirk held his bulky tricorder before him like a shield. His eyes darted from the readout to the surrounding terrain and back again. Tycho Prime was setting. The horizon blazed with the color of blood. But there were no readings.

"Captain, there's nothing out there!" Kirk's voice betrayed the tension he felt.

But the voice on the communicator remained calm. "Stay put and keep scanning, Lieutenant. You've got forward fire control till the main sensors are back in operation."

"Aye, sir," Kirk acknowledged. In standard orbit above him, the *Farragut*'s weapons were at his command. With no sensors to guide them, Kirk was now their targeting system. Somehow, the weight of that responsibility felt good.

A distant scream cut through the dusk, ending too abruptly. High-pitched. A woman.

Kirk held his position, heart hammering. He fought the urge to throw down his communicator and draw the laser pistol at his side. Garrovick had given him his orders, and there was nothing Kirk wouldn't do for his captain.

Garrovick was that kind of commander. That kind of man.

A figure ran for Kirk's boulder. It was nothing more than a red-tinged silhouette against the sunset. Kirk quickly checked his tricorder. The figure was human.

Androvar Drake.

The young lieutenant slid into position beside Kirk, out of breath, laser drawn. His short, bristle-cut blond hair was streaked with black volcanic ash. He glanced at Galt's body, but he showed no more reaction to it than a Vulcan might.

"That scream," Drake said, "it was Morgan."

Even as Kirk felt the shock twist through his chest, he saw the flicker of a smile on Drake's face. Faith Morgan was the *Farragut*'s weapons officer. For the last three months she had shared Kirk's quarters. As his lover.

Kirk wanted to grind Drake's smirk into the rocks of this place.

But he had his orders. Garrovick's orders. Starfleet orders. There was nothing more he could do for Faith Morgan, but the crew of the *Farragut* numbered four hundred. At least it *had,* when the ship had first entered this system.

Kirk waved his tricorder into the gloom. Still no readings. He felt angry tears sting his eyes, but he fought them back.

Before anything else, he was on duty.

Drake clicked through the power levels on his weapon, twisting the stubby barrel completely around to its highest setting.

Kirk reached out to stop him. "Lasers don't work on it." One of the sentries had managed to gasp that into her communicator before whatever it was had snuffed out her life.

"The creature can change its molecular form," Drake argued. "Maybe lasers can work on one form but not another."

Kirk rapidly changed the settings on his tricorder, scanned again, looking for a target. "Garrovick says *phasers* will do it." Phasers were the newest weapons in Starfleet's arsenal.

Drake gestured dismissively with his laser. "What does Garrovick know?"

Kirk slapped his communicator to his side, grabbed Drake by his collar, shoved him hard against the boulder. "He's the *captain,"* Kirk hissed. "He'll know how to get us out of this." As far as Kirk was concerned, that was what starship captains did. They were invincible. They had to be.

Drake looked amused by Kirk's emotional outburst. He smoothed his tunic where Kirk had crushed it. "He didn't do so well in orbit, did he?"

Kirk flipped open his communicator again, to keep his fist off Drake's jaw. Drake wasn't worth it. Kirk had found that out at Starfleet Academy. Their final after-class fight in the antigrav gym had cost Kirk two demerits. Kirk had won, barely. But the greater satisfaction had come when Kirk had edged out Drake by two percentiles and drawn first star duty in their class.

"Something caused a temporal shift in the sensor grid," Kirk said. It was the only explanation for how Garrovick had been taken by surprise.

Kirk had been on duty on the *Farragut's* bridge when it had happened. The sensor boards had lit up as the ship had been invaded by . . . something—a gas cloud, a creature? At the time there had been no way to be certain.

Garrovick had ordered shields to full strength. The creature responded by somehow vanishing from the sensors' sensitivity range. At the same time, an impossible temporal phase shift overloaded every key circuit in the *Farragut.* It might even have been a defensive move on the creature's part. But whatever had caused it, for a breathless hour it had seemed the ship might not be able to hold her orbit.

Garrovick had ordered the evacuation of all but a skeleton flight crew. Then he had saved the ship. Invincible.

But by then the creature had found the evacuation camp on the surface of Tycho IV. And it *was* a creature, there could be no doubt about that now. A creature that fed on the red blood cells of humanoid life-forms. Like Galt. And Faith. And all the others already cut down.

On the surface, the creature methodically probed their defenses. It overpowered their emergency forcefields. Withstood whatever the laser cannons could send into it. Enveloped everything with a sickly sweet smell—the smell of death on an already dying world.

Immediately, Garrovick had beamed down to the heart of the action, organizing the withdrawal of his crew. Fighting at their side.

Then, suddenly, halfway through the boarding process, the ship's transporters had stopped functioning. Too strained by the temporal overload and the first evacuation.

Garrovick had called down the shuttlecraft.

No one believed they would make it in time.

But Kirk never doubted that Garrovick would save them. Somehow.

He was the *captain.*

Something spiked on the tricorder's display.

Kirk fine-tuned the reading. Di-kironium. It meant nothing to him.

But then an unwelcome fragrance reached out to him. Too sweet, Overpowering.

"It's coming back . . ." Kirk said.

"Lieutenant!" Garrovick transmitted. "Where are those readings?"

Something moved out by the distant rocks.

No—not *moved—billowed.* Roiled forward against the scarlet sunset like a storm front from hell.

"Kirk?!" Garrovick repeated.

It was at this moment, in another time, another life, that Lieutenant Kirk froze. Faced with certain death, weighed down by the responsibility of his duty, he hesitated.

But not this time.

"Kirk to *Farragut!"* he shouted. "Target bearing thirty meters due west this location! All phaser banks *FIRE!"*

Instinctively Kirk charged Drake, forcing him down to cover as well. A heartbeat later, the heavens of Tycho IV were ripped open by twin lances of blue fire.

Kirk felt the ground shake as the eerie harmonics of phased energy tore apart the atoms of everything in its beam. He smelled burnt dust, heat, the tang of ozone released by atmospheric ionization.

The barrage ended.

Kirk peered past the edge of the boulder. A cloud of dust was lit from within by the glow of superheated rocks.

The creature was gone.

"We did it," Kirk exulted. He brought his communicator closer. "Captain Garrovick—we . . ."

A wispy tendril of white vapor twisted from the dust cloud like a tornado forming in reverse.

Kirk stopped talking.

The vapor stretched up from the ground, spinning faster, rising along the ionization trail left by the phaser beams.

Rising up to the *Farragut.*

"Dear God . . ." Kirk whispered.

He looked at Drake. Drake's eyes gleamed in the final trace of light from the sunset. His expression was unreadable.

"Kirk to *Farragut!* The creature is on an intercept course! Get out of there!"

Garrovick broke in on the transmission. *"Farragut!* Break orbit! Maximum warp! *Now!"*

The *Farragut's* science officer responded, her voice breaking up in static.

". . . shields down . . . coming in through . . . antimatter containment is . . ."

A new star blossomed directly overhead.

"Farragut?" Garrovick said. *"Farragut,* come in . . ."

Nothing. Not even static.

Kirk stared up at the flickering pinpoint of light. Two hundred crew. A Constitution-class starship. Reduced to one dying star among so many.

Now obscured by a slender coil of white vapor. Spiraling down from the heavens.

Coming back to claim them all.

Drake laughed beside Kirk. "Great instincts, Jimbo. See you in hell."

The descending cloud creature was almost on them. Kirk had run out of options. There was only one thing left to do.

"End program," he said.

Then the creature and Drake and Tycho IV dissolved into a holographic haze, back to the past where they belonged . . .

. . . and Kirk no longer did.

* * *

"Was the suit too heavy, sir?" The young Starfleet technician waited respectfully for Kirk's answer as Kirk slipped off the bulky encounter helmet he had worn during the simulation.

In the cavernous room in the subbasement of the Cochrane Physics Hall of Starfleet Academy, massive banks of machinery hummed. The unpainted, generic blocks and platforms that had recreated the rocky terrain of Tycho IV dutifully reset themselves into yellow-gridded walls.

Kirk's eyes ached where the visual input encoders had pressed against them. His back ached from the weight of the servo drivers that controlled the feedback web enclosing his body. The entire holoenvironment encounter rig *was* too heavy.

But Kirk wasn't going to be the one who complained about it.

He made a conscious effort to stand straighter, move his arms more quickly. He flashed a smile at the technician. "Felt fine," he said lightly. "Almost as if I were back in my old uniform."

The technician grinned, impressed. As if all he ever heard were complaints. He started disconnecting the feedback web.

"You know," the technician said as if Kirk were a familiar friend of his, "someday it should be possible to do away with the suit entirely. Use focused tractor beams. Microgravity control. Maybe even build some props with transporter matter replication."

Kirk groaned inwardly as he kept a patient smile on his face. In addition to its weight, the suit chafed in places he didn't want to rub with an audience around.

He let the technician babble on happily about the wondrous abilities of his gizmos and gadgets and the future of holographic simulations.

He hoped the technician would think the sweat streaming off his subject's forehead was the result of the encounter suit's skintight fit, and not the exertion that had left Kirk close to exhaustion. Or the pain in his shoulder not letting him forget the way he had hit the simulated ground and rolled behind the simulated boulder.

He thought it was too bad Starfleet engineers couldn't simulate the feeling of indestructibility he had had in his youth, when he could hit the real ground on a roll five times a day and never feel the consequences.

"Think of it," the technician continued with innocent enthusiasm. "Just walk into an empty room in your ordinary uniform and *zap!* Instantly you're surrounded by a holoenvironment so realistic you can't tell the difference between it and reality."

Kirk flexed his hands, remembering the weight of the old-fashioned tricorder he had carried during the simulation. The way the fabric around Drake's neck had compressed in his fist. All of it an illusion.

"Trust me. It's very realistic now," Kirk said. He meant it.

"So you can be sure that's what would have happened."

Kirk didn't understand. "What would have happened?"

"If you had fired at the cloud creature right away, instead of hesitating the way you really did."

Now Kirk understood. But he didn't want to talk about it. He hadn't thought about Faith Morgan in years. But he had never forgotten her. He would never forget any of them.

"You see, by not firing the phasers right away," the technician persisted, "the creature only attacked those crew members on the ground. The *Farragut* and everyone on her were safe. But if you *had* fired right away—based on the computer's reconstruction of the cloud creature's abilities, it would have returned to the *Farragut,* destroyed her, *then* finished off everyone else on the ground as well. So you did the right thing the first time round."

And Garrovick had died because of it, Kirk thought grimly. He changed the subject. "It should make for a wonderful training device."

The technician gave him a bewildered look. "Training? I guess. But how about for entertainment? The gaming possibilities alone are endless."

Kirk kicked off the heavy feedback boots that had made him feel as if he had crunched across volcanic soil. "You programmed all this for 'entertainment' purposes?" he asked.

The technician retained his puzzled expression as he retrieved Kirk's feedback boots, balancing the entire suit in an awkward position across his arms. "Sir, we've programmed almost *all* your early exploits into the system."

"*My* exploits?"

The technician nodded ardently. "This encounter with the cloud creature of Tycho IV, and your destruction of it eleven years later on stardate 3619.2. And stardate 3045.6—remember? Your encounter with the Metrons and hand-to-hand battle with the Gorn. And 3468.1—when you escaped from the alien on Pollux IV who claimed to be the Greek god Adonais. We've almost got them all, sir. More coming online each day."

Kirk felt rattled. He couldn't recall a single stardate from his first five-year mission on the *Enterprise* if his pension depended on it. "But why?"

The technician stared blankly at Kirk, as if he couldn't understand why the question had been asked. "Sir . . . you're a hero."

"Oh." *That again,* Kirk thought.

"Don't you feel that way, sir?"

Kirk hesitated. He didn't want to say the wrong thing. This young man had gone to a prodigious amount of effort to re-create an incident from Kirk's past in Starfleet's prototype holographic encounter suite. In incredible detail, as well. Even Kirk had forgotten the laser sidearms that used to be standard Starfleet issue.

He had, he admitted to himself, forgotten a great deal from those days.

He smiled at the technician, trying to soften the blow. "Those . . . 'exploits,' " he began.

"Yes, sir?"

"They were just my job," Kirk said simply. "A job I did a long time ago."

The technician regarded Kirk blankly for a moment, as if unsure how to respond.

"It was more than a job, sir. To us." With a nod he indicated his fellow technicians in the control room overlooking the encounter suite. Men and women, they were all the technician's age. Younger than Kirk could ever imagine having been. And all of them were lined up against the viewport, watching Kirk's every move. It was disconcerting to be under that close scrutiny.

Kirk could see the dawn of disillusionment in the young technician's eyes. "We'll never forget, sir."

With that, the young man turned and walked back to the control room.

Kirk held out his hand to stop him. He wanted to say something, anything, to erase the youth's disappointment.

But he didn't know how.

It wasn't the first time, either.

The problem was with expectations, Kirk knew. For all that it mattered to others, his past held little appeal for him. He had always looked toward the future, toward new challenges, not past accomplishments.

But his future was running out.

He was a starship captain without a starship. Unable to look back, unable to go forward. Trapped in the present. Pent up. Frustrated. Ready to go nova.

It was an intolerable state for James T. Kirk. And he knew he had to do something about it soon. Otherwise, he would have to give up. And giving up had never been an option for him.

He'd rather die first, and Kirk was not yet ready to face that final moment.

Though in time, he knew, even a starship captain must die.

TWO

No one knew who had built the Dark Range Platform.

The seemingly haphazard supports of the immense space station stretched out like demented spiders' webs. Coiled around a confusion of life-support spheres and cylinders installed by a dozen races over the platform's millennia of service.

Once, it might have been a transfer point for vast flotillas of starships. Some, perhaps, belonging to the Preservers themselves. It was that old.

But now it was a backwater refueling stop. A starting point for dreamers seeking fortune among the stars. A lair for the smugglers and cutthroats who would steal that fortune from them.

Alone, it drifted in the dark between the stars. At relative rest in the hinterlands of the Federation's frontier and the Klingon Empire's Old Regions. As telling testimony to the station's true worth, neither the Federation nor the Empire claimed it.

No one knew who had built Dark Range. What's more, no one cared.

But for Pavel Chekov on stardate 9854.1, it was the most

important thing in his life. Because the grime-covered walls of its access corridors might well be the last thing he would ever see.

The cold tip of the disruptor's emitter node dug deeper into Chekov's temple.

The leather-gloved hand tightened against his windpipe. It was impossible to breathe.

That was the point.

Kort, the one-eyed Klingon, breath reeking of bad *gagh,* leaned in closer, finger tightening on the trigger stud, counting down.

"*. . . hut . . . chorgh . . . soch . . .*"

In seven seconds, Chekov would be a cloud of disrupted subatomic particles. His only thought: *What would the captain do?*

"*. . . jav . . . vagh . . .*"

Chekov struggled uselessly against the Klingon's thickly muscled arm. "I vanted to get on with my life!" he gasped.

Kort stopped counting. Narrowed his one good eye at his captive. Infinitesimally lessened the tightness of his grip.

"That is why you *punched* an admiral?" Kort asked. His disbelief was evident. "Destroyed your career?" The deep ridges in the Klingon's heavy brow furrowed all the way down to the duranium plate that covered his useless eye socket.

"Vat career? Starfleet had nothing more to offer me." Chekov looked sideways along the barrel of the disruptor. Kort's breath made him want to gag. But he had the Klingon's attention as surely as the Klingon had his.

"Thirty-three years I had given them," Chekov continued. "And for vat? I vas still a commander—a *commander!* Always having to do vat the brass told me to do." The words came easily to Chekov now. He wasn't even aware of the disruptor's tip easing away from his temple. "'Readings, Mr. Chekov.' 'Run a sensor sveep, Mr. Chekov.' Alvays in someone else's shadow. Never a chance for *me.* To show vhat *I* could do."

Along the length of the disruptor's barrel, Chekov met Kort's icy one-eyed gaze. Held it. The weapon's ready light pulsed silently, fully charged.

"I vanted to let go of it. I didn't vant to be angry anymore."

At last, Kort pulled the weapon back. But still held its aim on Chekov's head. Still kept his hand on Chekov's throat. Water dripped somewhere. The slippery decks rumbled with the comings and goings of cargo shuttles from the nearby bays. Chekov counted heartbeats. Waiting.

Kort shot a glance across the shadowed corridor. To where the two Andorians held Uhura.

One delicate blue hand was clamped over Uhura's mouth. A ceremonial dagger precisely indented the skin under her jaw. The blade's silver sheen was marred by a pinprick of red blood. Human blood.

Kort nodded once.

Uhura tensed.

With great reluctance, the bulky Andorian in the fur vest took the dagger away. The slender Andorian in chain mail removed his hand from Uhura's face.

It was Uhura's turn to gasp for breath.

But still she couldn't move. The Andorians kept her pinned to the bulkhead.

"Is it true?" Kort asked Uhura.

Uhura's eyes darted to Chekov. Chekov saw the same thought hidden there. Knew what she was thinking.

"Don't look at *him!*" Kort shouted. His deep voice echoed along the twisting corridor of pipes and conduits. Was swallowed by the distant thrum of jury-rigged air purifiers and gravity generators.

Kort jabbed his disruptor back into Chekov's temple. "Is . . . it . . . true?" he repeated.

"Yes," Uhura said evenly. "For both of us."

Chekov counted ten heartbeats. An eternity.

Then Kort reholstered his weapon. Motioned to the Andorians to release Uhura.

Their antennae dipped in disappointment, but they did as they were told.

Kort grabbed Chekov by the shoulders. "So, even fabled Starfleet is no different than the Empire's navy. Step on a worm often enough, and even the lowliest will evolve wings!"

Chekov didn't bother trying to follow Kort's idiom. He only braced himself as the Klingon crushed him in a bear hug.

Ten more heartbeats passed. Chekov felt dizzy.

Kort released him. Gave him a pat on the cheek that was more an open-handed punch.

"They'll call you a traitor," Kort boomed.

Chekov rubbed the side of his face, trying to lessen the stinging. Unused to the stubble of beard that grew there. "They have called me vorse."

Kort looked at Uhura. "And you, the same."

Uhura flashed a savage smile. Chekov could see Kort's nostrils flare with interest.

"*I've* called *them* worse," Uhura said.

Kort reached inside his belt and pulled out two identity wafers.

"How unfortunate you didn't see the errors of Starfleet's ways a decade ago," the Klingon growled. He returned the wafers to Chekov and Uhura. "Then, by now, perhaps it would be the Empire gathering to gnaw at the Federation's bones."

Chekov slipped his forged identity wafer into a hidden pocket on his coat. For all the wafer had cost, it had been useless. Kort had been able to determine his and Uhura's true identities in less than ten hours—effortlessly discovering they both had left Starfleet under less than ideal circumstances six short months ago.

"I do not look upon vat ve are doing as gnawing the

Empire's bones," Chekov said. He adjusted the somber civilian clothes he wore. Uhura did the same.

Kort clamped an arm around Uhura's shoulder, drawing her near. "Of course, the law of the juggled." He managed to look almost wistful as he spoke. Not an easy task for a Klingon. "Eat or be dinner." He frowned at Chekov. "Yours is such an awkward language."

Chekov shrugged. "Vat happens now?"

Kort gave his new human friends a final painful squeeze and then released them roughly, causing both to stumble back into the Andorians.

"Now," Kort said, "we do what we came here to do. *Business!*"

He began to stride down the corridor, heading for Dark Range's habitat levels, his Andorians at his side. Kort's heavy, metal-shod boots clattered with each step. Chekov and Uhura took rapid double steps to keep up.

"Weapons-grade antimatter," Kort began, counting off his merchandise on his thick, hairy fingers. "Photon torpedoes—still in their crates. Disruptor cells. Warp cores." He suddenly stopped and spun around to leer at Uhura. "Dilithium crystals!"

"Vorthless," Chekov said.

Kort looked astounded.

"Ve can recrystallize them now."

Kort shook his shaggy mane in wonder. "Oh, brave new planet . . . how many times were our forces held back from dealing you a decisive blow because we had no dilithium?"

"Who cares?" Uhura interjected. "So far, all you've told us about is low-level matériel we could get from any two-credit smuggler. You told us you had access to *generals.*"

Kort grinned at Uhura. Chekov winced as he saw the twitching tail tip of a single *gagh* worm still caught between two of Kort's stained and yellow teeth.

"In your language, the Empire is having a going-out-of-business sale." Kort looked at Chekov. The grin vanished. "You also say: You get what you pay for."

"The people we represent are vell funded. If they vant veapons-grade antimatter, they can get it from their own contacts, direct from Starfleet."

Kort waited. Uhura didn't disappoint him.

"What we want is hardware," she said.

Kort gestured broadly, making a joke of Uhura's request. "But of course. A Bird-of-Prey? Maybe two?"

"No secondhand Romulan junk," Chekov snapped. "A cruiser."

"*K'tinga*-class," Uhura added. "Maybe two."

Kort's remaining eye widened.

"Of course," Chekov said coolly, "if that is beyond you . . ."

Kort grabbed Chekov's arm as if to keep him from walking away. "I had no idea," he said quickly. "When I found out your documents were forged . . . that you were Starfleet . . ."

"Ex-Starfleet," Uhura corrected.

"I thought this was, in your language, a stung."

"Sting," Chekov said.

"A cruiser?" Kort asked.

"Ve know there are generals who are . . . making them available."

Kort glowered. As if even a Klingon criminal had standards. As if somewhere beneath his avarice, his willingness to deal in the debris of his collapsing Empire, there still beat the heart of a patriot. Someone who still believed in his flag and his ruler.

Chekov wondered how much this transaction was really costing the Klingon. What price could there be on lost dreams?

But this was not the time for sentiment.

"Vith dilithium reserves so low," Chekov continued, "how much good does a powerless cruiser do the Empire, anyvay?"

Kort nodded. A serious expression clouded his dark face.

"Bones to be gnawed," he said. "With the Federation the vulture for once." He glanced at the Andorians. Chekov could sense that he had reached a decision.

"Cargo Bay Twelve," Kort briskly told Chekov. He held up two fingers. *"Cha' rep."*

"Two hours," Chekov agreed.

Kort nodded once to Uhura, then turned and clanked off down the corridor. His two Andorians hurried after him.

Uhura rubbed at the tiny scratch under her jaw. "Still think this is a good idea?" she asked.

"I enjoyed punching that admiral," Chekov answered with a shrug. "Besides, ve might end up vith a Klingon battle cruiser of our wery own."

Uhura put a hand on her hip and frowned at her co-conspirator. "And just what do you think you're going to do with a Klingon battle cruiser?"

Chekov smiled winningly. "A man can dream, can't he?"

Uhura shook her head and patted Chekov's cheek. "You keep dreaming, Pavel. That's what you're good at."

She glanced up and down the corridor. They were alone.

"Come on," she said. "We've got two hours to get our credits together."

But Chekov didn't move.

"What?" Uhura asked him.

"When Kort was getting ready to kill us . . . I saw vat you vere thinking. In your eyes."

Uhura waited.

"You vere thinking: Vat vould the keptin do now?"

She nodded, smiling. "The bluff worked, didn't it?"

"Da. But I vonder vat the keptin *is* doing now?"

Uhura pulled her cloak tighter around her. "If he's smart, he's trying to find an admiral of his own to punch."

Chekov was surprised. "And leave Starfleet?"

"And get on with his life," Uhura said. "Which is what we should do."

She started up the corridor then, not waiting for Chekov.

Chekov hung back for a moment, trying to think of Captain Kirk no longer being part of Starfleet.

It was easier to think of the Earth without the sun.

But still, after all that Kirk had accomplished in his career, what more could he want from Starfleet? What more could he expect?

A man could dream. But what dreams were left to a man who had already captured so many of them?

Chekov hurried along the corridor after Uhura.

He hoped never to live so long that he ran out of dreams.

He wished the same fate for his captain.

THREE

☆

Despite the best efforts of human mind and machine, it still rained without warning in San Francisco.

Kirk liked that.

Throughout the worlds of the Federation, Earth was hailed as some ethereal fairyland. Home of perfection. Free of want. Of need. Of disease. Of crime.

By the standards of the twentieth century, perhaps it was.

But every time some aspect of that perfect order broke down—even something as inconsequential as a late-summer thunderstorm arriving unannounced to thwart the Bureau of Weather Management—a part of Kirk rejoiced.

Who wanted to live in a perfect world?

He had seen too many of them in his voyages.

Perfection meant there were no more challenges.

It was as good a definition of death as Kirk could imagine.

He idly rocked the glass in his hand. Making the scotch swirl. The ice cubes clink. Blending with the soft patter of the raindrops on the window.

Spock could probably make a poem out of it, Kirk thought. The soft sounds of a sleeping city—San Francisco spread out below him, distant lights shimmering in the rain, fading away to nothing in the 3 A.M. mist. Now and then the slowly moving running lights of a flying car, or a shuttle, floated past like a firefly on an Iowa night.

But poems weren't Kirk's way.

He gulped a mouthful of scotch. Felt it burn his throat—ice cold and fire hot at the same time. That was his poetry. Sensation. Being alive. Imperfection in all its glory.

The gray clouds above flashed with inner lightning.

Kirk closed his eyes, waiting for the thunder to reach him. Dreading it.

Because it wasn't lightning. It wasn't thunder.

She was calling to him.

From up there.

Bound in spacedock. Awaiting the order that would turn her into scrap.

The thunder came. Rumbled past him. Made the window rattle.

Kirk saw the face of a horse he had cherished, lifetimes ago.

The look in the creature's eyes as it lay beyond the help of twenty-third-century veterinary science.

As Kirk's uncle had raised the short barrel of the laser rifle.

He couldn't remember how old he had been. Eight? Ten?

All he remembered was the horse's eye. Seeing in it the knowledge of the oblivion to come.

The horse had kicked feebly. Tried valiantly, heartbreakingly, one more time to stand. Knowing somehow that if it could just stand up one last time, then the man with the rifle would leave and everything would be as it was.

Tears streaming down his face, young Kirk, little Jimmy, had pulled on the horse's bridle, trying desperately to make it stand up. One last time.

But the horse couldn't stand. Jimmy's aunt pulled him gently away. He heard the soft pop of the laser. The last soft whisper of the horse as . . .

More lightning. More thunder.

The *Enterprise* called out to him. Beyond the clouds. Among the stars.

One last time.

Stand up.

The man with the rifle.

The knowledge of oblivion.

Alone . . .

"Come back to bed, Jim."

Kirk's eyes flew open. A flood of adrenaline shot through him. He hadn't heard Carol come up behind him. He had forgotten she was here.

He made himself smile before he turned around to face her.

It was her apartment, after all. Where he always returned.

His safe harbor. His spacedock.

Carol Marcus slipped a hand around Kirk's waist, snuggled under his arm, watched the city with him.

Kirk could see their reflections in the window. The smile became real. Starfleet's heroic starship captain and the Federation's best molecular biologist, nothing more than two middle-aged civilians in terry-cloth bathrobes. He wondered what the young virtual-reality technician from this afternoon would think.

Then, in a sudden flash of lightning, he saw himself and Carol as they had been when they were the technician's age. So full of dreams, of promise. As Spock would say, so full of *possibilities.*

But as quickly as the lightning faded, their youth fled once again.

Kirk sighed. His shoulder hurt from the holographic simulation this morning. He felt tired. He felt . . . old.

Carol hugged Kirk to her. "Thinking about the farm?"

Kirk shook his head. He had forgotten all about it, actually. The advocates handling his parents' estate were after him to decide what to do with the Kirk farm. His nephews had no plans to return to Earth. Kirk was the only family member left who might have an interest in maintaining it. But the demands of the paperwork associated with the decision had been incessant. Upsetting. Pushing any desire to deal with it out of his mind.

"They don't need a decision till the end of the month," Kirk said.

They stood together in silence for a minute more. Far away, the air-traffic warning lights on the Golden Gate Bridge pulsed weakly through the mist.

Carol nuzzled his shoulder. His bad one. Kirk winced.

"It's all right," Carol said. "Really."

Of all the troubles he faced in his cluttered, planetbound life, Kirk knew what she meant. He didn't want to discuss it. He drew away from her. Swallowed the rest of his scotch.

Carol misunderstood his action. His silence.

"It happens, Jim. To every man. Sooner or later."

Kirk could feel his cheeks burn. He knew his anger wasn't right, but it didn't change the way he felt.

He wasn't every man. He couldn't be.

"Jim, I don't know what we are to each other after all these years. More than friends. Certainly—" Carol reached out to turn his face to hers. "—certainly lovers. But I do know we've been through too much together for you to stand there . . . sulking."

"I am not sulking."

Carol's hand fell away from his face.

"Getting up in the middle of the night to drink scotch and stare out at the rain isn't my idea of having a good time."

"I like scotch. And rain. Especially when it isn't programmed."

Carol shook her head. Moved closer. "Come back to bed," she whispered.

She moved her hand inside his robe, pushed against the tie that held it in place, let it fall open.

"We'll try again." She kissed his neck. "As many times as it takes."

She took him in her hand.

But all was as it was before.

The fire had fled as surely as their youth.

Only ashes remained.

"Carol, don't." Kirk pulled away, tied up his robe. He turned away from her tears, unable to deal with them.

"Why do you keep doing this to me? To us?" she asked, voice breaking. "Why do you keep coming back?"

Kirk stared out at the storm. He had already asked those questions of himself. He had no answer.

"What do you want?" Carol asked—*demanded.*

But Kirk was too cold, too tired, too *old* to answer.

Lightning flashed. The thunder would come.

She cried out to him.

One last time . . .

"What do you want, Jim?"

The thunder arrived, enveloped him. He tensed. Waiting.

But it carried him nowhere.

"I don't know," Kirk said. A voice of defeat. He faltered as he heard it come from him, but could do nothing to temper it. "Not anymore."

Carol went back to her bedroom. Closed the door.

Kirk poured another scotch. Turned a chair so it faced toward the window.

The rain lasted all night.

Tears he couldn't shed.

FOUR

☆

Chekov shivered. The cavernous Dark Range cargo bay was that cold.

There was no forcefield to hold in atmospheric pressure and heat. Only large metal doors—uninsulated, obviously—a hundred meters across. All the air would have to be pumped out of the hold before those doors could be opened.

There were no tractor beam nodes in the splotched and flaking walls, either. Four shuttles were docked here—each older and bearing more hull patches than the next. Each would have to maneuver by station-keeping rockets or impulse power to leave under manual control. One misstep, and a bulkhead could be punctured, a door thrown out of alignment.

Chekov studied the welded panels and mismatched, frost-covered sheets of hull metal lining the hold. It appeared such missteps were not infrequent.

Disturbingly primitive, he decided. But then he remembered how old the Dark Range was. It was surprising that anything aboard it still worked at all.

Beside him, by a stack of modular cargo crates marked with Romulan warning symbols, Uhura pulled her collar up around her neck. For a moment, her teeth chattered. Her breath hung before her. One of the few working overhead lights caught it perfectly, a pale vapor ghost glowing against the hold's deep shadows.

But their "banker" showed no sign of the cold. The

compact, young human woman stood three meters away with her flight jacket open. As if ten degrees below freezing were her body's natural setpoint.

She noticed Chekov looking at her, returned his gaze. Attractive, Chekov thought. Finely drawn features. Dark complexion. A strong intelligence in her eyes. But a mouth that was not used to smiling.

As for her hair, that was hidden. She wore a tight flight hood favored by pilots who spent too much time in microgravity but didn't wish to shave their scalps.

By now the banker's expression had become one of challenge. Chekov had looked at her too long.

"Is there something you want?" she asked.

Her code name was *Jade*—the only designation Chekov and Uhura had been given. But Uhura had dubbed the woman "the banker" early on. An old Earth term, Uhura claimed. From the days when Earth had relied on money for financial transactions.

Chekov thought the term fitting. This far out on the frontier, where the Federation's massively complex economy had yet to be established, archaic institutions like banks had reason for existing.

In Jade's datacase were computer wafers holding enough exchange credits to buy a small planet. To say nothing of a Klingon battle fleet or two.

Chekov and Uhura had come through with their part of the bargain. Now it remained to be seen if their Klingon smuggler would come through with his.

And Kort was late.

Chekov looked at the time readout on his chronograph—a small pocket model with a few built-in sensor functions—the closest the civilian market could get to a decent tricorder out here. "Perhaps he is not going to show."

Jade's dark eyes burned into him. "He'll show," she said. "Even if he doesn't have access to battle cruisers, he won't be able to resist making a grab for this." She held up her datacase.

"I hadn't thought of that," Chekov muttered softly to Uhura.

"Maybe you're not cut out to be a criminal," Uhura said.

"Did *you* think of it?" Chekov asked indignantly. He felt very much the criminal type, given all he had been through in the past six months since leaving Starfleet.

Uhura answered by pulling her cloak open long enough for Chekov to see the full-sized phaser II pistol attached to her belt.

Chekov was surprised. "That's illegal," he hissed. Not to mention unsafe.

But Uhura rolled her eyes. "So's buying Klingon military hardware."

Chekov had left his own phaser—a palm-sized type I—in his quarters. With Kort's insistence on searching them at every meeting, it was the simplest thing to do. But he was regretting the decision.

Jade raised her hand and motioned to Chekov and Uhura to be silent.

Uhura heard it first. A communications expert's trained ears. As exceptional as any Vulcan's.

"Footsteps," she whispered to Chekov.

Chekov didn't hear them. He hadn't even heard a personnel door open into the hold. So how could there be anyone else here?

Unless someone had set up an ambush.

"Reach for the *Hovmey,*" Kort thundered from behind him. "And turn around. Slowly."

Chekov sighed. He was getting tired of this. Six months.

He turned with his hands held high. Uhura did the same beside him.

Kort and his two Andorians stood five meters away, all with disruptors drawn. Kort's metal-shod boots were wrapped in packing foam and made no sound against the deck. A banged-up Tellarite ore shuttle was directly behind them. The blackened phaser streaks on her side suggested she had hauled more than just ore in her day.

"I thought ve vere going to do *business,"* Chekov said. He didn't have to feign annoyance.

"Shut up or put down," Kort barked.

"Put up or shut up," Uhura corrected. "Maybe you should think about buying a Universal Trans—"

Kort's disruptor beam bubbled the deck plate metal just in front of Uhura's boots.

Then he aimed directly at Uhura. "Prove to me you can afford to buy what I have to sell."

"Wery vell," Chekov said. He began to speak over his shoulder. "This is . . . our banker . . ."

But there was no one behind him.

Jade was gone.

"I have no time for Terran games," Kort snarled.

"She vas just here," Chekov stammered.

"Who?"

A phaser whined. The large Andorian to Kort's side suddenly arched back. Burst into a blaze of blue energy.

Chekov was appalled. The disintegration could only mean that Jade was still here, and she had set her phaser to kill.

Kort and the thin Andorian fan-fired their disruptors to either side. Chekov hit the deck, rolling behind a Romulan crate.

Uhura's voice rang out in the cargo bay. "Don't even think about it, mister!"

Chekov peered around the crate.

Uhura held her phaser on Kort and the Andorian.

So Kort and the Andorian held their disruptors on Uhura.

"Two to one," Kort said. "Even a Federation *Qtalh* like you can figure those odds." But he kept glancing about. Still not sure of the source of the first phaser blast.

"Then I'll take one of you with me," Uhura said. "And I'm not aiming at the Andorian."

Chekov saw the Andorian's antennae prick up with interest.

Kort took a step sideways and behind the Andorian.

The Andorian moved sideways, exposing Kort again.

Chekov calculated the trajectory he needed. He lobbed his chronograph to the top of the Tellarite shuttle. It disappeared nicely in the dark shadows, out of sight, then clattered on the shuttle's hull.

Kort and the Andorian spun, disruptors firing against the shuttle's hull.

The Andorian fell to the deck as Uhura's phaser stunned him.

"The odds just evened," Uhura said.

"You led me into a trap," Kort hissed.

Uhura's aim was unwavering. "You drew first."

Chekov edged out from behind the crates, trying not to make a sound. Whatever Jade was up to, he couldn't wait for her. If Uhura could just keep Kort talking . . .

"And why shouldn't I?" Kort exclaimed. "Starfleet Intelligence agents everywhere. The Empire's own internal peace forces turning on their own. It is not an easy time to be in business for yourself."

Chekov moved carefully, quietly. He could hear the growing sense of unease in the Klingon's voice. Uhura wasn't his only adversary. He had to know there were at least two others in the hold with him—Chekov, and whoever had fired the fatal phaser blast.

Chekov peered past the glaring lights at the docked shuttles. Deep shadows stretched between haphazard stacks of crates. Still no sign of Jade. Chekov didn't understand her tactics. But he didn't waste time trying.

Right now he had to disarm Kort before he could fire at Uhura. Or before Jade could kill the Klingon.

Unless one of the wild bursts Kort and the Andorian had

fired had managed to kill Jade instead. That could explain why she hadn't fired again. It was easier than believing she wanted Chekov and Uhura out of the way.

Chekov eased between two large crates labeled FREEZE-DRIED STOMACHS in Klingon script. He didn't even want to *think* what they might be for.

All he could think of was Jade's datacase. Filled with credit wafers. Enough to buy a small planet.

A man *could* dream, Chekov decided.

He squinted around the edge of a crate.

Kort was one stack of crates over, backing up to the Tellarite shuttle.

He was near the pilot's hatch.

Chekov understood what Kort was planning. Saw his chance.

"I suggest we withdraw," Kort shouted to Uhura. "Begin negotiations again. By subspace."

"Negotiations end here and now," Uhura answered.

Kort's free hand came up behind him, feeling for the shuttle's hull. Found it. Moved to the hatch controls.

Chekov tensed. Muscles coiled.

Kort pressed the activate control.

The hatch puffed open.

The Klingon couldn't help himself—at the sound of the panel opening he *had* to check with just the barest movement of his eye. The slightest diversion of his attention.

Chekov sprang forth screaming—to startle Kort and to warn Uhura not to fire.

Somehow it worked.

Kort swung his disruptor toward Chekov. But Chekov plowed into his gut, bashing him backward.

Chekov felt something crunch in his own neck as Kort's massive body collapsed by the shuttle. He heard the Klingon's heavy head slam against the hull with a clang, the disruptor hitting the deck and clattering away, Uhura running forward.

He heard the *snick* of a coiled knife springing to life.

Knew what it meant.

No Klingon ever carried just *one* weapon.

Chekov also knew Uhura would never close the gap in time. He braced himself for the bite of the knife as it pierced his back. Thrusting for his heart, as he knew it must.

He wondered what his captain would do.

He was disappointed as he realized that this would be his dying thought.

But he didn't die.

Kort grunted.

Chekov opened his eyes. Looked up past Kort's bulk to see Jade—crouched beside Kort, a phaser jammed against the Klingon's thick neck, taking the uncoiled spring knife out of his glove.

Chekov got to his feet. Grimaced as a sharp pain from his wrenched neck flashed down through his arm. But he was alive, and Uhura was beside him.

"Vhat vere you thinking of?" Chekov yelled at Jade. "Vaiting so long?"

But the young woman just stared coolly at him, then swung her datacase onto Kort's chest. She popped it open, letting Kort see the credit wafers it held.

Kort strained to look into the case, almost comical.

"You know I could kill you," Jade said. Her words formed puffs of vapor. They swirled around the Klingon's shadowed face.

Kort coughed, then nodded once, as best he could under the pressure of Jade's phaser.

"But instead, I'm showing you more credits than you could earn in a dozen lifetimes."

Kort nodded again. His one eye strained to look up at his captor. His brow glittered with sweat even in the space cold air.

"What does that tell you?" Jade asked.

"B-business," Kort croaked. "You want to do business."

"*Very* good. And some people say Klingons don't have the brainstem of a mugato."

Kort's eye bulged at the insult, but he did nothing more.

Jade had accomplished what she had set out to do. Proven she was in control. She pulled the datacase back, flicked it shut, rocked back on her feet, stood up.

She motioned her phaser at Kort to stand as well.

Chekov didn't like it, but Uhura's eyes told him not to interfere. They were merely intermediaries here. Now that contact had been made, it was Jade's operation.

"No more small talk," Jade said to Kort. "*K'tinga*-class battle cruisers. How many can you get me?"

Kort rose painfully to his feet. He staggered toward the Tellarite shuttle. The stale smell of dried Tellarite ceremonial mud wafted from the shuttle's open hatch.

Kort eyed the datacase on the deck. More credits than he could earn in a dozen lifetimes.

He eyed the phaser in Jade's steady hand. Groaned in defeat.

"That . . . I cannot provide."

Chekov and Uhura exchanged a look of shock.

"Cannot . . . or will not?" Jade asked.

Kort seemed to shrink in stature. He could not meet Jade's eyes. He swallowed hard.

"Cannot."

Jade stared at the Klingon with unblinking intensity. Her face revealed none of the thoughts that Chekov knew must be spinning through her mind at warp speed.

The time that had been wasted locating Kort. The credits expended. The risks taken. And for what?

Without taking her eyes off the Klingon, Jade spoke to Chekov and Uhura. "Leave." She adjusted the setting on her phaser. "I don't want any witnesses."

Chekov froze. True, he wasn't used to thinking like a

criminal. But killing an unarmed prisoner? Such an act went beyond any bounds he was prepared to accept, even in this new life.

But before Chekov could object, Kort did. Shockingly.

"Please," the Klingon begged. He was so abject, so lacking in Klingon spirit, that Chekov had to wonder what atrocities Kort had encountered to lose his warrior's resolve and training so absolutely.

Klingons never begged.

At least, a decade ago they didn't.

Neither did they sell off parts of their Empire for quick profit.

Times were changing and Klingons with them.

"There are other goods I can provide," Kort pleaded, hands held together in supplication. "Weapons-grade antimatter. Photon—"

"Battle cruisers," Jade said implacably, repeating her demand.

"Surely . . . surely there is something more, out of all the mighty works of the Empire . . . ?"

Chekov couldn't believe it. The Klingon was groveling.

But Jade was like a statue. Her phaser arm unwavering. Her expression unchanging.

"What else could something as miserable as *you* know about the Empire's mighty works?" she said.

The deck creaked, responding to some slow temperature change. A flurry of ice particles slipped off one bulkhead and rattled across the side of a shuttle in a far corner of the bay.

To Chekov, Kort wore the expression of someone who had sunk to the deepest level of Klingon hell.

"I was a . . . datakeeper." Kort's rough voice was barely audible. "For the Imperial Forecasters."

Chekov saw Jade's cheek flutter as she tightened her jaw. Just once. A strong reaction for her.

"What level?" she asked.

Chekov didn't understand the question. He had never heard of the Imperial Forecasters before. They sounded like Klingon meteorologists.

"Crimson," Kort said wearily.

For the briefest instant, the corner of Jade's mouth flickered up.

"What is the path of the fourth-rank watch dragon?" she asked.

Kort reacted to the question in astonishment. "You know the code?" he blurted in shock.

"Answer me. If you wish to live."

"By Praxis' light, in seasons still to come." Kort intoned the phrases as if reciting poetry.

"I believe you, datakeeper. Now tell me, and I will ask only once, what was the secret in your Crimson Level that will make me spare your life?"

Kort tried to square his shoulders, but failed.

"Chalchaj . . ." he whispered, two soft guttural exclamations. To Chekov it sounded like a death rattle.

"Louder," Jade ordered.

"Chalchaj," Kort repeated. *"Chalchaj 'qmey."*

Chekov glanced at Uhura. Since the voyage to Camp Khitomer, she had labored hard to improve her spoken Klingon. But she looked puzzled. "Something about the sky and children," she said under her breath, answering Chekov's unspoken question. "But an odd construction."

Chekov glanced back at Jade. It was his turn to be astonished.

She was smiling.

It was as unnatural a sight as if he had seen Spock do the same.

"You know of the *Chal?"* Jade asked.

Kort nodded without taking his gaze off the deck.

Chekov instinctively knew that whatever the Klingon had revealed to Jade, it had cost him the last scrap of his honor.

But it must have done its job, because once again Jade adjusted the setting on her phaser.

Chekov wondered what secret the Klingon had just surrendered. He wondered how far he himself would have fallen, what secrets he might have been tempted to reveal, if he had been in Kort's place.

Chekov knew Kirk would have found a way to cheat death. Somehow. But was there a price that couldn't be paid, shouldn't be paid, even to escape annihilation?

Then, with a sudden rush of fear that matched exactly the startled grip Uhura took of his arm, Chekov realized he would never know the answer to that question.

Jade was aiming her phaser directly at him.

"No witnesses," she said, the horrible smile still on her face.

The blue beam was blinding.

Chekov's last thought was to wonder what his captain would have done.

A grime-covered wall of Dark Range Platform was the last thing he saw.

FIVE

☆

The first time Kirk had entered the Great Hall in Starfleet Headquarters, he had been a lowly lieutenant. Still two years from his captaincy.

He had been able to admire its grandeur then, uninterrupted. The soaring cathedral of its ceiling, hundreds of meters high, its immense dining floor, its raised orchestra balcony framed by the Seal of the Federation—a mosaic of stones indigenous to the founding worlds of that great undertaking.

But most of all, Kirk had been able to gaze undisturbed at the Mural. There was a long-winded, bureaucratically inspired plaque on the wall that gave its real title. But no one ever called it by that name. Let alone remembered it. Because no other name was needed.

The Mural swept wondrously around the Great Hall's curved walls, tracing the evolution of humanity's journey to the stars. From Icarus and the Montgolfier brothers, through Apollo, Pathfinder, Cochrane's *Bonaventure,* to the first joint missions with Vulcan vessels.

The Mural ended yet didn't end with the *U.S.S. Constitution,* the ship that had set the design standard for Kirk's own *Enterprise.* There was still room for many more vessels past that one, but the Mural itself was deliberately unfinished. Its last fifty meters faded to the white of the artist's blank canvas.

The message was clear.

Humanity's journey, like the artist's painting, would never be finished.

Kirk couldn't remember what had become of the artist, though.

But he had no time or opportunity to reflect on the significance of that thought now. Two thousand dignitaries filled the Great Hall this evening, and all of them knew him.

Or thought they did.

He had never gotten used to it.

It had begun slowly enough, this rise to celebrity. At its earliest stage, he would walk into a bar on a starbase, and a suddenly waving hand would rise from a table filled with gold shirts, beckoning him over.

It was fellow officers who recognized him then. They had

seen his face on his edited logs, circulated throughout the Fleet for general reference and review.

That's Kirk of the Enterprise, they'd say. They'd buy him a drink. *What was Elaan of Troyius* really *like? What sort of maneuvers did that Romulan vessel make out by the Neutral Zone?* The questions were unending, and at its earliest stage, he was flattered.

But then his recognition had moved beyond the Fleet. Civilians began approaching him, asking the same questions, seeking more details. Always details. After the incident with V'Ger, the floodgates had opened. All Earth claimed to know him. Most of the other worlds, too.

Now Kirk couldn't go anywhere without detecting the unsettling flash of recognition in strangers' eyes. All the more intense because, unlike the sudden recognition awarded a new sports star or politician, people had come to recognize him over decades of his career.

He was filed away in their brains with other long-term acquaintances, the same memory slots given over to family members and lifelong friends. So that's how they approached him now. People like the young technician who had grown up seeing his face in the news updates, reading of his adventures —his job. They felt they knew all about him. He was their friend. Their uncle. Their inspiration.

Kirk would be the first to admit he was in their debt. By their support of Starfleet and the Federation, they made what he had done possible. And for that he would always be grateful.

But the truth was, to Kirk, they were still no more than strangers.

After the millionth question had been asked about Elaan, after the millionth question about some Romulan commander, his reticence at appearing in public had little to do with the fact he could think of nothing new to say. It was more the feeling that there was nothing lonelier than a man with a million friends. For how could he ever return that true, yet false, debt of friendship?

It was a no-win situation, and Kirk had learned painfully that the best way to deal with those was to avoid them at all costs. Even if it meant that some of those strangers who once thought of him as friend now thought of him as enemy.

He had first paid that price long ago, and knew he would continue to pay it as long as people knew him.

Or thought they did.

At least at a formal Starfleet reception, his stature was not unique or remarkable. Indeed, there were many whom Kirk himself recognized from having seen their news updates and read about their exploits. The mutual recognition they shared with Kirk was a secret signal of shared commiseration. They were members of the same exalted and beleaguered club, unable to voice their complaints about public adulation without appearing spoiled and unworthy.

Kirk wondered if the others in the club knew the answer to the question that plagued him now. He wondered if there were any among them he could ever ask.

But, of course, there were.

They approached him now. One who looked even more uncomfortable in his formal uniform than Kirk felt. And the other who wouldn't look uncomfortable in an Iron Maiden with rats chewing at his toes.

Spock and McCoy.

For an instant, Kirk felt a wave of relief wash over him. Here was friendship he both understood and could return.

"Good evening, Captain."

Kirk grinned at Spock's greeting. So formal. So typical.

"Hiya, Jim. Quite a spread, isn't it?"

McCoy's smile was wider than Kirk's. And for good reason from McCoy's standpoint, Kirk knew.

The reception *was* a wonder to behold. The national costumes of Starfleet's guests, along with the rainbow hues of their skin—and fur, and scales, and feathers, and what-have-you—were an explosion of color. Matched only by the kaleidoscopic extravagance of the banquet tables laden with the bounty of uncounted worlds.

The only thing McCoy liked better than a good time was seeing others having a good time, too.

"Very impressive," Kirk answered. "Wouldn't you say, Mr. Spock?"

"Indeed," Spock admitted, with typical Vulcan detachment.

McCoy shook his head. "The biggest party to hit Starfleet in ten years. The top ambassadors from the Federation *and* the unaligned worlds. The Lunar Philharmonic up on the bandstand. And all you can say is, 'Indeed'?"

"What would you have me say, Doctor?"

McCoy gave full vent to his exasperation. "That you're having a good time."

"That would be—"

McCoy chimed in. "Don't say it. Illogical. I know."

"Perhaps there is hope for you yet," Spock observed.

McCoy rolled his eyes. "Don't count on it."

Kirk caught Spock studying him. "Are you well, Captain?"

"Isn't that my line?" McCoy said.

Kirk held up his hand to quiet the doctor. Trust Spock to see right through him.

"I didn't get much sleep last night."

Spock nodded. "Yes. The rain was unprogrammed."

"It wasn't the rain," Kirk said. He felt his mood sour as even the thought of last night reawakened the feelings he had wrestled with.

McCoy seemed to understand what might have happened. "Wasn't Carol going to come tonight?"

Kirk shrugged. Not much to say about that.

McCoy did understand. "Why don't I get us some drinks," he said.

"As long as you're prescribing."

McCoy started off through the crowd.

Kirk took a breath. Preparing himself for what he wanted to say to Spock. To try out the waters.

But Spock beat him to it.

"Captain, I will be leaving Starfleet at the end of the quarter."

Kirk opened his mouth. Said nothing. That was going to be *his* line.

"I will be joining the Vulcan Diplomatic Corps."

"Ah," Kirk said, still containing his surprise. "The family business."

Spock nodded thoughtfully. "I will be working with my father on a number of initiatives. Though the Romulan question is what I shall direct most of my efforts toward. It was a topic of considerable interest at the Khitomer conference."

"The Romulan question?"

"Unification," Spock said. "Vulcans and Romulans have been apart too long."

Kirk stifled a laugh of amazement. "Spock, that could take . . . decades. If not a century."

"I hope so, Captain. It would be interesting to see the process concluded in my lifetime."

Those simple words were like a slap to Kirk. Spock's Vulcan heritage meant he was barely at the midpoint in his life. Another century of full productive life was not out of the question.

Spock regarded Kirk with penetrating eyes. No secrets lost between the two friends.

"You had something to tell me?" Spock asked.

"I'm . . . thinking of leaving Starfleet, too." Kirk regretted the words as soon as he spoke them. They sounded foreign.

"I was wondering how long it would take you to reach that decision."

"Then you think it's a good idea?"

"It is not up to me to pass judgment on your plans."

"So . . . you're saying you think I should stay?"

Spock hesitated before replying. Choosing his words carefully, Kirk knew.

"Captain, wherever your future happiness lies, it will not be found in the pronouncements of others. Only you can make that kind of decision."

Kirk frowned. "You're not making this any easier."

"Such decisions seldom are."

McCoy barreled back through the crowd. "What decisions?" He held two tumblers of thick blue liquid. Shoved one into Kirk's hand.

McCoy waited expectantly.

Kirk stared dubiously at his drink.

"Bones, I swore off Romulan ale a year ago. You were there, remember?"

McCoy narrowed one eye. "What decisions?"

Spock looked innocently neutral. An expression he excelled at.

Kirk swallowed a shot of the ale. Surprised he had forgotten how intensely it burned the gullet.

"I've been think—" he began, then coughed. "I've been thinking—"

"CITIZENS OF THE FEDERATION AND ALL EXALTED GUESTS!"

The amplified voice boomed throughout the Great Hall, instantly stopping each conversation.

Kirk, Spock, and McCoy turned to the stage as did all the others. A ten-meter-tall hologram of the Federation Council president was projected above it. The president's holographic arms stretched out to encompass everyone.

The real president standing beneath the projection was a small figure, almost obscured by the assembled heads and other topmost limbs and protuberances of the guests standing in front of Kirk. He was recognizable only by his long mane and mustache of white hair.

Kirk was surprised to see a few Klingons in dress armor near the stage as well. There appeared to be no end to the Federation's attempts to reach out to the Empire.

"ON BEHALF OF THE FEDERATION COUNCIL, I BID YOU WELCOME."

The president then began to repeat his greeting in Vulcan.

McCoy whispered into Kirk's ear. "This should be good for the next half hour. *What* decisions?"

But Kirk didn't want to talk. Another figure was moving on stage to join the president. For now, he was just outside the focus of the holographic projector.

But Kirk saw the figure's burgundy uniform jacket and didn't have to see the admiral's bars on it to know who it would be. Though at this distance he couldn't tell which admiral it was.

"Shhh, Bones," Kirk said. "That's got to be him."

"Of course it is," McCoy said without shushing. "That's what this whole wingding's for."

Kirk sighed. "Well, I want to see who it is."

"You mean you don't know? It's got to be the worst-kept secret in Starfleet."

"Bones . . ."

". . . GREAT PLEASURE TO ANNOUNCE, WITH THE UNANIMOUS APPROVAL OF THE COUNCIL—"

The president had switched back to Federation Standard. He moved to the side. His hologram motioned to someone to join him.

"STARFLEET'S NEW, SUPREME COMMANDER IN CHIEF—"

The admiral stepped into the holographic projector's range. His ten-meter-tall projection took shape like a giant invading the hall.

Kirk felt his stomach twist as he finally recognized the admiral. It couldn't be true.

"ADMIRAL ANDROVAR DRAKE!"

The Great Hall thundered with applause.

Kirk was stunned.

The rival he had sworn never to forgive had just achieved an impossible position. On the same day Kirk had decided to give up the fight.

McCoy's voice betrayed his interest in Kirk's obvious discomfort. "You know him?"

"In the Academy," Kirk said, struggling to sound offhand. "Then on the *Farragut.*"

Kirk closed his eyes, saw Lieutenant Drake's sneering face on Tycho IV, laughing at the death of Faith Morgan. Kirk saw his own son, David, so innocently led into danger.

"Is something wrong?" McCoy asked.

Kirk knew everything was wrong. "If that's what's going to run Starfleet," he said, "then I was right. It's time for me to leave."

SIX

Chekov's first impression of death was that it was colder than Siberia.

He wasn't impressed.

It also smelled like a Tellarite mudbath.

That was when he decided he wasn't dead after all.

But he couldn't move. And he couldn't see. And his body ached with the all-too-familiar pains of a high-intensity phaser stun.

"She didn't kill us," he said aloud. His voice was dry, raspy, weak.

"Thank you, Mr. Obvious." That voice was as weak as Chekov's, but only a few centimeters away.

"Uhura? Vhere are ve?"

By now, Chekov had recovered sufficiently to know he was flat on his back on an ice-cold surface. His hands and legs were expertly bound, immovable. Gray shapes began to melt out of the darkness at the corners of his vision. Somewhere, however dim, there was light.

"Listen," Uhura said.

Chekov forced himself to concentrate on something other than the pounding of his heart. At first he heard the thrumming sounds of laboring equipment that told him he was still on Deep Range Platform. That was a good sign.

But there was some other sound there. Coming from above. Directly above. Almost random. A faint clicking or tapping. Getting stronger. Getting softer.

He heard a muffled snort.

The sounds made sense.

Hoofsteps.

Chekov moaned.

He and Uhura were under the Tellarite ore shuttle in the cargo bay and its crew was on board. He could hear them walking around in the shuttle's cabin.

"HELP!" Chekov yelled. His eardrums rang. The shuttle's lower hull was less than a handsbreadth above him.

"Forget it," Uhura said. "They're Tellarites. They'll never hear us through the hull plates."

Chekov's mind raced with potential strategies. "Can you hit the hull?" he asked. "Or kick it or *something?*"

"I can't move," Uhura said. "Can you?"

Chekov strained. It felt as if his legs and arms were bolted to the deck.

"Vhy has Jade done this to us?"

"She said it herself. No witnesses. But it's clear she needs bodies."

"Da," Chekov sighed. It *was* clear. When the time came for the shuttle to launch, whether or not it used maneuvering rockets or impulse engines to lift off the deck, he and Uhura would be scorched or irradiated to death. Presumably, whatever was holding them to the deck would be vaporized. And whatever passed for law enforcement on Deep Range would have two easily identifiable bodies. Death by misadventure. Freeing their erstwhile partner, Jade, to pursue her purchase of . . .

"Vhat was it the Klingon said to her?"

"Chalchaj 'qmey," Uhura said. "I still can't figure it out. Probably a code name of some kind. Maybe a type of experimental Klingon weapons system."

"Then it makes no sense Jade has done this to us," Chekov protested. "That's exactly vhat ve vere supposed to be buying."

"Not 'exactly,' Pavel. Otherwise we wouldn't be here."

Chekov didn't say anything. He listened for the Tellarites above him. They had stopped moving around the cabin. A bad sign. It meant they were strapped into their seats.

Preparing for launch.

"At least I figured out what the captain would do in a situation like this," Uhura said.

"Vhat?"

"Have a backup plan."

Chekov sighed. "Jade *vas* our backup plan."

A hum began. It came from the shuttle. Systems coming online.

"At least," Chekov said, "vhatever propulsion system they use, it vill be quick."

A new noise began. Closer, louder. A pulsing roar from beneath the deck.

"Wrong again, Pavel."

Air pumps.

The cargo bay was being depressurized.

"Vonderful," Chekov said. "Suffocation and *then* incineration."

"At least she's thorough."

Chekov grunted as he suddenly strained every muscle against his bonds.

Nothing gave.

He gasped for breath after his exertion.

"I'll miss you, Pavel."

"It's not over yet," Chekov said.

His gasping intensified, quickened. The hum from the shuttle became muffled as the air pressure diminished.

"The keptin vould never give up!"

He fought once more against his bonds. He heard Uhura do the same. The sounds of their struggles seemed to move farther and farther away as the air grew thinner.

Chekov's lungs ached. Black stars flared at the edges of his vision. But he wouldn't give up either.

He hated the idea of dying twice in one day.

Next time, he told himself, he'd be sure to have a backup plan.

And then there was no more air to breathe.

SEVEN

☆

In the end, Kirk had not left the reception and dinner for Starfleet's new commander in chief. That would have been admitting defeat. And Kirk *never* admitted defeat.

Instead, he had had three Romulan ales, effectively changing the rules of the game.

He simply no longer cared about Androvar Drake.

After three Romulan ales, it was difficult to care about anything.

Or so he told himself.

"Bones, you're supposed to be talking me out of this," Kirk said.

McCoy sat back in his chair, arms folded. The circular table was littered with the remains of the coffee and dessert course. Most of the guests were on the dance floor or talking in groups by one of the bars. But Kirk, McCoy, and Spock still sat together. Unspoken evidence of their knowledge that the times when all three of them could share their company this way were finite, and counting down.

"Why'd you join Starfleet?" McCoy asked.

Kirk grinned. Closed his eyes. Said the words so familiar to every cadet. "Why did anyone? 'To seek out new life and new civilizations . . .' "

McCoy pushed back on his chair, making it teeter two-legged, then rocked back with a thump. "And what are you doing for Starfleet now?"

Kirk's grin faded. "Teaching. Consulting. Chairing committees."

McCoy's gaze fixed on Kirk. "And you *want* to be talked out of leaving?"

Kirk didn't know the answer himself. Spock replied for him. "I believe the captain is undecided at the moment, because he has not yet determined what it is he should do upon leaving Starfleet."

"You 'believe' that, do you?" McCoy replied.

Kirk poured himself another cup of coffee to take up the fight against the Romulan ale. Hearing Spock and McCoy go at it was like listening to a live version of the debates he had been having with himself.

Sure enough, Spock took up the baton. "Do you know what *you* shall do upon *your* retirement from Starfleet, Doctor?"

"Who said I was retiring?"

Spock angled his head thoughtfully. "A man of your years—"

"Hold it right there! I might not have any of your damned green blood in my veins, but sixty-seven isn't what it used to be. I look at what passes for sickbay design in the new ships on the drawing boards and I tell you, I'm not leaving Starfleet till they carry me out. There's no heart to what they're thinking. No thought given to what goes on between patient and doctor. Someone's got to care about that part of it. And it looks like I'm the one who's got the job."

McCoy paused for breath. He saw that Kirk and Spock were both watching him carefully.

"Sorry," the doctor said tersely. He reached for the coffee. "I tend to get a bit passionate about Medical's policies."

Spock folded his hands together. "Which clearly accounts for your decision to remain in Starfleet. There is still a job you can do for the service which is useful, necessary, and for which you feel passion."

Spock looked then at Kirk.

Kirk didn't have to hear him say it. It *was* that obvious.

But Spock said it anyway. He was good at that. "In this case, Captain, passion *is* the most logical answer to the questions you are facing."

McCoy rolled his eyes. "Now I've heard everything, Jim. We're being lectured to about *passion* by a *Vulcan.*"

"Doctor, once again you remind me how little you know about the true nature of my people."

Kirk stared off across the Great Hall as Spock went on to tell McCoy how Vulcans really did have emotions and simply chose not to allow them to rule their lives.

McCoy, of course, rose to the bait, hotly disputing Spock's definitions.

They could go on for hours. On occasions, they had.

Without paying attention to the familiar arguments he had heard over the years, Kirk was struck by how much just the sounds of their voices brought an ease to him. As if he were a child again, sitting at the table in his mother's kitchen for a holiday meal, listening to his parents, grandparents, his brother, aunts and uncles, and the cousins. Their competing words raised in the noisy confusion of long acquaintance. The bonds of family.

That's what Spock and McCoy had become to him.

Family.

He was glad to have such friends in his life. Yet he knew there *had* to be more. . . .

Spock went on about Surak's teachings as McCoy snorted dismissively.

Kirk's attention wandered to the dance floor. A group of Klingons stood off to the side, unsuccessfully trying to hide their disdain for what passed as dancing on Earth.

Kirk had been to a Klingon dance once. McCoy had ended up giving him three protoplaser treatments to make the scars fade.

Klingons took the act of cutting in very literally.

Then Kirk saw that familiar flash in one of the Klingon's eyes. The Klingon recognized him, nodded at him—a sign of respect. Kirk returned the gesture, marveling how the day had ever come when he actually felt respect in turn for a Klingon.

But the events surrounding the attempted assassination at Camp Khitomer and the growing peace movement between the Federation and the Empire had changed many minds. Including his.

Kirk supposed he should be glad that he was not totally set in his ways. That he could still entertain new thoughts, new ideas.

Before Camp Khitomer, when Spock had told him that the explosion of the Praxis moon meant the Klingon race might perish, Kirk's first reaction had been to blurt out, *Then let them die.*

Almost at once he had realized how wrong those words were. How hurtful. How unfeeling. But once spoken, there had been no way to take them back, to soften their impact.

He regretted those words still.

Decades ago, he might have been unseasoned enough to have said those words and meant them. But not now. His voyages had not just been about making discoveries for the Federation. He had made them for himself, as well. And change had come because of what he had encountered, and what he had learned.

Kirk dreaded the day he would stop learning. Stop changing.

His gaze continued to sweep the room as Spock and McCoy companionably argued on in the background. He reflected on change. On passion. Other people on the dance floor caught his glance. Most smiled back at him. A few looked momentarily startled, as if they had never expected to see so notable a figure in the flesh. Kirk was used to all their reactions, had seen them all a thousand times before.

But then he found one person who was already looking directly at him before he saw her. It was Kirk's turn to be startled.

But he didn't know why.

Perhaps it was her eyes, he decided at first. Heavily lashed, dark and enticing . . . if he had been a twenty-year-old cadet he'd have been by her side in fifteen seconds. Ten seconds if he wanted to beat Gary Mitchell to asking her to dinner.

Then he was startled again as he suddenly realized those haunting eyes belonged to a Klingon. Her dark hair, dramatically swept back for the reception, revealed the ripples of her high-ridged brow. Though, oddly, it was not as pronounced as most females' he had seen.

He understood why when he saw her ears.

Pointed.

Klingon *and* Vulcan.

That was reason enough to be startled, Kirk decided. Just as people sometimes took a few seconds to place his identity after realizing that they recognized him, he decided his scrutiny must have taken in the young woman's unusual features, sensed the inherent contradiction of them, and then paused just long enough for the facts to come to the attention of his consciousness.

Which meant he was doing to her exactly what he disliked so much when it happened to him.

He was staring.

But she didn't seem to mind.

In fact, she smiled at him.

Not the giddy smile of someone recognizing a celebrity.

But a smile of success. Of finding something lost.

Kirk knew he shouldn't keep staring, but he couldn't *not* stare.

The smile transformed her face. Worked some magic that he couldn't comprehend.

Until his brain finally fought through the fog of Romulan ale and spoke plainly to him: *She's gorgeous. That's why you're staring. She's the most beautiful woman in the Hall. And she's letting you stare at her like a shuttle pilot who's been on solo duty for the past two years.*

Kirk's mouth suddenly felt dry. He felt the faint rush of

what had been a familiar sensation when he had been a twenty-year-old cadet and the whole galaxy lay waiting for him. A lightness in his chest. A thrill of anticipation in his stomach.

His brain kicked in again, like his own personal Spock offering observations untinged by emotion: *You're thinking as if you're twenty again, and she isn't even that. You're old enough to be her father. Hell, you're old enough to be her* grand*father.*

A dancing couple moved across his line of sight. The instant she was gone from his vision, Kirk shook his head, as if a spell had been broken.

"Don't you agree, Captain?" Spock asked.

"If you do," McCoy countered, "I'm through giving you advice."

Kirk had no idea what his friends had been discussing. "I think," he said cautiously, "the answer lies somewhere in the middle."

Spock and McCoy exchanged a look of surprise.

"Fascinating," Spock said.

But McCoy narrowed his eyes in disgust. "You didn't hear a word we said, did you?"

The music ended. The dancing couples on the floor began to drift back to their tables. Kirk put his hand on McCoy's arm, nodded out to the floor.

"Bones, that young woman over there. In the long dress . . ."

Kirk saw only a flash of her glittering gown moving amid the crush of people. His heart actually fluttered. She was moving in his direction.

"Where?" McCoy asked. "The one in red?"

"No," Kirk said. "You can't miss her. She's half-Vulcan, half-Klingon."

"A most improbable combination," Spock said.

McCoy frowned at Spock. "Look who's calling the kettle black. Or in your case, green."

Kirk turned to Spock. "She's right over there. Klingon brow. Vulcan ears."

"I see her," McCoy said brightly. "She's stunning. I wonder whose daughter she is?"

"Klingon-*Romulan* would be a more logical conclusion," Spock said.

Kirk could barely keep up with the doubled conversation. "Romulan?" he asked Spock. "At a *Starfleet* function?" He turned to McCoy. "What do you mean, 'daughter'?"

"Starfleet did invite several high-ranking Klingons to this reception,"Spock said. "Undoubtedly invitations would have gone out to the Romulan diplomatic missions as part of the ongoing move toward openness."

"She's very young, Jim," McCoy said. "Probably some diplomat's child."

Kirk's heart sank. "She's not that young." But he knew she was.

"Perhaps some diplomat's consort," Spock suggested.

Kirk's heart hit bottom.

McCoy gave him a quick look of understanding. "Oh, ho. About to add 'cradle-snatching' to your list of crimes against the Klingon Empire?"

Kirk felt his cheeks start to burn. "I was pardoned," he said. "So were you. All I was saying was that I thought she was . . . exceptionally lovely. And I wondered who she was. That's all. Completely innocent."

McCoy pursed his lips to keep a grin from spreading across his face.

Kirk scanned the crowd. Whoever she was, she was gone.

"If, indeed, she is a child of joint Klingon and Romulan heritage, her beauty should come as no surprise," Spock said.

"Is that so?" McCoy retorted. "In addition to passion, you're suddenly an expert on beauty?"

"The perception of beauty in most cultures is connected to symmetry of features. Symmetry of features indicates that an individual has not succumbed to any one of a number of diseases which affect growth during childhood and adolescence. Therefore, beauty equals symmetry equals robustness. And hybrids generally take on the most positive attributes of their parents, becoming, as it were, exceptional specimens."

"Such as yourself," McCoy stated dryly.

"As always, Doctor, the depth of your logic impresses me."

McCoy couldn't tell if he had just been tricked into complimenting Spock.

Kirk knew he had been.

Then the woman appeared in the crowd, only a few tables away, heading in Kirk's direction.

"Bones, Spock—there she is."

Kirk stood up as her eyes met his.

She moved so gracefully, it was as if he were watching a dancer perform.

She was slim, lithe, but despite McCoy's speculations, clearly a woman. No mere girl.

For a moment as he rose to his feet, Kirk almost forgot how old he had felt recently. He wanted desperately to know why she was coming over to him. He wanted to hear her voice, know her name. Know everything about her.

Spock was right. Passion *was* his answer.

But two tables over, she stopped.

Her entrancing face clouded. Her delicate brow ridges became much more pronounced, almost as if she were scowling.

Kirk started to hold out his hand.

But another hand came down on his shoulder, hard enough to surprise him. Kirk turned just as he saw the woman do the same—turn away.

"Jimbo! Glad you could make it to my little party!"

Kirk was face to face with Androvar Drake.

His new commander in chief.

"Admiral Drake" was all he said. He *loathed* "Jimbo."

He glanced back over his shoulder.

She was gone. Again.

Drake poked him in the stomach.

"Spending too much time behind a desk, Jimbo?"

Kirk concentrated on not making his hands into fists. Drake still kept his now white hair in a military bristle cut. His sharp features had filled in since the years he had been in Kirk's graduating class. The extra lines there, deeply etched, were kept company by a thin ragged scar over his right cheekbone. A protoplaser could take it away in a month. But Drake had earned it in battle, the story went. He had taken out a Klingon battle cruiser just before the Organian intervention. That scar was his badge of honor.

Or a relic from a bygone day, Kirk thought.

Drake put his fists on his hips. "We've both come a long way since the Academy, eh?"

Kirk didn't want to get drawn into anything with Drake. What had happened between them was long passed. David was at rest and nothing could bring him back.

"Congratulations," Kirk said simply.

Drake took that as an opportunity to pump Kirk's hand.

"Ever wonder what might have happened if you hadn't taken the *Enterprise* out again?"

Kirk shook his head. As captains, both he and Drake had taken out starships on five-year missions. Both had survived, returning as heroes within months of each other and receiving immediate promotion to the admiralty. And then, after V'Ger, Kirk had been unable to resist the siren call of the stars. He had turned his back on a career in Headquarters and had gone back out.

But Drake had remained.

Now, twenty-three years later, Kirk was a captain again. And Drake was still Drake. Even if he was commander in chief of the entire Fleet.

Four Romulan ales, Kirk thought, and I could probably get away with belting him. No matter what his rank.

But instead, he said, "May I introduce my friends—Captain Spock, Dr. McCoy."

Drake shook McCoy's hand. Then he respectfully raised his hand and gave Spock the Vulcan salute, instead of committing the faux pas of attempting to touch a Vulcan. Drake had obviously learned well during his years climbing the ladder at Headquarters.

"Know them well," Drake said enigmatically. "Always followed your career, Jimbo." His lips tightened. "Always impressed you were able to accomplish so much, after . . . well, you know." He laughed with a tone of calculated, hollow, camaraderie.

But Kirk didn't respond, by word or by gesture. He could sense McCoy's glance of curiosity. He knew Spock would be equally intrigued by Drake's statement, though of course he wouldn't show it. But the past was the past.

Drake was running Starfleet now.

Kirk had never wanted the job. But he knew in his heart that it had always been a possibility. He *could* have been commander in chief. If he had stayed behind as Drake had. Played the political games at Headquarters as well as he played the games of life-and-death on the frontier.

But Kirk hadn't chosen that path. It was no use thinking of what might have been.

"Can't stay long," Drake said.

"Pity," Kirk replied.

"But thought you might like to know—reviewed the Fleet status logs. The *Enterprise.* Decommissioned next month."

Kirk nodded, like hearing of a friend's terminal illness. "I know."

"Going to use it for wargames."

McCoy frowned. "Starfleet hasn't fought wargames for years."

Drake shrugged. "An oversight I intend to correct." He clapped Kirk on the shoulder, far too familiar. "The *Enterprise* will be a target ship. Try her out on a couple of the new photon torpedoes. Mark VIIIs. Twin vortices." He winked at Kirk. "Should go out in a real blaze of glory." His eyes were cold. "Thought you might like that, stuck behind a desk and all. At least something in your career will go out in a blaze of glory."

"Waste not, want not," Kirk said lightly.

Drake laughed. "Good one." He started to go. "See you at the decommissioning ceremony?"

Kirk shook his head. "I'll . . . be off planet."

Drake winked again. "I'll see that they save you a piece of her. Put it on a plaque, mount it over the fireplace. Tell the grandkids about—" Drake suddenly took on an expression of feigned sadness. "Oh, sorry, Jimbo. Forgot about your son. David, wasn't it? Klingons killing him, and that. There won't be any grandkids, will there."

With that, he was gone, swallowed into a crowd of well-wishers.

"What the hell was that all about?" McCoy sputtered.

"We go back," Kirk said. "Too far." He sat down again, more tired than when he had begun the evening. He looked for the young woman, but she was gone, too. As he knew she would be.

As the *Enterprise* would soon be gone.

As all things must go.

Passion among them.

McCoy and Spock exchanged a look of concern.

"You want another drink, Jim?"

Kirk shook his head. "I've had enough." It was late.

He would never hear the sound of her voice.

He would always remember Drake's.

"I've had enough," he said again.

He didn't mean Romulan ale.

EIGHT

☆

The outer doors in Cargo Bay Twelve opened before the straining pumps had removed all of the atmosphere.

A sudden storm of ice crystals plumed from the growing gap between the moving doors.

Inside the bay, loose debris swirled into empty space. The shafts of light from the ceiling fixtures faded without dust and moisture to define them.

On some of the cargo pallets, sealed drums and crates bulged in the absence of air pressure.

But there were no squeals of metal or plastic to accompany their deformations.

There was only the silence of vacuum.

Of space.

Of death.

The Tellarite ore shuttle in the cargo bay brought its maneuvering systems online.

Four thrusters on its battered lower hull vented pinpoint streams of hyperaccelerated plasma to lift the shuttle against the Platform's artificial gravity.

Any organic material within range of that plasma was only seconds from being carbonized.

The Tellarite shuttle rotated. Its nose pointed toward the open doors and the stars beyond. Its impulse ports glowed briefly, pushing it forward.

The plasma jets left blackened streaks on the deck plates.

The shuttle launched.

The doors ponderously closed behind it.

Nothing lived in Cargo Bay Twelve.

Pavel Chekov clenched his eyes shut to prevent the moisture coating them from sublimating in the vacuum. He gasped desperately for a last lungful of oxygen.

Air flooded his lungs so easily, he was shocked into opening one eye.

"Hikaru?"

Captain Hikaru Sulu grinned down at his friends. He offered both his hands to help them up.

Chekov and Uhura slowly got to their feet. They were on a transporter platform.

Uhura's face tightened in confusion as she looked around. "The *Excelsior?"* she asked.

Sulu's laugh was deep and genuine. Then he took on a serious expression. "I'm sorry. I know I shouldn't . . ." He grinned at Chekov again. "But the expression on your faces . . ."

Chekov didn't share Sulu's good humor. He was still shivering with the cold of space. His lungs still ached with the effort of trying to breathe vacuum.

Chekov's voice was coiled as tightly as a Klingon spring knife. "How long have you been tracking us?"

Sulu's smile melted in the force of Chekov's withering stare. "Pavel, calm down. You're safe now."

"How long?"

"Since the beginning of your mission," Sulu said.

Chekov could hear his heart thunder in his ears. He couldn't tell if he was shaking from the cold or from outrage. He hit his open hand against Sulu's shoulder. "So each time ve faced a disruptor, each time ve were scared to death someone vould catch on to us, you vere out here ready to snatch us to safety?"

Sulu's eyes grew wide. He took a step back.

But Chekov grabbed Sulu by his uniform jacket. "You bastard!" he shouted.

Sulu pushed at Chekov's hand, trying to disengage.

"Pavel, take it easy!"

"Take it *easy?* Six months undercover! My friends and family thinking I'm a criminal! *Living* vith *Klingons!* And you want me to . . ." Chekov's outburst choked off in rage.

There was only one way he could continue this conversation.

With a roar of anger he swung his fist into Sulu's nose.

Sulu grunted and stumbled back, completely taken by surprise.

A gout of blood exploded across his upper lip.

Chekov kept his grip on Sulu's jacket. Held him up.

"Vhat vere ve to you? Chess pieces to be moved around? To be sacrificed?"

On that last word, Chekov let Sulu have it again, this time releasing his hold so Sulu fell back against the transporter console.

Uhura tugged at Chekov's arm, trying to hold him back.

"Pavel! That's enough! Hikaru saved our lives!"

But Chekov straight-armed Uhura out of his way.

"Ve nearly died because of him!"

He swung at Sulu again.

But Sulu was ready this time.

He brought up an arm to deflect Chekov's wild swing. Leaned in with his shoulder to keep Chekov's center of gravity moving forward.

Sent Chekov over his back to thud against the deck.

Now Sulu grabbed Chekov by his jacket, leaned over him.

"Listen to me, Pavel!" Sulu hissed. "My orders came from Intelligence Oversight. Even the brass were excluded. If you knew you were being monitored by the *Excelsior,* and any of your Klingon contacts had used a mind-sifter to question your stories about quitting Starfleet . . ."

With the end of decades of military tension between the Federation and the Klingon Empire, the Klingon armed forces were falling into disarray. Weapons inventories were no longer secure. This section of the galaxy was especially vulnerable to the possible entry of Klingon armaments into the open market.

So Chekov and Uhura had sacrificed six months of their Starfleet careers and brought shame to their friends and families, who could not be told the truth. All to create a false background establishing them as illegal weapons dealers with extensive Starfleet connections.

"Oversight had nothing to do vith leaving us there—freezing to death—until the last second!"

Chekov kicked up and caught Sulu on the back of his leg.

Sulu let go of Chekov to jump away before he could lose his balance.

The two men faced each other, half-crouched. Chekov looked for an opening like a barroom brawler. Sulu turned sideways, hands positioned for the Vulcan *sal-tor-fee* defense.

The two men circled each other warily. Sulu tried again. "Pavel—you're overreacting. While you were on Dark Range, I had to keep the *Excelsior* at forty thousand kilometers, right at the transporter's maximum range."

Chekov swung. Sulu parried.

"I had to keep our sensors on their lowest setting so Kort wouldn't detect them."

Uhura tried to move between them again.

"Stop it, Pavel. Listen to him."

Sulu used Uhura's intervention to advance his argument. He spoke rapidly over Uhura's shoulder. "Sensors showed you two and Jade meeting with Kort and his Andorians in the cargo bay. They showed thc phaser emissions. But it wasn't until the others left that I knew you were remaining behind. And even then, because I was picking up life signs from you, I couldn't be certain it wasn't part of some plan you'd put together. Until the bay doors started to open."

"You see?" Uhura asked Chekov.

Some of Chekov's murderous rage began to diminish.

But not all of it.

"I had my orders," Sulu said. "I could only interfere if I thought you were in immediate danger of being killed."

Uhura put her hands on Chekov's shoulders, holding him back. "He got us out, Pavel. He got us out as soon as he could."

"We're on the same side," Sulu said. "Someone tried to kill you. Let's do something about it."

Chekov couldn't speak. He wanted to punch a hole through a bulkhead.

"It was Jade," Uhura said.

Sulu looked stunned. "But this was her operation. She's supposed to be one of the top agents in Starfleet Intelligence." He wiped at the blood streaming from his nose. His face betrayed his surprise at how much there was.

"Kort offered her something she couldn't refuse," Uhura said grimly. She pushed Chekov back. "Take a couple of deep breaths," she advised him.

Chekov unclenched his fists. Felt his whole body tremble. For six months he had believed that Uhura and he were living on the brink of instant death. All because Sulu had his orders.

He remained silent and sullen as Uhura told Sulu about the enigmatic exchange between Kort and Jade in the cargo bay.

When she had finished, Sulu walked around the transporter console, carefully giving Chekov a wide berth. He hit a control.

"Computer: Identify a Klingon organization designated 'Imperial Forecasters.' "

Without an instant of hesitation, the computer's distinctive voice responded from a console speaker.

"The Imperial Forecasters were a division of the Klingon Strategic Operations Bureau."

"What were their responsibilities?" Sulu asked.

"Using advanced wargaming and simulation techniques, they forecast probably outcomes to military scenarios."

Chekov shrugged. "So, they vere military planners. The Klingon Empire is a military culture."

But Sulu wasn't finished. "Computer: In the context of the Imperial Forecasters, what is the significance of the Crimson Level?"

"That classification corresponds to Starfleet's security classification, Ultra Secret."

Sulu glanced at Chekov and Uhura. "Now it's getting interesting." He addressed the computer again. "What aspects of military planning were the responsibility of the Crimson Level?"

Again, the computer didn't hesitate. "Doomsday scenarios."

Chekov heard Uhura's sharp intake of breath. He started to pay attention to what the computer was saying.

"Define," Sulu said.

The computer complied. "Scenarios concerning the effects of interplanetary famine, plague, and natural disasters on the ability of Klingon colony worlds and protectorates to support the Empire. Scenarios concerning the effects of political upheaval on the ability of the High Council to govern the Empire effectively. Scenarios concerning the effects of the military defeat and subjugation of the Empire by its enemies, on the ability of the Klingon race to survive."

"Definitely high-level material," Uhura said. "I don't think I'd like to know the Klingon response to the defeat of the Empire."

Sulu tapped a finger against the console. "In this context, what significance do the following phrases have: 'the path of the fourth-rank watch dragon,' and 'by Praxis' light, in seasons still to come'?"

"They are lines from the death poem of Molor."

Before Sulu could ask another question, Uhura said, "That

poem was in my upgrade courses. About fifteen hundred years ago, Kahless the Unforgettable defeated the tyrant Molor to found what became the Klingon Empire. It's considered a classic."

Chekov walked over to the console. He felt drained. He chose not to look at Sulu. "Kort referred to the lines as a code," he said.

Sulu did not respond to Chekov. He looked across the console at Uhura, instead. "Uhura, give the computer the Klingon phrase Jade found so interesting. I'll never be able to pronounce it."

Uhura cleared her throat. "Computer: Translate the Klingon phrase *chalchaj 'qmey."*

The computer complied at once. "Literally, the phrase translates as an archaic form of 'the sky's offspring.' "

"That's close to what I thought," Uhura said.

But the computer kept speaking. "In the context of the death poem of Molor, the phrase translates as 'the children of heaven,' referring to those who would inherit the lands destroyed by Molor during his final war against Kahless and his followers."

Sulu shook his head. "More code words?"

Chekov frowned. The *Excelsior's* captain was missing the point. "Computer: Vhat does the phrase 'children of heaven' mean in context of the Imperial Forecasters and the Crimson Level?"

This time the computer hesitated.

"That is restricted information."

Sulu gave Chekov a sardonic smile. "Computer: This is Captain Hikaru Sulu. Confirm voiceprint identification."

"Voiceprint identification confirmed."

"Security access code Sulu alpha-alpha-omicron-alpha. Identify the phrase."

Another hesitation. "That information is restricted."

It was Chekov's turn to smile. Sulu stared at the console in indignation. "Computer, I'm a starship captain. I have a level thirteen security clearance."

"That information is restricted to security clearance level seventeen."

Sulu looked up in amazement. "I thought there were only *fifteen* levels of clearance in all of Starfleet."

"That is restricted information," the computer replied.

Sulu unconsciously prodded his nose in thought. Chekov was pleased to see it seemed tender.

"A Klingon who was once involved in planning doomsday scenarios for the Empire . . ." Sulu said, thinking aloud. "Offers to share something so secret it's classified at one of Starfleet's highest levels . . . to what he believes is an illegal arms dealer."

Chekov stated the obvious, wondering why Sulu didn't see it. "It must be a veapon."

"Something exotic," Uhura added.

Sulu nodded. "And so terrible it would only be used in the event the Empire was defeated."

Chekov didn't like the implications. "There are those who vould say that given the current state of the Empire, it already has been defeated. Not by its enemies, but by history."

Sulu's scowl showed he didn't like the implications, either. For the first time since their fight, he looked at Chekov.

The tension was still thick between them.

"You're saying that someone might be deciding to use this weapon? Whatever it is?"

"I think that's obvious, gentlemen," Uhura said, trying to keep the two men from making matters personal again. "Whatever kind of weapon the 'Children of Heaven' is, it was enough to make a top Starfleet Intelligence agent willing to kill two other agents, so she could get the secret for herself."

"A renegade agent vith a Klingon doomsday veapon,"

Chekov sputtered. "This is far beyond the objectives of our mission."

"I agree," Sulu said. "You two will have to deliver a full report at once."

"Take us to a secure communications station," Chekov said. He began to walk toward the transporter room's doors.

"No," Sulu said.

Chekov turned to face him, ready to fight again if he had to.

"Vhat do you mean, 'no'?"

Six months of living like a criminal had had an effect on him.

Sulu remained calm. "Not by subspace. I think we have to assume that a Starfleet Intelligence agent like Jade has full access to current codes. It might be best for her to think you two really are dead. Otherwise, she might take extra precautions to make certain Starfleet can't find her."

"You want us to report in person?" Uhura asked.

"I don't even want to consider what a Klingon doomsday weapon might be capable of," Sulu said. "Their standard armaments are bad enough." He toggled another control on the console. "Captain to the bridge."

Sulu's science officer answered. "Bridge here, Captain."

"Lay in a course for Earth. Maximum warp. And maintain a communications blackout. I don't want anyone to know we're coming till we're there."

The science officer acknowledged her orders. "Bridge out."

"That serious?" Uhura said.

"That serious," Sulu confirmed. "We're going to have to take this to Admiral Drake himself."

"Admiral *Androwar* Drake?" Chekov repeated. "Vhy him?"

"He was just appointed commander in chief, Starfleet."

Chekov glared at Sulu with incredulous disgust.

Sulu's voice revealed he'd been unprepared for Chekov's

reaction. "Starfleet needed a new C in C to take over from the acting chief who replaced Cartwright."

Chekov headed for the transporter console and leaned against it for support. This changed everything.

Needing a replacement for Admiral Cartwright was old news. Because of Captain Kirk and his crew, Cartwright had been arrested at Camp Khitomer. He had been part of a conspiracy to restart hostilities between the Federation and the Klingon Empire.

In the aftermath of that arrest, Starfleet had been shaken to its core. Cartwright had been considered one of its ablest leaders. For someone of his reputation and stellar accomplishments to have been promoted to a position of absolute authority, while at the same time working against everything the Federation and Starfleet stood for, had been a depressing example of how far humanity still had to go. The twenty-third century was evidently not as perfect as some wished to believe.

"What's this about?" Sulu asked cautiously, apparently determined not to provoke Chekov again.

Chekov chose his words carefully. "Drake is not . . . commander in chief material," was all he would say.

Sulu's brow knitted in confusion. "What do you know that the Federation Council doesn't?"

But Chekov wouldn't answer. He couldn't.

He feared that despite the years they had spent on the *Enterprise,* a void had opened between himself and Sulu.

Chekov couldn't comment on Drake because Kirk had sworn him to secrecy.

And Chekov's loyalty to Kirk was absolute.

But Sulu was a starship captain now.

He had been willing to risk his friends' lives to follow orders to the letter.

Kirk would never have done that.

To Chekov, that meant Sulu had lost the capacity to think for himself, to question authority.

Which made him just the kind of officer who would blindly follow the orders of criminals like Admiral Drake.

Chekov left the transporter room without saying anything more.

As far as he was concerned, Sulu could no longer be trusted.

NINE

☆

The instant Kirk had coalesced from the transporter beam, he knew he had failed.

Again.

It was not an impression he was used to. He had always fought failure. He drew comfort from the certainty that this aspect of him, at least, would never change.

He shifted his boots in the sunbaked dust. He smelled the heat of the place, heard the silence. Felt its weight. He fought the impulse to grab his communicator and request an immediate beam out.

In the holographic environment simulator, he had found there were no answers for him in the past.

In the safe harbor of Carol Marcus's embrace, he had found there were no answers for him in comfort and distraction.

His Starfleet duties were little more than routine—filling his days with detail that in the end amounted to nothing.

His friends knew him well enough to support him, but never pretended they could give him direction.

So he had come here. To the final port in a fruitless mission.

And again there was nothing for him.

He might as well have stepped onto the sterile soil of a lifeless world.

But he was in Iowa.

On the farm.

Where he had been born. Where so long ago his father had held his hand on summer nights and first shown him the stars where he would find his first, best destiny.

With unsparing insight, Kirk knew he no longer belonged here, either. Hadn't for years.

Nor did he belong to any of the other worlds he had encountered in his travels.

He had no starting point to return to, no final destination that drew him.

He had no home.

Kirk inhaled deeply, sweeping the past from his mind, if not his heart.

He had often thought he could teach Spock a thing or two about controlling emotions.

He opened the front flap on his uniform jacket in a futile gesture against the heat. He walked toward the farmhouse. He tried not to remember how he once ran for it, bare feet kicking up dust, or sometimes mud, depending on the season.

His boots thudded on the worn wood of the porch steps. He tried not to remember how he once raced up them, hands and feet slapping the risers in giddy excitement, his brother Sam charging right behind him, because their father had returned from space.

He put his hand on the quartz screen of the lockplate by the front door. The scanning mechanism was a century old, an anachronistic antique, like most of the fixtures in the house. But it still worked.

The door lock clicked.

Kirk stepped into the front hall.

His bootsteps echoed. The house was empty. All the furniture long gone to cousins. He smiled fleetingly. His mother's three-hundred-year-old Amish rocker was in his nephew Peter's home on Deneva. What would its makers have thought to know the eventual fate of their work, hundreds of light-years from its birthplace?

He looked around the too-quiet house, thinking about the fate of *his* work. His job.

If he left Starfleet, he wouldn't have even that anymore.

The summer sun blazed through the windows. The dusty air was close and oppressive. Again, he turned away from his memories, of so many other summers when this house had been alive with hope and promise.

He went upstairs.

His room was much smaller than he remembered.

The doorframe still bore the marks his older brother had made to measure Kirk's growth.

Kirk ran his fingers over them, remembering how Sam had gouged them into the wood with a penknife.

His parents had protested each new mark Sam had added. But George Kirk had never repaired the damage.

His father had known. Memories were the markers of the journey through life. It was necessary to know where you had come from. Only then could you know where you were going.

Kirk ran his hand along the smooth upper reaches of the doorframe, where his height had never been recorded.

He knew where he was going. All humans did.

But how would he get there?

What would the rest of his journey bring before its inevitable end?

Wood creaked downstairs.

Kirk stopped breathing.

Another, barely perceptible scrape on the bare floor below.

The air in the old farmhouse was subtly different.

There was someone else here.

Kirk came alive.

His hand reached instinctively for his belt and his phaser.

But, of course, there was no weapon there. Weapons were no longer needed on this perfect Earth.

His mind quickly sifted through options and strategies. The intruder—how easily he fell into thinking like a starship captain—was most likely one of the advocates handling his parents' estate. That's why Kirk was here, after all. A final visit before deciding whether or not to sell the place.

But an advocate would have shouted out a greeting by now. An advocate would make more noise, having nothing to hide.

Kirk moved swiftly, silently, to the stairway. He knew the location of every loose floorboard. Each step revealed the depth of his education by experts in the martial arts of the Klingons and the ancient patterns of Vulcan self-defense.

Except for that damned nerve pinch, he had mastered them all.

The hallway was empty. He glided down the stairs, as silent as a Vulcan. Even the dust was not disturbed, so knowing was his step.

He saw a shadow move across the hallway floor, just for an instant blocking the sun. The intruder was in the kitchen.

Kirk was aware of every nerve end. His heart was calm, his breathing steady. But he was ready to uncoil. To be all that he had trained to be. All that he had been born to be.

Like smoke, he moved through the hallway of his home and into the kitchen doorway.

His hands were raised in the Klingon first position, his body tensed for impact.

He was prepared for anything.

Except for what he saw.

TEN

☆

She.

From the reception.

Of the Klingon brow, the Romulan ears.

She wore a black jumpsuit, so formfitting it would forever lay McCoy's concerns to rest. This was no girl, this was a woman—superbly muscled, an athlete by any standard. And though her costume seemed designed only to emphasize her form, there was something about it that might have made Kirk think it was some type of uniform.

If Kirk had been able to think.

But his only reaction to her was visceral, as it had been at the reception.

She exploded into his senses.

"At last," she said. Her voice rich, low, filling the kitchen, focusing Kirk's attention absolutely.

Dimly, he thought he should say something.

"Who . . . ?" But it was no good. His voice cracked, as if unused for years. As if words were not needed.

Her smile was instant. As if he had known her forever. As if this were a reunion and not a first meeting.

She moved toward him until she was so close, he could feel the heat of her.

"Teilani," she said.

Her breath carried flowers and soft winds, erasing the staleness of the empty house.

Kirk's heart thundered. He tried to speak again.

But she placed a hand to his face.

"Shhh," she admonished.

Her touch was incredible, both soft and bitingly electric at the same time.

The kitchen seemed to spin around Kirk.

Her arms moved around him, one hand pressing into his back, one hand forcing his head down, his lips to meet hers.

He was aware of nothing but the weight of her body against his. The yielding softness of her lips against his.

The taste of her. The scent of her.

He kissed her with an urgency he hadn't known in years, crushing her to him, closer and closer, feeling her back arch in response, until his body burned with the anticipation of the only way an embrace this intense could end.

It took that long for him to fully realize what he was doing.

For his consciousness to catch up to his senses.

With the clear thought that he would probably regret his decision for the rest of his life, Kirk pushed her away.

"No," he said.

He felt her surprise. Her dark eyes seemed to glow with the force of her energy. Or the sun from the kitchen windows.

"But, James, at the reception . . . I saw this in your eyes."

"Who are you?" he asked, keeping her away from him with his hands on her shoulders, fighting the need to be overwhelmed again.

"Teilani." She repeated her name as if it alone explained her existence.

"No," Kirk said. "*Who* are you? Where are you from? What are you doing in my parents' home?"

She took a step closer. "Why do you resist what you know your heart wants?"

Kirk did want her. He wasn't fooling himself any more than he was fooling her.

But he had long ago learned that mere appetite could not be allowed to rule his life.

He had not needed Spock to teach him about balance in all things. It was his nature.

He dropped his hands from her shoulders, moved back a step.

"How do you know me?"

She laughed, the sound thrilling, exotic.

"The whole galaxy knows you," she said simply, as if explaining something to a beloved child.

Kirk felt almost dizzy, intoxicated. He forced himself to think about pheromone scents. Subsonic fields that might affect his thought processes. Any one of dozens of possible technological explanations for what had happened to him. For how he *felt.*

McCoy's voice echoed in his ear. The words still possessed their bite. *You're old enough to be her* grand*father.*

"You're not answering my questions," he said.

She regarded him through half-closed eyes. The delicate tip of her tongue played tantalizingly across her lips. Their surface glistened. She moved a hand to the neck of her jumpsuit, to the tiny control switch of the fabric sealer.

"There's time enough for talk, later," she said, leaving no doubt as to what she expected to happen *now.*

She pressed a finger to the control. The fabric of her jumpsuit parted down her neck. She lifted her finger, held it poised, ready to part the fabric even more.

Kirk willed himself to keep his eyes locked on hers.

"There won't be a later," he said. "Unless you answer me now."

With that, everything changed.

Teilani's smile this time was one that encouraged friendship, not desire. She tugged once on her collar, an odd gesture. Her jumpsuit stayed open, though. A casual look. Not necessarily seductive.

Hell, Kirk thought. She's seductive just standing there.

"Ask me whatever you wish to know, James. I can have no

secrets from you." Then she turned her back to him and walked to the window over the kitchen sink.

Kirk's pupils automatically widened as his eyes traced the unbroken line of the jumpsuit along her back, down her legs, each curve undisguised. But he looked away. It was no time for distraction.

He moved to the other side of the kitchen, leaned against the counter. The sunlight shining through the window over the sink caught her hair in a mesmerizing interplay of light and shadow.

A halo, Kirk thought. As if his visitor were some mythic creature descended from the heavens.

"Why were you at the reception?" he asked, mentally shrugging off the vision. The question seemed so prosaic for one so celestial.

"I was invited."

She smiled again and this time he returned it, relaxing a fraction. It was to be a game, he decided with relief. He could deal with that. Enjoy it, even. The rules would give him a badly needed focus.

"And *why* were you invited?"

"To celebrate the selection of Starfleet's new commander in chief."

"That's not what I meant," Kirk said. "Invitations went out to Starfleet personnel, diplomats, industry leaders from the Federation—"

"And to the Klingon Empire," she continued. "The Romulan Star Empire. The First Federation. The unaligned worlds."

"And which are you?"

She looked down for a moment, as if the question were difficult, required thought.

"Unaligned," she said. "For now."

That made no sense to Kirk. The heritage of her brow and ears clearly said she was one of either the Klingon or Romulan empire. "But your . . . parents . . ." Kirk said, unsure as to how blunt he could be. Despite Spock's logic, one of her parents might even have been Vulcan.

Teilani traced a finger along the sweep of one delicately pointed ear. "Once, my home was a colony world." She neglected to say of which empire. "We opted for . . . independence, many years ago."

Kirk's instincts instantly told him her statement was the beginning of a story. Her initial, mind-dazzling approach to him had been some sort of smoke screen. She had something to tell him. Something she wanted from him.

He was pleased he had turned her advances aside, seen through her game before he knew it was even being played.

Good instincts, he decided. At least *they* still worked.

The afternoon was shaping up to be far more rewarding than he had first thought when he had arrived.

"Tell me, *Teilani,*" Kirk began. "Why is it—"

It was then the attack began.

ELEVEN

☆

Kirk saw it like a slow-replay holoprojection.

The kitchen window behind Teilani erupted in a starburst of glittering glassite shards. Each glint and sparkle of sunlight on the shattered fragments etched a pinpoint afterimage of black against his eyes.

A spray of green blood blossomed over her shoulder, expanding like a galaxy in space.

Her scream was low, drawn out, distorted.

Her arc through the air seemed effortless.

Kirk surged forward, trapped in dreamlike slow motion, as if the air had thickened, as if the kitchen expanded to stretch the distance between her and him.

She hit the floor, hair flying. She slid. Moaned. Blood smearing from the angry green gash atop her shoulder, the black jumpsuit torn.

Kirk heard the whistle of another projectile cutting through the air.

The far wall shuddered with a spray of plaster.

But Kirk was not distracted from what he knew he must do. Even as he scooped her into his arms, he assimilated the details of the attack, calculated his response.

Holding her securely, he burst through the kitchen doorway, heading for the stairway.

Teilani's eyes were shut tight with pain, though the bleeding had stopped already.

Kirk halted by the stairway. He heard footsteps running outside. Teilani stayed limp in his arms.

There were at least two attackers, Kirk knew. The angle of the two projectile blasts had told him that—each from a different location of cover. The first blast to hit the wall had come from beside the barn.

Kirk began to see his strategy. Projectile weapons meant the attackers weren't local. Local farmers who kept weapons preferred old-fashioned laser rifles. Times were slow to change in Iowa.

Projectile weapons also gave Kirk a clue to the attackers' motives. He considered it rapidly. If they had wanted to kidnap either Teilani or him, they'd be using phasers to stun them. If they had just wanted to kill Teilani or him, they'd have used more powerful phasers to disintegrate them.

Their use of projectile weapons indicated they wanted to kill someone, *and* have a body left to show for it. To prove that the job had been done, or to teach others a lesson.

Kirk could imagine there would be a few old-guard

Klingons who would want to phaser him out of existence. He knew there were others in the galaxy who'd pay to drag him back to some alien world for a slow and painful death. There were exceptions to every argument, Kirk knew, but he was certain even Spock would conclude that whoever was charging up the porch stairs of his family farmhouse, they weren't after James T. Kirk.

They were after Teilani.

He heard them fumble with the lockplate. They probably had transmitters that could open any lock made in the past fifty years. Kirk thanked his father for his love of antiques.

His glance swept upward. The stairs. The Academy taught that high ground was always preferable. But that meant it was always expected.

Kirk pushed his boot against a section of the wood paneling that ran up the side of the stairway.

A hidden, half-sized door popped open.

The damp smell of the cellar enveloped him.

It had been his playground as a child. He and his brother had fought many valiant last stands there in endless games of Humans and Romulans.

He ducked down, forcing his way through the small door as he heard a projectile blast the front door's ancient lockplate.

He winced as he realized that with his injured shoulder he could barely compensate for Teilani's added weight as he bent over.

He sat down heavily on the top step, still holding Teilani. She stirred and looked up at him.

He shook his head before she could speak, then reached out to find the crosspiece he knew so well on the small door and pulled it shut.

The instant after the cellar door clicked shut, Kirk heard the front door burst open.

The enemy entered his house.

He was surprised at the anger he felt.

Two harsh voices spoke. Their speech was clipped. He couldn't make out the language.

But it wasn't human.

Rapid footsteps rang out above them, past the hidden basement door into the kitchen. Kirk eased Teilani to the step below him. He placed a hand on her shoulder to guide her down the wooden stairs, into the darkness.

She moved silently. As if she was as classically trained as Kirk.

He followed behind her. Twelve steps down to the dirt floor.

The footsteps were slower now, more cautious. They retraced their direction to the hidden doorway. Then stopped.

Kirk nudged Teilani under the staircase.

She didn't resist. She didn't speak. She followed his unspoken orders. Whoever she was, Kirk guessed she wasn't a civilian.

His curiosity about her grew.

Then the footsteps resumed, became fainter. They moved upward, to the higher ground. Kirk was pleased. It meant the attackers had been classically trained, too. It also meant they didn't have anything resembling a tricorder that could scan for life signs.

Kirk smiled. This was going to be easy. He reached for his belt. Brought out his communicator. Held the mute button as he opened it, cutting off its distinctive chirp.

In the pale light of its status indicators, Kirk and Teilani looked at each other. Neither showed fear. There was only intense expectation.

Kirk knew the feeling well. Every time he faced death.

Kirk moved closer to Teilani and put her arm around his waist. He tapped the silent, emergency recall button on the communicator. In seconds, the Starfleet transporter grid would beam him and Teilani to an orbital station.

He braced for the cool wash of the transporter beam.

It didn't come.

Something thudded upstairs. He felt Teilani's arm tighten involuntarily around him. Classically trained for combat, he decided, but not experienced.

He risked opening an audible communications channel to see what had gone wrong.

For an instant, static hissed.

Kirk closed the communicator. Whoever the attackers were, they had a subspace jammer operating nearby. The transporter wasn't going to save the day.

But that suited Kirk.

The two intruders remained upstairs. Chances were they'd been briefed on the type of structure they might find on a human farm. That meant they'd know there was an attic to be searched. Eventually, they'd think about a cellar as well.

But chances also were they hadn't been given a full grounding in human history, and how humans had responded to various threats throughout the centuries.

Kirk moved out from under the stairs, drawing Teilani out with him. In the darkness, he guided her toward where he knew the far wall would be. He lifted his feet only a centimeter from the ground, sliding each forward slowly, just in case any boxes or furniture still remained down here. Without being told, Teilani matched her movements to his, exactly.

Though the farmhouse had been remodeled over the years, and the decades, most of it dated from almost two hundred and fifty years earlier. Good, solid, pre-World War III construction.

The Earth had been a different place then. Dark, paranoid, no one certain if the human race would survive long enough to use the incredible promise of Zefram Cochrane's startling breakthrough of warp propulsion.

So humans had taken measures to insure their survival.

The day that little Jimmy and his brother had found the old bomb shelter under their house had marked one of Kirk's most exciting summers.

Their parents hadn't wanted them playing down there, ten meters beneath the side yard. But Kirk and his brother had scavenged wood and plastic, rescued discarded furniture, made it their secret starbase.

And like all good secret starbases, it had secret entrances. One from the house. And one from the barn.

While the intruders investigated the high ground, Kirk and Teilani would outflank them.

Kirk reached out blindly and touched the cellar wall exactly where he estimated it should be. He slid his fingers along the rough polycrete, dislodging dust and old cobwebs, till he found the edge of the tunnel door. It wasn't disguised. He found the small handle. Twisted it.

The door was stuck.

He let go of Teilani, held one hand open and ready, then tugged on the handle. With a crack of old paint, the door popped open.

Kirk heard Teilani take a sharp breath and hold it.

He listened more carefully.

Nothing.

He had learned there was never any sense in hoping for the best in these conditions. The intruders must have heard the door open. They were just trying to decide from where the sound had come.

Kirk quickly reached into the tunnel and explored the wall's surface. He found the switch. Light channels flickered into subdued life on the ceiling.

Kirk motioned for Teilani to go first. She crouched down to fit under the tunnel's low ceiling and started forward.

Kirk listened one last time for footsteps. They were coming downstairs. Fast.

He crouched. Entered the tunnel. Pulled the door shut behind him. Threw the sliding lock.

"Run," he said. The time for silence was over.

They scrambled along the tunnel, passing through dark sections where the light channels had finally given out. It turned sharply at thirty meters, where the entrance to the bomb shelter was. Kirk felt it was a small victory. At least the enemy couldn't just pull open the door and fire wildly down the tunnel. Now he'd be able to hear them as they approached the turn.

Teilani slowed as she saw the bomb shelter's entrance. But it was not Kirk's destination. If they entered the shelter, it would only be a trap. There would be nothing to prevent one attacker from remaining on guard outside while the other went for a phaser, which could easily burn through the heavy metal door.

So Kirk urged Teilani to keep running. The door to the barn entrance was dead ahead. Once there, she moved to the side to let Kirk pass. He saw her frown, puzzled by the crude attempts at Romulan words Kirk and his brother had written on the tunnel wall in their childhood.

Kirk didn't bother to listen for their pursuers in the tunnel. He shoved open the door, pulled Teilani through, then closed it behind them.

They stood in a sunken stairwell, which was open to the barn. Kirk looked up to the rafters overhead. Enough sunlight filtered in through the old boards that he could see where he was going.

He sprinted up the polycrete stairs, no longer concerned about noise. Teilani followed. At the top of the stairs, Kirk paused, looked around. There were still some old hay bales by the empty horse stalls. He headed for them.

Together, he and Teilani tossed five bales into the stairwell. The attackers would have to dig their way out once they realized they couldn't open the door.

"I don't hear them," Teilani whispered.

For a brief moment, as he looked at her, Kirk couldn't help noticing the incongruous strands of hay in her hair.

"Maybe they haven't found the cellar yet," Kirk whispered back. He reached out to brush away the straw, remembering the romantic adventures he had had in this barn. All the hay he had had brushed from his own hair.

Then he heard the thud of a vehicle door outside.

He crept to a narrow gap between two boards in the barn's high wall. Teilani followed. Shoulder to shoulder they peered out through the slit.

An antigrav car was parked in the yard, halfway between the barn and the farmhouse. It was a late-model, self-drive rental, the kind that could fly off the programmed flight paths.

The attackers wore nondescript civilian clothes that would not attract attention on any world. One, with bare, hard-muscled arms and a long, sleeveless vest, sat in the passenger side, intent on adjusting some piece of equipment on his lap. The other, in a dull gray tunic, stood beside the open door, holding ready a gleaming silver projectile gun, looking anxiously about.

But their clothing, their weapons, and their equipment weren't the important details Kirk focused on.

His attackers' foreheads were furrowed like a Klingon's.

But their ears were pointed.

Just like Teilani. Youths, no older than she was. And in the same superb state of fitness.

"Do you know them?" Kirk whispered. For an instant, he took his eyes off the youth with the gun.

Teilani shook her head.

Kirk wasn't certain if he could believe her.

"But they're your people," he said.

"There are many like I am. I don't know them all."

"But you know who sent them," Kirk persisted. "Tell me why they want you."

Her dark eyes burned into him.

"They don't want *me,* James. They want *you.*"

TWELVE

☆

Kirk didn't believe her.

There was no reason for these youths to pursue him.

He didn't know them. Had never known anyone like them.

"Why?" he asked.

But close beside him, Teilani shook her head, held a finger to her lips. Listened intently.

The youths were talking. Kirk didn't understand a word. Their words were too faint, their language unknown.

But Teilani's ears were apparently as sensitive as Spock's. And she knew their language. "They think we might have transported away," she whispered.

"How could we? They're jamming my communicator."

"That's what they're checking now."

Kirk watched the two Klingon-Romulans in heated conversation. The one in the vehicle slammed shut the cover of the equipment on his lap. Kirk decided that was the subspace jammer. They would have to know it was functioning properly. They'd have to know that he and Teilani were still somewhere near.

Kirk stared at the antigrav car. Suddenly realized what he had missed.

"How did you get here?" he asked her.

"Car," Teilani said. "I parked it down by the gate."

Kirk calculated the odds. The gate was three hundred meters down the drive. Even at Teilani's age he couldn't outrun a projectile over that distance.

The youth in the car got out. Kirk watched the powerful muscles in his arms flex impatiently as he also drew a gleaming projectile gun from inside his vest.

Now both youths stood in the yard, dark eyes sweeping the area, weapons held ready.

"They're going to find us," Kirk said softly.

Teilani looked at him, alarmed. "You're giving up?"

Kirk felt insulted. "No. I'm stating the inevitable. If we're going to take control of the situation, we have to make them find us under *our* terms, not theirs."

Teilani raised an eyebrow in appreciation. Kirk almost smiled at how familiar her expression was.

"Tell me what to do," she said.

Kirk looked around the barn. It was all so familiar. He and Sam had saved the Federation a thousand times here.

He decided the enemy wouldn't have a chance.

It took less than a minute to set the trap. Baiting it would not be any additional trouble. The Klingon-Romulans were already beginning to move toward the barn.

Kirk watched them from his vantage point high in the hayloft. Teilani now crouched by the empty horse stalls. He signaled to her. She ducked down, out of sight. Kirk tossed a small piece of chipped polycrete so that it hit the barn door.

Instantly both Klingon-Romulans fired at the door, splintering its ancient wood. The barn reverberated with the twin explosions.

Then the youth in the gray tunic ran forward and kicked away the remains of two barn boards, creating a new entrance in the closed barn door.

He eased through slowly, gleaming weapon leading the way.

Then he was in the barn, looking all around.

"There is no escape!" the Klingon-Romulan called out, in precise Federation Standard. There was no trace of any accent Kirk could identify. "Accept your fate! Die honorably!"

Kirk held his position, knowing he could not be seen. The

youth's sentiments had more than a touch of Klingon sensibility to them. But Kirk thought it interesting that the hunter had not called out the name of his intended prey—either Kirk or Teilani.

The youth remained in position, unmoving. Kirk understood the strategy. Wait for your opponent to make a mistake.

But mistakes were for the impatient young. Kirk didn't make them anymore.

At least, not in situations like this.

In the end, Kirk's patience, and experience, won out.

The youth in gray said something over his shoulder, moved farther into the barn. His partner edged warily through the splintered door.

Kirk waited till the two Klingon-Romulans stood shoulder to shoulder, each checking a different angle of the barn's interior. Then Kirk tossed his second chip of polycrete.

It landed far back in the barn's depths.

An instant after it bounced against a wooden post, two explosions followed as the Klingon-Romulans fired.

Kirk was impressed by their reflexes.

But the chip hadn't been intended to draw their fire. It was Kirk's second signal to Teilani.

She made her move.

Like a molten shadow she flew from a stall, somersaulting over the half-height door, flipping over, landing precisely on her feet and continuing on.

The barn rang with the sounds of explosions as the attackers' shots traced Teilani's path, always a heartbeat behind.

But Kirk didn't stop to admire her acrobatics. He had no doubt she would end up vaulting onto the hay bales in the sunken stairwell, safely out of range of any more explosive shells. And by then, the enemy would no longer be a threat.

Kirk would see to that.

It was his turn.

Leaping from the hayloft. Rocketing down on the rope

looped around the old hay pulley. Pulling up his legs just *so* to hit each Klingon-Romulan squarely in the back with each boot.

The bare-armed youth just started to turn in time. Just managed to see Kirk's boot as it drove toward him.

The wrenching impact sent shocks of fire along Kirk's legs and up his back. His teeth clacked together, sending sparks of pain flashing through his jaw.

But the pain was easily ignored in the satisfaction of feeling his enemies' bodies become unresisting deadweights as they absorbed his charge.

Kirk released the rope and landed running. He spun around, ready to dive forward.

And he had to dive.

The youth in the gray tunic lay facedown on the barn's polycrete floor. But his bare-armed partner was on his knees, aiming his weapon.

Kirk hit the floor on his shoulder. He gasped in shock as his strained shoulder crunched on impact.

Reflexively he slapped the ground to absorb his momentum and spare further affront to his back and arm. The sudden stop of his forward motion saved his life as an explosive shell ripped out a hole in the polycrete just before him.

The left side of his face stung with a spray of stone chips.

Kirk jumped to his feet, ready to dodge again.

The kneeling youth brought his weapon up.

Teilani charged. Her bloodcurdling Klingon death cry filled the barn. The youth's weapon wavered.

That moment's distraction was all Kirk needed.

He leapt forward.

Teilani hit the floor and rolled at the exact instant a projectile blasted through the air above her.

Kirk hit the youth shoulder to chest.

It was the final indignity to Kirk's challenged muscles. Something tore in his shoulder. Kirk's teeth ground together.

He tasted blood from the cuts on his face. But still he grabbed the bare-armed youth by the front of his vest and drove in hard with a solid head butt.

Stars flashed before Kirk's eyes with the sharp crack of his forehead against the youth's heavy brow ridges.

But green blood flooded from the attacker's nose. His dark eyes lost focus.

Kirk let go of the fabric of the vest.

His adversary fell back with a moan.

Kirk longed to do the same. But he settled for sitting back on the floor, taking inventory of his aching joints and limbs.

He was disgusted to hear himself wheeze as he fought to recover his breath.

Right now, he felt old enough to be Teilani's *great*-grandfather.

She knelt beside him. She held both attackers' weapons. "You're hurt, James."

Kirk laughed at the understatement. The action sent a new wave of agony through his shoulder, forced him to gasp for breath. But he laughed again.

Teilani frowned. "You think this is . . . amusing?"

Kirk shook his head, barely able to speak. "No . . ." he gasped. "I was . . . I was just thinking . . . that I haven't felt . . . this good . . . in years."

He saw the baffled expression in her eyes. He couldn't help it. Laughter welled up in him, uncontrollable.

The pain only made it harder to stop.

THIRTEEN

☆

When he felt he could breathe without setting fire to his shoulder, Kirk stood. He even accepted Teilani's offered hand to help him to his feet.

For a moment, he felt light-headed. He didn't know if it was from oxygen starvation or adrenaline letdown. He didn't particularly care. From experience, he knew the sensation would pass, so the sensation could be ignored.

The first thing to be done was to consolidate his gains. He knelt beside one of the felled Klingon-Romulans, opened his vest, felt inside for an ID packet or set of credit wafers. But only found a clip of microexplosive projectiles.

Then Kirk realized that something wasn't right.

He held his hand to the youth's chest.

It wasn't moving.

He put his fingers to the youth's neck. Felt nothing where a human carotid artery would be. Moved farther back along the jaw to where the Vulcan and Romulan equivalent would be. Then pushed under the jaw for the Klingon pulse point.

The attacker was dead.

"I didn't hit him that hard," Kirk said.

He went to the second youth, still facedown on the floor. He rolled the body over. There was a small pool of coagulating blood from the youth's mouth, a few splattered drops of it on his gray tunic, but no more than would result from a split lip or dislodged tooth.

Yet this second youth was also dead.

"No," Kirk protested. It made no sense.

Teilani tried to comfort him. "But they were trying to kill *you*, James."

"That's not it," Kirk said. These were young men. Fit and strong. They weren't meant to die from a blow to the jaw or a kick to the back.

It was becoming apparent to Kirk that he had seen too much death in his years. More and more it sickened him to play a part in adding to the universe's store of it.

"*Why* were they trying to kill me?" Kirk asked. He felt the need to make their deaths count for something. Anything. He took Teilani by the shoulders again. "You owe me answers."

But she touched his face again, held out a single finger stained with red blood. Kirk's blood.

"There's a medkit in my car," she said.

Kirk looked down at the bodies of the two young Klingon-Romulans. They weren't going anyplace. He nodded wearily. He started for the barn door. Teilani quickly took hold of his hand, as if to steady him. He didn't protest her action. In the back of his mind came the terrible thought that he might stumble without her support.

Outside, Kirk paused before beginning the long walk to the gate and Teilani's car. He drew in a deep breath. The air had become sharper, sweeter, more intense than before.

Kirk knew the reason for the change.

Victory. Triumph. Life.

His life.

Will it always be this way? he wondered. Could he only find purpose in cheating death? And how much longer would his aging body *let* him cheat death? What would happen when his reflexes could no longer achieve what his instincts demanded?

An unwelcome memory surfaced. Captain Christopher Pike in his life-support chair. A starship captain reduced to little more than an inert receptacle for an imprisoned mind.

Kirk never wanted to face that—the day the mind outstripped the body. But as he limped along the dirt driveway to the gate, now with his arm around Teilani's shoulders, he had to admit that his body *was* beginning to succumb to the ravages of time.

"Tell me, Teilani," he said, each word an unexpected effort. "Why did they come here?"

"So you would not be able to help me."

"Help you do what?"

"Bring peace to my world."

She was almost as infuriating as Spock could be, answering only the specific question, never volunteering additional details.

"Where is your world? What's its name?"

Kirk caught Teilani smiling at him, affectionately. "Don't try to change the subject again," he warned. He knew the power over him that that smile unleashed.

"I'm not. It's just that I know you must be in pain, yet you still hunger for knowledge." She gave his hand a firm squeeze that was not necessary for support. "I was right to choose you."

Kirk groaned. She was maddening in many ways. "For *what?*"

They were almost at the gate. Kirk could see a groundcar parked behind it, on the shoulder of the country road. From a nearby stand of chestnut trees, he heard cicadas whine in the heat. Birds sang songs he remembered from childhood summers.

Teilani paused imperceptibly. She seemed to come to some decision. "My world has many designations, James, depending on whose charts it appears. But for those of us who were born there, who live there, we call it *Chal.*"

She looked at him as if testing him for any prior knowledge of what she was about to tell him. But the name of her planet meant nothing to Kirk.

"It began as a colony," she continued. "A joint venture of sorts. I think you can guess who its founders were."

Kirk nodded. "The Klingons, and the Romulans."

"One of many attempts to bring the two empires together." Teilani frowned. "And a failure, like all the others."

They were at the gate. Teilani carefully lifted Kirk's arm from around her shoulders so she could walk ahead and open the latch, swing the gate open. The gate wasn't a security device. Just a simple barricade to keep neighbors' livestock from wandering in.

"You said you opted for independence," Kirk prompted her. He fought to keep his balance without her young body to lean on.

"In the end, neither empire wanted us. So we chose to make our own way."

As Teilani swung the gate open, its old hinges squealed.

Feeling sudden kinship with the antiquated gate, Kirk awkwardly started for the groundcar. He squared his shoulders as best he could, somehow resisting the humiliating temptation to shuffle. He felt embarrassed by his condition. Exhausted. Vulnerable.

"I can't imagine either empire willingly giving up a colony world," he said. "Not if there was a chance the other side would claim it."

They stood before the groundcar—another self-drive rental. It was a touring model with an extended hull, and wide bench seats in the back under a clear viewing dome. Kirk knew it was a favorite of tourists who crossed the light-years to visit the Amish farms nearby.

"As far as either empire knew at the time, my world had nothing of value. Chal was nothing more than a failed experiment from the past. More regrettable than exploitable."

"At the time," Kirk repeated. "Then something has changed?" He stood back as Teilani punched in the operating code on the door. It swung up with a soft hiss of air.

"Yes," she said, and Kirk was surprised to hear in that one word the same weariness he felt. As if Teilani bore a burden far beyond her years. She lifted the door all the way open so

Kirk could enter. As he gripped the side of the car to step inside, he reflected on his new role—the one being protected, not protecting. It was . . . different.

Kirk chose a rear seat. Teilani entered a moment later and took the driver's seat. She punched more controls on the dash. Kirk felt cool air begin to circulate, cutting the heat that had built up beneath the dome.

Teilani pivoted the driver's seat around to face him, then reached below to open a small compartment marked with a red cross. The medkit was required equipment for all cars. An example of the pervasive regulations that made Earth what it was today.

"There's trouble on your world now, isn't there," Kirk said. He slipped easily into the diagnosis of conflict. The habit of too many years. Too much experience. "Two factions, at least. You represent one. Those people who tried to kill us, they represent the other."

Teilani laid out the contents of the medkit like a soldier. She ripped open a sterile swab.

"As you suspect, our world has something of value after all. Something neither empire knew of. Some on Chal want to profit from our past and our world's treasure. Pit both empires against each other and side with whichever promises the richer price." She fixed her lustrous eyes on Kirk. They were mesmerizing in their clarity and unwavering gaze. "But some of us don't want a return to the conflict and the violence of the past. We cannot allow our world to be plundered and exploited. Chal must be preserved for our children, and their children. Not squandered."

The spray hypo she held against his injured shoulder hissed against his skin. A cool sensation of relief eased the shoulder's pain.

Kirk had no doubt which side Teilani was on. He thought it odd that one so young should worry about the future. He hadn't when he had been her age. There had only been the eternal present for him. He tried to keep that same state of mind these days, but it was more difficult with each passing year.

Teilani reached out to wipe his face. But he stopped her.

"How about *your* shoulder?" he asked.

She touched the tear in her jumpsuit, crusted with blood. "It's fine," she said.

Again, Kirk didn't take her word as given. He took the swab from her, remembering the explosion of green that had burst from her.

"We'll look after you first," he said. "I've just got a few scrapes."

She tried to pull back, but he wouldn't let her. He braced her shoulder with one hand, then used his other hand to begin cleansing her wound with the swab.

The dried green blood flaked away.

Kirk stopped.

There *was* no wound.

Only a purplish green bruise and raised yellow welt. With no indication that the skin had ever been broken or blood had ever been spilled.

"I *saw* you get shot," Kirk said.

Teilani held his hand against her shoulder.

"There was blood," Kirk said. "The projectile *exploded. Threw* you across the kitchen. I *know* you were hurt."

Teilani's eyes sought his. Held them.

"I told you my world has a treasure, James."

He pulled on the fabric of her jumpsuit, exposing her shoulder, to be certain he was not mistaken.

Except for the bruise and welt beneath the original tear, her skin was unmarked and flawless.

"How is this possible?" Kirk demanded.

Teilani took his hand and held it to her shoulder. He could feel her pulse.

"This is the treasure of my world, James. The gift it bestows on all who live there."

Kirk felt the heat of her unblemished body warm his hand. But a chill spread through him, too.

"Come home to Chal with me, James. Come home with me and save my world." Her eyes bore into his like phasers set to an infinite power. "Come home, and be young *forever.*"

FOURTEEN

When that impossible day came to an end, Kirk had no clear memory of it.

Too much had happened. Too much had changed.

The bittersweet return to his boyhood home, perhaps for the final time. The disturbing shock of urgent passion triggered by Teilani's unexpected appearance. The fierce but welcome fight to cheat death one more time. The rebirth that followed survival. As it always followed.

And then—Teilani's revelation.

Of Chal and its secret.

A world where youth was eternal. Where death had no dominion.

As Teilani had tended his wounds, she told him more of Chal. Nameless to all but its colonists, poor in resources, a water world with only vegetation and a handful of animal species on its minuscule island landmasses. A distant, worthless world. On the farthest reaches of the two empires' reluctantly shared, often disputed border.

She had slipped off his jacket, his shirt. Her cool hands and skillful fingers had probed the muscles of his shoulder. Kirk had closed his eyes as her hands moved over him, kneading, caressing, somehow taking away the fire and the pain.

And then Teilani's touch had brought a sudden memory of being in a different place, being soothed the same way.

He smelled wood fire. Remembered Miramanee, the tribal priestess on the Preserver planet. Saw her dark hair swaying above him, bound by her headband, all that she wore. She moved her hands across him in an ancient ritual of her people, calling him Kirok, making him hers.

The memory flashed through him in an instant and he was with Teilani again. She told him of the fitful truce between the empires. The selection of her nameless world as a place to strengthen their bonds. In time, the empires had fallen apart again. Trade broke off. The colony world had been abandoned.

Eventually, even the founders left, returning to the more familiar, profitable worlds of their youth. But their children chose to remain behind with what was familiar to them. Hybrids all, Klingon *and* Romulan. With the perversity of youth, they had determined to side with neither empire, to strike off on their own.

And they had. Forging a new home. A new culture. Working for a distant future when they could bequeath an independent, functioning world to their children.

But Chal had changed their future. Even as their own children grew to adulthood, that first generation did not age.

Eventually, all had realized that illness never struck their world. Inevitable accidents, provided they weren't instantly fatal, resulted only in injuries that healed without trace. Almost at once.

Kirk moved his fingers across Teilani's unmarked shoulder.

Less than an hour after being shot, her wound was gone completely.

It was Teilani's turn to close her eyes, to push her shoulder into Kirk's hand, sighing as their flesh again made contact and she guided his hand beneath the fabric of her clothing.

"Chal needs a hero," she breathed into his ear. "*I* need a hero. To show us how to defend ourselves from those who would destroy us."

Her lips brushed his neck. Her hands moved across his back, delicately raking her sharp nails across his skin, awakening nerve endings to a heightened awareness of what it was possible to feel.

Kirk was engulfed by sensations he no longer wanted to question, no longer was able to question.

He moved his face against her shoulder, delighting in the warm scent of her hair, the delicacy of each tiny thread of it feathering the back of her neck.

Another memory claimed him, pulling him from the here and now. He was in his cabin on the *Enterprise*, tangled in the glittering bedspread. His lips trailed across the neck of Marlena Moreau. In another universe, a dark reflection of his own, she had been the captain's woman. *His* woman. In this instant, her scent still clung to him, blending with Teilani's.

Kirk brought himself back to the moment. Brushed his lips across Teilani's. Savored her sweetness. "You could go to the Federation Council," he said softly. "If Chal is unaligned, you could petition for membership, for protectorate status."

He listened to the words he said with a sense of unreality, as if someone else were speaking. One hand slipped to her waist, imprinting the feel and the shape of her into his senses.

The past claimed him again. He felt the smooth skin of Kelinda. The icy beauty of the Kelvan explorer afire with the sensations he brought to her for the first time in her human form.

Kirk knew what it was like to be overwhelmed by unexpected desire, as he had overwhelmed Kelinda. Teilani reawakened those same sensations in him now, as her hands caressed him.

"We cannot go to the Federation," Teilani said, her breath quickening in response to his own caress. Kirk felt as if two strangers conversed in the car while two others communed in an exchange far more primal. "We are too deep in Klingon territory, in Romulan territory, for either to accept a Federation claim."

Her hand captured his. Raised it to her lips. Moved her soft tongue against and between his fingers, taking his breath away.

"We must do this on our own," she whispered, "or not at all."

Her other hand sought the dash behind her, found a control.

Slowly, the viewing dome darkened into total opacity, encasing them in a cocoon of silence and privacy. A universe of their own.

"All or nothing," she said. They were her final words.

All else that followed was beyond language.

Each sound she made, each move, propelled Kirk further from himself, into a realm of inexpressible perception.

He was as overwhelmed as he had been by the tears of the Dohlman. Elaan of Troyius was within his arms again, demanding lips crushing his with a passion he had never encountered before.

But which he now encountered again.

Come home with me and be young forever.

Teilani had reawakened the youth of his past, given purpose to his present, and now she was giving him back his future.

His future.

In the soft lighting of the car, Teilani drew away from Kirk. Once more, she held her finger to the fabric sealer control at her neck, kept it there.

This time, the fabric of her jumpsuit parted completely, fell away from her, nothing hidden, all revealed.

Kirk held his breath at the beauty of her perfection.

She reached out for Kirk.

He did not hesitate.

He flew through the years—

. . . to the ruins of Triskelion and Shahna, the drill thrall, as her mane of auburn hair engulfed them both . . .

. . . to the haunting, empty duplicate of the *Enterprise,* where he was caught in the rapture of Odona's love, as she sought to save the people of Gideon but lost her heart to Kirk instead . . .

. . . to the hyperaccelerated realm of the Scalosians, where Queen Deela's pulse fluttered in time with his own, each second of passion stretched to last an hour . . .

Teilani was one and all women to him.

Each touch was familiar, calling forth cherished memories.

Each kiss was unique, searing new pathways through his senses.

Her hands, her lips, her body kept him trembling on the brink of an ecstasy he had never imagined.

Until all thought was finally driven from his mind.

Until all that could exist was the brilliant clarity of the moment.

A wave of cleansing resurrection.

For the first time in years, he was truly *alive.*

When Teilani adjusted the dome control again, the sky was red with sunset.

Kirk lay back on the bed they had made by folding the rear seats together. He gazed up at the darkening sky.

He knew the *Enterprise* was up there, as he always did. But in the sanctity of this moment, he couldn't hear her call to him.

He was at peace.

Teilani lay beside him, one hand tracing patterns on his chest, radiant with the same peace Kirk felt, glowing with the sheen of their exertions.

"So it's true," she said in a languid voice.

Kirk turned on his side. He ran his fingers through the satin waves of her hair. "What is?"

She raised herself up on one elbow to look at him directly. Her smile became wicked, delightful. "What they say about humans."

She laughed and Kirk felt his cheeks redden.

Suddenly she kissed him again. Deeply. Expertly.

The effect was literally breathtaking.

She rolled over on top of him. Held his face in both her hands. Her nose brushed his as she covered him with kisses, her hair falling forward in an enclosing curtain.

The fragrance of her hair, her breath, swept over him.

"Come back with me?" she asked.

Kirk narrowed his eyes, as if to reduce the influence her loveliness had on him. His finger lightly trailed along her body, traced the swell of her breast where she pressed against him, the curve of her hip. Flawless. Somehow more than perfect. "Why does a planet blessed with people like you, need someone like me?"

A small smile flickered across her face. She pushed herself up and sat back on him, knees tight against his sides. Her hands moved down his chest. "Experience," she said. "I can attest to its value."

And then—

—she *tickled* him, both hands digging into his ribs in a move so sudden and unexpected that Kirk choked in surprise. He couldn't remember the last time that anyone had tried that.

Years. Too many years.

She collapsed in giggles atop him. He had no choice but to burst into laughter as well. He reached up under her arms to give as good as he got.

The car rang with their laughter. Some part of Kirk thought it was as if two children were playing. *And what's wrong with that?* he asked himself.

Out of breath, Teilani stopped her attack, lay upon him. What had been playful one moment became intensely erotic the next.

Kirk felt exhilarated by the quick recovery of his desire.

For one long delicious moment, they stared at each other, each knowing where the next moment would lead.

Then the viewing dome vibrated.

Kirk recognized the sound that caused it. He pushed past Teilani, sat up, stared into the sunset.

Down by his parent's farmhouse, the attackers' antigrav car was taking off.

Teilani held on to his arm, watching with him as the car banked over the barn and sped off toward the north.

"There must have been *three* of them," she said.

Kirk stared after the car. "Then why didn't the third one come after us, too?"

Teilani's voice shook with a burst of anger, with hatred. "Why do they want to destroy my world? Why do they do *anything?*"

She pressed her head against Kirk's chest.

He held her close.

There were no more questions in his mind.

No more uncertainties.

Time was slipping too quickly through his fingers.

He would not let this second chance slip through as well.

FIFTEEN

☆

Leonard McCoy was immune to the Parisian cityscape spread out before him. It was aglow with entire galaxies of lights, drawing the eye unerringly to the floodlights bathing the newly restored Eiffel Tower. But the beauty of the ancient city held no charm for him tonight. He scowled over his mint julep.

"Our ancestors had a descriptive medical term for what you're going through, Jim."

"Did they?" Kirk asked, without enthusiasm. He had just finished telling his two closest friends about his intention to resign from Starfleet and accompany Teilani to Chal. But the evening was not progressing as smoothly as he had hoped. He should have realized. Things seldom did when both Spock and McCoy were involved.

The doctor sourly regarded his drink. "They called it 'middle-aged crazy.'"

By the kitchen alcove, Spock raised an eyebrow. "Indeed. A most fitting description."

Kirk slumped in his chair. An uncomfortable position because it was Vulcan, and most Vulcan chairs were not meant for anything other than ramrod-straight posture. "Spock, not you, too."

"What did you expect?" McCoy's exasperation was evident. It gave his voice an edgy tenseness that flattened the friendly warmth of his Southern drawl. Even to Kirk it was unsettling to hear strong emotions being voiced in the serene sanctuary of Spock's quarters in the Vulcan Embassy.

"I don't know what I expected," Kirk said. "But what I had hoped was that . . . you'd wish me well."

Spock handed Kirk a thimble-sized glass filled with a yellow liquid. Kirk looked at it skeptically. It smelled like licorice. "You keep the makings for McCoy's *mint julep* here, but no scotch?"

"The doctor is a frequent visitor," Spock said. "He maintains his own supply of refreshments."

Kirk looked at his two friends. McCoy was a *frequent* visitor? *Here?* He felt out of touch, as if he had ignored the people closest to him. After a few moment's thought, he realized he had. And regretted it. But it was still time to move on.

"As you must know," Spock continued, "we, of course, do support you in any decision you make and indeed wish you well."

"Even if we also think you're a horse's ass," McCoy grumbled.

Kirk couldn't take it anymore. "Didn't you hear a word I said?" He jumped to his feet, began to pace. "I *love* her, Bones."

McCoy was not impressed. "Didn't you hear a word *I* said? You're crazy!"

Spock stepped between the two men as a mediator. "Captain, if I may, you say you are 'in love.' How are we to expect that this time is different from any of the others?"

Kirk stared at Spock, surprised by the bluntness of his question. "The point is, *I'm* different. Don't you see . . ." Kirk looked around at the plain gray walls of the Vulcan-designed room. They were the same walls that confined his existence, pressing in on him from all sides, restricting movement and freedom and life itself. "Spock, I'm dying here."

McCoy couldn't let that go. "Speaking as your doctor: No, you're not."

Kirk ignored him. "That's not what I mean, and you know it. My time's running out. *Your* time. Spock's time. This past year it's been as if everyone expects me to sit in my rocker and stare at the sunset and wait for night to bring an end to everything. But now, Teilani's showing me . . . a new horizon."

"She's blinding you, is more like it," McCoy said.

Kirk had no argument with that. "Yes, she is. And I love it. I can't stop thinking about her, Bones. I can't stop remembering what it's like to be with her."

"Your hormone levels would probably short out my tricorder."

Kirk grinned. "Exactly. Can you know what it's like to feel that way again? Bones, she's . . . incredible. Beyond incredible. I mean, when she—"

McCoy turned away. "Spare me the details."

But Kirk wouldn't let himself be ignored. He couldn't keep Teilani bottled up inside him. "I feel like I'm twenty again. That thrill, that expectation, it's all come back to me. Each morning. Each day. Each *night.* Everything is new again. Everything, Bones."

"The only thing that's new is the *Enterprise*-B."

That stopped Kirk.

McCoy was visibly working to hold in his anger, now. "Almost finished. Up in spacedock. Going to be launched within the year. And she's already been assigned to Captain Harriman—*not* James T. Kirk."

Kirk angrily rejected the diagnosis. It was too simplistic. He felt his temper spiraling upward to match McCoy's. "You're not listening to me. This is *not* about the *Enterprise.* This is about me. My feelings. My needs." He turned to Spock. "Spock, you know, don't you? We spoke of passion. You said that's what I needed. And Teilani has made me feel that again."

"Of that, I have no doubt, Captain. But that same passion has adversely affected your judgment."

Kirk was astounded by Spock's blanket assessment. "Exactly how has my judgment been affected?"

"Have you stopped to consider what Teilani's motives in this matter may be?"

"Spock, what does it matter?"

McCoy stepped to Spock's side.

"It matters because she's using you, Jim."

Kirk spread his arms wide. "Then let her use me. My God, Bones. Do you know what it means to be useful again? You've got medicine. Spock's got diplomacy. But what do I have? What *did* I have until Teilani came to me and said her world needs me?"

McCoy shot Spock a sideways glance. "Well, I suppose it is a more original line than, 'Come here often, sailor.'"

Kirk didn't know how much more of this he wanted to hear. "Bones, Spock himself confirmed everything Teilani told me. The failed Klingon-Romulan colony. How neither side claimed it. How it declared independence."

"So she read the same handful of paragraphs in a Starfleet almanac that Spock did," McCoy said dismissively. "Ha. No one even knows the exact location of this Chal place."

Spock steepled his fingers in a meditative pose. "To be fair, Captain, the drastic nature of your intentions does not seem to coincide with the apparent threat faced by Chal. I therefore suspect you have not told us everything Teilani has revealed to you about her world and its predicament."

Kirk wore his best poker face, though he knew it had long since stopped working on Spock and McCoy. "I've told you everything that's pertinent. Some things, minor things, she did tell me in confidence. There's no need to repeat them."

He still found it difficult to believe in the amazing medical properties Teilani claimed for her world.

But if he dared tell anyone, even his friends, what Teilani had told him about . . . being young forever, they'd lock him up. The galaxy was littered with false fountains of youth. Not to mention the con artists who fleeced those desperate enough to believe in them. He had no intention of looking more foolish to his friends than he apparently already did.

"In confidence," McCoy sputtered in the midst of a sip. "Pillow talk is more like it."

"Bones, don't."

McCoy slammed down his glass, as if he'd lost his taste for his favorite drink. "And if I don't, who will? Face it, Jim, you've got all the symptoms of someone escaping reality at warp nine. We all know you need something to do. But to go off, you'll excuse the expression, half-cocked with this *child—*"

Kirk faced McCoy as if facing an accuser, shouted back at him, surprising himself as much as his friend. "She's an adult, Bones. She knows what she's doing. Her planet has no defense system, no military history. They need me . . . someone of my experience to . . . set up a police force, show them how to defend themselves, secure their world and their future."

"And you think there aren't a thousand consulting companies on a hundred worlds that are better equipped to do that than you? You don't think that the Federation would jump at a chance to set up a joint peacekeeping operation with the Klingons and the Romulans to improve relations?"

"There are other considerations," Kirk insisted.

"I'm sure there are. *Her* considerations!" McCoy held up his fingers as he counted them out. "*Your* reputation. *Your* prestige. *Your* instant access to virtually any level of government and industry in the Federation and almost anyplace else you'd care to mention." McCoy's eyes were wide with indignation. "How long do you think it's going to be before your little playmate snuggles up to you in bed some night and asks if you could set up a teeny-tiny meeting between her and some planetary official? Or some industrialist that she couldn't get to in ten years of negotiations?"

"What's wrong with *any* of that?" Kirk demanded.

McCoy shook his head in pity. "She's a third your age."

"Which is how she makes *me* feel!" Kirk took a deep breath. He hadn't wanted any of this to happen. "Bones, even if everything you say is true, what's *wrong* with it?" Kirk reached out to his friend, anger turning to a plea for understanding. "Teilani and I are *both* adults. We're *both* going into this with our eyes wide open. If I can take five steps with her, and then drop dead on the sixth, at least I will have had those first five."

Kirk turned to Spock. His Vulcan friend revealed no trace of what he was thinking. "Spock, you understand what I'm saying."

"I do," Spock said.

At last Kirk felt hope. Perhaps there was a way back from this emotional precipice after all. "Then help me here. Help Bones see that what I'm doing isn't wrong."

But Spock shook his head. "I cannot. For in this instance, I find myself in the unique position of agreeing with everything Dr. McCoy has said."

Those simple words, spoken so calmly, were more of a shock to Kirk than if McCoy had come right out and punched him.

"Spock . . . no."

"If you have been forthcoming with us, Captain, then I must say your actions involving this woman are uncharacteristic, unsuitable, and ill-serving your past reputation and accomplishments."

Kirk stared at Spock. Mortified. In his own Vulcan way, Spock was shouting at him, too.

"To abandon Starfleet and your career in order to become little more than a mercenary, apparently paid by the sexual favors of a young woman about whom you know little or nothing, is not an act of passion."

"Then just what is it?" Kirk demanded hotly.

"It is an act of desperation. And desperation is also an emotion with which I am familiar."

The silence in the room was physical, like a jungle to be hacked through.

"Spock," Kirk said quietly, "you once asked me if we had grown so old that we had outlived our usefulness. . . ."

"The times have changed, Captain. As have our abilities. Our functions and our goals must change with them. To refuse to accept the inevitable is the first step toward obsolescence, and extinction."

Suddenly, Kirk felt empty. There was no need to control his emotions. He no longer felt anything. "What if I don't want to change?" His voice sounded flat to him. As if it came from a great distance.

"Then that would be . . . unfortunate."

"Unfortunate . . ." Kirk said. Three decades of friendship dissolving in that one spoken word.

That one verdict.

Kirk faced Spock, and then McCoy, and it was as if he looked at strangers. Had they ever known him well? Had he ever understood them so little?

After almost thirty years, Kirk could think of nothing more to say to Spock or McCoy.

"It's late," Kirk said. He stared at them both, fixing them in his memory. In case he might never see them again. "I have to . . . take care of some loose ends."

Spock and McCoy let him go. In silence. As if they, too, could think of nothing more to say to him.

Times had changed.

Kirk continued on his journey.

Alone.

SIXTEEN

☆

With no hint of hyperbole, San Francisco Travelport called itself "The Crossroads of the Galaxy." And rightly so.

The vast central hall of the enormous complex echoed with a symphony of travel and commerce—boarding calls, arrival and departure times, lost-child announcements, commercial messages in all the languages of Earth.

Its very air was an overload of intermingled aromas—from the precise harshness of filtered and reconditioned air, to the exotic spices of food kiosks representing dozens of worlds, and the complex tapestry of scents and perfumes from the milling, passing crush of humanity and other species, in all their varied forms.

When Kirk had first come here as a boy to see his father off, the sights and sounds of this crossroads had overwhelmed him. Became magic to him. Claimed his imagination and his heart forever.

To step beyond any of the departure lounges was to go by suborbital shuttle to anywhere in the world in less than an hour. Or by impulse liner to the Moon in less than a day. The Martian Colonies in less than a week.

Or even by warp to the stars, for however long time itself might last.

But now, for all its romance, the teeming Travelport was little more than a meaningless way station to him. One last stop, one final obstacle to overcome before he could begin what he had to do.

Instead of magic, today—his first day out of Starfleet since enrolling in the Academy forty-four years ago—Kirk saw only aimlessness and confusion.

Cut off from the Starfleet infrastructure and orbital transporter grid he had come to accept as second nature, Kirk almost felt as if Earth had become an alien planet.

He had to think about *how* to do almost everything. Without a Starfleet communicator on his belt, he had to remember his personal transmitter code, how to access the commercial data spectrum, even endure listening to advertising messages as his request was passed through the worldwide computer nets.

It took five times as long to do anything.

Even leaving Earth was going to take hours.

So the Travelport he had once associated with unlimited possibilities had become nothing more than an infuriating bottleneck.

He knew what was beyond each of the departure lounges.

He knew exactly where he wanted to go.

But he couldn't just say "One to beam up" anymore.

James T. Kirk was a civilian.

As a student of anachronistic language constructions might have put it, he thought it sucked.

Finally, the computer screen Kirk stood before in the Travelport's Public Communications Hub changed to show his call had been put through.

Kirk sighed. It was about time. He tensed for what was to come. The conversation he had put off till the very last.

But Carol Marcus wasn't home.

Kirk relaxed.

Carol could never be one of his "loose ends." They had loved each other once. Made a son. Only time and the stars had been able to pull them apart. Only heartbreak and circumstance had been able to bring them back together.

The memory of what had been between them still remained. But it was clear to both of them now that that memory was no longer enough.

Kirk felt certain Teilani had nothing to do with his achieving this insight, except to accelerate his recognition of the inevitable. It was time for Carol and him to continue their own lives. Otherwise, both risked descending into the stultifying abyss of habit and familiarity that had drawn him back to her on his return from Khitomer, and the *Enterprise*'s last voyage.

The computer screen waited for Kirk to indicate whether he wished to leave a message or make a further call.

Kirk hesitated. Carol deserved more than the brief farewells he had recorded for his office staff at the Academy. But he didn't know how much more than that he had to give right now.

In the end, instinct won out. Whenever the urge to hesitate grew too strong in him, Kirk knew it was the signal that he must take action. Only then could he continue to move forward.

He touched the message bar on the screen.

The computer said it was recording.

"Carol . . . I know what I want now." But how could he explain it to her? "I . . . uh, you helped me find it." He felt flustered. It was not like him to struggle for words. But all his skills, all his bravado, evaporated when it came to facing and expressing his own desires. "Thank you for . . . everything you've brought to me, shared with me." He placed his hand on the screen, picturing Carol on the other side, sometime later this day, watching her messages, her fingers joining the phantom images of his own. "I'll always love you," Kirk said. A universe of emotion in that simple promise. Then he disconnected.

Maybe that was always part of the problem, he thought. He loved them all. And always would.

The insight made him stop and stare at the patient computer screen for a few silent moments. There was no question that he knew the finality of his next action. What he was leaving behind. Who he was leaving behind. Forever.

But he *was* moving forward again. Contemplating the risks and the chaos that might accompany the voyage only filled him with anticipation, even excitement.

With a lightness of being he had not felt since his return, Kirk turned away from the computer. He headed toward the central hall of the Travelport.

Teilani waited for him there, under the holographic display that showed the times and dates on Earth, the Moon, and Mars.

Her face lit up as she saw him emerge from the crowd.

Kirk increased his stride, moving with purpose again. He felt himself quicken in return.

He didn't know what would happen next in his life.

But here at the crossroads of the galaxy, he was no longer without direction.

Once again, Teilani surprised him.

Kirk was beginning to think he should come to expect that as normal.

As it turned out, they didn't have to wait hours to book last-minute passage on a shuttle. Teilani had a private yacht. Standing by, already cleared for launch.

Customs and immigration clearance was no more difficult than slipping an ID wafer into a reader and having a retina pattern confirmed.

As Kirk and Teilani were swept along a moving walkway toward a private shuttle pad, she told him that the simplified procedures were part of the diplomatic privileges of her invitation to Admiral Drake's reception the week before.

That detail *had* been troubling Kirk. "If your world is so distant, considered so inconsequential, why did the Federation decide to invite someone from Chal?" he asked.

"We're not unknown to the Federation, James. Over the years we've set up specialized trade relations with various groups. We do have accounts in most of the key interstellar exchanges." She put her hand on his, where he held the moving handrail. "And I *asked* to be invited. I'm sure the Federation Protocol Office didn't have to think twice about complying. It was a large reception, and an invitation to delegates from Chal could be considered a gesture of good-will. To both the Romulan *and* Klingon empires,"

Kirk turned his hand over to grasp hers in his. They were nearing the pad. He could smell fresh air blowing into the transfer tunnel.

"But you didn't talk to me at the reception," he said, remembering his first glimpse of Teilani. When he had first felt the need to be with her. Like this.

"I wanted to. But you were with your friends. And the admiral." Teilani shrugged.

Kirk relived the moment Teilani had turned away—the moment Androvar Drake had stopped at his table.

"Do you know Admiral Drake?" he asked suddenly. He couldn't be certain, but he thought he recalled seeing a flicker of recognition in her eyes that night. Although those three Romulan ales still cast a pall on a full recollection of the evening.

But Teilani said, "No."

The walkway slowed and they stepped off. Teilani had no luggage. Kirk carried a single, soft-sided bag. Inside were two real books, a few treasured computer wafers with images of friends and family, and a change of clothes. The contents of the bag were all he truly wanted to take with him. A lifetime distilled into less than four kilograms of idiosyncratic, personal belongings. Everything else he had collected over the years was in long-term storage. The prospect of walking away from so much of the accumulated detritus of life added to his sense of liberation.

They emerged from the tunnel, onto the tarmac.

Teilani's sleek yacht was caught in a web of floodlights. Its smooth white hull glowed stark against the night.

Kirk's eyes brightened. Starfleet craft were of necessity designed for multipurpose applications, resulting in solid, utilitarian designs.

But the manufacturers of private spacecraft were under no such restrictions.

Teilani's yacht not only *could* travel at warp one, it *looked* as if it could. An aggressive set of double curves swept around from the flight-deck windows to flow smoothly over the long blisters of the miniaturized warp nacelles tracing the lower edge of each side.

"I like it," he said with understatement. He began to walk around the yacht in the center of the pad, giving it a pilot's traditional preflight visual inspection. Teilani accompanied him. "But I've never flown anything like it."

"Oh, you don't have to fly it, James."

Kirk froze as he passed by the flight deck. Not because of what Teilani said, but because of what he saw.

One of the attackers from the farm.

Alive.

Kirk instantly pushed Teilani behind him.

The youth looked up, startled. He had been doing something inside an open access panel on the yacht's hull.

Kirk rushed forward, pressing the advantage of surprise.

"James, no!" Teilani shouted after him. "He's the *pilot!*"

Kirk's upraised fist paused a split second. Just long enough for Kirk to take in his target's features.

He was one of Teilani's hybrid race—furrowed brow, pointed ears. Young like her. Like the two attackers who had tried to kill them.

But in the brilliant glare of the floodlights, he also saw that Teilani was right.

Kirk had never seen this youth before. Though the pilot

resembled the attackers so strongly that Kirk at once wondered if he might be related to them.

The shaken pilot held out a hand to Kirk. "I am Esys," he said nervously. "It is a great honor to meet you, sir."

Kirk slowly lowered his fist to take the offered hand. "I apologize. Teilani and I had some—"

"The attack, sir," Esys interrupted. "Yes, she told me. The Anarchists are everywhere."

"Anarchists?" Kirk asked.

Teilani took Kirk's arm. "He means the people who are against us. It's as good a word as any. They want to tear apart our culture, yet offer nothing to replace it."

Teilani saw the shadow of a smile cross Kirk's face.

"Does that amuse you?" she asked.

"Different worlds, different ways," Kirk said. "I was just thinking that on Earth, it's more traditional that young people like you are in favor of anarchy."

"On Chal," Teilani said, "we are *all* young." Her eyes met Kirk's and held them. "As you will be."

Kirk's smile faded. He hadn't admitted that part of Teilani's story to Spock and McCoy because he still couldn't accept it himself. Because, if everything he had done since meeting Teilani—abandoning his friends, giving up Starfleet, hurting Carol—was simply the result of a desperate desire to recapture his youth at any cost, then his friends would be proven right.

James T. Kirk would be nothing more than a self-obsessed fool who had selfishly gambled away everything he held dear in a vain attempt to deny and delay the inescapable passage of time.

Kirk refused to so define himself. He *knew* he loved Teilani. He wanted—needed—to be with her for whatever time remained to him.

That was what had driven him to abandon everything for Chal.

Passion. Not desperation.

Love. Not an impossible dream of youth, however appealing, however real.

But Kirk also knew, better than anyone, the greatest fear of a man who had been a starship captain. That, in the end, he was just like everyone else.

Full of hope, rejecting doubt, Kirk held Teilani's hand tightly as they boarded the yacht.

He had made his decision.

He chose the future.

SEVENTEEN

Teilani's yacht shot up through the night as if it had gone to warp.

Kirk was unprepared for the g-forces that slammed him back into the copilot's seat.

"What's wrong with your inertial dampers?" he asked, trying not to sound as if he were gasping for breath.

Esys shot him a glance. "Oh, sorry, sir." He ran his fingers over some controls.

A moment later, all sensation of movement vanished as the inertial dampers absorbed and redirected the momentum of everything within the speeding craft. Kirk shifted in his chair, grateful he could breathe again.

Esys shrugged apologetically. "I sort of keep the dampers tuned down. So I can feel how I'm flying."

Kirk nodded, feeling foolish. He used to do that himself at the Academy. All young pilots did. Half the fun of flying trainers had been to see who could set their dampers the lowest. The resulting g-forces and inertia would wrench the fledgling pilots against their seat harnesses and slam them from side to side in the cramped, one-person flight cabins, ideally without causing blackouts as blood rushed from the bravest pilot's head. How had he forgotten what it was like to be that young?

Kirk felt Teilani put her hand on his arm, leaning forward from the passenger seat behind him. "Not quite like Starfleet?" she asked.

"Just like Starfleet," Kirk answered.

Through the flight-deck viewport, the last retreating wisps of cloud were visible only because of the ocean of light from San Francisco that dramatically lit them from below.

Ahead, the stars brightened. As the yacht rose and the atmosphere thinned, their twinkling ceased.

Eyes fixed on the stars, Kirk felt an unexpected but familiar sensation of anticipation come over him. He was going back. Where he belonged.

Though the manner in which he was returning was not familiar.

On this voyage, Kirk was a passenger. Teilani had still not shared with him any details of the trip ahead of them. Because she was still finalizing them, she had told him.

Kirk turned in his seat to look at Teilani. "Is your ship as impressive as your yacht?"

She nodded. "Even more, I'm told." She smiled playfully.

Kirk was coming to know her well enough that he recognized her expression. She was deliberately withholding information, making him work to obtain it. Making the conversation a game.

He liked that in her. He remembered doing the same when he was her age—*No!* he warned himself. *Don't start thinking like that.* Once a person was an adult, age should no longer matter.

But the inner voice in his head—perhaps Spock's, perhaps McCoy's—told him he was wrong.

Again, he ignored it.

He saw Teilani watching him carefully, as if she could recognize *his* feelings through *his* expressions. He winked at her, then settled back into his seat, eyes front.

Esys handled the controls smoothly.

The stars were crisp and unwavering.

Kirk was back in space.

With satisfaction, he watched the western seaboard of North America recede on a flight-console viewscreen. He had assumed they were headed for a low orbit to rendezvous with Teilani's ship. But they were still climbing.

Kirk spoke over his shoulder. "Is your ship in free orbit, or docked?"

"Docked," Teilani said.

Kirk patiently folded his hands together. He tried to concentrate on not thinking about how *he* would fly the yacht if he were at the controls. Chal was several weeks away at maximum warp. No doubt Teilani's ship had required servicing for the voyage ahead.

But judging from their continued ascent, Esys was taking them past the orbital plane of most commercial spacedocks.

"Are we going to the Moon?" Kirk asked. There were still shipyards there, though most specialized in manufacturing with lunar materials, rather than providing service and repairs.

He heard Teilani's amusement in her cryptic answer. "No." Whatever was going on, she was enjoying herself.

"Coming up on terminator," Esys announced.

The stars shifted past the viewport as the yacht's orientation changed.

Kirk saw the curve of the Earth below them, a dark hemisphere wrapped in the glowing strands of transport ways. At major hubs and intersections, vaguely defining the shape of the continents they served, cities clumped like sparkling dew on a spider's web.

Above it all, the impossibly thin arc of Earth's atmosphere began to stand out in a pale blue glow. The yacht hurtled toward dawn at thousands of kilometers per hour.

"On docking approach," Esys said. His eyes darted from his controls to the viewport and back again.

Kirk stared dead ahead, but saw nothing.

At this speed, he didn't expect to. That's what sensors were for.

The curve of the atmosphere brightened. Kirk squinted at the hotspot that announced where the sun would appear.

Then the Earth's thin layer of air flashed red, flared blue-white, and the sun was before them.

In the sudden wash of that brilliant dawn, Kirk saw at last his destination.

He gasped. Teilani had struck again.

Kirk *was* back where he belonged.

Teilani's ship was the *Enterprise.*

EIGHTEEN

☆

The mighty starship still bore the damage of her final battle over Khitomer. Angry scorches marred her saucer and her engineering hull. A double hull breach yawned wide on the saucer where General Chang's final photon torpedo had punched through her.

Apart from her battle damage, empty gaps were apparent in

her main sensor array, where industrious Starfleet engineers had reclaimed state-of-the-art equipment not permitted on the civilian market.

Her name was gone, too. Blasted from her hull by particle etching beams, along with her registration numbers and Starfleet colors.

But there was no disguising her identity from Kirk.

In his eyes, she was beautiful still.

Gleaming white in the orbital dawn.

A steed of incomparable heart, rising nobly on a mountaintop, eager to renew the pursuit.

"How . . . ?" Kirk began to ask. But his throat, his chest, his *heart* were so full of emotion, he could say nothing more.

Teilani left her seat and knelt by Kirk's. "My planet negotiated for her, James."

"But . . . she was going to be used in wargames." *A blaze of glory,* Drake had told him.

"A goodwill gesture on the Federation's part. She's to become the first ship in Chal's planetary defense group." Teilani lightly kissed Kirk's cheek as he marveled at the vision she had arranged for him.

But Kirk barely felt Teilani's caress as Esys guided the yacht around the *Enterprise.* Lights burned in some of her decks, though her running lights and sensor array were dark.

"Of course," Teilani continued, "she's not quite the ship you remember. The closest things to weapons she has are navigational deflectors and tractor beams. Sensor capability has been downgraded by fifty percent. The Fleet communications system has been replaced with a civilian model."

What did any of that matter? It was the *Enterprise.*

"But I thought you could live with those changes," Teilani said.

Kirk still had a hard time grasping the reality of what had happened. "You *own* her now?" He turned to her. He had to know.

"She's *yours,* now, James. Free and clear. A gift from my world. To you."

"I . . . don't know what to say."

"It's not what you say—it's what you'll do."

At that moment, Kirk feared he would do anything.

Esys guided the yacht toward the hangar bay.

The *Enterprise* called out to Kirk.

Beyond the clouds. Among the stars.

One last time.

And Kirk, at last, could answer that call.

The turbolift doors parted and Kirk stepped onto the bridge of the *Enterprise* for the first time in months. It was an action he had never expected to take again.

He sensed Teilani and Esys remain behind in the lift, giving him this moment.

Kirk paused on the upper deck, immersing himself in the sensations of his return. The artificial gravity felt right. The air smelled a bit too much like chemical cleansers, but the temperature was set precisely where he preferred it. As if his personal preference file had not been deleted from the ship's computer.

Overall, though, Teilani was right. The *Enterprise* was different.

Most noticeably, her warp generators were offline. He missed the almost subliminal hum of them, vibrating through every rigid part of the ship's superstructure.

The bridge environment was quieter, too. Without the background chatter of department heads and more than four hundred crew working together. Replaced instead by the slow flickering of the status lights on her new, automated control stations.

Uhura's communications board was just an empty hole in the back wall. Her chair remained, but the extensive nerve center of the *Enterprise*'s comm system, linking her with

Starfleet and from there the universe, had been replaced with a few gray boxes of ordinary switches and automated controls.

Similar holes existed in the tactical console, where weapons panels had been removed.

The *Enterprise* had a makeshift, unfinished feel to her.

But Kirk had seen her and her namesake in worse condition. Given the choice—and Kirk always made certain he *was* given the choice—he preferred to think of his starship now as half-built, not half-disassembled.

The greatest change of all, though, was not in the hardware of the vessel. It was in the crew.

They were all Teilani's people.

Young Klingon-Romulans in such robust and dynamic health that Kirk felt another year older for each one he saw.

They took up most of the control positions on the bridge. Impossibly young, unlined faces working efficiently, with total concentration. By now, their ridged Klingon brows almost appeared to Kirk to be a natural match for their sharply angled Romulan ears.

There wasn't a Starfleet uniform in sight, either. They wore a series of variations on what Kirk took to be the clothes of their world—loose-fitting white trousers and tops, some with sleeves, some without, some with splashes of color, some unadorned. Yet the simplicity of the designs did nothing to hide the perfect muscles that sculpted their lithe, lean forms.

The young Chal crew nodded respectfully to Kirk as he went to the center of the bridge. His chair, at least, hadn't been changed or removed. He was glad. It always took too long to get used to a new one.

He sat in it. Put his hands on either arm.

It felt good to be back.

But not right.

He glanced to his right.

Spock's science station was dark.

He idly tapped his finger above the control that would send

his voice to McCoy's sickbay. But he doubted anyone was there to answer.

Except ghosts.

Kirk sighed. Teilani came down to the lower deck to stand by him. He saw concern in her eyes. Esys took the navigator's chair at the helm console.

"Is something wrong?" Teilani asked.

But before Kirk could answer, something changed.

He held up his finger, asking Teilani to stay quiet.

He leaned forward, ears straining.

But it wasn't a sound. It was a vibration.

The matter-antimatter reactor had just started up. The warp engines were online again. As smooth as they had ever been.

The heart of the *Enterprise* had been restored.

Kirk smiled.

Some of his new young crew smiled back, though it was clear they weren't sure what had prompted his reaction.

Kirk studied his crew again.

The oldest Chal he had seen was no more than twenty-five standard years. But a matter-antimatter reactor like the one that powered the *Enterprise* was a hellishly complex device that could take at least that long to master.

How could these *children* have brought this ship back to life? Unless . . . ?

Without looking, Kirk touched the control that opened a line to the engine room.

"Kirk to Engineering."

"Scott, here, Captain."

To Kirk, it was as right to hear the warm Scottish lilt in that greeting as it was to be on the bridge again. And he wasn't surprised to hear it, either. Perhaps because the *Enterprise* and her engineer shared a bond as strong as his own with his ship.

"Mr. Scott, I thought you had retired."

"Aye. So did I."

Kirk grinned. He had long ago learned that Scotty was only happy when he had something to complain about. "Then I trust Starfleet came up with a suitable reward for duty above and beyond."

"Starfleet has nothin' t' do with me being here, Captain."

That *was* surprising.

"'Twas the lass. Teilani. Starfleet put her in touch with me, and she told me what it was she was planning to do with the *Enterprise.* I figured if the time wasn't quite right for the old girl t' retire, then it wasn't quite right for me, either."

Kirk wasn't going to argue with him. When was it ever right to give up doing what you lived to do?

"You've done a magnificent job with her, Scotty."

"Och, if ye could see the shambles the reclamation team left this engine room in, you'd call it a bloody miracle."

"When you're involved, Mr. Scott, I always do. Glad to have you aboard."

Kirk was about to sign off, but Scott wasn't finished.

"Captain, just so you know . . . th' *Enterprise,* sir . . . well, she's . . ."

Kirk knew what Scott was trying to say. The signs were everywhere. "I know. She's been through a lot."

"That's puttin' it mildly, sir." It was Scotty's turn to sigh. "She was never repaired properly after that last go-round with Chang. And the best parts of her, well, Starfleet's taken those back. Left her in a kind of depleted condition, if ye know what I mean."

Kirk knew. "The question is, will she get us to Chal, Mr. Scott?"

"Aye, I'll see to that. But afterward . . . I don't know if she'll be up to much in th' way of planetary defense. Without a complete overhaul, I mean."

"And that's not very likely, is it, Mr. Scott?"

The chief engineer sounded as if he were speaking about the death of a dear friend. "This is an old design, sir. I'd never say it to an admiral's face, but there was good reason for scheduling her to be decommissioned."

"Your secret's safe with me, Mr. Scott."

Scott chuckled. "Aye. We oldsters have to stick t'gether, don't we?"

Kirk winced.

"Warp power is online and ready when ye need it, Captain."

"Thank you, Mr. Scott," Kirk said. "I think."

"Scott out."

Kirk caught Teilani's sly grin. But before he could say anything, she took his hand, kissed it.

"On Chal, none of that will matter anymore. Young, old . . . everyone will be the same."

"Did you tell Scotty what to expect there?"

Teilani shook her head. "He'll find out when we arrive."

"Will he be able to stay?"

"If he wants to."

It struck Kirk that what Teilani said was odd. Who wouldn't want to stay on a planet where there was no aging, and no death?

Unless there was something else she hadn't told him. If there was some price to be paid for what Chal offered.

But he didn't care. There was a price to be paid for everything, and for Teilani's love, no price was too high.

"Are we expecting any more passengers or supplies?" Kirk asked.

Teilani shook her head. "You may give the word anytime, James."

Kirk faced forward. The Earth filled the viewscreen, clouds white, oceans sparkling.

A place he no longer belonged.

"Mr. Su—" he began, then caught himself. "Mr. *Esys,* lay in a course for Chal. Best possible speed."

Esys adjusted the helm controls. "Course laid in, Mr. Kirk."

Kirk shifted uncomfortably in his chair. He hadn't been called "mister" since he had been an ensign.

"Take us out of orbit," Kirk said. "Ahead, warp factor one."

The *Enterprise* hummed to life around him.

The sensor image of Earth shrank in the viewscreen as he left her at the speed of light.

Once again, Kirk went where he had *always* gone before.

Into the unknown.

Even as the *Enterprise* streaked from Earth and the heart of Sector 001, the *Excelsior* returned.

The sleek starship under Hikaru Sulu's command traveled under a total communications blackout.

Kirk's aging starship, rescued from her inglorious fate as an expendable target, hurtled out of Sol system on a flight path duly registered with the sector's traffic-control computers. As commander of a civilian vessel, Kirk was under no obligation to communicate with Starfleet Command.

Within the faster-than-light infinities of warp space, the *Enterprise* and the *Excelsior* passed each other by tens of thousands of kilometers. Each ship registered as nothing more than a nonthreatening sensor blip on the other's navigational-hazard display.

The encounter lasted less than a ten-thousandth of a second.

Then the *Enterprise* accelerated to warp seven and in a heartbeat left the entire system light-hours behind.

At the same time, the *Excelsior* dropped to sublight velocity and put out a priority call to Starfleet Headquarters.

Now traveling away from each other at millions of kilometers per second, the commanders of both vessels had nonetheless committed themselves to a deadly collision course.

NINETEEN

☆

Chekov found Androvar Drake's sprawling house in San Francisco's old Presidio district vaguely unsettling.

It wasn't a home, he decided. It was a military museum.

Of the worst kind.

Everywhere he looked in Drake's study, there was another reminder of humans' ongoing need to subjugate one another. Antique plasma guns. An entire suit of combat armor belonging to a mid-twenty-first century Fourth World Mercenary, complete with a drug-delivery inhaler mounted on its chest. Battle flags from Colonel Green's genocidal campaigns. A set of slowguns from some long-forgotten colonial uprising, ingeniously designed to fire projectiles that would kill people without puncturing environmental domes.

Worst of all, each weapon, each emblem, each uniform, was reverently displayed in elegant cabinets or mounted in spotlit frames on the wood-paneled walls. As if each were a work of art.

Androvar Drake was a product of the past, Chekov decided. Unfortunately, he was now one of the most powerful individuals of the present.

It was not a reassuring juxtaposition.

Then Chekov was startled from his reverie by Admiral Drake himself. "You don't approve of my collection, do you, Commander?"

Unlike his collection, Drake seemed surprisingly warm and welcoming. He had greeted Chekov, Sulu, and Uhura as if they were intimate friends. Prepared tea for them himself. Ushered them from his private transporter pad into his study only after taking them aside for a few moments to admire the spectacular view over the Bay.

"Your 'collection' does seem to concentrate on some of the worst moments of history," Chekov said.

Drake nodded, unperturbed. "Precisely its purpose." He got up from behind his massive mahogany desk and opened a display cabinet near a freestanding bookcase filled with real books. He withdrew a small booklet containing several plastic tickets, and handed it to Chekov.

Chekov read the fine print on the tickets. "A ration book?" he asked.

"From Tarsus IV," Drake confirmed. "Half the colony. Four thousand colonists. Massacred. Because the food supply was destroyed. And Starfleet couldn't provide support in time." He gestured to encompass the room. "Everything here. A reminder of those dark times that have tried human souls and dignity. Since the era of interstellar exploration began."

Chekov studied Drake. The admiral's pale eyes were intense. But Chekov saw no sign of compassion in his words.

"Everything here. A reminder that we must not let any of it happen again. That in my new position, *I* must not let any of it happen again."

Chekov handed back the ration booklet. Of course Drake was good. He had to be. He had convinced the Council to put him in total command of Starfleet.

But he didn't fool Chekov.

Chekov was certain Drake didn't keep that ration book from Tarsus IV as a reminder of Starfleet's obligation to provide for endangered colonies.

James Kirk had been at Tarsus IV. As a young teenager.

Kirk had seen the four thousand colonists massacred before his eyes.

Their deaths haunted the captain to this day. He had told Chekov so.

Chekov was convinced Drake kept that ration book because it was a reminder of something that had hurt Kirk long ago.

"A very admirable goal," Uhura said.

She exchanged a look with Chekov. She wasn't convinced by Drake's act, either.

But Sulu avoided looking at Chekov. Publicly, he was maintaining a more neutral demeanor, as befitting his rank. But this past week on the *Excelsior,* he and Chekov had barely spoken. That suited Chekov.

"Then you understand why we requested this urgent meeting with you," Sulu said, attempting to get Drake back on topic.

"Absolutely," Drake confirmed. "A rogue agent presents an unacceptable risk to Starfleet's integrity. The mere possibility of a Klingon superweapon going on the open market could destabilize a dozen nonaligned systems. To say nothing of what it might do to the ongoing peace process between the Federation and the Empire."

Drake placed the ration book back in its case, then returned to his desk.

Chekov, Uhura, and Sulu sat across from him, each in a separate chair. Drake appeared to be thinking something over. No one disturbed him.

"You all have exemplary records," he said at last.

No one responded. Chekov could sense a big "but" coming. It was clear that Drake was leading up to something.

"Commander Chekov, Commander Uhura, Starfleet recognizes and especially appreciates your valor and self-sacrifice in undertaking a potentially deadly covert assignment to stop the flow of Klingon armaments to the illegal market. Captain Sulu, your exploits on the *Excelsior* are carving a place in history alongside Jim Kirk's himself."

Chekov shot another glance at Uhura. He could see that she also felt Drake was piling it on thick enough to choke a Gorn.

"Which is why I have decided to bring you all on board another, ultrasecret operation, already under way."

Chekov was shocked. Knowing what he did about Drake, he had been expecting Drake to thank them and say good-bye, sweeping their concerns about Jade and the Klingon superweapon into a black hole.

"What kind of operation, sir?" Sulu asked.

Drake's friendly attitude disappeared. He became distant and formal. He pressed a control on the computer screen beside him. Chekov saw a red light on the screen start to blink.

"I am now recording this conversation," Drake announced. "Everything I am about to tell you is classified at the highest level. If you cause to be made known anything of what you learn here today, to any party other than those directly connected to the operation, you will be subject to indefinite solitary confinement in a Starfleet detention center. Before you leave this meeting, you will be required to sign a formal security oath agreeing to these conditions." Drake looked each of them in the eye, beginning with Chekov. "Is that clear? Please reply audibly."

One by one, Chekov, Sulu, and Uhura stated that they understood and agreed to the conditions Drake had set out.

Chekov felt uneasy, not knowing what would follow. He knew Uhura well enough to sense the same reticence in her.

But there was no way to be certain what Sulu thought of this escalation of the meeting.

Drake held his finger over another desk control. "I am now going to ask two other officers to join us. They are also involved in this operation." He pressed the control. "Gentlemen, if you would be so kind."

A side door in the study opened inward.

"Come in," Drake said. A small enigmatic smile flashed across his face for an instant. "I believe you all know each other."

Chekov, Uhura, and Sulu instantly stood.

The two other officers were Spock and McCoy.

At any other time, an impromptu party might have begun as the former *Enterprise* crewmates unexpectedly met again.

But the surreal surroundings and Drake's presence precluded anything like that from even beginning.

The admiral directed Spock and McCoy to take their seats, then began his briefing.

"Bottom line: Admiral Cartwright and his co-conspirators appear to have been the tip of the proverbial iceberg. I regret to inform you that the entire Starfleet command structure might be compromised by a cabal of senior officers. Traitors who will stop at nothing to prevent the Federation from achieving a secure peace agreement with the Klingon Empire."

Chekov was shocked.

But Sulu asked the first and most obvious question. "Does the Council know that?"

Drake didn't appreciate the interruption. "That's why *I* was selected commander in chief, Captain Sulu. Certainly there were other candidates more qualified in areas of diplomacy and exploration. But my background in security was considered essential to what the Fleet needs most under present conditions."

"And because you're drawing us in," Uhura added, "you must think that this rogue agent, Jade, is somehow connected to the renegade command officers."

Spock nodded his head at Uhura. "A logical inference, Commander. And a correct one."

Sulu turned to Spock. "You already know what happened at Dark Range Platform?"

Again Spock nodded. "Admiral Drake shared your report with us just prior to this meeting."

Drake waved an imperious hand to silence them, determined not to allow any further interruptions or exchanges he did not invite.

"Because of the checks and balances in Starfleet Intelligence, it is almost impossible for an agent to go rogue," Drake explained, "*without* some type of support from within Starfleet itself."

"Admiral, I don't understand," Sulu said. "Doesn't a rogue agent, by definition, have to be acting alone?"

But Drake shook his head. "Every computer record pertaining to the agent code-named Jade has been selectively deleted from Starfleet's databanks. We have no identification picture, no fingerprints, no DNA structure. We will be able to reconstruct a great deal of it. But the process will take weeks. That all points to an inside accomplice."

"Sir, are you seriously postulating a connection between a rogue agent, a Klingon superweapon, and a conspiracy within Starfleet?" Sulu asked.

Spock calmly steepled his fingers. "Consider this, Captain Sulu. Fortunately, the diplomats and negotiators for both the Federation and the Klingon Empire are aware of the strong, antireconciliation sentiments within their own camps. They understand that random acts of terrorism undertaken by a handful of detractors do not mean each government is not committed to peace."

Chekov felt himself begin to relax. It was almost soothing to hear Spock lay out a rational explanation for something that had so confused and upset him. He noticed that Drake also seemed pleased by Spock's analysis, because the admiral let Spock continue.

"Consider, however," Spock continued, "what might happen if a Klingon 'doomsday' weapon were used. Not just to destroy a ship or a colony, but to lay waste a planet. Perhaps Earth or Vulcan itself. Consider also the ramifications of an investigation into the use of the weapon. An investigation which finds no evidence of any Klingon conspiracy to employ it."

Sulu understood what Spock's logic had described. "Because the weapon would have been used by a group within Starfleet."

"Precisely," Spock confirmed. "If an official investigation cannot show any evidence of a Klingon conspiracy, then the public conclusion must be that the investigation was conducted in bad faith. That would logically lead to the further conclusion that the weapon was therefore used *with* the support of the Klingon government."

"Damned if you do, damned if you don't," Uhura added. "If the official investigation does find evidence of a *Starfleet* conspiracy to use the weapon, then the public conclusion will be that it was a Klingon plot to shift blame from the Empire."

Spock proceeded to forge the remaining links in the chain of logic. "In the confusion that would follow, the individual worlds of the Federation would have to choose sides. No doubt, some would withdraw. Treaties would be abrogated. Trade agreements canceled. The Council would be in chaos."

McCoy shook his head at Spock. "It's a wonder you can ever sleep at night."

Drake wrapped up the analysis with the ultimate conclusion. "And under those conditions, the Federation would be vulnerable to Klingon attack."

"But surely the Klingons have no motive to attack us anymore," Sulu said.

Drake fixed him with a stern gaze. "The Empire has no motive to attack a *strong* and *secure* Federation. But if they see us begin to fall apart? If they think we would use an attack on the Klingon Empire as a way to reunite our members. Then the Empire will have no choice but to strike first."

"And," Spock added, "knowing that is the likely Klingon action, the conspirators still within Starfleet could convincingly argue that the Federation should therefore launch a preemptive strike."

"Good Lord," Dr. McCoy moaned. "It's World War III all over again. Everyone trying to second guess everyone else."

"Which is why Starfleet needs all of you to help stop that Klingon weapon from falling into the wrong hands," Drake concluded.

Chekov started to ask if anyone had any idea what the weapon code-named Children of Heaven might be. But he stopped. He looked at McCoy and Spock.

He had been so surprised to see them, and so pleased, that he hadn't stopped to wonder *why* they were part of this meeting.

"Excuse me, Keptin Spock, I know vhy the rest of us are here. But vhy are you and Dr. McCoy part of this operation?"

McCoy and Spock looked to Drake.

Drake looked uncomfortable. "This is an extremely difficult situation for me," he said.

"For all of us," McCoy snapped.

Drake continued. "I have been conducting an internal investigation. A very discreet one. Attempting to ascertain the sympathies of various Starfleet officers in sensitive positions. Looking for at least one individual who is unquestionably connected to the conspiracy within Starfleet to start a war with the Klingon Empire."

"And have you found someone?" Uhura asked.

Drake nodded gravely. "I have."

Chekov couldn't stand the suspense.

"Vell, who is it?"

Drake's answer struck Chekov like lightning.

"James T. Kirk," the admiral said.

TWENTY

☆

Chekov was outraged and didn't bother to hide it. "That is *impossible!*"

Drake raised his voice without shouting. His words echoed off the hard-paneled walls of the study. "Don't you think that's what *I* said?"

Silence reigned.

"But then," Drake said in a lowered voice, "I saw proof."

"Pah," Chekov spat. "Vhat proof?"

Slowly, almost reluctantly, Spock stood up.

Drake pressed a control and a section of wall slid away to reveal a display screen. There was a picture on it of a beautiful young Klingon woman in a black jumpsuit. Or *was* she Klingon?

"The young woman's name," Spock said, "is Teilani. She is a hybrid—her parents were Klingon and Romulan."

The picture changed. The young woman was now in a formal gown, her dark hair swept up to reveal her pointed ears. There was a large party of some sort going on behind her. Chekov concluded these were surveillance images, likely taken without the young woman's knowledge.

"As far as Starfleet Intelligence can ascertain, despite her relatively young age, she is a high-ranking official in her planetary government."

"What planet?" Uhura asked.

"A colony world somewhere on the frontier between the Klingon and Romulan empires," Spock said. "Jointly settled by both empires approximately forty years ago, during one of their sporadic periods of truce. The planet's name is Chal." Spock gave Uhura a significant look. "A Klingon term for 'heaven.'"

"The Children of Heaven," Uhura murmured.

Spock continued. "Given what we know about the Crimson Level of the Imperial Forecasters, it is logical to conclude that some of their more extreme weapons were developed on planets far removed from Klingon centers of population. In the event something went wrong."

McCoy muttered in disgust. "Same as testing fusion bombs on Pacific islands in the twentieth century."

"Precisely, Doctor. All evidence to date suggests the joint Romulan-Klingon colony on Chal was the center for the development, construction, and storage of a weapon. The weapon was code-named Children of Heaven. It was intended to be used only in the event of the total defeat of the Klingon Empire."

"But vhat does *any* of this have to do with Keptin Kirk?" Chekov demanded.

The picture changed again.

Kirk and Teilani.

Both in civilian clothes.

Locked in each other's arms. Kissing.

The background of the picture showed more civilians, some carrying luggage. Chekov guessed it had been taken at a travelport somewhere on Earth.

"Three days ago, Jim Kirk resigned from Starfleet," Drake said. "He didn't talk to anyone. He didn't deliver his resignation in person. He simply logged his resignation request onto his personnel file, and left."

Chekov found that difficult to believe. He knew the captain had been scheduled to retire after returning from Khitomer. But Kirk had since taken on so many committee appointments and teaching assignments that Chekov had decided he'd have to stay in the Fleet forever, just to complete them.

"Left?" Sulu asked. "For where?"

"Presumably, Chal," Spock answered. "Twenty hours ago."

Uhura stood up. "I, for one, don't like where this is going."

"Where *do* you see it going, Commander?" Drake asked.

"You're making the captain out to be one of your conspirators. And that's ridiculous. Captain Kirk might have played hard and fast with the rules in his day, but I refuse to believe he's a traitor."

"So do I," Chekov added. He stood to join Uhura.

"As do I," Sulu agreed. He rose to his feet to stand with Uhura and Chekov.

But Drake told them to sit down again. That there was no need for confrontation. "You'll get no argument from me. Jim Kirk is one of the most dedicated officers ever to wear a Starfleet uniform. But the point is, he's not wearing that uniform anymore."

Sulu reacted with exasperation. "A man like the captain does not change his beliefs overnight."

Chekov was gratified by Sulu's support of Kirk. He was also surprised that he was willing to argue with his commander in chief.

"Usually, no," Drake agreed. "But look at that picture, Captain. Jim is sixty-two years old. That woman is what, *maybe* twenty?"

"They are both adults," Chekov said stiffly.

Drake looked at him with a pitying expression. "I'm not going to pretend that Jim and I are close friends. But listen to what Captain Spock has to say."

Spock folded his hands behind his back. "The captain's behavior in the week leading up to his resignation was emotionally erratic."

Uhura batted her eyes at Spock. "Maybe he's in love, Mr. Spock."

"He believes he is," Spock stated.

Sulu shrugged. "For the captain, that could explain a great deal."

"But not treason," Chekov said firmly.

"She is a very attractive young woman," Drake pointed out. "And I regret to say that there sometimes comes a point in a man's life when he begins to wonder if he is still attractive to others. If he still has what it takes to—"

"I am not prepared to believe that Keptin Kirk vould throw avay everything he believed in because of . . . some pretty face!" Chekov interrupted.

"Teilani is only part of the bargain," Drake said.

"Bargain?" Uhura repeated.

"Kirk's new job is coordinator of Chal's planetary defenses. His payment is a unique one. In fact, the only inducement his psych profile suggests might cause him to abandon his most deeply held convictions."

"Believe me," Chekov scoffed, "there is nothing that Keptin Kirk vould vant that badly."

Spock cleared his throat. "Teilani's government has given the captain the *Enterprise.*"

Chekov's jaw dropped open. "Is that . . . possible?"

"She'd been decommissioned," Drake explained. "She was slated to be a target in some field trials we're running. Then one of the resource-management departments received an inquiry about converting her to civilian use. Starfleet has a long-standing commitment to recycling and reusing obsolete equipment for the benefit of colony worlds, so Chal's request was in order."

"That ship was part of him," Uhura said quietly.

Chekov felt as if Drake had somehow engineered all this. He hated the look of false disappointment on the admiral's face. Disappointment in James Kirk.

"I trust you all agree that the gift of it to Kirk does put a different light on his actions," Drake said. He looked directly at Chekov. "Believe *me,* Commander, I'm not for a moment suggesting that Jim has been a willing member of any conspiracy in Starfleet—if such a conspiracy really does exist.

But what I'm afraid the evidence does suggest is that he might be being *used* by the conspirators."

Drake settled back in his chair. "At least you must admit the possibility that Jim might not be questioning this young woman's motives too closely. His career was essentially over. What did he have to look forward to? Suddenly a beautiful young woman comes into his life, gives him a purpose, and hands over the one thing that means more to him than anything else—his ship." Drake looked sternly at Chekov. "Whatever else Jim Kirk has been in his day, he's still human. That means he can make mistakes."

Chekov didn't know what to say.

What Drake said seemed plausible—for anyone except James Kirk.

But Spock was part of this. And McCoy.

Could the captain, in the end, simply be someone who finally made a wrong choice, blinded by the desire to have one last adventure in life?

Could Kirk really be that *ordinary?*

"Admiral, what *are* Teilani's motives?" Sulu asked.

Drake looked at Spock. Spock answered once again.

"It is the admiral's belief that Captain Kirk is being deliberately manipulated as a pawn. Someone is using him in an attempt to turn the *Enterprise* into a delivery system for the Children of Heaven weapon. What that weapon is, where it is intended to be used . . . these are questions which Starfleet has yet to answer."

But Chekov knew Spock well enough to read between the lines of what he said.

"Captain Spock, vhat are *your* beliefs?"

Spock gave Chekov a look of total disinterest. "I am puzzled that you ask that question, Commander Chekov. Surely you know that under these speculative conditions, personal beliefs are not logical."

Chekov was in no mood to take that kind of evasion from

Spock. He was surprised that Spock would even attempt to so deflect him. But before he could press his questioning, he saw something in Spock's eye . . . just what, he couldn't define.

But they had served together for almost thirty years.

Spock was sending him some kind of message, some kind of—

The realization of what was happening in this room suddenly burst through Chekov like a nova.

Spock was lying.

Chekov turned away from Spock and faced Drake. The dynamics of this meeting were suddenly much clearer.

Spock didn't trust Starfleet's new commander in chief either.

McCoy was being unnaturally quiet, so Chekov had to assume that he was in unspoken agreement with Spock as well.

But Drake didn't appear to recognize Spock's distrust of him. Which wasn't surprising. People who didn't know Vulcans well tended to take them at face value. They even believed the old story that Vulcans never lied.

But Chekov had learned that Vulcans were extremely adaptable. Given the right motive, a *logical* motive which did not involve personal gain, few Vulcans would have any reservations about exaggerating or withholding information.

And Chekov had absolute faith in Spock's motives, whatever they might be.

"So," Chekov said, playing Spock's game, "does Starfleet consider Keptin Kirk to be a security risk?"

"I hesitate to characterize the situation in that manner," Drake said disarmingly. As if he were trying to protect Kirk's good name.

Chekov caught Uhura's eye. He saw the doubt she hid there. She had sensed what Spock was doing as well.

Only Sulu remained an enigma. Chekov still had not forgiven his friend for delaying Chekov's and Uhura's rescue from Dark Range Platform. Unquestionably, each Starfleet officer had a duty to follow orders. But on the frontier, days and weeks away from command, Starfleet officers also had a duty to adapt to emerging situations. Sulu's refusal to do anything at Dark Range except follow the letter of his orders unsettled Chekov. He no longer had any idea what Sulu was thinking.

"How *vould* you characterize it, Admiral?" Chekov asked.

Drake looked at the ceiling as if the right words might be written there. "A *potential* security threat." He adopted a rueful expression, as if he were saddened that Kirk's career had come to this. "I know as well as you that Jim would never willfully do anything harmful to Starfleet or the Federation. But the evidence being what it is, we can't rule out any inadvertent action on his part. Just think of the Starfleet secrets he's had access to in his career."

"If he represents such a 'potential' threat," Chekov said bitterly, "then vhy the hell did Starfleet allow him to get the *Enterprise* in the first place?"

Drake looked at Sulu. "That's where you come in, Captain. You people served with Kirk. No one knows him better."

Sulu didn't understand. Neither did Chekov.

Drake spoke as if making a confession. "We don't know where Chal is."

"But Spock told us," Uhura said. "In the Klingon-Romulan frontier."

"Which comprises more than thirty-three hundred stars," Drake said. "Remember: Chal was a product of the Klingons' Crimson Level. Starfleet Intelligence has never come across any reference to it in any computer records it's obtained from Klingon or Romulan sources."

"So Starfleet has made Captain Kirk a pawn as well," Sulu reasoned. "And you want the *Excelsior* to track the *Enterprise* in order to locate Chal."

Drake nodded. "And then return with the Children of Heaven. Whatever it is."

"What about Captain Kirk?" Sulu asked.

"Oh, I want him back, too," Drake said. "Preferably alive."

For the first time in the meeting, Chekov was heartened to see Sulu show an emotional response. "Are you saying Captain Kirk is *expendable?*"

Drake remained seated, his tone, calm. Though the sudden chill in his voice was menacing. "Are *you* suggesting one man is more important than the safety and security of the Federation? If you can't handle your assignment, *Captain,* tell me now so I can put someone else in command of the *Excelsior.*"

Chekov wondered if Sulu still had the fire to question authority. If the drive and desire for seeking the truth of the matter, which had fueled his promotion to starship captain, had survived the burden of command.

But Spock defused any potential confrontation.

"You must excuse Captain Sulu, Admiral. Dr. McCoy and I have had ample opportunity to digest the current state of affairs. But it is still a considerable shock to those who are new to the operation."

Drake's attitude softened. Slightly. "What do you say to that, Captain?"

Sulu took a breath. Stood at attention. "Captain Spock is correct, sir. I apologize. Of course I will follow my orders, track the *Enterprise,* and return to Earth with the Children of Heaven *and* Captain Kirk."

Chekov was disappointed but not surprised by Sulu's ready capitulation.

Drake leaned back in his chair. "Very good. When can you be ready to leave?"

"Four hours."

"Make it two."

"Yes, sir."

Then Drake surveyed the others. "No doubt you will have other technical questions. But before you ask them, Captain Spock will provide you with background files on what we know about Teilani, Chal, and the Imperial Forecasters. *After* you sign your security oaths." Drake held a finger over the record control on his computer screen.

One by one, he looked at everyone else.

No one had anything more to say.

"I believe we're finished for now. Thank you, one and all. And Godspeed." He stopped recording. The side door swung open again. Spock led the way through it.

Chekov was the last to leave. At the doorway, he looked over his shoulder.

Drake was looking at him as if he had expected Chekov to turn around. He waved farewell as if they were friends.

He's good, Chekov thought as he walked through the door and heard it swing shut behind him. *But the captain's better.*

Then the door clicked and Chekov heard the faint buzz of a security screen.

Drake had locked his study and sealed it with a forcefield.

Chekov stared at the door.

He wondered what secrets Drake was hiding behind it, and from whom.

TWENTY-ONE

☆

The *Excelsior* was Sulu's ship, but at this moment everyone looked to Spock.

He, Chekov, Sulu, Uhura, and McCoy had gathered in a briefing room as soon as they had beamed aboard the starship from Drake's home.

By unspoken agreement, no one had discussed their meeting with Drake. Until they could be sure they were in secure surroundings.

But as soon as the briefing-room doors slid shut, Spock began speaking. He was framed against the room's large display screen. A color schematic of the *Excelsior* filled it.

"As I see it," he said without preamble, "we are faced with three possibilities."

Everyone settled back into his and her high-backed conference chair. They had all come to trust Spock's logic over the years.

"First, it may be that events are exactly as Admiral Drake has described them to us. Captain Kirk, for personal reasons, has become an unwitting pawn in an attempt to discover the secret of a powerful Klingon doomsday weapon. The organizers of this attempt are members of a conspiracy within Starfleet to stop the peace process between the Federation and the Klingon Empire, and one member of that conspiracy is the Starfleet Intelligence agent code-named Jade. When Jade discovered information pertaining to the Children of Heaven, Captain Kirk was put into motion as someone who could act on that information to locate the weapon, without realizing his role."

"But put into motion by whom?" Sulu asked.

"In the first scenario, by the alleged conspirators within Starfleet." Spock explained. "However, the second possibility is that Teilani's people themselves may be responsible for involving the captain. When they learned that Starfleet Intelligence had uncovered the location of the *Chalchaj 'qmey,* they may have decided to seek the help of a protector. Captain Kirk and the *Enterprise* make a most formidable first line of defense."

"And the third possibility?" Uhura asked.

"That nothing Admiral Drake said to us is correct."

"Are you saying the commander in chief of Starfleet lied to us?" McCoy asked. He was the only one at the table who did not appear to be reassured by Spock's analysis.

"That cannot be discounted," Spock admitted. "Which is why I did not offer any of these theories to Admiral Drake in our meeting with him. However, it may simply be that the admiral himself is not aware of the true state of affairs, and passed on incorrect information without intent to mislead us."

McCoy wasn't happy with that answer, either. "But, if what Drake told us is a lie, Spock, what's the truth?"

Spock thought a moment before replying. "I believe the truth is known only to one person involved in these events. Captain Kirk."

"Is that what your damned logic dictates?" McCoy asked.

"Where the captain is concerned, logic seldom applies. However, based on our past experience with him, it seems reasonable that he is in some way driving these events, and not merely an observer of them."

"Captain Spock," Sulu said, "in light of these three possibilities, can you suggest what our course of action should be?" No matter what was discussed in this gathering, on this ship the command decisions were Sulu's to make.

"You should, of course, follow orders," Spock answered. "I am not altogether comfortable with having to question the motives of Starfleet's commander in chief. Making contact with Captain Kirk is likely to help us discover the true state of affairs."

Chekov had reached his breaking point. Despite his promise to Kirk, he had to confide in someone. Who better than those in this room?

"Excuse me, Captain Spock," Chekov said, "but I feel it is wery important that we do question Drake's motives. *Especially* since they somehow involve Captain Kirk."

All eyes turned to Chekov.

"Admiral Drake and the captain have had . . . their differences in the past," he began.

"We know that," McCoy said. "Jim and Drake were in the same class at the Academy. Served on the *Farragut* together."

A frown clouded McCoy's face. Everyone who had served under Kirk on the *Enterprise* knew what had happened on the *Farragut.* The *Enterprise* had almost suffered the same fate when the deadly cloud creature had reappeared and threatened her.

"And after that, they ended up in separate postings," Chekov continued. "They became keptins vithin a month of each other. Each vas assigned von of the first twelve Constitution-class starships."

Sulu nodded appreciatively. The competition for those early command positions had been fierce.

"Each vent out on a five-year mission. They returned vithin six months of each other. Both vere immediately promoted to the admiralty."

McCoy looked at Chekov with suspicion. "It sounds as if you've compiled a dossier on Drake."

Chekov folded his hands together on the table, knowing what he was about to set in motion. "I have."

But Sulu reacted with impatience. He didn't appear to be interested in pursuing what Chekov had to say. "Then it couldn't have amounted to anything. The results of any investigation conducted by Starfleet Intelligence would have been turned over to the Council. If you had turned up anything that might indicate Drake wasn't fit to be C in C, he wouldn't have gotten the job."

"I didn't inwestigate Drake for Starfleet Intelligence," Chekov said. "I inwestigated him for Keptin Kirk."

Spock gave Chekov a curious look. "Commander Chekov, are we to understand that you used the facilities of Starfleet Intelligence for a *personal* inquiry?"

Chekov shrugged. "There is no one in this room who has not bent the rules for the keptin."

Uhura laughed. "Bent the rules? Pavel, we've demolished them."

"And ve have been justified each time."

Spock took a chair at the table, giving the floor to Chekov. "Please continue, Commander," he said.

Chekov addressed everyone. "After their return, for two and a half years Drake and Kirk vere posted to Headquarters. Kirk vas chief of operations. Drake became a deputy chief in Security Services."

McCoy tried to speed along the account. "And after the V'Ger incident, Jim took command of the *Enterprise* again and gave up his career path at headquarters. This is ancient history."

Chekov waved a hand for emphasis. "But Admiral Drake did *not* give up his career path. And, as of ten years ago, he vas in charge of Starfleet's adwanced strategic technology dewelopment programs. Veapons research."

Spock remained noncommittal. "Ten years ago, we could have gone to war with the Klingons at any moment. Starfleet has always had a military responsibility, and does to this day."

"Von of the projects Drake headed vas code-named Rising Star."

Spock shook his head. The name meant nothing to him. Nor to anyone else in the briefing room.

"It vas a feasibility study for deweloping veapons using protomatter."

That meant something to everyone.

Protomatter was one of the most volatile forms of matter known to exist. So hazardous that most ethical scientists had long ago denounced its use in any type of research.

But protomatter *had* been used in at least one notable scientific project in recent memory. And had yielded predictably tragic results.

"Genesis?" McCoy asked.

Chekov nodded. Project Genesis had been an ambitious research program to develop a process by which uninhabitable planets could become life-bearing. It had been directed by

Dr. Carol Marcus, aided by her son—and Kirk's—David Marcus.

Though the initial results had been promising, the process had been abandoned when it was discovered that the only reason Genesis worked was because David Marcus had used protomatter in the initializing matrix. All products of the reaction were thereby rendered dangerously unstable.

Spock seemed concerned by the implications of Chekov's revelation. "I find it most difficult to accept that the Genesis Project was a secret Starfleet weapons research program from the beginning."

"Genesis had nothing to do with Starfleet," Chekov said. "It *vas* a legitimate scientific inwestigation, completely independent of any military application or influence. Carol Marcus vould not have pursued it under any other conditions. But, after the keptin's son vas murdered by the Klingons, *on* the Genesis Planet, Keptin Kirk became . . . obsessed. He vanted to know everything about the project."

"So he asked you to investigate Carol Marcus?" McCoy asked. His skeptical tone said how unlikely he thought that was.

But Chekov said, "No. Only von Genesis scientist acted outside of the project's strict guidelines. The keptin's son." Chekov stared down at his hands on the tabletop. He remembered how distraught Kirk had been over David's death. "The keptin asked me to find out how David had obtained the protomatter he used in his vork."

Spock made the connection at once. "Admiral Drake."

"The admiral vas sharply critical of Starfleet's decision to abandon protomatter veapons research. Yet, vhen it vas abandoned, his department became responsible for storing the protomatter Starfleet had already manufactured, until means for its safe disposal could be deweloped."

McCoy seemed as if he could barely stay seated. "And you're saying Drake deliberately provided some of that protomatter to David Marcus, knowing it would be incorporated into the Genesis Device?"

"Exactly," Chekov said. His voice trembled with indignation. "Just to see vhat vould happen. Veapons research by proxy."

Spock was the only one at the table who remained calm. "Commander Chekov, you have raised a series of most disturbing allegations. If what you say is true, then Admiral Drake could face a court-martial. Indeed, he *should* be court-martialed. Why didn't you and the captain present your findings to Command?"

Chekov had wrestled with that question for almost a decade. The answer was inadequate, but unavoidable. "Because Drake had spent sixteen years at Starfleet Headquarters. He knew how its bureaucracy vorked better than anyone. There vere no records that could be traced. No direct connection between David and Starfleet at any level. I don't believe the keptin's son ever found out vhat the original source of his protomatter vas."

Uhura sat forward. "Pavel, does Captain Kirk believe Drake is responsible for the death of his son?"

"Not exactly," Chekov said. "He accepts that David vas . . . his father's son. He made his own choices. Even if he didn't have the experience to understand vhat might happen because of them. But the keptin also knows that David might not have been *able* to make the choices he did if Admiral Drake had not been there, tempting him with protomatter to begin vith."

"What did you do with your report?" Spock asked.

"I gave it to the keptin."

"What did he do with it?"

"Vhat could be done? There vas no proof of any misconduct on Admiral Drake's part. Shortly after the Genesis Planet self-destructed, Starfleet disposed of its entire supply of protomatter. Vonce that happened, there vas no vay to determine if any of it had gone missing."

"Didn't *Starfleet* try to find out where David had obtained his protomatter?" McCoy asked.

"Of course," Chekov said. "But because Admiral Drake vas able to produce records showing that all of Starfleet's supply vas accounted for before it vas destroyed, the Genesis Investigation Committee didn't pursue that part of their inwestigation. The official werdict vas that David had obtained protomatter from an unknown source outside the Federation. Possibly the Klingons."

McCoy settled back in his chair, suddenly looking older than his years. "Do you have any idea how serious these charges are?"

"Vhich is vhy I cannot believe the Council woted for Drake."

McCoy sighed, looked across the table at Spock. "So what does this do to your logic?"

"It appears to be an unrelated fact," Spock said.

"How can it be?" Chekov demanded.

"Even if everything you have told us is true, Commander, Drake's involvement in the death of David Marcus could be nothing more than a coincidence. If you had uncovered evidence suggesting that Drake had deliberately provided protomatter to David, *knowing* he was Jim's son, then a causal connection to the current situation might be made."

"What 'causal connection'?" McCoy asked.

"That Admiral Drake specifically manipulated events to propel Jim on his journey to Chal, knowing it would place him in great danger."

"It makes sense to me," Chekov said.

"But it is not logical," Spock countered. "A rivalry stemming from Academy days is hardly motive enough for what you are attempting to accuse the admiral of. Without a motive for the admiral's actions, his possible complicity in supplying protomatter to David and Jim's involvement with the Children of Heaven cannot be linked. We are, I regret to say, back where we started from, with no indication Admiral Drake intends to do the captain harm."

Chekov disagreed. "But Sulu's orders say ve're to enlist the keptin's help in taking possession of the Children of Heawen, vhatever it is. And if the keptin does not cooperate, then ve are to use force."

Sulu glanced at Chekov in annoyance. "I am aware of what my orders entail, Commander."

Everyone looked uncomfortable with that exchange. No one at this table could ever conceive of a situation in which they would take arms against Kirk.

But Sulu was a Starfleet officer *and* a starship captain.

Under orders.

Chekov could no longer be sure what Sulu would do when forced to choose between his personal wishes and his sworn duty. Not after Dark Range.

McCoy voiced the frustration Chekov felt. "So, what's the key to all this, Spock?"

"In what way, Doctor?"

"What's the piece of information you need that'll tell you what possibility we're dealing with here?"

Spock looked thoughtful, as if he had never considered the question before.

"At the heart of these events is a single unexplained coincidence," Spock finally said. "On the frontier, on Dark Range Platform, a Starfleet Intelligence agent makes contact with a Klingon who can tell her about the *Chalchaj 'qmey.* That agent immediately goes rogue. At almost the exact same time, a young Klingon-Romulan woman makes contact with Captain Kirk, and invites him to journey to the presumed location of the very same Children of Heaven."

Spock looked around at everyone at the conference table. He had their full attention. "There was ample time for Jade to transmit a coded subspace message from Dark Range to someone here on Earth. The question is: To whom?"

Spock paused. No one spoke.

"I believe if we can find out who the link is between Jade and Teilani, then we will know the truth about Captain Kirk. And Admiral Drake."

"Unfortunately, we have no time to do that," Sulu said. "We're leaving orbit in ninety minutes."

"Then we must accept that we are on our own," Spock concluded. "And finding Captain Kirk is our best strategy."

Sulu stood. The meeting was over.

Chekov could sense the conflict in the room.

If the *Excelsior* found the *Enterprise,* everyone here would have to follow orders and confront Kirk, pitting loyalty to Starfleet against loyalty to the truth.

It was a no-win scenario the equal of the *Kobayashi Maru.*

But at least Chekov knew that comparison would give them the clue they needed to find the proper action to take.

As Captain Kirk had long ago shown them that, when forced to choose between two equally undesirable options, the only thing to do was to change the rules.

All they had to do now was to figure out what game was being played.

As Chekov left the conference room, he thought again of Admiral Drake's study. Of the sealed door.

And of the secrets behind it.

TWENTY-TWO

☆

Even as the door to Drake's study sealed itself behind its forcefield, another door had opened.

An inner door.

Hidden behind the display case that held the uniform of a Fourth World Mercenary.

As Chekov and his crewmates signed their security oaths in an anteroom, a woman had stepped through that hidden door.

She was compact, attractive, with finely drawn features and dark complexion, a strong intelligence in her eyes. But her mouth was not used to smiling.

She still wore the flight suit and tight-fitting hood she had worn on Dark Range Platform.

Drake rose to greet her.

"You heard?" he asked.

The woman pulled off her flight hood, shaking loose her dark hair.

A streak of white blazed through it.

The starkness of the color made the resemblance between Drake and the woman more striking.

Her code name had been Jade. But her real name was Ariadne.

Drake.

Father and daughter.

"I should have disintegrated them in the cargo bay when I

had the chance," Ariadne said. "Or ejected them from the airlock when I got rid of Kort."

Then she kissed her father's cheek.

His eyes kindled with pride. For her and all she had done.

"No," he told her. "You did the right thing. If Chekov and Uhura had disappeared altogether, Intelligence would have launched a full investigation."

Drake's daughter made a playful face. "You're saying they're not going to investigate *my* disappearance from their ranks?"

She went to a small cabinet against the wall, pressed a hidden switch. The cabinet unfolded into a bar.

Drake joined her there, gloating. "No one even knows you've disappeared, my dear. Kirk created such a paranoid group of officers that they actually came to me first, convinced no one else could be trusted. So the situation is contained. Intelligence doesn't know any of you are back on Earth. They think you're all still deep under cover, hunting Klingon generals who've gone into business for themselves."

The woman gave her father a snifter of brandy, poured the same for herself, then lifted her glass in a toast to her father's success.

"What if *Kirk* goes into business for himself?" She closed her eyes, savoring the brandy's aroma. "We've been after the *Chalchaj 'qmey* for years. That pathetic Klingon on Dark Range final'y gave us the connection to Chal that we needed. But now we're tossing a potential superweapon into Kirk's lap."

Drake sipped his brandy, unconcerned. "Kirk is a man of the moment. He has no vision. So he'll do exactly what we want him to do. Lead us to Chal. And to the Children of Heaven. Then, one way or another, he'll be . . . superseded."

Ariadne drank the contents of her glass in one quick toss. "I still think torturing Teilani would have been simpler."

Drake put down his snifter and rubbed at his face. He'd

been working twenty-hour days since obtaining his new position.

"That wouldn't have been wise. Or profitable. We tried interrogating some of her compatriots right after Khitomer. When the Chal first started inquiring about membership in the Federation. No matter what we did to them, we learned nothing to indicate any of them knew what their world is sitting on. And they have incredible control over their autonomic nervous systems. As soon as they realized there was no escape, they literally willed themselves to death."

Drake poured more brandy into Ariadne's glass, then his own. "It was one thing for a few aides to disappear. Accidents still do happen, even on Earth. But we can't risk Teilani suddenly vanishing. Someone might start asking questions."

Ariadne frowned. "'Willed themselves to death'? They're half Klingon. They should have died trying to escape. How could they commit *suicide?*"

Drake patted her hand with paternal condescension. "Klingons are animals, Ariadne. Never forget that."

Drake stared up at a two-dimensional photoprint framed above the bar. He was in it, much younger. The handsome woman beside him looked out with a face softened by love. Together, they held a small girl on their laps. A streak of white blazed through the child's dark hair.

Drake's face darkened as he looked at the image of his wife. The family he used to have.

"Never forget that," he said again.

"How did you manage to get Teilani to go after Kirk?"

In a lightning change of mood, Drake winked at Ariadne. "I told her to."

Ariadne laughed scornfully "And Kirk doesn't suspect?"

Drake shook his head. "I gave her his complete psych file. Told her how sorry I was that Starfleet couldn't get involved in defending a planet so deep in Klingon-Romulan territory. But suggested—off the record, mind you—that Kirk couldn't refuse the challenge. As far as I can tell from the surveillance we ran on him before they left, she's using everything in his file. Pulling his strings as if he's her personal puppet."

"What if she tells him that recruiting him was your idea?"

"She won't. Kirk's a proud man. I made it clear to her that if he got any hint that he's been manipulated into helping Chal, he'd walk away at once."

Ariadne walked over to an armchair, sat down, hooking one leg over the arm, letting it swing. "How'd anyone that predictable ever last so long in the service? Let alone command a starship?"

Drake grinned, the smile of a predator. "Thirty years ago, he was different. Would have ripped the throat out of a Klingon with his teeth if he had to. But the years have not been kind to Kirk." Drake chuckled. "I've done my best to keep it that way."

Ariadne gave her father a curious look. "Why so personal? What did Kirk ever do to you?"

Drake's eyes flamed with sudden anger. "This isn't personal! Kirk is the epitome of the cancer weakening Starfleet and the Federation. To stay strong, we have to remain intact. Pure. There's no more room for Klingons and aliens. Our borders have to be secure. We have to look to ourselves, not to outsiders. Cartwright knew that. But he wasn't careful."

"At least Cartwright didn't talk about us at his trial," Ariadne said.

"Only because he knows we're the last ones left of his organization. If he ever dares breathe a word about us, he knows he'll never get out of confinement." Drake sat back down behind his desk. "We're Admiral Cartwright's last hope for freedom. And we're the Federation's best hope for security."

"So what's Kirk?" Ariadne asked.

"Debris. To be tossed aside by the waves of history."

"From what I've heard, he doesn't sound the type to let himself be tossed aside."

"He doesn't have a choice anymore," Drake said with venom in his voice. "Kirk's day is over. Starfleet knows it. His friends know it. And *I* know it." He settled back in his chair, hands clasped behind his head. "And I intend to see the expression on Kirk's face when he knows it, too."

"Whatever you've got planned for him," Ariadne said dryly, "I'm glad to know it *isn't* personal."

Drake frowned.

Sometimes children could be such a burden.

TWENTY-THREE

☆

Kirk missed his Starfleet sideburns.

He had had them ever since the Academy. A tradition whose origins were lost in time.

But two days ago, Teilani had carefully shaved them off.

Slowly. With a naked Klingon *SeymoH* blade.

After covering him with hot lather.

Kirk had heard stories of the *SeymoH* blade and how the Klingons employed it. Not for cutting, but for delicate, maddening, and indescribable scraping.

He used to think it would be an experience he would never have. Simply because he would never trust any Klingon to get that close to him with a drawn knife.

But Teilani was something different. Something special.

And smart.

She had told him that his Starfleet sideburns would cause him to stand out where they were going.

Not on Chal. But on Prestor V.

It was a bleak, backwater planet just inside the boundaries of the Klingon Empire, close to the Federation's watchposts.

For generations, Prestor V's only industry had been provided by the Klingon garrison that was stationed there. But with the Empire's recent military cutbacks, the garrison had been recalled.

Prestor V then became the latest in a long list of planets to look elsewhere for support in the new era of peace. So, like many others before it, the colonial government solved its problems by turning to institutionalized piracy and theft.

Prestor V was also to be the *Enterprise*'s first port of call on her voyage to Chal.

For supplies, Teilani had said. And equipment.

She had explained everything to Kirk as she had drawn the edge of the blade across his skin, awakening each nerve ending with a combination of exquisite pressure and the constant danger of serious injury.

Kirk hadn't said much during the discussion. Teilani had proven herself very resourceful in redirecting his attention.

Meanwhile, the *Enterprise* had arrived at Prestor V on schedule.

Now Kirk and Scott sat at a wobbling table in a dingy spaceport bar, on the outskirts of the planet's capital city. They were waiting for Teilani to join them.

Neither had their Starfleet sideburns anymore. Though Scott had had to shave his off himself.

Looking around the bar, Kirk could see that Teilani had been correct in suggesting the sideburns go. It was not a Starfleet-friendly environment.

Like any good Klingon drinking establishment, this one had a number of ears nailed to the wall behind the bartender's station. Most of them human. Kirk wondered if any had fallen to a *SeymoH* blade in the hands of a jealous lover.

Probably not, he decided. If a spurned Klingon lover had a *SeymoH* blade handy, an ear might not be the first trophy taken.

Kirk looked away from the collection of ears and smiled at Scott.

Scott smiled back.

Both smiles were forced.

The silence was awkward.

"We haven't done this for a long time, have we?" Kirk said. "Sit in a bar, wear civilian clothes for a change, have a few drinks."

"No," Scott agreed. "We haven't."

Kirk sipped what passed for this planet's beer. Scott did the same.

More awkward silence.

"After Khitomer, I got very busy," Kirk said. "At headquarters."

"So I understand."

Kirk couldn't stand the tension any longer. He used to like touring alien bars with Mr. Scott.

"Scotty, is there something wrong?"

"Why? Should there be?"

Kirk shrugged. He wasn't sure what he was trying to say. "I don't know. It's just that . . . you and me . . . here in this bar . . . shouldn't we be having . . . *fun?*"

Scotty sighed noisily. The Prestor beer left an attractive little fringe of blue foam on his mustache.

"Captain, we've been traveling on th' *Enterprise* for th' past eight days and you've barely said two words t' me that weren't havin' t' do with th' engines."

Kirk grimaced. What could he say? "Scotty . . . I've been . . . busy."

"Aye, sir, that ye have been." Scott poured a fresh glass of the blue beer from the copper pitcher on the table. Something small and green with too many legs shot out from beneath the pitcher the instant Scott lifted it. "But the point of the matter is, you're always busy."

Kirk heard the recrimination in Scotty's tone. He knew he couldn't make up for anything he might have done, or not done in the past. But at least he could try and change things for the future.

"Mr. Scott, I am not busy now." Kirk raised his glass in a toast. "I am sitting in this fine establishment hoping to have a drink with an old friend."

Scotty didn't look convinced, but he appreciated the effort. He clinked his glass against Kirk's.

"To old times," Scott said.

Kirk disagreed. "To new times."

Scott countered with the one toast neither could argue with. "To th' *Enterprise.* Th' finest ship Starfleet ever saw."

"And to her crew," Kirk added.

At least this time when silence followed, there was some semblance of a connection between the two men.

Kirk couldn't help himself.

"So, how *are* the engines?"

Scott's eyes twinkled. There was a reason most of Kirk's conversations with him revolved around technical matters.

"I've had to rework th' intervalve couplings t' keep th' power groupings online," Scott said. "And with th' new disruptor cannons being installed, I've—"

"Excuse me?" Kirk interrupted. "Disruptors?"

"Aye," Scott said innocently.

Kirk stared at his chief engineer. *"Klingon* disruptor cannons . . . on the *Enterprise?"*

"Captain, we don't have any phasers. Our tractor beams have been downgraded. And all but one photon tube has been welded over with duranium." Scott leaned forward and dropped his voice. "If th' *Enterprise* is t' be part of a planetary defense system, then she needs something t' defend herself with, don't ye think?"

Kirk couldn't argue with that. "But where did we get disruptor cannons?"

Scotty smiled. "Ask me nae questions, I'll tell ye nae lies. Teilani was the one who did the dealing. Right here in this bar I'm told."

"She *bought* them," Kirk said, not quite believing it.

"We're in Klingon territory, sir. And in Klingon territory, currency is still widespread. As are a number of ex-officers who see nothing wrong in selling surplus equipment t' th' highest bidders. Let me add that Teilani is quite th' negotiator, too."

Kirk smiled inwardly at that. He knew from experience that she was skilled at getting her own way.

"Is there anything else being installed on my ship I should know about?"

Scott scratched at his mustache. "A few antimatter pods. Ten photon torpedoes. Twin disruptor cannons. Shield augmenters. Tractor enhancers." Scott looked at Kirk. "That's about the lot."

"That's just about everything Starfleet took out of her when she was decommissioned."

"Aye. I never would have thought it, but with th' new equipment and a few more weeks' work, I should have th' old girl back close t' her original condition."

"Except she'll have Klingon disruptors instead of phasers."

Scott finished off his glass of beer and wiped his mustache free of foam. "The pieces all fit in the holes Starfleet left. So why not? After all, there're not a great many Starfleet officers willin' to sell off parts of their own Fleet."

Don't be so sure, Kirk thought. He looked around the bar. It was still fairly early in the evening and only half the tables were filled. Almost all of the clientele were Klingon. None of them appeared to be paying any attention to the two humans sitting by themselves.

Just the same, Kirk leaned forward and gave Scott a conspiratorial whisper. "Does any of this refitting make sense to you, Scotty?"

The whisper made Scott nervous. He leaned forward to speak in the same hushed tone. "Why not? Ye've got t' want t' have a whole ship to command, don't ye?"

"Chal is deep within the Klingon-Romulan frontier. At

worst, we're going to face a few Orion pirates. As long as our shields are up to strength, a few photon torpedoes are all we need."

"Teilani seems t' know what she wants."

"Don't I know it," Kirk said with a smile.

Scott poured the last of the blue beer from the copper pitcher. Something thick and green plopped out of the pitcher and into his glass. Scott eyed it warily. But it didn't move on its own.

"Could be that Teilani knows more about what t' expect around Chal than we do," he suggested.

"I have no doubt of that," Kirk agreed.

Scott shrugged. "When in Rome." He upended his glass and bravely swallowed the thick green sludge.

Kirk flinched. "Scotty. How could you?"

"Trust me, Captain. There's nothing that could be alive in a brew as foul as this one."

Kirk's first impulse was to thank Scotty for calling him "captain" again. But he decided not to. The title had probably just slipped out without Scott being aware of what he said.

The surly Klingon bartender lumbered over to Kirk's table with another battered copper pitcher of blue beer. She was old and deeply wrinkled with a mane of pure white hair. Her leather apron carried an ominous collection of stains. It looked ready to burst from the pressure it exerted on her massive breasts crammed under her armor chest plate.

Kirk tried to send the pitcher back but the bartender muttered that it was free.

"Free?" Kirk asked.

The bartender said any customer who ate the green sludge got a free pitcher. It was house policy.

"What, exactly, is the green sludge?" Scott asked politely.

The bartender gaped at Scott in admiration. Her deeply ridged brow rippled as her eyes widened. "You didn't know?" she mumbled.

Scott shook his head.

The bartender erupted with a bone-chilling howl of Klingon laughter, whomped Scott on the back, then went back to her bar, still snorting in amazement.

A look of panic crossed Scott's face.

Kirk pushed the copper pitcher closer to the engineer. "Drink up, Scotty. Who knows what you get for doing it twice?"

Before Scott could reply, Kirk suddenly felt familiar hands move across his back and slide around his chest.

He lost his breath as quickly as that.

Teilani whirled him around and kissed him. Innovatively. Thoroughly. But only for a second.

It was her usual dramatic entrance.

"I'm done," she announced as she dragged over a chair and sat at the table.

Her dark jumpsuit clung to her curves. Her exotic face was flushed, vibrant with satisfaction. The energy she radiated was nothing less than blinding. As always.

Kirk felt the pull of her nearness, as if he were a moon trapped in helpless orbit, drawn by irresistible force.

"I didn't know you had anything more to do," he said. He decided he could stare at her for hours. He wondered how he could ever have thought that a Klingon brow was ungainly, or that pointed ears were alien.

Both features looked perfect to him now, especially the way they blended in Teilani.

"The *Enterprise* is a big ship, James." She reached out to pour herself a glass of beer. "She needs a great deal of supplies."

Scott held out a cautioning hand. "Careful of the sludge, lass."

"I know," Teilani told him. "If you accidentally eat any of it, they have to give you a free pitcher to help dredge the worms out of your system."

Kirk was impressed by how quickly the color drained from Scotty's face.

The engineer quickly excused himself.

As soon as he was gone, Teilani reached across the table and squeezed Kirk's hand.

"Happy?" she asked.

"Exhausted," Kirk answered.

For all the time they had been spending in his quarters, sleep had been a low priority for both of them.

Teilani liked his answer. "Ready to start work?"

Kirk was puzzled.

"As coordinator of Chal's planetary defense force," Teilani explained.

"Now?" Kirk asked.

Teilani's face became serious. "We're being followed."

Kirk immediately glanced around the bar. No one was overtly looking at them.

"Not *here,*" Teilani said. "In space."

"Who?"

"The people who went after you on the farm."

"What sort of ship do they have?"

"A Tholian starcruiser. Emerald class."

Kirk knew the vessel well. A crystal-faceted teardrop hull, similar to the ships that had once captured the *Enterprise.* A crew of twenty, maximum cruising factor of seven point five, exceptional shields. But little in the way of firepower.

"We can outrun it," he said. "Or outfight it."

"Good," Teilani said. "Then I think we should outrun it."

"We'll still meet up on Chal, won't we?"

"Not if they don't think we're going there."

Kirk didn't follow her reasoning. "Where else would they think we were going?"

Teilani wasn't taking this as seriously as Kirk thought she should.

"They're going to be able to track us here, to Prestor V, easily. They're also going to find out about all the equipment we've taken on board. So what we have to do is make them think we've gone to another system, looking for spacedock facilities. So we can install everything."

"That means they don't know about Scotty," Kirk said. "He could refit the ship holding his breath, walking her hull in a pair of magnetic boots. No spacedock required."

"But since they won't know Scotty, when we leave Prestor V, I think we should set up a false trail. Just to give us some extra time to . . . prepare for things on Chal."

It was Kirk's turn to be serious. "You still haven't told me what we're going to face on your homeworld."

Teilani bit her lip, hesitating.

"Scotty told me about all the weapons systems you were having installed aboard the *Enterprise.* Is that why you wanted me down here most of the day?"

"James, no. I'm not hiding anything from you."

Kirk believed her, if for no other reason than his heart longed for her. "Then at least tell me who those weapons are intended to be used against. I know it's not just a Tholian starcruiser."

Teilani looked away from him, making up her mind.

"If things work out the way I hope," she said, "they won't have to be used against anyone. Just the fact that we have them should be enough to get the other side to the negotiating table."

"What other side?" Kirk asked.

"The Anarchists, of course. Those among us who want to destroy Chal."

"How?"

"By telling the galaxy what we have to offer."

"If that's all they have to do, then why haven't they done it already?" Kirk asked. "A few broadbeam subspace transmissions and the whole quadrant would know about your world in weeks."

Teilani wrapped both hands around her glass of beer. "They're not that fanatical, James. The Anarchists know Chal could never withstand the billions who would come to it after that kind of announcement. No, what they intend to do is keep its location a secret, so they can sell access to Chal to a select few."

"Teilani, is that so wrong?"

She lifted her chin in determination. "When you see Chal you'll understand why even that level of exploitation is intolerable."

Kirk allowed himself to be completely captivated by her eyes. "What *is* Chal like?"

She eased forward over the table, until her lips brushed against his, full of promise.

"Ten more days," she whispered. "Then you'll see for yourself."

TWENTY-FOUR

Ten days later, the *Enterprise* slipped into standard orbit of Chal.

Kirk almost felt like a boy again.

He remembered the excitement he had felt on his first school trip to Tranquility Base. The first time he had left Earth to set foot on another world.

This was better.

He couldn't explain why.

He stared through the forward viewport of Teilani's yacht as the *Enterprise*'s hangar doors ponderously opened.

A welcoming blue glow—reflected light from the world below—swept into the hangar deck.

Kirk watched as Esys reset the yacht's controls for manual flight. He saw the young Klingon-Romulan adjust the inertial dampers to full strength.

"That's all right," Kirk said. "Leave them at minimum."

Kirk wanted to feel what it was like to *fly* to Chal.

He felt Teilani touch his shoulder from the seat behind him, understanding his excitement.

The sleek yacht rose from the hangar deck, slowly floated toward the open doors under automatic tractor-beam control.

Passing from the hangar to space was like moving from the darkness of a cave to a lustrous summer day.

Chal was a sapphire before him.

Rich deep blue beyond any word Kirk knew in any language.

An ocean world, ninety percent of her pure azure waters, scrolled in elegant curlicues of brilliant white clouds.

The yacht banked away from the *Enterprise,* moving down. Kirk felt the shudder as Esys took control from the tractor beam.

The binary suns of Chal glinted from the world's vast ocean, leaving dark spots in Kirk's vision.

It was as if every summer day on every beach that ever was had been collapsed into one perfect, shimmering blue moment.

"What does 'Chal' mean?" Kirk asked. He had heard so many different names for worlds that he had never thought to ask.

"Heaven," Teilani said.

Kirk understood.

He fell toward paradise.

The yacht shook satisfyingly as it entered Chal's atmosphere.

Kirk grinned along with Esys as the dampers did little to dilute the sheer sensations of speed and descent.

Ahead, on the distant horizon, rapidly losing its curve as

they neared the surface, Kirk saw a string of islands rise from the sea.

They were one of four archipelagoes that daubed the ocean like artist's brushstrokes.

The largest island, in the archipelago closest the equator, was where the colony of Chal had first been founded, where its first and only city remained. It had a population of almost one thousand, Teilani said. Small enough that they had little impact on the world's ecology. That there was food enough for the taking, without requiring anyone to work in agriculture for more than a few weeks in any year.

Neither was there much work required in the way of support services or maintenance. The building materials used and technological infrastructure the colony's founders had installed were robust and capable of self-repair.

By all accounts, to Kirk the colony sounded more like a resort camp than a working community. It was almost as if the Klingons and Romulans who had created the colony had intended that their descendants would never have to work to maintain their blissful existence.

The air of Chal whistled past the yacht as Esys slowed the craft to subsonic velocity.

They flew a few hundred meters above the ocean.

The main island rushed at them like a wave of green, held apart from the ocean by a border of white sand.

"Almost home," Teilani said.

They raced along the shore, twisting and curving with it. Completely inefficient, but unquestionably *fun.*

Kirk watched deep jungle flash by to the side, highlighted by vivid explosions of color from flowers that beggared those of Earth.

He saw a handful of ground vehicles parked on the beach below them. Groupings of Chal looked up from the sand on which they lay and from the water in which they swam.

Sports and games were high among the pursuits enjoyed by the Chal, Teilani had explained. Loosely organized committees arranged the minimal work schedules. A more formal group of volunteers formed the planet's government, such that it was. Teilani was the one responsible for maintaining contact with other worlds.

With no industry and no exports, Kirk was uncertain where Chal's trade credits originally came from. Teilani had no answers either. She had merely taken over her position, inheriting a system set in place from the beginning. Computers provided almost all the suggestions and advice for running the colony. And with only a thousand or so inhabitants to cater to, with food and shelter and recreation abundant for all, actual government involvement in anyone's daily life was rare and inconsequential.

Kirk was surprised that the colony had been provided with such a stable organization from the beginning. Most colonies served as laboratories for creating new forms of social interaction.

The yacht eased to the right, following the curve of the shore. The city was before them.

Nestled in green. Clear, clean stripes of beige and cream and pale pink walls and roofs arranged like scattered seashells, raised on a small outcropping of black volcanic rock, caught in the jungle's edge, overlooking the sweep of a protected harbor and kilometers of wide white beach.

There was a central structure larger than any other building—a covered stadium, Kirk guessed. But all around it, everything was low and simple. Nothing more than two stories. Nothing that could get in the way of the glorious sunlight that bathed the scene.

Esys brought the yacht around, slowing it gradually.

Kirk saw a series of circular landing pads carved into the black rock at the city's edge.

Yellow concentric circles glowed. Numbers written in Romulan script identified them.

Gently, the yacht touched down.

At the same instant, the yacht's hatch sprang open.

Kirk gasped as the rich air of Chal flooded the cabin.

He smelled the ocean, the flowers, the damp green of the jungle.

For a moment, he felt dizzy. His skin tingled. His heart raced.

Esys and Teilani were standing already.

He pushed himself out of his seat.

There was something different about the action.

"What's your gravity here?" Kirk asked.

Teilani smiled at him as she stood in the hatchway. Beyond her, Kirk could see lush jungle fronds sway in the breeze.

"Point nine eight," she said.

Kirk worked it out. That only meant a difference in his weight of about a kilogram and a half. Not enough to account for the ease of movement he felt.

"Oxygen content of the atmosphere?" he asked.

Teilani's smile grew puzzled. "Twenty-one percent."

Again, just slightly off Earth normal. But not enough to account for the undercurrent of energy surging through his body. He felt a rush of exhilaration.

"Are you all right, James?" Teilani asked.

He joined her at the hatchway, swung her off her feet, hugged her, smothered her laughing face with kisses. That was his answer.

Esys laughed as he passed them in the hatchway.

Kirk knew he would hear a lot of laughter on this planet.

He decided he was going to like it here.

Everything was new.

Because of Teilani.

TWENTY-FIVE

☆

The *Excelsior* dropped from warp and smoothly banked on impulse to enter standard orbit of Prestor V.

On the spacious bridge, Chekov looked up from the security officer's station. "Ve have them," he announced.

Sulu swiveled in his center chair to look over at Spock.

Spock had taken over the science station.

Chekov knew some of Sulu's bridge crew hadn't been pleased to relinquish their key positions to what were, after all, interlopers. But the ease with which those of the *Enterprise* had fallen into their old routines was remarkable to witness. It was as if not a day had gone by since their first five-year mission.

Even Lieutenant Janice Rand, once Captain Kirk's yeoman, now Sulu's communications officer, worked perfectly with Uhura at the station they shared.

Spock confirmed Chekov's readings.

"Sensors are picking up impulse ionization readings consistent with the *Enterprise*'s engines. I estimate she was in orbit here, within the past eight to twelve days."

"Any idea how long she stayed?" Sulu asked.

"Judging from the residual ionization trails, multiple orbits. Two to three days at least," Spock said.

Sulu looked ahead at the main viewscreen. Prestor V was a scabrous brown and purple planet below them. "Then that means she did some business here."

He tapped his finger on the side of his chair. Chekov could

see him working out the sequence of orders he was going to give. The expression on his face, the position he assumed in the chair, all reminded Chekov of Kirk.

"Mr. Chekov," Sulu began, "continue an intensive sweep for the *Enterprise*'s warp signature. Just in case they remained in orbit a few days longer and we can still pick up their warp heading. Commander Uhura, contact all orbital docking facilities. Ask if the *Enterprise* has booked space in them in the past two weeks."

"Ask?" Uhura said. "Sir, this is a Klingon borderworld. No one's going to answer any questions a Starfleet ship *asks.*"

Chekov hid his smile as Sulu frowned, the rhythm of his orders lost.

"Very well," Sulu said with a sigh. "Find out what they use for currency here, withdraw it from ship's stores, and assemble landing parties to beam over to the docking platforms and inquire about the *Enterprise* in person."

"You mean, bribe the dockmasters," Uhura said, looking for clarification.

"Whatever it takes," Sulu acknowledged.

He stood up to face the viewscreen. "The *Enterprise* came here for a purpose. I'm going to guess it was to replace some of the equipment Starfleet removed from her. So far there's been no evidence that Captain Kirk has been trying to hide his trail. But once the *Enterprise* was resupplied, he might have changed tactics."

Chekov thought Sulu was stating the obvious. If anything was consistent about Kirk's tactics, it was the frequency with which he changed them.

Spock looked up from his science station. "Captain Sulu, if Captain Kirk wished to replace all the equipment Starfleet removed from the *Enterprise,* then that would include weapons systems."

"Of course," Sulu said.

"Then I submit that he must have dealt in extralegal channels."

"It's a Klingon borderworld," Uhura reminded Spock. "The whole planet is extralegal."

Spock was unperturbed. "There are various levels of extralegal activity, Commander. To replace weapons systems, I suggest Captain Kirk would have made contact with suppliers close to the old Klingon garrison that was stationed on this world. Logically, they would be the ones with access to any military matériel that was left behind."

"Or stolen," Chekov added.

"As I said," Spock agreed, "there are various levels of extralegal activity."

Sulu nodded, surrendering to Spock's logic. "I'll want landing parties to go to the surface, as well. To look into 'extralegal' supply options." He glanced at Spock. "Will that be sufficient?"

"Again, the inhabitants of Prestor V might not be willing to aid Starfleet personnel in their inquiries."

"Undercover, Captain Spock?" Sulu asked.

"That would be the logical approach."

Sulu looked in Chekov's direction. Chekov could see what the captain was thinking.

"Pavel, I believe you're our designated criminal," Sulu said.

Chekov heard Uhura chuckle at her station.

"All right," Chekov said. "But this time, *I* get to carry the money."

TWENTY-SIX

☆

Kirk thundered across the sands of Chal.

He stayed crouched and low in his saddle as his mount pounded along the beach, sending billowing clouds of glittering sand flying with each hoofbeat.

Teilani rode at his side, hair streaming in the wind of their race.

He caught her eye.

The suns of Chal sparkled in her. The passion of their contest. Of their lovemaking only an hour ago. The joy of home. Everything united in that one expression that transformed her face. Making her beauty transcendent.

She snapped her reins and yelled at her steed to spur it on.

The horselike creature, glossy brown and native to a distant Romulan colony world, snorted and took off, its powerful legs driving against the beach.

Kirk urged his own mount on. He gulped down air as if he had been drowning. He had never known breathing to be so elemental an experience.

Even as he closed the gap between them, Kirk wondered what a thorough analysis of Chal's atmosphere would find. He had only been here a single day, but had felt the planet's influence from the moment he first landed.

The treasure of this world, Teilani called it.

Be young forever.

Only a length ahead of him, Teilani guided her mount

around a jagged black rock and hauled back on the reins to bring the race to an end.

Kirk was still getting used to the creatures. They weren't the same as the horses he was familiar with on Earth. He overshot Teilani, had to circle back.

She was waiting for him, resplendent in the simple white clothes she wore. They were decoration more than protection in Chal's benign climate—loose, open, innocently plain yet captivatingly sexy.

Kirk wore a version of the same. As did everyone else he had met on Chal. Everything, even these clothes, was a celebration here, of unfettered life and love.

It seemed as if there was nothing to hide on this world. Nothing to be denied.

Kirk dismounted, went to Teilani. He was out of breath. She teased him for it. Then apologized with a kiss.

They walked to the water's edge.

Gentle waves bordered by translucent foam lapped at the white sand.

Tiny flying creatures chased the water. Some skittered on impossibly tiny feet, leaving delicate tracks in the sand. Others glided gracefully on the soft breeze, skimming the curl of the gentle surf.

On the horizon, brightly colored sails of small boats darted swiftly between air and sea.

This world wasn't a resort. It was a playground.

Everything about it had been designed from the beginning to offer a world without stress, without need.

Kirk slipped his arm around Teilani. She leaned her head on his shoulder.

"Now I know why you want to keep this world a secret," Kirk told her.

"Do you?" Teilani asked.

Chal's binary suns hung like an hourglass in an unbroken blue sky. The primary star was yellow-white, the smaller secondary orange-yellow. From space Kirk had seen the incandescent plasma bridge that joined the two, as the primary stripped off gases from the secondary that spiraled around it.

But the light those suns cast on this alien shore was warm and inviting.

"If people knew what it was like here, you'd be beach-to-beach hotels and travelports inside a year," Kirk said. His words seemed banal to him, in the face of such perfection.

"And that would be the end of everything." She held him closer. "But that's why you're here."

Kirk looked into her eyes. The face of his old enemies—Klingon and Romulan—improbably joined, looked back.

But they were enemies no longer.

In Teilani's arms, he had left the past behind.

"I'm here because of you," Kirk said. He nuzzled her wind-tossed hair. "You told me you needed someone to save your world, remember? And then you brought me to . . . heaven."

She held his hand to the side of her face. Pressed her open lips against his sun-warmed skin. "Were you expecting a war zone?"

"Some sign of imminent danger at least," Kirk said. His fingers traced the ridges of her forehead.

"There is danger all around us, James."

"I thought the *Enterprise* would put an end to that. That just her presence would bring the other side—the Anarchists—to the negotiating table." He moved his fingers down the side of her head, pushed her hair away from her ear, kissed its curves, drinking in the intermingled scent of sun and sand and sea and her.

"But that's just here on Chal," she whispered into his ear. Her breath was warmer than the sun, melting him.

Kirk ran his hands along her back, the silky fabric of her light tunic no barrier to the softness of her skin. "You have other enemies?" he asked.

Teilani stepped back from him, holding his hands against the sides of her waist.

"You're feeling the effects of Chal, aren't you?" she asked, as if she hadn't heard his question.

"Yes," Kirk admitted. Nothing to hide, nothing denied. "I feel . . . young . . . younger . . . more alive than I have in . . . years."

"What is that worth, James? Not just to you, but to entire planets? Entire empires?" She released his hands. Slowly lifted her own hands to the neck of her tunic. "Youth is the ultimate limited resource. Chal has survived these past years because no one knew of her. But now, with the changes in the Klingon Empire, the old secrets are being revealed."

She unfastened the top closure on her tunic, moved down to the second.

"Chal cannot remain a secret for much longer. But to survive, she must."

The second closure parted.

Her skin was intoxicating.

Her tunic slipped from her shoulders.

She was intoxicating.

Kirk was undone.

His hands encircled her. He brought his lips down to hers.

But he didn't kiss her as she expected.

"Is there something you aren't telling me?" he whispered.

"Make love to me, James."

She drew his own tunic from his shoulders, pushed it away so their skin met as she pressed against him.

"Who is your enemy?"

"James, please."

Her hands stroked his back. Their pressure hypnotic.

But Kirk stepped back. Breaking contact.

They stood, poised on the brink of their desires.

"Teilani, I need to talk," Kirk said.

Teasingly, she reached out for the drawstring of his pants. "But *I* need you," she said.

Kirk surrendered. How could he not?

With Teilani at his side, time had no meaning.

They could talk whenever, love whenever, do whatever their hearts desired, whenever and for as long as they wanted.

Kirk had found his Eden.

Perhaps, he thought, *I have found my home.*

A deep rumble resonated through the air.

Kirk turned to look past the jagged rock, along the beach toward the city.

It was kilometers away, hidden by a curve of jungle.

But from behind that curve, a billowing fireball blossomed, rising into the air on a trail of black smoke.

Teilani's face was white with fear. Or rage. Kirk didn't know.

"They're attacking again!" she said. "They said they would talk but they're attacking *again!*"

"Who's attacking?" Kirk demanded. "The Anarchists?"

"Yes," she said. "The Anarchists. The old ones. Our *parents.*"

TWENTY-SEVEN

Kirk stared at Teilani for a moment, then decided it was not the time or place for more questions.

He sprinted across the sand, back to his mount.

In his saddlebag, he found his communicator.

He flipped it open.

"Kirk to *Enterprise.*"

Scott answered.

Kirk gave his orders.

Everything happened at once.

Within seconds Kirk and Teilani were beamed from the beach to the landing pads by the city. Right beside Teilani's yacht.

Kirk felt the heat from the new fireball that exploded not more than a kilometer away in the jungle.

Smoke wafted through the lush growth toward the simple city buildings. He could hear screams and shouting voices carried on the wind.

A new transporter column sparkled into being.

Kirk ran to it.

He pulled on the jacket that lay atop the equipment Scott had beamed down. He tossed the second one to Teilani. Then he strapped on the equipment belt, adjusted the position of the Klingon disruptor pistol that hung from it.

He flipped open the screen on his tactical scanner.

"Transmit," he said into his communicator.

The screen came alive with moving dots of color.

Teilani watched over his shoulder as she sealed her jacket. "What is it, James?"

"The *Enterprise* is sweeping the area with her sensors. This screen shows the position of the attackers."

There seemed to be twenty of them, moving in from the jungle.

He heard the whistle of a shell screaming through the sky. Instinctively he pulled Teilani to the landing pad, hunched over her.

An explosion rocked the next pad, spraying shattered stones to rattle off the hull of the yacht by Kirk.

"Scotty," Kirk yelled into his communicator. "Can you pick those shells off in flight?"

"Negative, Captain. We don't have the precision aim we used t'."

Kirk dragged Teilani toward the shelter of the yacht. He studied the screen.

"What sort of defense does the city have?" he asked.

Teilani looked helpless. "Hand disruptors. Projectile guns."

"That's it?"

She nodded, an expression of shock distorting her features.

"What are they after?"

Teilani stared blankly at him.

"The Anarchists! What's their objective?"

Teilani was frightened. Kirk filed her reaction. She hadn't behaved this way when they had been under attack at the farm.

"Teilani! I can't help you unless you tell me what they're trying to do!"

"The power station," she said. "In the center of town."

"The large domed building?"

She nodded.

Kirk found the building on the tactical screen. It was the structure he had thought looked like a covered stadium.

The Anarchists were about three kilometers distant from it.

Whatever they were using to launch the explosive shells had more than enough range to reach the station. The fact that they weren't shelling it told Kirk their objective was to get *to* the station, not destroy it.

That made defense easier.

"Scotty—can you lock transporters onto the twenty or so life signs in the jungle to the north of the city?"

That would be the easy way, Kirk knew. Transport all the Anarchists directly to the *Enterprise*'s brig.

"Sorry, sir. The jungle is full of life signs, birds and animals I'm guessing, and we just don't have precise enough control to isolate the attackers. Unless ye could talk them int' carrying communicators."

"How about a low-intensity disruptor burst?"

"Aye," Scott answered. "If ye don't mind knockin' out a few wee beasties, too."

Kirk looked at Teilani. "What are the life-forms here like? Can they stand up to a stun setting?"

"I . . . I think so," Teilani said.

She flinched and shrank as another explosion rocked the landing pads.

Kirk coughed as a gust of fine powder and dirt rushed past him.

"Do it, Scotty."

"Targeting now, Captain. Setting disruptor cannons to lowest power. Ye might want to cover your eyes. . . ."

A section of sky to the north of the city suddenly flared with orange light.

Kirk checked his tactical screen.

The dots that represented the Anarchists were still there, indicating they were still alive.

But they weren't moving.

"Good shooting, Mr. Scott."

"Fish in a barrel, sir."

Kirk told Scott to stand by, then flipped his communicator closed. "It's over," he said to Teilani. The *Enterprise* had worked her magic.

"Only for now," she said. "They aren't the only ones who threaten us."

Kirk stood and brushed the dust from his jacket and pants.

The jacket Teilani wore was too big for her.

For just this moment, it made her look too much like a young girl, frightened and alone.

Kirk hugged her. With compassion this time and for no other reason.

"Vacation's over," he said gently to her. "No more secrets."

He felt her nod against his chest.

"Tell me everything," Kirk said.

Teilani held nothing back.

TWENTY-EIGHT

It was night in Prestor V's main city. A light rain fell, coating the corroded streets with an oily yellow sheen. The air stank of sulfur.

There were public streetlights lining all the thoroughfares in the warehouse district surrounding the spaceport. But none of them worked. The only light came from windows haphazardly shuttered by twisted blast shields.

The Klingon engineers who had built this city fifty years earlier had not intended their temporary structures to last. And they hadn't.

Down one narrow street, a glowing sign sputtered and sparked, creating a pool of flickering red light.

Chekov paused in that light. To check out his "associates" one last time.

He was not filled with optimism.

"Please," Chekov pleaded as he adjusted Dr. McCoy's collar, "look more . . . menacing."

"How am I supposed to do that?" McCoy grumbled.

"Scowl," Chekov said. "Hunch your shoulders. Do *something* to make them think you're a vanted, desperate man."

McCoy snapped the collar of his long dark coat even higher around his neck, shoved his hands deep into his pocket. He glared in an expression of . . . annoyance.

Chekov sighed. He looked at Spock.

Spock hesitated a moment, then snapped up his own collar. "How is this?" he asked.

His neutral expression hadn't changed.

"Perfect," Chekov said without enthusiasm. He hoped Uhura was having better luck with her landing party on the other side of the spaceport. "Come vith me."

He led Spock and McCoy into the bar.

The sulfurous smell from outside had permeated the low-ceilinged room they entered. So had the mist.

Chekov peered through it, counted the ears nailed up behind the bar. He saw Spock and McCoy looking at them as well.

"At least," Chekov whispered, "none of them are pointed."

"There's always a first time for everything," McCoy said cheerfully, looking at Spock.

Chekov walked over to an empty table and sat down, trying to swagger as best he could.

As Spock and McCoy joined him, a nearby table of Klingons made a show of smelling a terrible odor and changed to a table farther away.

The bartender, a craggy old Klingon female with an explosion of thick white hair, approached Chekov's table. Before Chekov could order, she slapped down a copper pitcher filled with something blue and foamy. Three chipped glasses followed.

"Two credits," the bartender wheezed.

Chekov thought, Here goes. He locked eyes with her.

"*Federation* credits? Vhat do you take us for?" Chekov dropped a Klingon colonial coin on the wooden table. "Ve deal only in talons."

The bartender reached under her stained apron and brought out a tiny scanner, no larger than one of McCoy's medical sensors. She held the device over the coin. The scanner glowed orange on one end.

The bartender pocketed the scanner and the coin.

"Anything else?" she growled. Her tone was slightly less belligerent.

Chekov motioned for the bartender to lean closer. "Ve are in need of some . . . equipment."

The bartender grunted. "This is a bar, not a shopping mart."

"Perhaps I misunderstood my friend's adwice," Chekov said.

The bartender eyed him suspiciously. "Who's your friend?"

"Kort," Chekov said. He dropped his voice. "Of the Imperial Forecasters."

Chekov was pleased with the way in which the bartender tried not to let her surprise show. "Kort! How is the old bladder these days?" she asked.

"Not too vell. Life on the Dark Range is getting . . . difficult. His sources of supply are being compromised by Starfleet Intelligence, and the Empire's own internal peace forces."

"And he sent you here?"

Chekov could tell the bartender was intrigued, though still not convinced. He played his final card.

"Vhat is the path of the fourth-rank vatch dragon?" he asked her.

The bartender's mouth sagged open in astonishment as Chekov quoted the death poem of Molor.

Chekov had no idea of the significance of the words. Only that they had had a powerful effect on Kort when Jade had used them in the cargo bay. Judging from the bartender's reaction, they were still useful.

"Vell?" Chekov prompted.

"By Praxis' light, in seasons still to come," the bartender muttered nervously.

"Wery good," Chekov said. He placed five more talon coins on the table and slid them toward the bartender.

The bartender sat down, passed her arm over the coins. They disappeared without so much as a single clink.

Years of practice, Chekov decided.

Then the bartender nodded her head at Spock and McCoy. Strands of white hair fell over her eyes. "Who are they?"

"I am a dealer in kevas and trillium," Spock said. "My name is Sarin and I was born—"

Chekov kicked Spock's boot under the table, interrupting his recitation of the backstory Chekov had created for him.

"My talkative friend is . . . a client," Chekov explained. "They both are."

"A *Vulcan?*" the bartender asked. "For a client?"

Chekov shrugged. "Times are tough. And a customer is a customer."

The bartender leaned closer over the table. She smelled terrible.

"So what do you need, friend of Kort?"

"A starship," McCoy said brightly. Then he cleared his throat, scowled unconvincingly. "A starship," he repeated in a rougher tone.

Chekov felt embarrassed. "Something discreet," he added.

The bartender studied McCoy with a frown. "*Another* dealer in kevas and trillium?"

"That's vhat it says on the cargo manifests," Chekov explained. "You see, for the most part, my clients' dealings vith the authorities are wery cordial. They pay the . . . 'inspection' fees, and the border patrols inspect only the manifests."

The bartender looked at Spock with a glimmer of respect. "Smuggling, eh? An honorable profession."

"Except," Chekov said, "border patrols are not the only parties interested in my clients' shipments."

"Orion pirates?" the bartender asked.

"No vonder Kort likes you," Chekov said approvingly.

The bartender looked pleased. "So . . . you're looking for something to fight them off. A Bird-of-Prey?"

Chekov lowered his voice conspiratorially. "Actually, ve vere thinking of something that might stop a fight before it even began."

The bartender waited.

Chekov also waited.

He looked at McCoy.

McCoy looked startled. He'd forgotten his line.

"Oh," the doctor stumbled, "a starship! A *Starfleet* starship."

The Klingon reared back with a scornful laugh. She didn't bother to keep her voice low. Several patrons looked at her with curious expressions.

"You come to the Klingon Empire to buy a Starfleet vessel? You might as well go to Earth to buy a *QIghpej.*"

Chekov had no idea what a *QIghpej* was and had no desire to find out. He spoke quickly to keep the bartender's interest alive.

"Ve understand there vas a Starfleet wessel here not too long ago."

The bartender's laughter died abruptly. She pushed her long white hair back from her forehead with an indescribably filthy hand. "So what if there were?"

"Ve vould like to . . . obtain it."

"You and which spacefleet?" Her cooperation and respect obviously had limits. Even for a friend of Kort's.

Chekov pulled a small datacase from his jacket and flipped it open like a communicator. There was a credit wafer inside. The denomination on it was astronomical. And it was drawn on a nonaligned repository.

Chekov bared his teeth in what he hoped approximated the Klingon style of smiling. "Kort suggested you might be the person to arrange a boarding party."

The bartender immediately checked to see that no eyes were upon them. Then she reached out to touch the credit wafer. Her eyes widened with avarice. Chekov snapped the small case shut, then slipped it back inside his jacket.

The bartender looked at him intently, obviously calculating her chances on taking the datacase by force.

"Don't do anything you vill regret," Chekov warned.

He waited for Spock to make his move.

The bartender's hairy hands slid back across the table, as if getting ready to pull something else out from behind her apron.

Chekov kicked Spock's boot again.

"I *said:* Don't do anything you vill regret."

Spock hurriedly opened his cloak to show the butt of a phaser II.

The bartender's hands stopped.

"I've shown you ve can pay," Chekov stated. "Now . . . can you deliwer?"

The bartender nodded slowly. "I can field three ships. Twenty soldiers per crew. Fully armed. The Starfleet vessel is undercrewed, improperly armed. We can take it with a minimum of damage. I guarantee it."

Chekov remained calm. He hoped McCoy would remember to do the same.

"Then there *vas* a Starfleet wessel here recently."

"In private hands," the bartender confirmed. She grinned unpleasantly. Her stained teeth were as unpleasant as Kort's had been. "Ripe pickings."

"But only if ve know vhere it is *now.*"

Chekov pulled out another handful of metal *talons.* He held them in his fist in front of the bartender.

"The spacedocks at Delstin VIII," the bartender said slowly, keeping her eyes fixed on Chekov's fist.

"You're certain?" Chekov asked.

The bartender nodded. "Her master came to this very bar." She pointed two tables over. "Sat at that very table with his female and his engineer. Talked about how hard it was going to be to install the equipment they had purchased. How they had to find facilities to refit their ship before they could continue to wherever it was they were going."

Chekov shook his head slowly. "I'd like to believe you. But

people have been known to lie vhen so many talons are at stake."

The bartender bared her ghastly teeth. But it was no smile. "Do you question my honor?"

"That depends," Chekov said, deeply grateful for his six months of experience in undercover negotiations, even if his teacher had been Jade. "Describe the ship's master to me."

Her face wrinkled in distaste. "He was . . . human. Pasty. Pinkish. No fangs to speak of. A disgracefully smooth forehead, with not even a single ridge of a warrior." The bartender shrugged dismissively. "What can I tell you? You all look alike."

"Vhat about the others?" Chekov persisted. "The engineer?"

The bartender smacked her lips together. "Ah, now he was more formidable. A large man, more powerful. True, his forehead also lacked character, but he did wear a warrior's mustache."

"That sounds like Scotty," McCoy said.

The bartender shot a suspicious glance at the doctor. "You know the people on the ship?"

Chekov rubbed his hand over his face, thinking dark thoughts about amateurs.

But at least they had what they needed. Now all that remained was getting out in one piece.

"A lucky guess," Chekov said firmly. He began to stand.

The bartender's hand shot out and grabbed the wrist of Chekov's clenched fist.

"The master of that ship was a Federation lackey," the bartender snarled. "As was the engineer. So what does that make *you?*" She stared at Spock and McCoy. "And your clients?"

"Ve are not looking for trouble," Chekov said evenly. He looked at Spock and nodded.

Spock took an interminably long moment to realize what Chekov intended.

He opened his cloak again to show his phaser.

The bartender did not release Chekov's wrist.

"Now you tell me," she hissed. "What is the path of the *fifth*-rank watch dragon?" she asked.

Chekov didn't have the slightest idea what the rest of the code might be.

The longer he went without speaking, the more twisted the bartender's expression became.

"Answer . . . or die!"

Chekov could do nothing except wait for Spock to use his phaser. *If* he remembered he was *supposed* to use it. Undercover work was turning out not to be among Spock's many areas of expertise.

But it was McCoy who acted first.

"The path of the fifth-rank watch dragon is . . ." he began.

The bartender looked at him. "Yesss?"

"The yellow brick road!" McCoy hollered, and flipped the table into the air.

The copper pitcher smacked the bartender on her forehead, sending forth an explosion of foam that turned her white hair blue.

The coins from Chekov's almost-numb hand clattered against the upended table and scattered across the floor.

All through the bar, chairs fell over and tables squealed as customers leapt to their feet, drawing daggers and pistols and even a few swords.

The bartender still hadn't released Chekov's wrist. So Chekov pulled her forward and chopped at her shoulder.

She shrieked at him, nearly felling him with the foul blast of her breath.

A chair smashed into kindling against the back of her head.

She spun around to confront her attacker.

McCoy stared at the two small useless pieces of chair back he still gripped.

The bartender flung Chekov to the side and leapt at McCoy.

McCoy threw the pieces of chair away as he jumped backward.

Chekov recovered and dove at the bartender's waist, knocking her down before she could reach McCoy.

With an earsplitting screech, she bucked wildly, knocking him off her back.

Chekov landed on another table, flattening it as he crashed to floor.

His lungs emptied of air in an explosive wheeze. He gaped uselessly for a breath like a suffocating fish.

The bartender loomed over him. Both hands plunged beneath her apron and reemerged bearing ornate knife handles.

She flicked the handles and gleaming blades snicked into position.

Spock's hand came down on her shoulder, thumb and forefinger poised for a nerve pinch.

The bartender roared and shook Spock's hand free.

Spock raised an eyebrow.

The bartender elbowed him in the stomach, grabbed his phaser, then tossed it across the room.

Spock doubled over.

She turned back to Chekov, hurled a knife.

It thunked into the shattered tabletop beside his head. His breath returned to him a split second later.

The bartender raised her arm to throw again.

Spock straightened up behind her, reached out, and tore a strip from the top of her apron to expose the leather armor she wore over her shoulder.

The bartender wheeled, her arm descending on an arc toward Spock's neck.

McCoy grabbed at her arm, deflecting her aim, then hung on gamely as she shook him back and forth, screaming.

But McCoy didn't let go, even as he lost his footing.

Then Spock attached himself to her other arm.

Chekov decided if he lived through this night, he'd be able to laugh at the image of the Klingon bartender draped with McCoy and Spock. It looked like the performance of some avant-garde dance troupe.

Then Spock succeeded in snapping the armor off the bartender's shoulder to gently squeeze the bare flesh at the base of her neck.

The bartender hit the floor a second later, landing on top of McCoy.

Chekov struggled to his feet, almost able to breathe normally.

McCoy kicked and twisted to roll the bartender off him.

For the first time since the fight began, Chekov remembered the others in the bar. He realized he should brace for another attack. But all around them, the bar's other customers were busy with their own fights. At least ten were under way that Chekov could see.

No one else cared about them or the bartender.

Klingon death cries rang out in the establishment. Coins changed hands as bets were made. A free-for-all raged on behind the bar, where every drink was now on the house.

Wood splintered. Glass shattered.

Chekov looked back to Spock and McCoy, standing over the bartender's unconscious form.

They were arguing.

Chekov couldn't believe it.

"That's why *you* had the *phaser,* Spock!"

"There were too many innocent bystanders, Doctor."

"She was going to *kill* Chekov!"

"Doctor, please. It was obvious she intended to maim him first. His life was not in immediate danger."

Chekov barreled toward the two officers, hooked his arms through theirs, and dragged them toward the door.

Neither seemed to notice.

"You were going to let her *break* his arm?"

"My nerve pinch stopped her."

"On the *third* try!"

Chekov burst through the door and onto the street.

He inhaled deeply, desperate for fresh air.

But he had forgotten about the sulfurous rain. He started coughing.

Spock supported him. McCoy thumped his back.

"Good thing you had us along, isn't it," McCoy said.

Chekov moaned. He reached for his communicator.

"Chekov to *Excelsior*. Three to beam up."

This part of the mission had succeeded, at least. They knew where Captain Kirk had headed after leaving Prestor V.

Somehow, Chekov hadn't expected that following the captain would be so easy.

Unless, of course, Kirk had arranged things so it only seemed to be easy.

Chekov decided he wouldn't be surprised if that was the truth of the matter.

But what did continue to surprise him was that Spock and McCoy kept up their argument even as the transporter dissolved them.

Some things never change, Chekov thought. But who would want them to?

TWENTY-NINE

Kirk hefted the crate of emergency shelter supplies, pivoted, and threw it to the top of the cargo pallet.

The stacking indentations on the modular crate's bottom meshed with the matching pattern on the crate below it, locking both into place.

The pallet was full.

Kirk wiped his hand across his forehead to clear the sweat away. With so much work being done in the *Enterprise*'s cargo transporter room, the air was getting thick.

But Kirk didn't mind the heat. It wasn't slowing him down.

He rotated his shoulder, raising his arm over his head.

There was no resistance from strained muscles or ligaments. Only ease of motion. Freedom.

He slapped the side of the stack of crates.

"This one's done," he told the transporter tech.

The young Klingon-Romulan at the transporter console activated her controls.

The cargo pallet shimmered, then vanished.

A moment later the youth reported that the base on the planet's surface confirmed transport of supplies.

Kirk clapped his hands together, turned to his work crew—seven of Teilani's people. Their simple clothing, also drenched in sweat, clung to their supple forms.

But none of them looked tired.

In fact, Kirk thought, *they look the way I feel.*

Ready for more.

"Two to go," he told them.

They started eagerly for the doors leading to one of the *Enterprise*'s cargo bays.

Kirk followed, falling in with their energetic stride.

The doors to the corridor opened.

Scott stepped in, scowling.

Kirk hesitated in midstep. "You want to see me?" he asked, already knowing the answer.

Scott frowned. "I *was* lookin' for Bonnie Prince Charlie. But I suppose ye'll have t' do."

Kirk told the others in the cargo crew to continue without him, then went into the corridor to find Mr. Scott.

The engineer was waiting by a Jefferies tube.

Kirk assessed Scott's mood as he approached, tried to make light of it. "Scotty, you look as happy as a Klingon with a tribble in his pants."

The engineer was not amused. "We're not in Starfleet anymore, sir."

"That's right," Kirk agreed cautiously.

"So I feel I'm within my rights to ask ye what in thunderin' blue blazes is goin' on around here."

Kirk felt relieved. He thought Scott was coming to him with a serious problem.

"Scotty, we're saving a world."

"That's what Teilani told me when she offered me this job. But I've nae seen any sign of any world-saving goin' on. All I see is my diagnostics tellin' me th' poor transporter phase coils are overloadin'. Captain, we've got *shuttles* for routine cargo transport. Why not use them till I get th' *Enterprise* back in trim?"

Kirk leaned against the wall by the Jefferies tube. It seemed odd to look down the *Enterprise*'s corridor and not see any Starfleet personnel moving through it. The ship felt deserted with only a few dozen Chal aboard.

"Teilani's city is under siege. The shuttles might be shot at."

"Under siege by who?" Scott asked. "I thought we were supposed to be part of a planetary defense system for a world establishing her independence. I tell ye, I'm not comfortable with turnin' the *Enterprise* into a gunboat just to resolve some local political squabble. It's nae right."

Kirk understood Scott's position, but he felt his temper rise, nonetheless. "First of all, Mr. Scott—the *Enterprise* has never been, and *will* never be, a gunboat. And what Teilani's world is facing is not some 'local political squabble.' They're fighting for their lives down there."

"But *who's* fighting, Captain? I know ye keep wantin' me t' beam down and look around for m'self, but there's so much work t' be done up here . . ."

Kirk could see that Scott was preparing to draw a line.

"Captain, I have t' know that what we're doin' here is on the up-and-up."

"Scotty, you don't trust me?"

The engineer looked pained. "Och, don't put it that way. But the fact of th' matter is, th' way ye've been carrying on with that young lass—"

"She's not that young."

"—I sometimes have t' wonder if ye know what ye're doin'." Scott took a deep breath, as if what he had just said had taken considerable effort. "Ye can see th' predicament I'm in, can't ye?"

Kirk decided there were only a handful of people in this universe who could question him as Scott just did. The engineer could be prickly at times, outright rude at others, but the years they had spent together, fighting on the same side, added up to a friendship between them that was deeper than either would admit.

Kirk put his hand on Scott's shoulder. "I apologize, Scotty. You tried to tell me your concerns in the bar on Prestor V, and I should have done a better job of listening. It's just that you're so good at what you do, that sometimes I think you'd do just as well without me."

"We're part of a team, sir."

Kirk nodded. "And I have taken that for granted. Far too often." He looked around at his beautiful, empty ship. For all the accomplishments he had achieved with her, he was beginning to realize he had missed a great many opportunities as well.

Kirk looked down at his clothes. He needed to change.

"Walk with me, Scotty. I'll tell you everything Teilani's told me."

The captain and the engineer headed down the corridor together. Kirk felt as if he were back in uniform, giving a briefing.

"Chal was originally a joint colony founded by Klingons and Romulans during one of their truces."

"Aye, that much is in th' computers."

"But it has nothing in the way of exploitable resources. So when tensions rose between the empires, both withdrew their support."

"Leaving the original colonists' children behind." Scott seemed impatient. "I did know enough t' ask Teilani about her world."

Kirk and Scott came to a turbolift, waited for a car to arrive and the doors to open.

"They weren't *left* behind," Kirk said. "They *chose* to stay. To their parents, it was a colony world, different from their own. But to the first generation born there . . ."

"Aye, 'twas their home."

The lift doors puffed open. Kirk and Scott entered.

"Deck Five," Kirk said. The turbolift sped up through the ship as Kirk continued. "For forty years, they lived in peace, completely ignored by the rest of the galaxy."

"Because no one knew where they were," Scott said.

The lift slowed, then stopped. The doors opened. Kirk and Scott continued their walk.

"Teilani doesn't know how, but all records of Chal's location were purged from the central surveys of the two empires. Some think it was a final gift from one of the original colonists, to insure their children wouldn't be disturbed."

"Wishful thinkin'," Scott said.

"In any event, time passed Chal by. It became a forgotten paradise."

"With trouble brewin'."

"I'm coming to that," Kirk said.

They had arrived at his quarters. The doors opened. Kirk saw Scott purse his lips disapprovingly at the disarray. But there was nothing Kirk could do about that. He and Teilani had been energetic in their use of the quarters, to say the least.

Scott remained by the open doors while Kirk dug through his closet, searching for fresh clothes.

"As it turns out, Chal does have one resource that is imminently exploitable. What to do about it caused a split among its inhabitants. Along generational lines."

"What kind of resource would that be?" Scott asked. "I've looked at th' sensor results and I haven't seen anything worth comin' all this way for."

"Trust me," Kirk said. "It's there. If word gets out, then both empires will want to restake their claim to it. Chal will be torn apart."

"No secret that powerful can be kept for long," Scott said skeptically.

Kirk found a set of civilian clothes he had brought from Earth. He slipped them on. They felt looser.

"In this case," Kirk said, "even the older generation who wants to exploit the planet knows what would happen if they went public. So they want to keep the secret to themselves, too, and exploit it a little bit at a time. Sell what they have to sell without letting anyone know where it came from."

"But sell what?" Scott asked.

Kirk continued to ignore Scott's questions. "Teilani is part of the younger generation—those who don't want Chal to be exploited at all. They fear that even controlled access to their planet's treasure will eventually result in everyone finding out about it. Leading to the same probability of war between the empires."

"Captain," Scott interrupted. "What *is* this 'treasure'?"

Kirk lifted a hand to restrain the engineer's questions. "For now, Teilani's group is in control of the city and the small spaceport and the subspace transmitting station. As long as they maintain that control, the secret remains contained on Chal. That's where we come in."

"Are ye going t' tell me or not?"

"The older generation who want to exploit Chal have become anarchists. They're trying to tear down Chal's society, cause chaos, so they can steal a spacecraft or take control of the transmitting station. So far, they refuse to negotiate with their children."

Scott's face was nearly purple with frustration. "For pity's sake, what aren't ye telling me, man?"

Kirk adjusted his new shirt, turned on the fabric sealer to close it. "I'll tell you everything if you'll just be patient."

Scott folded his arms with a huff.

"Scotty, the *Enterprise* is here to get the Anarchists to the bargaining table. You saw how easily we stopped the attack this morning. You know very well that even with commercial sensor equipment, the *Enterprise* can track down any group of Anarchists on this planet. With her disruptors, she could destroy them, too."

Scott looked alarmed. "Not while I'm aboard her."

"Relax, Scotty. I wouldn't allow that to happen either. Even Teilani doesn't want that to happen. She simply wants to make certain that the Anarchists stay confined to Chal and eventually realize that they have to work out a compromise. Because as long as the *Enterprise* is here, they can't possibly win by violence."

Scotty stroked his mustache. "So where does th' Prime Directive fit int' all this?"

"It doesn't," Kirk said. "Chal is an independent world with

warp technology. An authorized member of her government, recognized by the Federation, has requested aid. The Prime Directive does not apply."

"So we're here to stop a fight, not start one?"

"Exactly."

Scott threw his hands into the air. "So what's Chal got that's so bloody valuable?"

Kirk tugged on his shirt. "Notice anything different about me, Scotty?"

Scott didn't understand the question. "What? Other than ye've been walkin' around like a schoolboy in a daze over a . . . a schoolgirl."

"Look at me," Kirk said. He swung his arms around in the air.

Scott blinked in total lack of comprehension.

"Two weeks ago, I couldn't have done that," Kirk explained. He rubbed at his shoulder. "My shoulder had been acting up. One too many jars and bumps, I guess. I was stiff, sore."

"Tell me about it," Scott said with sudden empathy. "My knees need replacement and some days my back doesn't loosen up till I've been on the go half the day."

Kirk paused. He hadn't intended this to turn into a comparison of old war stories.

"The point is," he said, "I have full movement in both shoulders now."

Scott looked at Kirk, about to ask a question. But all he could manage was, "So?"

"Look at me, Scotty! I feel wonderful! Charged with energy! Ready for . . . for anything! And I've only been on Chal for three days."

Scott tapped his foot against the carpeted deck. "I think ye'd better spell this one out for me, sir."

"It's the treasure of Chal, Scotty. Restoration. Rejuvenation. *Youth.*"

Scotty looked troubled. "Captain, no. You cannae believe that."

"I don't have to *believe,* Scotty. I've been down there. I know how I feel."

"I wish Dr. McCoy were here to give ye a full medical scan. T' find out what they've been puttin' in your coffee."

Kirk turned to the built-in desk, opened a drawer, pulled out a Starfleet-issue medical tricorder.

"That's what *I* thought. But look at these readings."

Kirk handed the tricorder over to Scott. The engineer scrolled through the display screens.

"Nothing," Kirk said. "No drugs, no chemicals, no stimulants natural or otherwise."

Scott shut off the tricorder, handed it back.

"It's Chal," Kirk said. "Just as Teilani said it would be."

Scott thought for long moments.

"Captain, I'm an engineer, not a doctor. But I cannae see how such a thing could be possible without some terrible price. And I cannae understand how you could fall for such a swindle."

Kirk carefully put the tricorder down. "It's not a swindle. You've seen Teilani. You've seen the others like her. If you'd just beam down and spend a day there yourself, you'd feel it, too."

Scott's eyes seemed to well up with tears. "Captain Kirk, I know we've had our differences in th' past. But I've always respected ye. And it tears me apart to see ye caught up in this."

"Caught up in what?"

"Whatever it is this lass has done t' ye."

"Scotty, Teilani hasn't done anything to me. I love her. I—"

"How can ye?"

Kirk didn't understand Scott's discomfort. "I know enough to leave explanations for love to the poets."

"That's not it. I mean, what do ye know about the lass? Really know about her? Aye, she's young, attractive, I'm nae blind to that. But how can ye think there can ever be anything more than just . . . just this carryin' on like jackrabbits between ye?"

Kirk frowned at Scotty's characterization.

"Seriously," the engineer continued. "I've nothing t' say one way or another about two grown people havin' a fling that's not hurtin' anyone else. But it's not just a fling t' ye. Ye've thrown away your life, your career, your—"

Kirk had had enough. *"Scotty!* I've moved on! I have a new life now. A new mission."

Scott shook his head with a sorrowful expression. "I don't care how ye justify it t' yourself. But I know what I see. She's pullin' your strings like you're her—"

Kirk clenched his jaw, determined not to lose his temper with Scott the way he had with Spock and McCoy. *"Mr.* Scott—you're stepping over the line here."

"Because you're refusin' to. I don't know. Maybe deep inside ye know you're foolin' yourself, not thinkin' things through. I hope so, 'cause it's not a pretty picture seein' ye playin' the fool to her."

Kirk took a deep breath. Thought of Chal's beaches and jungles and piercingly blue skies. Felt calm returning. "Come down with me, Scotty."

But Scott drew back. "I'll not be tormenting myself with impossible dreams. We had our chance at youth. We used it well. We pushed some boundaries, I'll admit. But now our day is almost over. It's the nature of things, sir. We have t' accept that."

"Scotty—think of all the miracles we've seen in our voyages. All the different ways that space and time and living flesh have been changed and altered. What's wrong with continuing to push at those boundaries? *Why* must we accept . . . *anything?"*

Scott gave Kirk a look of abject pity. He spoke slowly, sorrow in his voice. "Because otherwise, sir, we will surely go mad, desperately seekin' that which we cannae have."

Kirk didn't know what to say. The line Scott had drawn had become a wall.

"It appears I'm onboard for th' duration," Scott said stiffly. "And I shall do my best t' keep this fine ship t'gether for ye. But I will nae be a party t' attacks on anyone below. And I will nae be leaving the *Enterprise.* Until ye come t' your senses."

Scott turned to go.

"Now, if you'll excuse me, I'm needed in th' engine room."

The doors slid shut behind him.

Kirk stood alone in his empty quarters.

But Scott's words remained.

Maybe deep inside you know you're fooling yourself, not thinking things through.

Might it be true? Could it be?

Kirk had always been the master of the bluff and the well-crafted lie. How else had he survived for so long? Cheated death so often?

But what if he had taken that characteristic of survival and pushed it that one step too far?

What if he had come all this way, burned so many bridges, because he *was* desperate for something he could never have again?

Could his friends be right?

For all the times he had lied to others to wrest victory from defeat, what if this time he was simply lying to himself?

Kirk had crossed half the sector to solve the mystery of Chal.

But now he feared he had found a mystery more profound.

Himself.

THIRTY

☆

Five light-years from the spacedocks at Delstin VIII, the *Excelsior* dropped out of warp and came to relative stop.

The trail of the *Enterprise* had abruptly disappeared.

On the *Excelsior*'s bridge, Chekov worked with Spock to reconfigure the main sensors.

Sulu waited impatiently in the center chair.

But for all the increased activity on the bridge, no one was surprised by what had happened.

They had all served with Captain Kirk. They had seen him cover his tracks too many times to think following him would be easy.

Chekov finished entering the final adjustments on his tactical board. "Sensors reconfigured," he announced.

"Commencing scan," Spock said from his science station.

All waited while the *Excelsior*'s elaborate system of sensors probed the surrounding vacuum for any trace of the *Enterprise*'s distinct warp signature. Almost imperceptible distortions in subspace sometimes lingered after a starship's passage at faster-than-light velocities, like the wake left by an oceangoing vessel—sometimes for days.

The *Excelsior* had followed just such a wake on a direct course from Prestor V to Delstin VIII, precisely where the Klingon bartender had said Kirk was taking his ship.

Any other commander might have saved time by not bothering to scan continuously for the *Enterprise*'s warp signature along the entire route until arriving at the ship's stated destination.

But Sulu had wisely tracked it all the way, waiting for it to cease abruptly, as he knew it must.

The instant it had, Kirk's crew immediately knew that this was the point at which the *Enterprise* had left warp, changed heading, and then continued on her way.

Any other commander would have missed the end of the trail and arrived at Delstin VIII. There, a day would have been lost to frantic scanning to determine that the *Enterprise* had never arrived. Then the commander would have been forced to backtrack. Slowly. To find the point along the projected route where the *Enterprise* had surreptitiously changed course.

By that time, the *Enterprise*'s warp signature would have faded into the natural background ebb and flow of subspace, undetectable.

But Sulu wasn't any other commander.

"Sensors have made contact," Spock said. "Subspace disturbance at bearing one four four mark twenty."

Chekov confirmed the distortion pattern. "It is the *Enterprise*'s varp signature."

The helmsman, a young human, asked if he should lay in a course to match the new trail.

Chekov saw Sulu smile knowingly. "Negative, Mr. Curtis. If I know Captain Kirk, we should find at least *three* warp trails from this location."

In the end, they found four.

Kirk had looped back three times to muddy the subspace waters, laying false trails.

The most obvious trail to follow was on a bearing that headed toward the Klingon-Romulan frontier, the general location of Chal.

Sulu discounted that one right away as being far too obvious.

Of the other three trails, one headed back to the Federation, one to the Klingon Empire, and one straight out of the galactic ecliptic.

Sulu chose to follow the course heading for the Klingon Empire, because who would ever believe Captain Kirk would willingly return there? No one except his former crew, who knew Kirk could be counted upon to do the unexpected.

Chekov knew that if Sulu had guessed wrong, then within six hours the warp trail would end with a return loop, indicating it had been a false heading. Meanwhile, the *Enterprise*'s real path would have become even more difficult to locate.

But Sulu hadn't guessed wrong.

Five hours later, the *Enterprise*'s trail ended again, but without a return loop, indicating that Kirk had once again dropped from warp to change course.

This time, they found three possible trails.

Chekov was impressed by Captain Kirk's efforts.

But McCoy was puzzled. "Who did he think was following him?" he muttered as he sat by Uhura's communications post. "My ex-wife?"

"Whoever it was," Sulu said, "he couldn't be expecting it to be us. We'll find his pattern."

Spock confirmed the method behind Kirk's evasive maneuvers. "It is a feint he has used in chess many times, to hide the true focus of attack through misdirection."

Chekov looked up from his tactical displays. "It is not like the keptin to repeat himself."

"No, it is not," Spock agreed.

"Unless," McCoy suggested, "he laid down a series of course changes that would throw *everyone* off his trail—*except* for his friends."

"An intriguing speculation," Spock allowed. "But given the captain's somewhat erratic emotional state in his final days on Earth, I find it . . . unlikely."

Everyone looked at Sulu. It was time to choose which of the three warp trails to follow.

"Logically, we should choose the trail that leads away from the obvious choice," Spock suggested.

McCoy stood behind Sulu's chair and objected. "C'mon, Spock. Who the hell would know what the 'obvious' choice was except someone who's spent the past thirty years wrangling with Jim over a chess board? You said it yourself: Where Jim's concerned, logic seldom applies."

McCoy folded his arms and stared at Spock, as if daring him to top his argument.

Sulu glanced back at McCoy, then at Spock again.

Chekov had seen Kirk caught in the same position uncountable times.

Logic versus gut feeling.

Sulu made his decision.

"Commander Spock, if we are seeing a repeat of one of Captain Kirk's chess strategies, which trail is the obvious one?"

Spock gave the bearing.

"Mr. Curtis," Sulu said, "lay in a course on that bearing. Commander Chekov, resume tracing the *Enterprise*'s warp signature."

The bridge crew acknowledged their orders.

"Ahead, maximum warp," Sulu ordered.

The *Excelsior* smoothly stretched into the infinite realms of warp speed.

McCoy beamed at Sulu. "You make a damned fine captain, Sulu. Keep it up."

Chekov knew the real purpose of what McCoy had said. He glanced over at Spock.

Spock betrayed no reaction to McCoy's dig.

But Chekov suspected he was already plotting some form of logical, unemotional revenge. After thirty years, how could he not?

Chekov smiled to himself. It was almost like being back on the *Enterprise*.

Then the *Excelsior* hit a brick wall.

The main viewscreen flared orange white.

Collision alarms sounded.

The bridge lurched as the inertial dampers failed to keep up with the ship's sudden loss of warp drive.

An environmental station shorted out in an explosion of sparks.

Power to the bridge failed, then instantly reset.

"What the hell was that?" Sulu said.

Chekov pulled himself back to his tactical board. His fingers flew over the controls. There was nothing . . . nothing . . .

. . . and then, where there had been nothing—

—there was something.

The viewscreen showed it best.

Three Klingon battle cruisers dropped from warp dead ahead.

"Damage is consistent with photon torpedo impact," Spock announced.

"Captain," Uhura shouted over the alarms, "we are being hailed."

"Onscreen."

Chekov's eyes widened as the viewscreen image changed to show a Klingon bridge.

The Klingon commander was young, eager eyes gleaming viciously.

"Federation starship," he barked. "You have intruded in restricted Klingon space." His yellow teeth grinned through his wispy beard.

"Surrender . . . or *die!*"

THIRTY-ONE

☆

Kirk was one with the night.

He leaned with his back against the rough bark of an alien tree, listening to the sounds of the jungle around him.

Eerie calls from night-feeding birds. The chitter and hissing of unseen insects. The random rustle of leaves and branches as arboreal creatures swung through the jungle's canopy overhead.

But he heard nothing that betrayed the presence of the fifteen Chal who moved through the jungle with him, closing in on the Anarchists' base.

His soldiers.

Kirk wished he could take credit for their training. But, in truth, they had none.

Instead, the Chal's innate abilities to move stealthily, to follow orders, to think in tactical terms, all seemed to stem from their childhood games.

Elaborate games of hunts and chases through the jungle. Intricate strategy and tactics played out with twigs and stones on squares drawn into sand on the beach.

As Teilani had explained those children's pastimes to him, Kirk had first been astounded by the complexity of the military concepts contained within them. But then he had reminded himself that he wasn't dealing with a human culture.

Teilani and her people apparently had had a typical Klingon and Romulan upbringing.

They had learned their lessons well.

In the jungle, a shadow moved toward Kirk. His hand tightened on the grip of the disruptor at his side. Then relaxed as a faint shaft of light from Chal's glimmering moon revealed to him an unmistakable silhouette.

Making not a sound, Teilani crept up beside him.

Like Kirk, she wore the dark jumpsuit that was the uniform of those who fought for Chal. Like Kirk, her face was darkened with camouflage to better hide within the night.

But unlike Kirk, this was the first time she had faced real battle.

With swift but cautious movements, Teilani brought out her combat tricorder and showed its display to Kirk.

Sixteen muted green dots were arranged in a half circle around the target's coordinates.

Each Chal was in position. Each of Kirk's soldiers.

All that remained was for him to give the word.

He hesitated on the brink of action, savoring the anticipation of the moment when his plans would be unleashed.

The people of Chal had been in conflict for years. The city-dwellers had the advantage of a defensible position and hard technology. The Anarchists had the advantage of the jungle and elaborate jamming devices.

Only Mr. Scott's wizardry with the *Enterprise*'s weakened sensors had enabled Kirk to finally locate the Anarchists' stronghold, two hundred kilometers from Chal's main city.

But the stronghold was protected by a complex web of sensor screens, forcefields, and jammers. Its presence ruled out any attempt to stun its fighters by low-power disruptor fire from orbit. Neither could Kirk capture them by transporter or even beam in a sneak attack.

High-powered disruptor beams could punch through the relatively weak forcefields. Two photon torpedoes could decimate the Anarchists' entire compound along with several square kilometers of surrounding jungle.

But that was not the reason Kirk had come to Chal.

Lasting peace and reconciliation were never a question of brute force.

He was here to bring both sides in the conflict together. And the *only* way to accomplish that was by direct, physical confrontation.

Nothing could have pleased Kirk more.

He slipped his disruptor from its holster and checked again that it was at its stun setting.

He looked at Teilani, saw the faint reflection of moonlight in her eyes.

She reached out to touch Kirk's face, a silent gesture of her feelings. Her hand slid down to his neck. She tugged on the collar of his jumpsuit as if adjusting it.

"Now," he whispered.

The Anarchists' first perimeter line was only twenty meters ahead of them.

Teilani cupped a hand to her mouth. She made the sound of a nightfeeder, shrill and piercing. A sound that belonged to the jungles of Chal.

Then she made it again.

The signal had been given.

Kirk pushed away from the alien tree and began moving carefully through the darkness.

Teilani at his side.

In his mind, Kirk saw his strategy played out as if looking down at the levels of a chess board.

Fortunately, Spock was not on the board's other side.

The clearing came up before him.

Because of the moon and the stars, the night sky of Chal was slightly brighter than the stark black shadows of the surrounding trees and the Anarchists' watchtowers. The towers were each five meters tall, roughly constructed of wood and vines. Surveillance had shown that each held two guards, linked to the perimeter sensor web.

They were Kirk's first target.

Teilani silently held her combat tricorder out for Kirk to see.

Its pale screen showed they were a meter from the first sensor alarm threshold.

Kirk nodded.

Teilani repeated the nightfeeder's cry. Three times.

Kirk counted down from five. Then charged forward.

In his mind, he saw his soldiers move in perfect coordination with him.

Instantly the jungle roared to life with disruptor firings as each watchtower was hit by multiple beams.

Cries of surprise followed as the Anarchists behind the defensive perimeters heard the sensor alarms.

Then there were explosions.

Kirk recognized their distinctive sound.

Microexplosive shells from projectile weapons like those used by the attackers at the farm on Earth.

Those weapons had been his chief concern for this attack.

The jumpsuits used by the Chal contained an energy mesh that could dissipate much of the force of a disruptor beam. Even if the Anarchists set their weapons to kill, it would be unlikely if any of Kirk's attacking force would suffer more than a heavy stun.

But the explosive shells could be fatal.

It had been Teilani who told Kirk not to be overly worried about them. The Anarchists were unskilled with weapons, she said. They were unlikely to hit anyone they aimed at.

That contradicted what Kirk had seen at the farm. But he hadn't pressed the matter. If all went according to plan, the Anarchists would have little time to fight back.

Kirk ran past the closest watchtower.

There was no covering fire from it. Its guards had been stunned as planned.

The first stage of the attack was complete.

Ahead of them now was a wooden barricade reinforced

with metal sheets from old shipping containers. Beyond it, Scotty's low-resolution sensor scans had revealed a compound of wooden huts—the Anarchists' camp.

Teilani swung her projectile gun up. Fired a burst of shells set for contact detonation.

A section of the barricade disintegrated in flame. Over the din surrounding them, Kirk could hear simultaneous explosions nearby as the other Chal reached their sections of the wood and metal structure.

Before the smoke had thinned, Kirk had hurled himself toward the opening. The blast-torn edges of wood crackled with flames.

Kirk leapt forward through the smoke and the fire, arms outstretched.

His trajectory carried him low even as he heard the whistle of shells streak over him.

He hit on his shoulder, flipped over, was firing his disruptor even as he came to his feet.

Three Anarchists dropped in the orange glow of the disruptor beam.

Kirk ran on.

His breath came easily. His shoulder felt no different after his fall and tumble.

He exulted in his renewed vigor.

He *was* twenty again.

More explosions shattered the jungle night.

An enormous fireball flared overhead as a munitions crate erupted.

Flickering red light played across the compound. He ran on.

Kirk saw dark figures rushing about in confusion—the Anarchists, completely taken by surprise.

Kirk saw his soldiers—the Chal, efficiently picking off each Anarchist with disruptor stuns.

Kirk paused in the center of the storm he had unleashed. In control. Triumphant.

Teilani rushed to his side, combat tricorder in hand.

"Each team is in!" she shouted in her excitement. "No casualties!"

Kirk flipped open his communicator. His voice strong and clear. "Scotty—beam in the second wave!"

Instantly the warble of transporter beams blended with the cries and explosions of the compound.

In groups of six, three more teams of Chal took form near the breeched barricade.

Each member of the second team carried medical tricorders and multiple sets of prisoner restraints.

As Kirk and his soldiers continued to mop up, his plan dictated that the second wave would locate the stunned Anarchists, then disarm and bind them.

Four days ago, the Chal had made no effort to capture the Anarchists who had attacked the city. As soon as they had recovered from Scott's low-level disruptor stun, they had disappeared back into the jungle. Under his leadership, Kirk would not allow the Chal to make that mistake again.

Both sides *must* be brought together.

Teilani watched the second-wave teams fan out through the compound. "James—it's going perfectly."

"It's not over yet," Kirk cautioned.

"Soon," Teilani said. She ran off to help with the capture of the Anarchists.

Kirk checked the compound. The sounds of combat were diminishing. But he saw four Anarchists run between two huts. There was no sense of panic or confusion to their movements. They knew where they were going, what they were doing.

Kirk recognized the signs of a counterattack in the making. He sprinted toward the huts they had run between, slid to a stop by the corner of one. Carefully peered around the edge.

He heard an antigrav generator come online.

Kirk charged around the corner, swinging his disruptor up.

Ten meters away, a hover truck lifted into the air.

One Anarchist drove it. The other three operated the smart cannon mounted on its cargo bed.

The hover truck's headlight flared into life, blinding Kirk.

He heard its impeller fans whine as it flew straight for him.

Unable to see, he fired his disruptor, then dove to the side, feeling the bulk of the speeding truck closing.

He hit the ground hard.

The scream of the hover truck's engine became the thunderous explosion of a wooden hut.

Kirk looked up, realizing he had managed to stun the driver.

The truck was embedded in the ruins of a hut.

One Anarchist leapt from the truck's cargo bed, saw Kirk.

Ran at him.

The disruptor had slipped from Kirk's hand, wrenched out by the impact of his fall.

Kirk saw it, out of reach.

He rolled to the side, leapt to his feet.

The Anarchist trained his projectile gun on him.

He was just like any other Chal.

Though an Anarchist, a member of the world's first generation, he looked no older than Teilani.

But there was murderous rage in his eyes. He aimed his weapon.

Kirk was out of options. He knew a single shell from the gun could tear him in half.

There was only one thing to do.

He charged.

The Anarchist fired twice, point-blank, before Kirk slammed into him.

Kirk didn't even hear the whistle of the shells.

He only felt the impact of his fist on the Anarchist's jaw.

He only tasted the dust of the ground as they rolled against it.

The Anarchist swung his weapon for Kirk's head.

Kirk blocked the blow, punched again.

The Anarchist slumped back. The weapon fell from his hand.

Kirk smelled the acrid odor of the shells' propellant. He looked down at his chest.

The projectiles had missed.

For an instant, Kirk saw Teilani spinning through the air in his parents' barn, a string of projectile explosives missing her by a heartbeat.

Kirk reached up to his collar. Felt a small, curved, metal tube coiled inside the fabric.

Teilani had adjusted it just before the attack began.

He saw her standing by the kitchen window, hand on her collar, an instant before the projectile had hit her shoulder.

Grazed her shoulder.

Kirk's stomach tightened.

What else was before him that he hadn't seen?

In his mind, Spock, McCoy, and Scotty all seemed to answer at once.

And the answer they gave was *Teilani.*

THIRTY-TWO

☆

Kirk glanced around the Anarchists' compound. No other Chal were nearby. The sounds of fighting had ended. The battle had been fought and won.

But Kirk knew a different war on Chal was still in progress. The device hidden in his collar was proof of it.

He hauled the unconscious Anarchist to his feet. Flipped open his communicator.

"Kirk to *Enterprise.*"

"Scott here, Captain."

"I've got a prisoner with me, Scotty. I want you to beam us both directly to the brig."

Scott took so long to answer that Kirk almost added, *Scotty, that's an order.*

"I take it there's more goin' on down there than you've told me, isn't there?" Scott said.

"Please, Mr. Scott." Kirk could hear footsteps approaching from around the corner of the nearest hut.

Scott sighed over the open channel. "Energizin'."

The dark jungle compound dissolved around Kirk, changing into the bright, plain walls of the *Enterprise*'s brig.

Kirk's prisoner moaned, coming around. Kirk eased him onto a bench in one of the holding cells, then stepped out and activated the security field. Blue forcefield emitters glowed around the cell's opening.

The Anarchist shook his head, looked around. Saw Kirk.

Stared at him with hatred. Then pushed himself to his feet to face his captor eye to eye.

"Where have you brought me?"

"You're on the *Enterprise,"* Kirk said. "A starship orbiting Chal. My name's Kirk."

The Anarchist blinked in surprise, took another look around. "A *Federation* ship?"

Kirk heard the fear in his prisoner's voice. Wondered why.

"No. It's . . . a private ship. Serving Teilani."

At the mention of Teilani, the Anarchist spit at Kirk's feet. The spittle crackled as it hit the security forcefield and vaporized.

"You're in no danger," Kirk said. "After we've talked, you're free to return to Chal."

That confused the Anarchist. "Talk about what?" He eyed Kirk warily.

"To begin with, what's your name?"

The Anarchist seemed puzzled by the question. "Torl."

"Fine, Torl. How old are you?"

Torl became even more confused. "In your standard years, forty-two."

Kirk studied his prisoner carefully, looking for any sign that he was lying. Saw nothing. Only a youth no older than twenty.

"Then it's true. There's something on Chal—in the air or the water—that keeps people . . . young."

Torl's mouth opened in astonishment. "What?"

Kirk skipped a beat. He hadn't expected that reaction. "You all look about the same age. Your generation, Teilani's generation. Isn't that the result of living on your world?"

Torl smiled with sudden knowledge. Baring his teeth, he looked disconcertingly like a full-blooded Klingon.

"Tell me what Teilani told you, human."

It took Kirk only an instant to make his decision. As long as Torl was locked in that cell, Kirk had nothing to lose by revealing all that he knew. Or thought he knew.

"The colony on Chal was jointly founded by the Klingons and the Romulans," Kirk began.

"Correct."

"It was deemed a failure, and abandoned by both sides."

Torl snorted in derision. "It was an unqualified *success.*"

Kirk didn't see where that fit in. "Then why were you abandoned by both Empires?"

"We weren't abandoned. We were hidden."

"Why?"

Torl stepped closer to the security screen, as if conducting his own examination of Kirk's honesty.

"You really don't know who we are, do you?" Torl asked. "You have no idea *what* we are."

Kirk gestured with open hands, as if grasping for some truth just out of reach.

"You're the children of the original colonists—Klingon *and* Romulan."

"Children of the original colonists?!" Torl laughed. "Only half correct. We are the Children of Heaven."

"The children of . . . Chal?" Kirk asked, trying to reconcile Teilani's revelations with what his prisoner was saying.

Torl's smile disappeared. "The *Chalchaj 'qmey.*"

Kirk recognized the phrase as Klingon, but beyond that, it meant nothing to him.

Kirk's prisoner looked troubled. He held out a hand as if to touch the almost invisible security screen. "Why are you here, human? What business of yours is Chal?"

"I'm trying to help stop the fighting."

"Why?"

"So this planet will be at peace."

"Why?"

Kirk took control of the conversation again. "Do you *want* to keep fighting?"

"No," Torl said simply. "I want to destroy Teilani and her people. Then the fighting will stop."

"So you can sell the secret of Chal to the rest of the galaxy."

Torl struck out against the security screen in anger, then flew back from the crackling impact.

He collapsed onto the bench, looked up at Kirk, and actually snarled.

"Is that what *she* told you we were trying to do?"

"Yes. That you want to exploit Chal."

"Human, we want to *bury* Chal. To wipe it out of existence."

"Why? It's a paradise."

Torl jumped to his feet in rage. "It is an obscenity!"

Kirk would not accept that. "I've been down there," he argued. "I've felt its influence. It's one of the most beautiful worlds I've ever seen. Filled with bright, healthy people."

Torl's eyes smoldered with repressed fury. "At what cost?"

"You tell me."

Torl thought a moment. "Has she shown you the Armory?"

Kirk shook his head. He had never heard of an armory on Chal.

"The large building. In the center of the city."

"That's an armory? With weapons?"

"If you believe truth is a weapon."

Kirk had had enough. "What *is* the truth?"

Unexpectedly, the prisoner's expression changed once more. To mournful sorrow. "Evil, human. This world is not *chalchaj*. It is *chalwutlh*. The underworld, not heaven." He looked out at Kirk, his anger gone. "I don't know who you are or why you're here, but you must know that peace grows between our kind. The Klingon Empire and the Federation reach out to each other. If their fragile efforts succeed, the Romulans cannot stand against them. They must lay down their arms as well. Do you believe that is a good thing?"

"Yes."

"Then for peace to have its chance, let this world die. And all its secrets with it."

"*What* secrets?" Kirk asked.

Torl seemed to age before Kirk's eyes. His shoulders

slumped. His hands hung loosely at his side. "For what I am going to tell you, please forgive me. Remember that in the decades past our people were manipulated by their rulers to hate you. To consider your species as nothing more than animals."

He sat down on the bench. He leaned back wearily against the wall. He began to weep.

Kirk felt the hairs bristle on his arms. Torl wept as if he was torn apart by monumental anguish. Shame.

"What secrets?" Kirk asked again, almost afraid of the answer he was about to hear.

Then a new voice rang out in the brig.

"Mr. Kirk! Stand back!"

Kirk spun around. Two Chal stood in the doorway leading to the corridor. Each held a disruptor, aimed past Kirk.

Kirk recognized them.

The attackers from the farm.

The attackers who had died.

He read their intent in their eyes.

"No!" Kirk shouted. He stepped in front of Torl, blocking the attackers' line of sight.

One of them twisted the setting stud on his gun.

An instant later, Kirk felt himself fly backward, each nerve on fire with the all-too familiar sting of a disruptor set to stun.

He fell into the security screen.

A new wave of agony erupted against his back as he was thrown forward again, ears ringing with the crackle of the forcefield.

He hit the deck hard, unable to use his arms to break his fall.

His chest was paralyzed. He couldn't breathe.

The attackers walked past him.

Lungs burning with unspeakable pain, Kirk forced himself onto his back.

Just in time to see two disruptor beams hit Torl.

Just in time to see Torl fall back, body glowing with the incandescent light of a heavy stun.

The attackers looked down at Kirk. Reluctantly, they put away their weapons.

Kirk sensed a third person entering the brig.

Teilani.

Her face was still dark with camouflage. She knelt by him, spoke softly.

"It's over, James." He could barely hear her through the ringing in his ears. "They're our prisoners now. All of them."

Kirk was finally able to gasp for air. It tore through his lungs like liquid fire. The deck spun beneath him. He felt himself begin to fall.

"Thanks to you, James," Teilani said. "We won."

As the darkness claimed Kirk, he thought he could still hear Torl weeping.

THIRTY-THREE

"Go to hell," Sulu said to the Klingon commander. To his crew he added, "Go to red alert. Full power to shields. Phasers on standby."

The *Excelsior* prepared for battle.

Chekov read his tactical displays. "All three cruisers have locked veapons on us."

Sulu stood to face the viewscreen. "Klingon commander. I am Captain Sulu of the starship *Excelsior*. We are searching for a Federation vessel under the authority of—"

"You have five seconds to lower your shields and prepare for boarding," the Klingon snarled.

Sulu ignored him. "*Under* the *authority* of Chancellor Azetbur."

The Klingon blinked. "How dare you invoke the name of our chancellor for your foul crimes."

"I say again—the *Excelsior* has full diplomatic clearance to conduct her search in Klingon territory. Contact your central command for verification. Then I'll be more than happy to accept your apology." Sulu turned to Uhura. "Close the channel."

The viewscreen returned to an image of the three Klingon vessels hanging ominously in space.

"Veapons still locked on," Chekov said. He wondered how far Sulu was prepared to push the confrontation. "You know, the *Excelsior* can outrun them," he added, trying to be helpful.

Sulu sat back in his command chair. "I know the speed of my own ship, Pavel. But where could we go? Deeper into Klingon space, there're bound to be other cruisers in position to intercept us. The only direction open to us is back to the Federation. And then we'll have lost any chance of picking up the *Enterprise's* warp trail."

"I thought Admiral Drake personally cleared all this through Azetbur," McCoy said.

"Presumably, we're about to find out," Uhura said. "I'm picking up a flurry of encrypted messages. They're all going out from the Klingon lead ship. They're attempting to contact their central command."

"Can you decode?" Sulu asked.

Janice Rand activated the translator subroutines. "That's odd," she said. "It's an old code. We can crack it. Two minutes, maybe three."

"Any idea how long it will take for them to get a reply?" Sulu asked.

Chekov saw Uhura look to the ceiling as she worked out the

time and distance. "If they have to get a message all the way back to their homeworld, it could take half a day for a reply."

"We can't wait half a day," Sulu said.

McCoy offered his opinion. "Since we *can* outrun them, why not just keep going after the *Enterprise?* While they're chasing us, they might hear back from command and call the whole thing off."

Spock rose from his science station. "Doctor, what if Admiral Drake has *not* obtained the necessary clearance for us?"

McCoy spoke sharply. "What do you mean? He told us himself that Azetbur had okayed the mission."

"Admiral Drake has told us a number of things," Spock said blandly. "That does not make them true."

"It doesn't matter either way," Sulu said. "At the speed we'd have to go to keep ahead of those ships, we wouldn't be able to scan for the *Enterprise*'s wake. If Captain Kirk changed course again, we'd miss the changeover point completely."

The bridge fell silent. It seemed there was nothing they could do.

A damage-control team arrived to begin replacing the modular components of the damaged environmental station.

The battle readiness of the Klingon cruisers remained unchanged.

Lieutenant Rand announced that the computer had decoded the Klingon's message to central command.

"But . . . I don't understand," she said as she read the results onscreen. "It's . . . just random bits."

Sulu checked the screen over her shoulder. "Is it a code within a code?"

"Nothing the computer's seen before," Rand said. "Nothing I've seen either."

"Lieutenant, please transfer the output to my system," Spock said.

Rand did so. Even Spock was puzzled.

"The only logical way this message makes sense is if we assume it is a prearranged signal. That is, it is not the content of the message that is important, merely the fact that this particular pattern has been sent."

"But that would mean the Klingons were expecting to intercept us," Sulu said. "Even though they claim to be unaware of our mission."

"Curiouser and curiouser," Spock agreed.

Finally, ten minutes after the Klingon's message had been sent, Uhura announced that a reply was returning. "There must be a command ship nearby," she said.

"The return message is in the same code," Rand reported.

Sulu returned to his command chair. "On your toes, everyone. What's happening, Uhura?"

Uhura held her earpiece close. "Ship-to-ship communications . . . all encrypted . . . sounds like—" She looked up in alarm. "Sir! They're initiating a countdown!"

Sulu's hand hit the comm controls on his chair. "Engineering! I want—"

Two of the Klingon cruisers disappeared from the viewscreen.

"Damn!" Chekov said as his sensors told him what had happened. "Ve've been englobed."

At warp speed, the two cruisers had positioned themselves 120 degrees from the first and from each other, in a circle around the *Excelsior*. The *Excelsior* could run. But the Klingons had made sure that at least two or three photon torpedoes would impact before she had reached her top speed.

"The Klingon commander is hailing us," Uhura said.

Sulu glowered. "Open a channel."

The Klingon commander reappeared on the viewscreen, sprawled comfortably in his chair, a position of supreme confidence.

"Captain Sulu of the *Starship Excelsior,*" he said with mock deference, "my central command has no record of any diplomatic clearance being given to you or your vessel. Therefore, I give you your choice. Prepare to be boarded. Or prepare to die." The Klingon scratched delicately at his beard. "And by the way, your ten seconds are up. So I would appreciate hearing your answer—*now!*"

"Unfortunately," Sulu said, "I know you're lying. We decoded your message. You didn't ask your central command about—"

"baH cha!" the Klingon shouted, then disappeared from the screen.

"Torpedoes launched!" Chekov warned.

Instantly, the *Excelsior* rocked with multiple impacts.

"Shields at ninety percent!" Chekov reported. "They are firing again!"

Sulu jumped from his command chair and went to the helm. "I'll take over, Mr. Curtis."

The young helmsman left his position as Sulu slid into his chair.

The captain's fingers flew over the controls.

"Engineering, prepare for warp pulse—on my mark!" Sulu said.

The *Excelsior* rocked again. The torpedoes were being concentrated on screen overlaps, where the shields were weakest.

Chekov saw what was coming. The Klingons were going to punch through the weakened areas of overlap with their disruptors.

"Keptin! Ve have to move!"

"So they can send one up our tailpipe?" Sulu muttered as he reset fine controls on the navigation board. "I don't think so."

"Shields at seventy-eight percent!" Chekov shouted. "Ve are experiencing fluctuation feedback!"

"Brace yourselves!" Sulu ordered.

His finger jabbed at his board.

Instantly the single cruiser on the viewscreen expanded as the *Excelsior* accelerated for it at the speed of light.

Chekov held on to his tactical board, bracing for the moment of impact.

But the *Excelsior* swept beneath the cruiser—missing its shields by only the six meters Chekov read wonderingly from his controls. Then the warp pulse ended. The *Excelsior* lurched ninety degrees from her warp heading to bob up behind the cruiser. Again Sulu's ship escaped devastating impact with its shields by less than the length of a shuttle.

For one instant, Chekov had no idea what Sulu was trying to do, other than prove he was a madman.

But then Chekov saw the torpedo traces on his board.

Their targeting computers hadn't been able to make sense of Sulu's maneuvers either. They were locked on to the—

The viewscreen flared white as the *K'tinga*-class cruiser fell victim to the torpedoes launched by its sister ships.

Its shields had been tuned against Starfleet weapons, not Klingon.

Chekov cheered. He glanced at Sulu. "Vhere did you learn to fly like that?"

Sulu looked pleased. "Captain Kirk once told me he had always wanted to try that maneuver."

The bridge angled as Sulu spun his ship around in place.

The *Excelsior's* shields registered multiple hits from floating debris—the wreckage of the destroyed cruiser.

"Two-to-one odds we can handle easily," Sulu said. "Uhura—open a channel, please."

The cloud of debris was replaced by the astonished face of the Klingon commander.

"I'm not looking for a fight," Sulu said. "All I want you to do is shut down your warp cores."

"So we will be left here defenseless?" the Klingon sneered.

"No," Sulu said patiently. "So I know it will take you at least six hours to power up again before you can follow us."

"I am willing to die!" the commander proclaimed with clenched fist.

"That is also an option," Sulu said. "Now, shut down your warp cores. Or we will shut them down for you."

He nodded at Uhura. She cut the channel.

The viewscreen showed a long view with a Klingon cruiser hanging in opposite corners.

"Damage report?" Sulu asked.

Chekov was unused to a starship's commander being beside him at the helm.

"No damage, Keptin. Shields at eighty-eight percent and climbing."

"Weapons status of the cruisers?"

But before Chekov could report, his long-range sensor display lit up.

"Incoming wessel!" He had to check the readings twice. "At . . . varp factor ten!"

"Reinforcements?" Sulu asked.

"I . . . don't know. It is such a small ship."

"I recognize the configuration," Spock said unexpectedly. "It is a Vulcan warp shuttle."

"A shuttle? This far out?" McCoy asked.

"At varp ten, Doctor, wery few places are far avay." Chekov adjusted his sensors. "Coming into wisual range."

The viewscreen image changed again to show the small, angular craft on approach. Six of them in a row would barely be as long as one of the *Excelsior*'s warp nacelles.

"What kind of *shuttle* can reach warp ten?" McCoy asked.

As the shuttle came closer, Chekov adjusted the sensor image to maximum magnification. The first detail he noticed was a third nacelle in the center of the shuttle's propulsion carriage, accounting for its improbable speed. Then he saw the colors painted on its hull. "Vell, that answers that," he said.

It was a Starfleet vessel.

Uhura looked up from her station, hand to her earpiece. "The shuttle is hailing us, Captain."

"What are the Klingons doing?" Sulu asked.

Chekov scanned them. "Their varp cores are still online. But no veapons are locked."

"Onscreen," Sulu said.

It was Drake.

Chekov could see that the admiral was seated in the shuttle's forward section. Other than the pilot who was off to the side of the screen, there appeared to be no one else on board.

"Captain Sulu," the admiral said, "lower your shields so I can dock."

"Sir, we are involved in a firefight with two Klingon cruisers. I must request that you withdraw to a safe distance."

"Leave the Klingons to me, Captain. I've got a coded message for them from their High Council." Drake adjusted some controls on the console in front of him. "Stand by, *Excelsior.*"

"The shuttle is transmitting to the Klingon ships," Uhura said. "A new type of encryption code."

"What's their response?" Sulu asked.

Chekov watched his board. Conducted a second scan. "They're . . . powering down their veapons. Keptin—they're dropping their shields."

Sulu stood up from his helm position. Mr. Curtis replaced him at once. Chekov guessed the captain of this ship often took control of her himself. Captain's privileges.

"Admiral Drake," Sulu began, "may I ask what you're doing here?"

"I'll come aboard as soon as I dock, Captain. The message I've relayed to the Klingons explains the situation to them, and gives them their orders."

"Their orders, sir?"

Drake grinned. Chekov hated the look of it, so patently calculated. "It seems we've been caught up in the middle of some typical Klingon skulduggery, Captain. The orders Azetbur issued giving you diplomatic clearance were held up by the homeworld's bureaucracy. These ships were just doing their duty. But now they're ordered to escort us as we track the *Enterprise.*"

Sulu looked appalled. "Sir, I don't think the commander is going to want to escort us. We've just destroyed one of his ships."

"So I can see," Drake replied. "But, *c'est la guerre.* Now lower your shields."

Sulu went back to his command chair. "Mr. Curtis," he said to the helmsman. "Bring the ship around to give the admiral a straight path. Commander Chekov, lower the aft shields—but only around the docking bay. Then raise them as soon as the shuttle has docked."

"Thank you, Captain Sulu," Drake acknowledged. The viewscreen returned to an image of the shuttle moving closer, its passenger cabin separating for docking.

Sulu looked over to Spock. "Captain Spock, what would you say the odds were for the commander in chief of Starfleet to come this far into Klingon space without an entire flotilla for security?"

"Incalculable," Spock said.

"What?" McCoy exclaimed. "Did I hear right? You're admitting statistical defeat?"

"Without all the facts at my disposal, Doctor, I cannot begin to assess any of the reasons why Admiral Drake has undertaken such a dangerous and apparently foolhardy mission in what can be considered enemy territory."

"The shuttle has docked," Chekov said. "Shields are up. Still no response from the Klingons."

Sulu stood. "Captain Spock, Doctor McCoy, Commanders Uhura and Chekov—I'd appreciate it if you would accompany me to greet the admiral. Mr. Curtis, you have the conn."

The young helmsman took the center chair. The four officers went with Sulu to the turbolift. Chekov understood that Sulu was hoping Drake was going to offer them another briefing on their mission to find Captain Kirk.

But Chekov wondered what good it would do. Drake's presence had unquestionably changed the nature of their original mission.

The *Excelsior* and her crew were no longing tracking Kirk for Starfleet and the good of the Federation.

As far as Chekov could tell, they were hunting him for Admiral Androvar Drake.

THIRTY-FOUR

☆

Drake's shuttle thudded gently against the *Excelsior*'s aft airlock. The computer confirmed a solid docking.

In the pilot's chair, Ariadne shut down the maneuvering thrusters. She turned to her father.

But he cut her off before she could begin again. "Don't worry about it."

"But they destroyed one of our cruisers. How are the mercenaries going to react to that?"

Drake got out of his passenger seat. "They've already agreed to betray their empire. Besides, the loss of a third of them means their payment isn't split as many ways. And we *can* finish the mission with only two cruisers. Remember, the *Excelsior* is on our side."

"I wouldn't trust Sulu."

"He's a Starfleet officer and I'm his commander in chief."

"But he served with Kirk." Ariadne left her seat as well.

"Chekov and Uhura, the whole time we were undercover on Dark Range, Kirk was all they talked about. I don't think you understand the loyalty they have to him."

"They're all good officers," Drake said. "Starfleet's finest. The loyalty they have is to the chain of command."

Drake took his daughter by her shoulders, smiled at her warmly, no hint of calculation.

"This is why I've worked so hard to get to this position. If I have to, I *can* replace Sulu as commander of the *Excelsior.* I can have his entire command crew thrown into the brig. I *am* Starfleet."

"That's what Cartwright and Colonel West thought."

Drake's smile faded. "Every war has casualties."

"The assassination at Khitomer was exposed because Cartwright underestimated Kirk."

Drake looked aft as he heard the *Excelsior's* airlock hiss open. He hugged his daughter.

"Ariadne, ever since Kirk killed your mother, he has always underestimated *me."*

Ariadne stepped back from Drake. "Father, the *Klingons* killed Mother."

Drake's face hardened. "And Kirk let them get away with it." He lifted his kit bag from its storage alcove behind the passenger seat. "But once we have control of the *Chalchaj 'qmey,* once I can dangle that before our friends on the Federation Council, war will be inevitable. The Klingon Empire will be crushed. And Kirk and all his bleeding-heart sympathizers with it."

Drake handed Ariadne her flight helmet. "Keep that on, and make certain all the comm imagers are offline. I'll say my pilot has to stay on alert status in the shuttle in case of emergency evacuation."

Ariadne pulled on her helmet, stuffed her hair into place beneath it.

Drake gave his daughter's hand a squeeze.

"I'm doing this for you," he said. "For the future."

But even as he said that, Ariadne feared her father might become a casualty of the past, fighting a war that had ended years ago.

THIRTY-FIVE

☆

In his dream, Kirk held his child in his arms.

David. Three months old. So fragile. So full of life and promise.

The baby's tiny, perfect fist held Kirk's finger, squeezing mightily.

"Look at that grip," Kirk said. "Definitely going to be a starship captain. I should probably reserve a space in the Academy right now."

But Carol Marcus didn't return Kirk's smile.

She slipped her arm beneath David's thick blankets, lifted him from Kirk's embrace.

"When are you shipping out?" she asked.

Kirk knew what was coming. He was prepared for it. "I don't have to ship out, Carol."

He could tell she didn't believe him.

He tried to convince her. "Pike's ship, the *Enterprise,* she's coming back. She's going to be in spacedock for more than a year. They need an exec to handle the refit."

"And then what?" Carol asked.

Kirk didn't understand the question. "More than a year, Carol. I can live here, on Earth. With you and David. Help look after him. And you."

Carol's lower lip trembled. She fought back tears. "And *then* what? When the refit is over? Are you going to ship out on the *Enterprise?"*

Kirk didn't speak because she wouldn't like what he had to say. If things went the way he planned, he'd be the *Enterprise's* next captain.

But speaking wasn't necessary. Carol read his answer in his eyes. "I thought so."

Kirk caressed his son's delicate scalp, silken with tiny blond curls. "A year, Carol. Maybe two. With you and the baby."

"It's not enough, Jim." She couldn't hold back the tears. "He needs more than that. *I* need more than that."

"Carol . . . I love you."

She shook her head sadly. The baby stared up at her. Fascinated by her tear-filled eyes. "That's not enough, either."

This time Kirk didn't speak because he could think of nothing to say. This couldn't be happening. Not to him.

"I don't want you helping me," Carol said. "Or David."

"I'm his father."

"You fathered him. There's a difference."

"Carol . . . don't."

"I know what's right for my child, Jim. I don't want you involved."

"Carol, don't push me away."

She looked at him with such pity that Kirk felt shocked. "Jim, I don't have to push you away. Sooner or later, you'll go away yourself. Don't you see that? Don't you know what that does to me? What it will do to David?" Her voice rose in distress.

The baby began to cry.

Kirk reached out for him but Carol hugged their baby closer, gently rocking his small, bundled form.

"I won't have my son raised by a ghost a thousand light-years from home. I won't have him celebrate his birthdays with month-old subspace messages." She closed her eyes, wrapped herself around her child. "I won't have him look up at the stars and know his father died among them. I won't have that."

Kirk felt his heart torn from his chest. Every particle of him cried out for him to fight. To reject this banishment.

But he did love Carol. He knew she loved their child. And because he wasn't certain what to do, he offered no resistance.

Like a tumbling asteroid spinning away in space, he watched as Carol and David fell from him and his life.

The hole they left was never filled, but the pain it caused strengthened him.

That was the last time he ever let anyone take control from him without a fight. That was the last time he let anyone make his decisions for him.

From that day, he had strived to do nothing that would leave him with any regrets.

Each day became his best day. Each goal achieved or he knew the reason why.

Two years later, he was the new captain of the *Enterprise,* setting out on a five-year mission.

Against incredible odds, he brought his ship home.

And every time he faced defeat, every time he faced death, he remembered the feel of his small son in his arms, so fragile, so full of life and promise.

Nothing can take that from me, he told himself. Life is too precious. The promise of the future too vital.

From the day that Carol had asked him to leave, each fight had been for the children. Not just for his child, but for all children. For the future, for everyone. There was nothing more important.

All he had to do was remember his baby in his arms.

It was what Kirk remembered now.

In his dream.

Feeling a cool cloth press against his forehead.

Smelling the rich jungle scents of Chal.

His eyes fluttered open.

A face hovered close to his.

"Carol?" he asked uncertainly.

The face came into focus.

"Teilani," she said softly.

As quickly as that, Kirk was alert.

He had lost a battle. But the war continued.

He rolled off the bed, pushing his way through the filmy gauze that hung around it.

He was in Teilani's house.

Two walls were open to a sunlit courtyard surrounded by dense green vegetation.

The exotic birdlike creatures of Chal serenaded them from nearby trees.

He stood naked on the cool tiled floors. He moved his arms and shoulders. No trace of any injury from the disruptor stun or his fall against the security screen.

Teilani slipped off the bed, wearing only a wrap of fabric as transparent as the gauze around the bed.

But her beauty had no effect on him.

Kirk escalated the stakes, changed the rules.

His heart ached more than he could bear, but Teilani was the enemy now.

"Where are my clothes?" he demanded.

She smiled playfully, oblivious to his mood. "Come to bed, James. I want to see if you've fully recovered."

She reached out for him.

But Kirk turned from her and went to a wooden chest. Inside were his civilian clothes from Earth. He began to put them on. He wished they were his Starfleet uniform.

"James, what's wrong?"

"The attackers at the farm—they were *your* people, not Anarchists."

Teilani moved closer to Kirk, slipped her arms around him. "How could they be? They tried to kill you."

He twisted away from her. "That game's over."

He looked around the spacious room. He saw his jumpsuit lying with hers on a chair. Stormed over to it.

"They *couldn't* kill me," he said. He tore at the collar of the jumpsuit. Ripped out the silver coil of metal hidden in it. He pressed the activation switch on one end, saw a small ready light glow.

"Some sort of forcefield emitter, isn't it?" he said as he threw it at her. "Diverts the projectiles. That's why you told me not to worry about the projectile guns last night. That's why you tugged on my collar just before we attacked—to turn it on. And that's why I could be shot point-blank and not get touched."

Teilani stood her ground. "But, James, at the farm, you saw me get shot."

Kirk grabbed his shirt and yanked it over his head. "I saw you tug on your collar just as you turned your back to the window in the kitchen. A second later, the shot *grazed* your shoulder. Wouldn't surprise me if you could dial the emitter up and down like inertial dampers. Make the projectiles swerve around you—or just nick you to make it look good."

"You don't have to do this, James. The Anarchists' threat has ended."

Kirk pulled on his jacket, looked for his boots.

Scott had been right. Deep inside, perhaps he had always questioned Teilani and her motives. But he had been so caught up in the adventure of being with her that he had refused to question himself and his motives.

"The Anarchist in the brig was shot by the same two Chal who were at the farm. You must have some innate Vulcan abilities on your Romulan side. Meditative control of the autonomic system? Is that it? Make your heart stop for a few minutes to fool the human into helping out?"

Teilani still held to her injured innocence. "I haven't tried to fool you."

Kirk sat on the edge of the bed as he pulled on his boots. He knew the anger he felt was at his own stupidity. But he directed it at her. "You've lied to me from the beginning, haven't you? From that first meeting on the farm."

"You fell in love with me that day."

"We made love," Kirk said. "There's a difference."

"I won't believe you don't care for me."

Kirk reached out to touch her face. "I can see now how well you played me. First, you threw yourself at me. But I said no. So a minute later we're running for our lives, fighting side by side . . . and then . . ."

Teilani held his hand in place, kissed it. "And then you felt what I felt."

Kirk took his hand away. "You offered me a challenge when I didn't have one. You offered me a chance to save a world. That's my job, Teilani. It's what I do. Who I am. I couldn't refuse you and you knew it."

Teilani remained indignant. "Tell me you never loved me. That you don't love me still."

Kirk just felt embarrassed. "It made perfect sense to me that something connected to the Romulans and Klingons was something Starfleet couldn't get involved with. It made perfect sense that there was something I could do as a civilian."

Teilani raised her voice. "I want to hear you say you don't love me."

Kirk didn't take his eyes from hers. "I love my work."

Teilani slapped him. Her Klingon nails raked his cheek.

Kirk felt the scrapes she had left. Looked at the dabs of blood on his fingers.

"I can still help you," he said quietly. "There is a secret on this world that I think even you don't know about."

Teilani's face twisted in anger. "What lies did the Anarchist tell you?"

"Have you ever been in the Armory?" Kirk asked.

He saw her flinch.

"How you blinded me. How I let myself be blinded. That first attack should have made me suspect it wasn't your power station. If the Anarchists had really wanted to bring chaos to your society, they would have concentrated their shelling on it, to destroy it. But they wanted to *get* to it. They wanted to get inside. Why?"

Teilani's jaw tightened. She looked ready to explode.

"What's in there, Teilani?"

She turned away from him. "I don't know."

Kirk was surprised to sense that she was telling the truth.

He went to her. Put his hands on her shoulders. "Then go there with me."

He felt her shiver.

"Why won't you just accept that you've done what you were supposed to do?" she said. "We've won! Chal is safe! You can stay here and be young with me forever."

Kirk turned her around to face him, looked down into her eyes.

"You don't know how much I want to do exactly that," Kirk said gently. "But from what the Anarchist said, there might be more to that secret of Chal, too."

She leaned against him. Her head beneath his chin. "I know you love me." He felt her tremble.

"That's not enough," Kirk said.

His communicator chirped.

Kirk pulled it from his jacket, opened it, acknowledged the call.

"Scott here, Captain. I'm picking up vessels approaching at high warp. At least two of them are Klingon."

"Civilian?"

"From their power curves, I'd have t' say they were battle cruisers."

"How soon till they're here, Scotty?"

"Only six minutes. These sensors just aren't th' same as the old ones."

Teilani held a hand over the communicator. "You didn't stop the Anarchists in time, after all."

"In time for what?" Kirk asked.

"What we feared. If they couldn't destroy us, then it was

just a matter of time before they approached someone who could. Just as I approached someone I thought would be able to save us."

"Are those Klingon ships coming here to destroy Chal?"

"That's why we wanted you to have a starship, fully armed and shielded."

"The truth would have been more useful than a starship," Kirk said. "The Federation is at peace with the Klingons. At least we're trying to be."

He pulled the communicator away from her.

"Scotty, beam me directly to the bridge."

"Will that be one to beam up?" Scott asked.

Kirk stepped back from Teilani. "One, Mr. Scott."

But as soon as he said those words, Kirk knew Teilani would take them as a challenge.

The beam dissolved him just as she fell into his arms.

THIRTY-SIX

"Put your eyes back in your head, Mr. Scott. I want you on tactical."

The engineer blinked in embarrassment as Teilani stepped away from Kirk on the bridge of the *Enterprise.* Her transparent wrap offered little more than the suggestion of clothes.

Kirk took the center chair.

Esys was at the helm. Scott left the engineering substation for tactical beside him. Two other Chal held positions at communications and the science station. About twenty others were scattered through the ship, in Engineering, the disruptor banks, and the remaining photon-torpedo launch tube. Automated controls handled the rest of the ship.

"Can you put the ships onscreen?" Kirk asked.

Teilani came to stand by his chair.

"Still beyond visual range," Scott said. "But two of them are definitely Klingon battle cruisers."

"Full power to shields, Mr. Scott. Any idea what the third one is?"

"'Tis not in th' database that came with th' sensors," Scott said. "I'll try a manual scan."

"Um, Mr. Kirk?"

Kirk turned to the Chal at communications.

"I, uh, believe we're being hailed, sir."

Kirk remained calm. "The third switch on the left. The green one. That's it. Press it."

The young Chal hit the right switch. Kirk now had control of ship-to-ship communications from his chair.

Kirk opened the channel and turned back to the viewscreen.

And nearly jumped from his chair.

It was Sulu.

"Captain Kirk," his former helmsman said. "Good to see you again."

Kirk saw Sulu react to Teilani's almost clothed presence.

"Sulu—are you traveling with Klingons?"

"We're being 'escorted,' sir."

Kirk heard the qualification Sulu put on the word. "I see. Is this a social visit?" he asked lightly.

Sulu was about to answer, but his attention was caught by something to the side, offscreen. Instead, he sat back as someone else moved into view.

Kirk gripped the arms of his chair so tightly the frame creaked.

Drake.

"Hello, Jim."

"Admiral."

Kirk watched Drake's eyes move, obviously taking in Teilani on the *Excelsior*'s viewscreen. "I see you're enjoying yourself. As usual."

"Th' ships have dropped from warp," Scotty announced. "They're moving to match our orbit."

Kirk shifted in his chair. More than anything, he wanted to take Teilani aside for any information she could provide explaining how Chal had come to be caught up between the Klingon Empire and the Federation. But Kirk knew better than to turn his back on Drake for an instant.

"You're a long way from home, Admiral. Anything I should know about?"

Drake adopted a serious expression. Kirk visualized his fist driving into the middle of it.

"Sorry, Jim. This is Starfleet business."

"Depending on whose charts you believe, this is either Klingon or Romulan space."

Drake's serious expression became stern. "I'm here under the combined authority of Starfleet and the Klingon High Council."

"Authority to do what?" Kirk asked.

"That's classified, Jim."

Kirk tapped his fingers on the side of his chair. He could wait.

Drake remained silent for a few moments longer, then spoke over his shoulder to Sulu.

"Captain, send down the security details to secure the city."

Kirk had no idea what Drake was up to, but for the simple reason that it was something Drake wanted to do, Kirk was going to stop him.

"Mr. Scott, I want a level-seven photon discharge into the ionosphere over the city."

Scott didn't question the order. "Aye, sir." The bridge rumbled with the launching of three photon torpedoes, one after the other.

Kirk received his third surprise of the day when he heard Spock's voice come from the *Excelsior*'s bridge.

"Admiral Drake, the *Enterprise* has created an area of high ionization over the Chal city. We will be unable to beam anyone down for at least twenty minutes."

"Spock, is that you?"

Spock stepped onscreen behind Sulu. "Greetings, Captain."

Then McCoy stepped on from the other side. "Fancy meeting you here." McCoy's eyes widened more than Scott's as he saw Teilani.

Kirk sat back in his chair, feeling that the odds might have shifted back in his favor.

But Drake cut in. "This isn't a reunion, Jim. This is a Starfleet matter. I am ordering you to withdraw."

"I am not a Starfleet officer. This is not a Starfleet vessel. You are not in Federation space. Do I have to make it more clear than that?"

"Commander Krult," Drake said. *"Cha yIghus!"*

Scott spun around from his tactical board. "Captain, the Klingons are bringing their weapons online."

Drake grinned coldly. "Do I have to make it more clear to *you,* Jim?" He stepped forward. "I am now advising you that you are operating an illegally armed vessel in a restricted area of Klingon space. Your actions here could set back the new era of detente between the Federation and the Klingon Empire. For that reason, I am *suggesting* you withdraw from this system." He smiled in challenge. "Or face the consequences."

Kirk had had enough. "Sulu, what is that pompous ass going on about?"

Drake raised his hand as if to give an order to fire. But Sulu stepped down from his chair.

"Admiral, if I could have a moment?" Sulu asked.

Drake nodded curtly.

"Captain Kirk," Sulu began. "I know this is an awkward position for all of us to be in. But Starfleet *is* in possession of classified information suggesting that Chal could pose a threat to the peace process between the Federation and the Empire."

Kirk knew his former crew well. Sulu wasn't lying. He was incapable of lying.

"What are your intentions?" Kirk asked.

Sulu took a breath, clearly more uncomfortable than Kirk. "My *orders* are to dispatch security teams to the planet's surface and secure any war matériel we find. We do have the authority from the Empire, sir."

That information made several pieces fall together to form a pattern. Drake wanted war matériel. The central structure in the city was an armory. The Anarchist Kirk had questioned in the *Enterprise*'s brig seemed to think that the secrets contained in that armory were worth destroying a planet for peace to have a chance.

"Just so I'm sure I understand, Sulu. You say you are to *secure* whatever war matériel you find?"

"Yes, sir."

Kirk watched Drake carefully. The Anarchist had wanted to destroy something. Drake wanted to obtain it.

"Would this have anything to do with the *Chalchaj 'qmey?"* Kirk asked.

Teilani grabbed Kirk's arm at the same instant he saw Drake's eyes darken.

Sulu reacted as well.

Kirk realized that while everyone else recognized what the Klingon phrase meant, he himself was apparently not expected to.

"What do you know about the *Chalchaj 'qmey?"* Drake said coldly.

"Enough to know that I'm not letting you get near it," Kirk bluffed. "Captain Sulu, you are in violation of Chal orbital space. I ask you to withdraw."

Sulu bit his lip and looked at Drake.

"Captain Sulu," Drake ordered. "The *Enterprise* is a threat to this mission. I am ordering you to neutralize that threat."

Kirk ignored Drake. "Spock, talk some sense into the admiral. The Federation recognizes Chal as an independent world. Starfleet has no authority here."

Spock displayed no sign of conflict. "Unfortunately, Captain, the Empire does *not* recognize Chal's independence. However, the planet's cooperation in this matter might move the High Council to change its view."

"Spock, listen to me. If you proceed with what Drake is planning, you'll be following orders, but you will not be doing the right thing."

Spock drew himself up, held his hands behind his back. "Captain, with respect, sir. Can you be sure *you* are doing the right thing?"

McCoy turned to Spock. "Spock! Are you out of your mind?"

Spock kept his eyes locked on the hidden imager on the *Excelsior*'s bridge, so it was as if he stared directly at Kirk. "Doctor, I merely point out that since none of us know exactly what the *Chalchaj 'qmey* is, it hardly seems logical to fight over it."

Thank you, Spock, Kirk thought. Drake was on a fishing expedition.

On the *Excelsior*'s bridge, Drake realized that Spock was giving away secrets, too. "That's enough, Captain Spock." He stared at Sulu. "Captain—you have your orders."

For a moment, Sulu appeared torn by indecision. But starship captains could not be indecisive. "Weapons officer," he said. "Target the *Enterprise*'s impulse thrusters."

"Sulu," Kirk warned. "Withdraw or be fired upon."

McCoy threw up his hands in disgust. "Is everybody crazy?"

Sulu shook his head. "Captain Kirk, I'm sorry."

Kirk knew Sulu had no choice. He was doing what he thought was a reasonable compromise—disabling the *Enterprise* until the mystery could be solved. Any attempt on his part to delay acting on Drake's orders would be mutiny. Knowing Drake's excesses, it might even be treason.

Kirk closed the channel to the *Excelsior* and brought a tactical display up on the viewscreen. "Mr. Esys—set course bearing eighty-five, mark zero."

Esys started to turn in his chair. "But, that'll put us right in—"

"Do it, lad!" Scotty barked. "Th' captain knows what he's doin'."

"Full impulse, Mr. Scott. *Now!*"

The *Enterprise* shuddered as she blazed toward Chal.

Teilani held on to Kirk's chair as the bridge bucked and a new sound rarely heard on a starship thundered through the bulkheads—the scream of air being ripped asunder as the ship descended through atmosphere.

"Entering the zone of ionization," Scott confirmed.

"How long can we stay in it, Scotty?"

Scott had to shout to be heard over the howling wind.

"Thirty seconds!"

"James! What are you doing?"

Kirk reached out for Teilani's hand, trying to reassure her. "Disappearing," he said. "They won't be able to lock on to us through the ionized area we made."

"But for less than a minute?" Teilani said. "What good is that?"

"A few seconds will be long enough. Prepare for warp, Mr. Scott."

Kirk didn't hear Scott's reply. He thought it was just as well.

But Esys, who was not Starfleet-trained, questioned Kirk again. "You can't go to warp in the atmosphere!"

"Who would you rather believe, Mr. Esys—someone who's done it, or the textbooks?" Kirk smiled at the young Chal. "Set course bearing two four five, mark one eighty."

Kirk saw Scott shake his head in despair.

"She'll hold, Scotty!" Kirk shouted.

"Aye," Scott called back. "But will I?"

"Warp one . . . *now!"* Kirk commanded.

The *Enterprise* groaned as she was suddenly torn from the atmosphere of Chal at the speed of light, traveling back on a reverse course that would put her only a few kilometers behind the *Excelsior* and her Klingon escorts.

"On standard orbit!" Scott shouted, still caught up in the moment though the roar of rushing air had instantly stopped.

"Take out those Klingons," Kirk said. "Photon torpedoes—full spread."

That was too much for Scott. Even he had to question Kirk's plan now. "Sir, th' disruptors would have more of a chance!"

"No disruptors!" Kirk ordered. "Fire torpedoes!"

Scott muttered again but four more torpedoes launched sequentially, overloading the Klingons' aft shields.

"They never saw us comin'!" the engineer exclaimed. Then his tone changed abruptly as he added, "The *Excelsior* is comin' about."

"Put the Klingons between her and us, Mr. Esys."

The *Enterprise* shuddered as Esys overcompensated and almost collided with a battlecruiser.

It swerved away, forcing the second cruiser to change course.

Kirk watched the chain reaction spread on the tactical display. Now the careening Klingon ships were forcing the *Excelsior* to pull back.

But the first Klingon cruiser executed a roll to slide past the second and began firing.

The *Enterprise* absorbed the first shots easily.

"Do I return fire?" Scott asked urgently.

"Wait for the second cruiser to come about," Kirk said.

"The *Excelsior* is locking phasers!"

"Wait for the second cruiser, Mr. Scott. . . ."

"They're getting ready to fire!" Scott warned.

Teilani's nails dug into Kirk's arm.

The *Enterprise* shuddered as the second cruiser finally fired along with the first.

"Fire full disruptors!" Kirk shouted.

The orange beams blasted forth from the *Enterprise*'s saucer.

They passed through the first battle cruiser's shields as if they weren't even there.

Its bridge erupted into a tiny nova as the main hull began to spiral away, passing into the beams hitting the second cruiser.

Caught in those beams, the first cruiser's main hull blew apart in a string of small explosions as her antimatter containment bottles failed.

But by absorbing the second set of beams, she let the second cruiser escape.

"What happened?" Teilani asked.

"They assumed we had phasers," Kirk said, "and set their shields accordingly." He sighed. "I always wanted to try that."

He reopened a channel to the *Excelsior.*

Drake was in the command chair. His expression was the same as it been on Tycho IV when he had told Kirk of Faith Morgan's death.

"Excelsior," Kirk said. "Once again I ask you to withdraw."

Drake's reply was emotionless. "You're dead, Kirk. Do you hear me?"

"Put Captain Sulu on," Kirk said. "I want to talk with someone who's responsible."

"Weapons officer," Drake ordered. "Retarget the *Enterprise.* All phasers on the bridge."

"We took a beatin' in the atmosphere," Scott whispered. "Shields won't hold more than a minute under all that."

But with any luck, Kirk knew, the *Enterprise* wouldn't have to face that fire. By changing his orders, Drake had just given Sulu and his crew an opportunity to withdraw. Provided they saw the situation the way Kirk did.

"Admiral Drake," Kirk said, "am I to understand that you have just given orders to destroy a ship belonging to a sovereign world because it has tried to preserve its territorial integrity?"

"Your atoms will orbit Chal until its sun goes nova," Drake promised.

"Mr. Spock—isn't Admiral Drake's order a violation of Starfleet general policy?"

Spock stepped up beside Drake. He raised an eyebrow. "Starfleet does specify that in matters of self-defense, Starfleet vessels will respond to force with equal force, and no more."

Good, Kirk thought. *Spock knows where I'm going.*

"He attacked us," Drake told Spock.

"No," Kirk corrected. "I attacked the Klingons. Mr. Spock, has this vessel directed any fire toward the *Excelsior,* or any other Starfleet vessel?"

"No, sir, she has not."

"So, in your opinion, is Admiral Drake justified in ordering the *Enterprise*'s destruction?"

Spock nodded his head a fraction of a centimeter, letting Kirk know he had found a way out.

"Technically, a case could be made that the admiral's orders are in violation of Starfleet command directives," Spock acknowledged.

"Now, I know I'm no longer part of Starfleet," Kirk said as he saw Drake smolder, "but in my day, such violations were grounds for a general inquiry."

"As they are today, sir," Spock agreed.

"Fire!" Drake ordered.

Kirk braced for impact.

Nothing.

"Fire, damn you!" Drake said as he sprang to his feet. "Fire or you'll all be charged with mutiny!"

Sulu returned to the viewscreen. "Admiral Drake, with respect, sir. You are in violation of Starfleet command directives. I must request that you relinquish command of this vessel in order that we may convene a general inquiry."

"This won't work and you know it," Drake said. "We're in battle."

"Shut down the disruptors," Kirk ordered Scott.

Sulu looked offscreen. "Commander Chekov, is the *Excelsior* in danger of attack by the *Enterprise?*"

Chekov's there, too, Kirk thought. No wonder the *Excelsior* didn't fire on Drake's command.

"No, sir," Kirk heard Chekov reply. "The *Enterprise*'s disruptors are powered down."

"Admiral, please," Sulu insisted. "I don't wish to invoke General Order One-oh-four, Section C."

Drake stared at Sulu. "You wouldn't dare."

"*He* doesn't have to dare," McCoy said as he joined the line of officers standing up to Drake. "I'm senior ship's surgeon and I'd love to give you a medical exam to establish your frame of mind."

Chekov stepped onscreen. "I am villing to testify about the improper orders he gave me."

Even Uhura was there. She joined Chekov. "I have placed all bridge recordings on a message buoy, Captain Sulu, for transmission to Starfleet Command."

Kirk watched as Drake looked at each of the former *Enterprise* officers assembled before him.

Without any trace of emotion, he stepped down.

"You will hold the inquiry *now,*" he said to Sulu.

"After we have withdrawn from this system." Sulu took over his chair. "Captain Kirk, this could take several hours. But I suspect we will be returning after that."

"Understood, Captain Sulu," Kirk acknowledged. "Thank you."

"Thank *you,* sir. I didn't see how we could get out of that one. Sulu out."

The viewscreen flashed back to an image of Chal.

The *Excelsior* streaked away into warp.

There was no trace of the second Klingon cruiser, only debris from the first.

Scott spun around in his chair. His forehead dripped with sweat. "I swear ye have the luck o' th' d'vil."

"Wrong afterworld, Mr. Scott," Kirk said. "This is heaven, remember?"

Kirk got up and went to Teilani.

He tried to be gentle. "You know the lies have to end now, don't you. Whatever you've been keeping from me, the Federation knows about it. And the Klingons. How soon before the Romulans get here? Who knows how many others?"

Teilani couldn't meet his eyes.

"Teilani, your Anarchists had nothing to do with what just happened here. The one I talked to yesterday was ready to die rather than let anyone know what's in the Armory. Whatever secrets you're trying to hide, you're no longer in control of them. And that makes them dangerous."

"I don't know what to do, James."

He tilted her head up, to make her look at him, to see there was no anger in his eyes.

"I understand why you brought me here, now. To take care of a problem you felt you couldn't. But it is Chal's problem. Your problem. Not mine."

Panic flashed through her eyes. "You're leaving?"

"No," Kirk said. "But I can only *help* you. I can't take responsibility for you. You have to do that for yourself."

"How?" she asked.

With that plaintive question, Kirk saw she was a child in so many ways.

But she could not remain a child forever.

No one could.

"What is the *Chalchaj 'qmey?"* Kirk asked.

Teilani took a deep breath. "I . . . don't know, James. It's . . . it's whatever is in the Armory."

"And you've never been there?"

She shook her head.

"I'm afraid, James."

"That's part of growing up," he said. "And that's what you have to do, now. It's what all your people have to do."

She held his hand, not to distract him, but for support.

"Are you ever afraid?" she asked.

Kirk smiled at her. He leaned down to whisper his secret into her ear. "All the time."

She looked at him in wonder.

"I just don't let it get in the way."

A new look came to Teilani's eyes. Kirk guessed it was disillusionment. But there was nothing wrong with that. Generally, that was what inspired people to make a change.

Teilani looked down at her transparent wrap. "I suppose I should get some clothes on," she said.

"And then we'll go down to the armory?" Kirk asked.

"Together," she said.

Kirk took her hand.

The future waited. This time, for both of them.

THIRTY-SEVEN

When the *Excelsior* had withdrawn a light-year from Chal's territorial spacc, the ship's main briefing room was set up for a formal inquiry.

The large display screen no longer showed the starship's schematic. Instead, a series of still frames from the bridge recorders filled the screen. They showed the sequence of events leading up to Sulu's requesting that Drake step down from command. Time codes ran under each image. Uhura had been busy.

Like the others gathered in the room, Chekov had not yet taken his seat. Admiral Drake had still to arrive. Everyone was too tense to pretend that what would happen next was merely a formality.

"So what are the odds this time, Spock?" McCoy asked.

Uhura, Sulu, and Chekov ceased their own conversation, waiting for Spock's reply.

"For what, Doctor?"

"For us getting away with this."

Spock thought a moment. "If we analyze our present situation according to regulations, we have done nothing wrong. Therefore, there is nothing to 'get away with,' as you put it."

"And if we don't go by regulations?" McCoy prodded.

"Anything is possible," Spock said.

McCoy rolled his eyes. "Thank you for those reassuring words."

"They were not meant to reassure."

"No kidding."

"Doctor, even to you it should come as no surprise that we are in a precarious position."

"Well," McCoy said, "you were going to leave Starfleet anyway, so what's a discharge a few months early going to matter?"

"I do not refer to our position within Starfleet. That is covered by regulation and we were justified in pointing out to Admiral Drake that his orders were inappropriate."

"Then what do you mean by precarious?"

"The admiral does not appear to be engaged in a Starfleet mission."

That got everyone's attention.

Sulu sat down on the corner of the conference table. He

knew how Spock's mind worked. "What did we miss, Captain Spock?"

"When the admiral was confronting Captain Kirk, he ordered our Klingon escorts to prepare to fire their torpedoes," Spock said. "No matter how far along the peace process is with the Empire, it is highly improbable that any Klingon commander would place his ship in a position where it would be expected to take orders from a Starfleet officer."

Chekov remembered the readings on his tactical display. "But Keptin Spock, as soon as the admiral gave that order, the Klingon wessels did arm their torpedoes."

"Precisely, Commander," Spock agreed. "Which I take as evidence that the Klingon ships may be other than Klingon armed forces."

"Mercenaries," Uhura said. "In battle cruisers."

"That has some significance to you?" Spock asked.

"They vere our mission objectives," Chekov answered. "When ve vere undercover."

"Fascinating," Spock said.

McCoy looked back and forth from Spock to Chekov and Uhura, missing something. "The commander in chief of *Starfleet* is commanding Klingon mercenary ships? How in blazes does that happen?"

"The answer to your question lies in the sequence of events, Doctor. Following the events at Khitomer and the arrest of Admiral Cartwright, Starfleet Intelligence began an intensive effort to halt the sale of Klingon armaments on the illegal markets. That effort was specifically directed at obtaining the type of vessels now apparently under Admiral Drake's command." Spock looked at Chekov and Uhura. "During your mission, were you successful in negotiating the sale of Klingon battle cruisers?"

"At least five attempts led to arrests," Uhura said.

"Do you know the disposition of those vessels?"

Chekov shrugged. "Ve vere used to initiate the deals. Jade

vould take over for the money negotiations, and then other agents vould make the arrests."

Spock nodded. "And because you were out of direct contact with Starfleet, you had no way of knowing the end results of your efforts."

Uhura frowned. "Only what Jade told us."

"So," Spock concluded, "the Klingon vessels accompanying the admiral may have been obtained as a result of coopting the efforts of Starfleet Intelligence."

Sulu interrupted. "Captain Spock, with respect, sir, this is all circumstantial."

"What is?" Spock asked.

"This case you seem to be building that Admiral Drake is connected to Jade's efforts to get the Children of Heaven."

"He is here," Spock said patiently. "If obtaining the Children of Heaven were a Starfleet objective, there are many other commanders to whom the task could have been delegated. The fact that Drake is personally involved, backed by Klingon mercenary ships, suggests this is not a Starfleet operation."

"You're forgetting, Captain Spock," Sulu said. "The admiral is also backed up by the *Excelsior.*"

"Vhat has *happened* to you?!" Chekov exploded. "Starfleet gives you command of this ship and you lose your common sense?"

Sulu did not respond to Chekov's anger. "I worked hard for this ship, Pavel. I respect the chain of command that gave it to me."

"It sounds more like you vorship them."

Sulu got to his feet and jabbed a finger at Chekov. "Don't push our friendship. *Or* your luck. I can understand the pressure you've been under. But this isn't Dark Range anymore. We're professionals who have a job to do."

Uhura crossed her arms and stood shoulder to shoulder with Chekov. "Then do it."

Sulu seemed surprised that a confrontation was developing. "I am."

McCoy put himself between Sulu on one side and Chekov and Uhura on the other. "I don't think that's what she means, Captain."

For the first time, a glimmer of anger broke through Sulu's professional detachment. "There is nothing going on here that is not covered by regulations, Doctor. I am—we are *all* compelled to follow our orders until such time as conditions warrant otherwise."

Chekov took a step forward. As far as he was concerned, Sulu might need another punch in the nose to get his thinking in gear. "You're vorking for Drake, aren't you?"

Sulu started forward, only to be restrained by McCoy. "I'm working for Starfleet! The way you should be!"

Chekov wasn't prepared to push past the doctor. He turned to Spock. "Are you going to let him get avay vith this?"

Without hesitation, Spock took up a position beside Sulu.

Chekov was shocked.

"Commander Chekov," Spock said, "I assure you Captain Sulu's actions are logical, legal, and proper."

"But are they right?" Chekov asked.

"As he has pointed out," Spock explained, "all we have are suspicions. Nothing concrete."

McCoy kept his position in the middle. "What's it going to take to convince you one way or the other, Spock?"

"That will depend on Admiral Drake's next action. If it is reasonable, then—"

"Vhy must ve wait for *him?* Vhy can't ve take the next action?" Chekov interrupted.

McCoy flashed a strained smile at Chekov, trying to defuse the tension. "Commander, perhaps you've been undercover too long."

"So now you're on *his* side?"

"We're all on the same side. All that's going on here is a disagreement over tactics."

"There is no 'disagreement,'" Sulu said sternly. "This is my ship. I'm in command."

That was Chekov's breaking point. "And you're putting Captain Kirk in danger!" He pushed forward, forcing McCoy out of the way.

Uhura grabbed at Chekov's uniform jacket.

Sulu turned sideways, ready to defend himself.

Spock pulled Sulu back, positioning himself before Chekov.

One more second, and the first blow would be struck.

The briefing room doors slid open.

Everyone froze as Admiral Drake stepped in.

For a moment, his eyes widened as he realized what he had just interrupted.

Then he brought his wide, insincere grin into play. "Normally, I'd say 'As you were.' But in this case, I think I'll just ask everyone to take a seat."

Chekov and Sulu exchanged an angry glance. Chekov tugged on his jacket.

He and Uhura sat at one end of the briefing table. Sulu and Spock sat at the other. McCoy chose the middle.

Drake walked over to the display screen, studying the images. Then he turned to face his audience.

"Those records won't be necessary," he said. "Captain Sulu . . . all of you . . . I am prepared to acknowledge that you were performing your duty when you . . . 'reminded' me of Starfleet regulations."

Instantly, Chekov knew Drake was setting them up for something. His opening statement could only be a distraction.

"However," Drake continued, "to perform my duty, I must point out to you that there are certain diplomatic concerns at stake here. Which I cannot reveal to you." Drake's eyes narrowed as his smile vanished. "And, if I choose to, those concerns are more than enough to authorize me to place all of you in the brig pending court-martial."

He looked them all in the eye again, then turned the smile back on.

"But I, for one, understand the mitigating circumstances of the intense, personal loyalty you feel to your old captain. And I salute you for it."

Chekov was confused. Everything he had come to know about Drake had led him to expect some form of censure, if not punishment.

McCoy voiced the confusion Chekov felt. "So what's the purpose of this damned inquiry, Admiral?"

Drake gestured magnanimously. "There is no inquiry. Simple as that. Because this is a delicate situation, I will make a full report to the Federation president and Chancellor Azetbur, asking for their explicit direction. I will make their responses known to you, so that you will understand the reasoning behind your orders. Since that process will take at least two days, in the meantime I will direct the *Excelsior* to monitor the *Enterprise*'s location. As long as the *Enterprise* remains within the Chal system, we will stand by."

"What if the *Enterprise* leaves?" Sulu asked.

"Then we will follow. At a distance. Until we receive further instructions. Is that acceptable, Captain Sulu?"

The commander in chief of Starfleet had just asked a captain if his orders were suitable. Chekov was glad to see Sulu look uncomfortable.

"It seems to fall within regulations," Sulu answered.

"Vhat about the Klingons?" Chekov asked.

Drake nodded, as if that were a question Chekov was within his rights to ask. "They will stand by with us."

No one said anything else.

"Thank you for your . . . indulgence," Drake said, "in what is a difficult situation." He headed for the doors. "That is all."

In a moment, he was gone.

The silence he had left behind was brittle.

"Well?" McCoy asked Spock. "Was that reasonable enough?"

"Too reasonable," Spock said.

McCoy sighed. "How can you be *too* reasonable?"

"We challenged the admiral's authority and he has accepted and excused it without a formal inquiry. That can only mean he has something to hide."

"Or," Uhura said, "he's in a hurry to do something else."

"But what?" Sulu asked. "Think about what you're suggesting. I mean, how can a traitor possibly be chosen by the Federation Council to be Starfleet's commander in chief? Starfleet Intelligence would have to be . . ." Sulu hesitated. He looked at Chekov, then glanced away.

"It all comes back to Starfleet Intelligence, doesn't it?" Chekov said darkly.

"But how could Drake compromise the entire division so quickly?" Sulu continued, speaking to himself as much as to anyone else at the table. "He's only been C in C for a handful of days."

"Perhaps Admiral Drake is part of a larger process," Spock suggested. "I for one would be most interested in knowing his relationship with Admiral Cartwright."

Sulu looked pained. "That first time we met with Drake. He told us he suspected Starfleet Command had been infiltrated by a cabal of senior officers. That Cartwright was just the tip."

"Perhaps," Spock suggested, "that was one of the few times when the admiral was telling us the truth. He only neglected to mention that he himself was part of that cabal."

"So vhat do ve do now?" Chekov asked.

All eyes turned to Sulu.

The *Excelsior* was his ship.

The next move was up to him.

Chekov wondered if he had the strength to make the right one.

THIRTY-EIGHT

☆

Kirk and Teilani took their positions on the transporter pads in the *Enterprise.* Kirk still wore his civilian clothes, though he was outfitted with a disruptor pistol, communicator, and combat tricorder. Teilani wore her jumpsuit, similarly equipped.

In Kirk's eyes, the outfit added to her years. She looked ready for a fight in a way she hadn't before the jungle assault.

Innocence lost, Kirk thought.

Scott adjusted his controls at the operator's console. "Locked on t' the Armory's coordinates." He made a soft whistle. "That's a large installation."

"It's the biggest structure on Chal," Kirk said.

"More than that, sir. It extends underground through almost the entire city."

Kirk looked at Teilani but saw no comprehension in her eyes. "As far as we've ever been told, the Armory's our power station," she said.

"What about it, Scotty? Any sign of power generators?"

"Aye. But they only make up about a fraction of what's down there."

"Any idea what *is* down there?"

Scott looked puzzled. "Not with these sensors. Lots of equipment. Most of it dormant." His puzzlement turned to a frown. "That's a sly little trick."

"What is?" Kirk asked.

"They've got a transporter shield over the place. Hidden in

th' power generator fields so it would disperse any beam that struck it before an operator could recover the signal."

Kirk attention sharpened. The sensor maps of the Armory's exterior had revealed no entrances. Teilani had confirmed that the Chal were aware of no way in.

"Someone's gone t' a lot of trouble to keep visitors out," Scott said. His fingers tapped over the controls. "But the modulation routines are fairly old-fashioned."

"Forty years?" Kirk asked. That was when the colony had been founded.

"That would be about right," Scotty said absently. Then he smiled. "We're through!"

"No chance we'll be scattered?" Kirk asked.

"None at all," Scott said proudly.

"In that case, keep a lock on us the whole time we're down there, and energize."

The transporter chime grew as the surrounding room seemed to break apart into glowing bits of energy.

"Of course," Kirk heard Scotty's warbling voice say, "when I say 'none,' I mean very little. . . ."

Before Kirk could respond, a new location formed around him.

He saw it only in the glow from the transporter effect.

When he felt solid, he was in utter darkness.

"James?" Teilani asked from beside him.

"I'm right here," Kirk said. "Don't move. We'll ask Mr. Scott to beam down some lights and then . . ."

Lights flickered overhead.

Far overhead. Two hundred meters at least, Kirk estimated.

A geodesic pattern of glowing light channels took form. There was something odd about it, though. Their pattern was precisely regular, but they only covered half the enormous ceiling.

Then they brightened enough that Kirk could see there was something hanging above him, directly overhead, blocking almost half the ceiling from his view.

The light channels continued to intensify until the enclosure Kirk and Teilani had transported to was as bright as day.

The object above them was a Romulan Bird-of-Prey. An old one.

Kirk had seen one just like it, almost thirty years earlier, when the first cloaked Romulan vessel had tested Federation resolve at the Neutral Zone.

Teilani stared up at it. "James, what is it?"

"An old Romulan starship. But it can't possibly be here. It must be a holoprojection of some sort."

Kirk used his combat tricorder.

The ship was real.

"Why would they *bury* a starship?" Kirk asked.

"James, look over there."

One hundred meters away, new lights were coming on. They seemed to originate from within a series of transparent display cases which ringed the wide plaza on which Kirk and Teilani now stood. Directly behind and on top of the display cases, Kirk recognized Romulan data conduits. The flickering status lights that lit the dull gray tubes indicated the presence of a major computer complex.

"There must be some type of life-form sensor operating," Kirk said. "When our presence was detected, the installation was switched on." Kirk aimed his tricorder at the lit display cases.

"But why?" Teilani asked.

Kirk's tricorder registered no energy sources other than the light fixtures and the computer pathways. No explosives. No booby traps.

"Time to find out," he said.

The floor they crossed was polished black stone. Kirk recognized the patterns in it as the same in the rock around Chal's city. Whatever the purpose of the structure they were in, it had apparently been carved from solid rock.

By the time Kirk saw what was in the first display case, though, the Armory's purpose was becoming clearer.

"It's a museum," Kirk told Teilani.

The display before them contained a mannequin outfitted in a Romulan warrior's uniform, again forty years old in style.

Mounted beside it, a series of hand weapons were also on exhibit, power cells removed.

There was a white floor panel before the display case. Kirk's tricorder identified a pressure mechanism under it. Teilani tapped her foot against the panel.

A voice spoke to them from a grille above the display case. At the same time, a spotlight shone on the first weapon—a small hand disruptor.

"Is the voice Romulan?" Kirk asked.

Teilani nodded. "It's explaining how to use the weapon."

"I suppose your colony's founders didn't want you to lose your heritage."

The voice paused as the spotlight dimmed. Then a second weapon was illuminated and the voice began again.

"Unusual," Teilani said.

"What?"

"The last thing the recording said." She looked up at Kirk. "There are ten thousand of those hand disruptors stored here."

"The Armory," Kirk murmured. The name suddenly made perfect sense. "It's not a museum, it's a munitions dump."

"For what purpose?"

Kirk shrugged. What other purpose could there be. "War."

"With whom?"

Kirk tapped his chest. "With me. The Federation."

He glanced down the curving wall of display cases. Many held other mannequins. Some in environmental suits. Some in camouflage.

"Forty years ago, the Romulans and the Klingons must have been preparing for an all-out war with the Federation. So they founded Chal to be a secret supply base. In case the Federation overwhelmed either or both empires, Chal could supply a surviving force with the weapons they needed to continue the fight."

Teilani stared in at the Romulan weapons.

Kirk watched her reflection in the clear panel.

He could see what she was thinking.

That she and her kind were one of those weapons.

Teilani began walking along the curve of the cases.

Each pressure panel she stepped on began an informational sequence.

Dozens of recorded Romulan voices whispered in the Armory. Spotlights flared and dimmed on hand weapons, medical equipment, computer consoles, ration containers, navigation and communication devices, protective clothing, tactical bombs, enough supplies for an army.

Kirk stared up at the Bird-of-Prey. He could see the pylons holding it in position. One of the display cases would no doubt contain the information for opening the roof of the Armory and flying the spacecraft skyward.

He wouldn't be surprised to find a Klingon battle cruiser down here, as well. Perhaps an entire section filled with Klingon display cases.

Teilani had moved ahead of him as he had studied the starship.

He saw her in front of the first display case in the series.

Her hands were pressed against its clear viewing panel.

He went to her side.

It was the proof of her suspicions.

What Kirk had expected.

The mannequins were more lifelike in this display.

A Romulan male and a Klingon female held a baby.

The baby had a furrowed brow. Pointed ears.

A holographic projection came to life. DNA molecules spun within it. Separated, moved together in combination.

Parts of the twisted molecule were trimmed by quick flashes of atomically precise particle beams.

Another display showed egg cells being mechanically opened by microscalpels, so their dark nucleii could be replaced with new ones.

"We were *made,*" Teilani said. She looked at her hands. "Genetically engineered."

Kirk put his hand on her shoulder. Remembered how quickly it had healed. Understood the reason why.

"There is no shame in that, Teilani."

She shrugged loose from his touch. Turned around the corner.

He gave her her privacy.

He thought about the marks Sam had carved into the frame of his bedroom door, charting his growth.

He remembered his father's wisdom.

It was necessary to know where you had come from. Only then could you know where you were going.

This was the beginning for Teilani.

He heard her gasp.

Kirk sped around the corner.

Another curve of display cases ran there, also backed by enormous data conduits. Teilani leaned against the tenth case along, her fist against the clear panel. Her cheek pressed against it.

Kirk glanced into the cases as he passed.

Holographic images flashed before him.

Federation starships laying waste to planets.

Romulan and Klingon cities in ruins.

Kirk recognized them as scenarios for battles feared but never fought.

In another case, another display.

Klingon and Romulan bodies among the ruins.

It was as if Kirk looked through a window he had never known. Is this what had driven the two empires? This fear of annihilation? Not knowing that the Federation would never have pursued such destruction. That their fears were groundless.

Among the holographically constructed ruins, Chal emerged.

Male and female Chal, combining the heritage of their creators.

Images flashed.

The Chal worked among the ruins. Lived among the ruins. Children played around them as the ruins were re-formed. As a devastated world was rebuilt.

As the holographic images of the Chal grew old.

Kirk stopped a few meters from Teilani. "Don't you see," he said. "You're not genetically engineered to *fight*. You're genetically engineered to *thrive* in environments polluted by energy radiation, biological warfare agents. You're survivors."

Spock had said it that night at the reception in Starfleet's Great Hall. *Hybrids generally take on the most positive attributes of their parents, becoming exceptional specimens.*

But when Teilani looked at him, tears streaked her young face.

"Teilani, no," Kirk said gently. He reached out to brush the tears and the sorrow from her. "The people who founded this colony loved you. You were their hope for the future. Even if their civilization crumbled in a war that could never happen, you, your brothers and sisters, would carry on to the future. You are their children."

Kirk understood the Klingon phrase now. *Chalchaj 'qmey.* "The Children of Heaven," he said. "All that is good."

But Teilani slowly shook her head. Turned back to the display case. As if mesmerized by its contents.

Kirk moved to her side. Placed an arm around her shoulders.

Looked in.

Saw the holographic displays that so held her.

Felt his stomach tighten.

For what I am going to tell you, please forgive me, Torl had said while captive in the *Enterprise*'s brig. *Remember that in the decades past our people were manipulated by their rulers to hate you. To consider your species as nothing more than animals.*

Genetic engineering was only part of what made the Chal so fit, so strong, so impervious to injury.

There had also been operations.

Transplants. Of tissues and organs.

From *humans.*

This case didn't project holographic simulations.

They were actual real-time images of men and women, some in forty-year-old Starfleet uniforms.

Butchered. By alien surgeons. For the organic material necessary to create each Child of Heaven.

Teilani threw herself into Kirk's rigid arms.

"Forgive me," she cried, racked with sobs.

Torl had called this world an *obscenity.*

For peace to have its chance, let this world die. And all its)secrets with it, he had pleaded.

Kirk understood why now.

So did Teilani.

"The Anarchists are right," she wept. "Chal must be destroyed."

Kirk turned his eyes from the atrocities before him.

The origin of Chal could not be forgotten.

Could never be forgotten.

But the innocent could not be punished with the guilty.

"No," Kirk told Teilani.

She looked up at him in shock. Kirk went on, realizing that each word he said to her was a word he should say to himself.

"Teilani, we're not responsible for the world we're born into. Only for the world we leave when we die. So we have to accept what's gone before us in the past, and work to change the only thing we can—the future."

Teilani's fingers pressed against the display case. "How can I change *this?*"

"You can't."

"Then what's the point of anything?"

Kirk remembered the words Scott had said. *Because otherwise, we will surely go mad, desperately seeking that which we cannae have.* He remembered what Spock had said. *To refuse to accept the inevitable is the first step toward obsolescence, and extinction.*

Kirk wondered how he could have ignored his friends for so long. To not see the treasures that were already part of his life.

"The point is to change what we can. To leave this universe so that others can make it even better. And not to turn away from the challenges it gives us."

McCoy's words came back to him. *The only thing that's new is the* Enterprise-*B*.

For an instant, he saw the new ship's command chair.

And in that instant, he knew he could ignore its siren call.

That chair would be Harriman's challenge.

Kirk knew there would be others for himself.

Not distractions. Not escapes.

But work.

His work.

"Show me how, James. Show me how to not turn away."

Kirk drew Teilani to him and held her close. Without the passion of the past. But with love.

"You already know how," he said gently. "Just by coming down here, you showed you know how."

And Kirk knew how, too.

He had crossed the light-years to discover what he had always known, but never understood.

Life was for living.

No more. No less.

And to wait for it to end, as it must, was to waste it.

His horizon was near.

But for the first time in his life, he felt ready to meet it.

As he felt ready to meet all the challenges of his life.

On his own terms.

"I don't know if the Chal can live with their secret," Teilani said. She forced a smile through her tears. "But I can help them try."

Kirk hugged Teilani.

It was like holding a child in his arms.

A child of the future.

A future he had helped to survive.

"Thank you, James. For being the hero we needed. That I needed."

He kissed her forehead. Her warrior's brow.

"I should thank you," he said. "I suppose we both should—"

"Drop your weapons and raise your hands," a stranger said.

Kirk and Teilani spun around to face a human woman whose drawn phaser was leveled at them.

Kirk had no idea how long she might have been in the Armory with them.

"Who the hell are you?" Kirk asked.

"What a fitting choice of words," the woman said. "I'm Ariadne Drake. And that's where you're headed."

THIRTY-NINE

☆

As soon as she voiced her name, Kirk saw the resemblance, knew who she must be.

"Can't your father fight his own battles?" Kirk asked.

Ariadne flashed a smile, as cold and unfeeling as Kirk remembered Androvar Drake's to be.

"You aren't a battle, Kirk. You're a mopping-up exercise."

She motioned with her phaser. Kirk recognized it as Starfleet-issue.

"Move away from the display case," Ariadne said.

Teilani looked to Kirk. He shook his head.

Teilani stood her ground.

"Isn't that touching," Ariadne said. "You're willing to die for him."

"For my world," Teilani said defiantly.

"What world? Chal is a test tube. And you're just a medical experiment."

Kirk knew he could never draw his disruptor fast enough to drop Ariadne before she fired. So he calculated how many steps it would take to reach her. When she could be expected to fire, how he might roll to avoid it.

But if she didn't track him, she'd be able to hit Teilani.

He wasn't willing to risk that. Not at these odds.

"I won't say it again—move away from the case."

Kirk held his place. The only reason he could see for why Ariadne didn't shoot right away was because she was worried about damaging whatever was in the case. He thought he could use that against her. "You'll never learn what's in it," he said.

"I already know what's there," Ariadne told him. She held up a tricorder. More Starfleet equipment. "I've been watching you and recording since you got here and activated the displays. You see, they aren't triggered by human life signs. Only by animals like her."

"The Chal are not animals," Kirk said.

Ariadne cool glance chilled him. "You've seen how they were bred, how they were *manufactured.* If you can still believe they're human, then my father was right about you. You've lost whatever fire you had."

"At least I haven't lost my mind," Kirk said.

"But you've lost your honor."

Kirk thought that was an odd thing to say. But Teilani reacted more strongly.

Of course, Kirk thought. Her Klingon upbringing. A charge of lost honor was the ultimate insult.

Ariadne was trying to break the bond they shared. Divide and conquer.

"That's a lie," Teilani warned.

"It's the truth," Ariadne said. "He even lied to you about why he came here."

Involuntarily, Teilani glanced at Kirk. She had no experience in confrontations such as this.

"She's just trying to provoke you," Kirk said.

"Go ahead," Ariadne taunted, "ask him why he's here with you."

"He came because he loves me," Teilani said.

Ariadne laughed. She gestured at Kirk with her phaser. "Fool. He's been at war with the Klingon Empire—*and* the Romulans—since before you were born."

"That war's over and done with," Kirk said. He looked at Ariadne. "Put down your phaser. There's nothing here for you."

"Oh, yes there is. I want what *you* came for. Eternal youth."

"There is no youth here," Kirk said. And with that he finally accepted the truth for himself. In a world undamaged by war, Teilani and her people would stay young for decades. It was in their genetic structure. But there was nothing on Chal that he had not brought himself.

Love. Excitement. Challenge.

Passion.

Spock had been right.

Teilani looked at Kirk, confused. "But James, you said you felt younger. You are younger."

Kirk couldn't help smiling, in spite of Ariadne's phaser. "You didn't give me any choice. Keeping up with you is like training for a marathon."

"He's lying to you," Ariadne sneered. "He's known all about the Children of Heaven project from the beginning. What it could mean to him."

"It can mean *nothing* to me," Kirk said. "The Chal have been genetically engineered for health and youth. Their bodies' systems have been augmented by transplants."

"Human transplants," Ariadne said with a terrible smile. "And that works both ways."

Kirk saw instantly what Ariadne meant.

But Teilani didn't.

"Eternal youth—from the combination of Klingon and Romulan genetics, and human tissue," Ariadne explained. "For the process to work on the Chal, their creators used transplants from human donors of tissues that could not be cloned. But humans already have those tissues. So for the process to work on us, all we will need will be transplants from the Chal."

Teilani grabbed Kirk's arm. "James, is that true?"

Kirk's expression confirmed her fears.

"See?" Ariadne gloated. "That's all you are to Kirk. That's all any of the Chal are to humans. Cattle. Bred as a source of transplant tissues."

Teilani looked at Kirk with an expression of betrayal. *"Did* you know about us?"

"No," Kirk said.

"Ask him if he wanted youth," Ariadne said.

Kirk didn't wait to be asked. "I came here because of you, Teilani."

"But who brought you to the Armory?" Ariadne asked. "Kirk did. Because of the library computer. He knows it has all the medical files he needs to understand the process that created you. So he can be young forever."

Teilani had no defenses against the poison Ariadne spewed.

But Kirk did. And Kirk had heard the one piece of information he had been missing.

The library computer. Ariadne said he wanted the files in it. Which meant *she* wanted the files.

That was why she hadn't killed them where they stood. Phaser emissions might disrupt the energy flow in the data conduits that ringed the display cases.

"For the last time," Ariadne said. "Move away."

Kirk took Teilani into his arms. She fought against him but he hissed a question into her ear.

"How long can you stop your heart?"

The question stopped her.

"Step away from her!" Ariadne warned.

"How long?" Kirk repeated.

"Three minutes, maybe four," Teilani said.

"If you want to know the truth, do it," Kirk whispered.

"Now!" Ariadne shouted.

Kirk stepped back from Teilani. "I had to say good-bye."

Ariadne aimed her phaser.

Kirk began to move to the side, away from the case.

"You, too," Ariadne told Teilani.

Teilani's eyes rolled up to show her whites.

With a moan, she slumped to the floor.

The attackers at the farm had used the same trick of autonomic self-control to make Kirk think he had killed them. So he would leave their bodies and allow them to escape.

"I'm not falling for that," Ariadne said. "If you—"

In the absence of Klingon-Romulan life signs, the lights of the Armory cut out.

Instantly, Kirk was enveloped in absolute darkness.

He heard Ariadne swear. Heard her phaser beep as she adjusted its power settings.

But by then his disruptor was in his hand and he fired.

Full power.

In the strobelike flashes of the weapon's discharge, the display case exploded.

Kirk dropped to the floor, skidded to the side as Ariadne fired a stun burst where he had been standing.

He fired again, into the data conduits.

A chain reaction sped along the gray panels behind the row of cases.

Ariadne's voice rose with rage.

Kirk changed position again.

But this time Ariadne didn't fire.

He heard her boots charge across the stone floor even as a series of explosions blossomed at connecting points along the data conduits.

The lights in the Armory began to power up again.

Kirk ran to Teilani as she returned to consciousness.

She looked around in confusion, silently asking what happened.

"I destroyed the computer."

Teilani stared at him intently, seeking truth. Seeking honor.

"Then you've destroyed the secret that could have made you young forever."

Kirk thought of Torl's words.

"But at what cost?"

Kirk heard Ariadne curse.

He left Teilani, ran to the woman.

She had broken the transparent panel of a different display

case, stepped into it. There was a library computer console inside. She was frantically trying to pull datachips from it.

But flames flickered at its side. The metal was blistering hot.

Ariadne's fingers were streaked with blood.

Kirk reached through the shattered panel and pulled her out.

She kicked and struggled in his grip.

"You fool! You don't know what you've done!"

"Yes, I do," Kirk told her.

He grabbed Ariadne's phaser from her belt. It was set to kill. But before he could adjust it, he heard a transporter cascade begin.

Five meters away, four columns of light took form.

Orange columns, not blue.

Klingons.

And Androvar Drake was with them.

FORTY

Kirk held the phaser to Ariadne's head.

But the three Klingons aimed their disruptors at Kirk as if Ariadne weren't present.

The commander in chief of Starfleet simply smiled.

"Go ahead, Jimbo. Press the firing stud."

"At this range," Kirk warned, "even stun can be fatal."

"C'est la guerre," the admiral said. "Isn't that right, Commander Drake?"

Ariadne didn't struggle against Kirk's chokehold. "I'm ready to die for what I believe in."

Admiral Drake folded his hands behind his back. "Like father like daughter, eh, Jimbo?" He took a step forward.

Kirk felt the heat from the flames in the shattered display case behind him. Teilani ran to his side.

One Klingon tracked her with his disruptor as if he were computer-guided.

"What's keeping you, Jimbo?" Drake taunted. "Oh, that's right, I forgot. You're the fraud in Starfleet. The famous starship captain who chokes when it counts."

Kirk shoved the emitter node of the phaser against Ariadne's temple, making her gasp with surprise. "I'm not in Starfleet anymore. I've got nothing to lose."

"Except your nerve. Isn't that right, Jimbo?" Drake advanced another step. "Like when you hesitated on Tycho IV? You think Captain Garrovick would believe you now? Do you think he'd believe you might actually *do* something?"

"I did the right thing on Tycho IV, Drake. More than you know."

"What excuse have you got for the war, Jimbo?"

Kirk didn't follow Drake's reasoning. He glanced at the Klingons. One was making hand gestures to the other. A battle code, Kirk knew. But he couldn't decipher it.

"What war?"

"*The* war," Drake said. "The great war that never happened. Because of you. And you don't even remember, do you?"

Kirk shook his head. The Klingons began to spread out, keeping Kirk, Ariadne, and Teilani in their crossfire.

Admiral Drake looked up at the distant ceiling, admiring the Bird-of-Prey.

"Twenty-seven, twenty-eight years ago. Stardate 3198.4. Doesn't ring a bell? I was in the Kalinora Sector. Two Klingon battle cruisers had picked off a Starfleet hospital ship. Said it was on a spying mission." Drake looked back at Kirk. Something had changed in him. His eyes were even colder, emptier.

"A spying mission, Jimbo. Women and children were on that ship. *My wife* was on that ship."

Kirk stepped back, closer to the flames. Teilani followed. Ariadne didn't fight him. The curve of the display cases meant the Klingons couldn't flank him. But Kirk knew that if Drake really did believe his daughter was expendable, they could drop Kirk at any moment.

"The galaxy was different back then," Kirk said. "We were on the brink of war."

"Oh, we weren't on the brink of war, Jimbo. We were *at* war. I chased those Klingon ships." Drake ran a finger along his scar. "Got this blowing the first one out of space. Told Starfleet what had happened. The Code One signal went out. We *were* at war."

Kirk remembered that. Not the date, but Starfleet's declaration of war. It seemed fitting to Kirk that that low point in Federation history had somehow been precipitated by Drake.

Kirk tightened his grip around Ariadne's shoulders and neck. It was clear that the Klingons were going to try and stun him from different angles at once, hoping he wouldn't be able to discharge the phaser in time. It was a risky strategy. A disruptor stun made muscles contract. Even in the face of a heavy disruptor fire, Kirk would be able to fire the phaser. "That war never went anywhere," Kirk said.

"Because of you," Drake shot back. A vein pulsed in his neck. "You brought the Organians into the war. And the Organians stopped it before it could begin. Before I could punish the Klingons who had killed my wife."

"If your Klingons fire now, you'll be killing your own daughter."

"But I'll be able to take revenge on the one responsible, won't I?"

For just an instant, Kirk wondered what it would be like to tighten his arm against Ariadne's throat. To feel her struggle. Go limp. Die by his hand. "You already have," he said quietly.

Drake cocked his head, as if not quite understanding what Kirk meant.

Then Drake smiled.

Genuinely.

"Ah, you found out about David. The young man eager to make a name for himself. Hungry for protomatter."

An explosion echoed through the vast chamber. The Klingons turned their heads to see a ball of flame roll along the data conduit opposite Kirk's position. Whatever chain reaction Kirk had set off inside the library computer, it was spreading.

But Drake was not distracted. His complete attention focused on Kirk. As it had been since they'd first met at the Academy.

"You should be proud of your son," Drake said. "Thanks to his pioneering work and great sacrifices, Starfleet will be resuming protomatter research. Under my direction. In fact, when we test the first protobomb, you can be sure I'll give David the public honor he's due."

"He was a child!" Kirk said. "He didn't know the risks!"

"Neither do you, Jimbo." Drake shook his head in scorn. "Now, either kill my daughter or drop your weapon. For once in your life, do something!"

Kirk thought of David. He increased the pressure on the firing stud.

He wanted to see Drake broken.

Defeated by the greatest loss a parent could know.

As Kirk had been defeated on the Genesis Planet.

And it would be so easy now.

But at what cost?

Kirk dropped the phaser, kicked it away. Released Ariadne.

She hesitated a moment, then rushed to her father's side.

Drake smirked at him. "I always knew you were a coward, Kirk."

Teilani stayed with Kirk. Held his arm. Protected. Not protecting.

"I know what it's like to lose a child," Kirk said. "I won't be a party to that. Even to stop you."

Drake walked over to retrieve Ariadne's phaser. "I'm so very deeply touched. As will be my associates in Starfleet Command." Drake changed the setting on the phaser. Pointed it at Kirk. "There're are seven of us left. Not even Cartwright knew us all. Safer that way."

"Who are they?" Kirk asked.

"All you need to know is that they're patriots, dedicated to keeping the Federation free of alien influences. We've had too much of that recently." Drake waved the phaser at Teilani. "That's all right, Teilani. The charade is over. You can come back to me, now."

Kirk knew Drake had said that only to hurt him. But then he felt Teilani shrink closer to him.

"That's right," Drake said with amusement. "She's been working for me all along."

Kirk looked into Teilani's eyes. The flames from the display case and the data conduits flashed madly in them. Along with the truth.

"I'm sorry, James."

It explained so much Kirk wasn't even surprised.

"That's why you didn't approach me at the reception, isn't it? Because Drake was with me. And you knew him."

"He told me you wouldn't understand."

"But I do."

"My people needed help to survive the Anarchists' attacks. My aides said the admiral was going to be the new commander of Starfleet. That I should go to him. But Drake said the Federation couldn't get involved in a Klingon-Romulan matter. He said you were retiring. That you'd accept the challenge."

"I gave her your psych file," Drake snickered. "You were an open book."

Kirk wouldn't give Drake the satisfaction of seeing how he really felt.

"You did what you had to do," he told Teilani. An innocent pawn in a game between Kirk and an old enemy.

She squeezed his hand. "But I did fall in love with you. You must believe that."

Kirk raised her hand to his lips and kissed it. "I do."

Then Kirk turned to face Drake. "I think I can put the rest together. How you needed someone not involved in Starfleet to locate Chal."

Drake nodded imperiously.

"I'm curious. What were you going to do with the Children of Heaven process?" Kirk asked. "Bribe Federation officials with eternal youth? Get them to overturn treaties? Stop the peace talks?"

"Everyone has a price, Jimbo. Yours has always been your vanity."

"I think you're underestimating the people we have in Starfleet," Kirk said. "They won't accept such outright manipulation."

Drake's phaser never wavered. "Think again, Jimbo. Cartwright *almost* succeeded. Throw in a few assassinations, a border incident or two, and the paranoia so recently buried in humanity will come back in force. I guarantee it. I've made an exhaustive study of it. Under my guidance, my vision, the Federation will become stronger than ever before. It's the only way it can survive."

Kirk slipped his arm around Teilani, holding her closely to him.

"Study your history, Drake. If threats of war, bribery, and murder are the only way the Federation can survive, then it doesn't deserve to."

Drake smiled. He handed his phaser to his daughter. "That kind of attitude only proves your cowardice, Jimbo. You know what your problem is? You just can't see the future. Never have. Never will."

Kirk's grip on Teilani was like duranium. "I can see the future well enough." As if adjusting his collar, he tugged on the lapel of his jacket. Drake didn't even blink at the tiny movement. "That's why I didn't even think of coming here without knowing how to get back."

Drake frowned uneasily. He turned to his daughter.

Then Kirk gave an order he had never given before.

"Beam me up, Scotty."

As the Armory dissolved into energy around him, Kirk had the fleeting impression of a phaser beam crackling through the space he had occupied a heartbeat before.

But it had no effect on him or Teilani.

Drake had lost his battle.

Now it was time to make certain he lost the war.

FORTY-ONE

Kirk stepped down from the transporter platform the instant the beam released him.

"Scotty—tell whoever's on communications to raise the *Excelsior.* We have to get a message to Starfleet Command *now.*"

Scott grinned from behind the transporter console. "I think ye'd better talk to communications yerself, sir."

Kirk wasn't in the mood for games. He hit the transmit control on the console. "Kirk to bridge."

"Spock here, Captain."

"Spock?" Kirk slowly realized that he was standing with his mouth open. "What are you doing here?"

"It appears I am waiting for your orders."

Kirk looked at Scott.

Scott shrugged. "Captain Spock and the others thought ye might need a wee bit o' help."

"The others?"

"Aye. It's like old home week, if ye ask me."

Kirk told Teilani to follow him. He ran out the doors toward the closest turbolift. He was on the bridge in less than a minute.

Spock was in the center chair, vacating it the instant Kirk stepped from the turbolift.

Uhura was at what was left of communications.

Chekov was at tactical.

And McCoy was trying to stay out of the way at the engineering station. Which is exactly where Scott headed, sending the doctor grumbling over to environmental.

Kirk had to pause for a moment to take it all in.

He was back.

They were *all* back. Except for Sulu.

"I . . . I don't know what to say," Kirk stammered.

The *Enterprise* suddenly rocked with the impact of a direct disruptor hit.

"'Go to Red Alert' might be appropriate," Spock suggested.

Kirk jumped into his chair. "Red alert! Full shields! Chekov—report!"

"Drake has transported back to the Klingon wessel, Keptin! He is attacking!"

Kirk gripped the arms of his chair as the *Enterprise* rocked again. "Mr. Esys, bring us about. Chekov, lock phase—*disruptors* on Drake's ship. Spock—what happened after you withdrew?"

"Admiral Drake did not pursue our insubordination with a formal inquiry."

"Disruptors locked on, sir!"

"See what they've got, Mr. Chekov. Fire!"

On the main viewscreen, the Klingon battle cruiser shuddered as its shields flared in a sphere of glowing orange light.

"Their shields are tuned to disruptor fire," Chekov reported with disappointment.

"Photon torpedoes, Mr. Chekov. Target their port nacelle."

Kirk turned back to Spock. "Didn't hold an inquiry? So you immediately knew he had something to hide."

"Precisely," Spock said.

McCoy stepped down behind Kirk's chair. Kirk twisted around. "Teilani, may I introduce Dr. Leonard McCoy. Dr. McCoy—Teilani."

Teilani raised an amused eyebrow at Kirk as McCoy kissed the back of her hand.

"Charmed, m'dear," McCoy said with his best Southern drawl.

"James has told me a great deal about you, Doctor."

"Very little of it is true, I can assure you."

"Torpedoes loaded!" Chekov announced.

"Fire at will."

The inductance twang of the torpedo launcher echoed twice in the bridge.

Two explosions flared off the Klingon's shields.

"Their shields are at ninety percent," Spock said. "As are ours."

"So we're evenly matched?" Kirk asked. He was surprised at how good it felt to be back in the midst of action. Even battle.

"Not exactly," Spock said. "We do have the *Excelsior* standing by."

"Uhura, hail Captain Sulu."

"Aye, Captain."

An instant later, Sulu was on the main viewscreen. He looked contrite.

"Captain Kirk, I believe I owe you an apology."

But Kirk would not accept it. "None needed, Captain Sulu. I'm well aware of the chain of command. You handled a difficult situation with—"

Bridge lights flashed as a Klingon torpedo hit the *Enterprise*'s shields.

"No damage," Spock said.

"Return fire, Mr. Chekov," Kirk ordered. Then he turned his attention back to Sulu. "As I was saying, I'm well aware of how awkward it is to be caught in the middle like that."

Sulu looked relieved. "Thank you, sir. With Admiral Drake on one side—"

"Oh, I didn't mean Drake," Kirk interrupted. "I meant Spock and McCoy."

Sulu laughed.

"You did what you had to do," Kirk continued, suddenly serious. "As a starship captain, you had no other choice."

"Our disruptors aren't making any dent in her shields," Chekov said. He looked at Kirk. Then at Sulu on the viewscreen. For all they had been through, there were no hard feelings between them.

Chekov sighed. It seemed he still had a great deal to learn about starship captains.

"Captain Sulu, stand ready to make your presence known," Kirk said. "Uhura, hail the Klingon vessel."

Sulu flickered off the viewscreen to be replaced by Drake, calmly sitting in the Klingon ship's center chair.

"Do you want to hear my terms for your surrender, Jimbo?" Drake asked.

"That won't be necessary, Drake. Captain Sulu, take out the Klingon's nacelles, please."

Drake gripped the sides of his chair as the Klingon bridge twisted under the *Excelsior*'s phaser barrage.

Drake barked out commands in Klingon.

Kirk heard photon torpedoes being launched over the Klingon audio pickup.

"The *Excelsior* is evading fire," Spock announced.

"Very good," Kirk told the admiral. "But you can't keep up firepower like that forever."

"I don't have to," Drake said. "As far as I'm concerned, you lost this fight the day you arrived."

The viewscreen cut back to an image of near space in Chal orbit. Drake's battle cruiser began to bank.

"His warp engines are powering up," Chekov said.

Kirk was puzzled. It wasn't like Drake to run from a fight.

Then the Klingon ship stretched into a rainbow streak and was gone.

"Heading, Mr. Chekov?"

"Out of the system, sir. No obvious destination."

Teilani grabbed Kirk and kissed him. Kirk saw McCoy and Uhura's surprised reactions.

But he didn't care.

"James! You beat him!"

"Not yet," Kirk said. He glanced over at Spock. "We have to keep Drake from contacting any of his co-conspirators in Starfleet Command. Start tracking him, Mr. Esys."

Then Sulu came back onscreen. "Captain Kirk, are you analyzing Drake's course?"

Kirk looked down at Chekov. "Mr. Chekov?"

Chekov shook his head. "These sensors can't track him at high varp speed."

"Is there a problem, Sulu?"

Sulu looked as if there were. "I'm transmitting our sensor readings to your science station."

A few moments later, Spock looked up from his viewers. After thirty years of friendship, Kirk could read the signs of alarm in Spock's placid expression.

"The admiral is moving into a slingshot trajectory."

"No," McCoy said in shock.

"What does that mean, James?"

Kirk pounded his fist against the arm of his chair. "He's attempting to go back through time. Probably to ambush us a week ago, before I had a chance to destroy the library computer in the Armory. That's what he meant when he said I had lost the day I had arrived here."

"Can he really go back to the past?"

"Unfortunately." Kirk turned back to Sulu. "Captain Sulu, has any ship of the *Excelsior*'s design ever undergone a temporal slingshot maneuver?"

Grimly, Sulu shook his head.

"The *Enterprise* has," Kirk said.

"But not in its present configuration," Spock cautioned.

"Close enough, Spock." Kirk held out his hand to Sulu. "What do you say, Captain? One last time around the block?"

Sulu grinned. "I always seem to say that. Stand by, *Enterprise.*"

The viewscreen jumped back to show Chal.

"James, I don't understand."

"Sulu has navigated us through the slingshot maneuver several times," Kirk said. "Better drop shields, Mr. Chekov."

A moment after Chekov's acknowledgment, a transporter beam formed before the viewscreen.

Sulu stepped from it.

"Request permission to come aboard," he said. Then he went straight to the navigator's station.

Mr. Esys slipped out of his chair.

"Captain Sulu," Kirk said. "Lay in an intercept course and proceed."

Sulu manipulated the helm controls like a concert pianist. Chal fell away from the viewscreen and the stars began to smear as the *Enterprise* jumped to warp.

Scott leaned down by Kirk. "I dinna know if this is th' time t' be tellin' ye, but I dinna think th' *Enterprise* can withstand a temporal jump."

Kirk felt like laughing. He was back in a life-or-death chase on the bridge of the *Enterprise,* with his full command crew at his side.

All of them. Even Sulu.

No matter what the future held, he knew he could not lose today.

"With any luck, Mr. Scott, we'll intercept Drake before he snaps around the sun."

The bridge rumbled with the whine of the warp engines. But the stars moved faster. The *Enterprise* still accelerated.

"We're going to hit some gravimetric turbulence," Sulu warned. "That's a binary sun."

"The Klingon ship's not built for this kind of action," Kirk said. "Just get us within disruptor range so we can spoil his trajectory. Uhura, keep us in touch with the *Excelsior.* We'll want her in position when Drake comes around the primary star."

Then Kirk kept his eyes fixed on the viewscreen. Chal's binary suns began to fill it. Drake's vessel was a slender streak of silver light heading between them.

"Drake is close to temporal dislocation," Spock said.

"Faster, Captain Sulu."

The bridge began to vibrate.

Scott's eyes widened nervously.

Kirk winked at him. "She'll hold," he mouthed silently. He could feel it.

"Coming up on disruptor range," Chekov said.

"Twenty seconds from temporal dislocation," Spock announced.

"Lock disruptors," Kirk ordered.

The viewscreen blazed with the yellow primary and orange secondary sun. The plasma bridge between them writhed like a living creature.

"Fifteen seconds," Spock said.

"Disruptors locked—but she's still out of range, Keptin."

Kirk felt Teilani's hand tighten on his arm. "James, what happens if Drake gets away?"

"Don't worry, if he *had* escaped, we wouldn't be here to chase him," Kirk said. "Right, Spock?"

"Actually, Captain, no. This could just be an alternate timeline in which the quantum probability waves—"

Kirk held up his hand to stop his science officer. "You know time travel gives me a headache, Spock."

"Ten seconds," Spock said.

"Entering the plasma bridge," Sulu shouted.

On the viewscreen, the yellow primary rushed to one side as the orange secondary rushed past the other.

Now the screen was filled with twisting tendrils of superheated plasma—the surface of the smaller star being peeled away by the awesome gravitational forces of the larger star.

Slicing through those tendrils, Drake's ship was a dark dagger.

A warning chime sounded.

"Shields at seventy-three percent and falling," Scott said. "She canna take these temperatures for long."

"Five . . ." Spock counted down. "Four . . . three . . ."

"In range!"

"Fire!"

The viewscreen flared with flickering disruptor feedback.

The *Enterprise* screamed as her frame twisted from her passage through the plasma bridge and the opposing gravitational fields of the stars.

"Got her!" Chekov shouted.

"Drake's ship has dropped from warp," Spock said. "He did not achieve temporal dislocation."

"Full magnification!"

On the viewscreen, Drake's ship cartwheeled slowly through the plasma streams, disappearing into a wall of seething light.

"Stay with her, Sulu." In the time it had taken Kirk to give that order, the *Enterprise* had overshot Drake's crippled ship by tens of thousands of kilometers. But Sulu brought the ship around and dropped her to impulse speeds as well, returning her to the point of last contact.

Kirk scanned the glowing patterns of braided light on the viewscreen. "Where is he?" Kirk asked.

"There is no sign of the Klingon ship, Captain. But our sensor capabilities are degrading." There was unexpected tension in Spock's voice. "We cannot scan more than a few hundred kilometers in any direction."

"Any sign of debris?" Kirk asked.

"The exterior temperature is in excess of thirty thousand degrees Kelvin. If Drake's shields have failed, physical debris would exist for only a few seconds at most."

"Any sign that's what happened?"

"No, sir," Spock said. "And no indication of an operative impulse drive either."

"Then we have to assume that he's in here with us. Either lying in wait or needing rescue." Kirk shifted in his chair. He wiped at the sweat on his forehead. It wasn't a good sign. The bridge felt a good ten degrees warmer than usual. "How are we doing, Scotty?"

The engineer answered from his station behind Kirk. "Not too well, sir. Our radiation shields can only take another twenty minutes o' this punishment. So we'll have t' pull out in ten."

Kirk didn't understand. "Scotty, at full impulse we can be out of the plasma in under thirty seconds."

But Scott shook his head. "We canna go t' full impulse in this kind of environment, sir. We canna afford to reduce our shields even a tiny bit to vent our impulse exhaust, so we're limited to no more than ten percent."

Kirk knew better than to argue with Scott about absolutes. "Did you hear that, Captain Sulu?" Kirk said. "We have ten minutes to find Drake."

McCoy moved around to where Kirk could see him. "Jim, is that a good idea? What if he's already out of here? He could be trying another slingshot run right now."

"Unlikely, Doctor," Spock said from his science station. "Drake knows the *Excelsior* is still on patrol. He will no longer have the element of surprise on his side, and so cannot reasonably expect to succeed in another attempt to slingshot."

"So what are you saying, Spock? He's hanging around in this garden spot looking for us?"

"If his ship was not too badly damaged by our disruptor blast, his shields and sensors will be up to full military strength. He will, therefore, be in a position of strength in this environment."

McCoy frowned at Kirk. "If you need a translation, Jim, I think that means we should get out of here."

Kirk listened carefully to each word Spock and McCoy said. But he didn't take his eyes off the viewscreen.

The plasma threads were hypnotic.

They flowed past the *Enterprise* like glowing currents of luminous water.

Kirk thought of Chal. The way the waves rippled up on the beach.

The planet had been one type of paradise.

But this ship was another.

The one that counted.

"Picking up something," Chekov said tentatively.

Spock studied his readouts. "It could be a ship," he said.

"But which one?" Kirk asked. "Drake's or the *Excelsior?*"

"We should know in a moment. . . . We're getting a stronger—"

Then the viewscreen flared brilliant white and even as Kirk flew from his chair, he knew his ship had been hit by a photon torpedo.

FORTY-TWO

☆

Ariadne turned around from her weapons station on the bridge of the Klingon cruiser.

"Direct hit!"

Drake leaned forward in his command chair. His eyes drank in the scintillating whorls and eddies of the plasma bridge between the stars.

And *there*—one dark spinning spot dead ahead—was the *Enterprise.*

With James T. Kirk trapped helplessly inside her.

All that Drake hated. And feared.

Small enough to be blotted out with his thumb.

"QIH poj!" Drake commanded.

The Klingon science officer analyzed his readings. "Damage as follows . . . no impulse engines . . . shields at thirty-three percent . . . failure estimated within five minutes."

Drake sat back in his chair, overcome with contentment. "Navigator, take us in. I want a clear view."

The navigator hesitated only long enough that Drake knew something was wrong. But the cruiser slipped forward, gently buffeted by the jets of starstuff.

"Admiral," the science officer said uncertainly, "may I remind you that *our* shields are only at forty-two percent. We cannot last much longer than the Federation vessel."

"But we *can* last longer," Drake said. "Which means we can last forever, compared with Kirk."

Drake stepped down from his chair and stood behind his

daughter. Placed his hand on her shoulder. Felt her take his hand in hers.

"Now that you've met him," Drake said, "you understand, don't you?"

"Why you hate him?" Ariadne asked.

Drake nodded.

She shrugged. "To tell the truth, he reminded me of you."

Drake's hand closed tighter and tighter on his daughter's hand until she pulled it away from him. "Except for one thing," he told her. "I am better than Kirk and always have been. This day proves that. Finally."

The *Enterprise* floated in the center of the screen, slowly turning in the pressure of the raging plasma currents.

"No inertial control," Drake said. "That means they're putting all their power into shields."

"Tuned to radiation only," the science officer confirmed. "Sensors show artificial gravity is also off."

"Ahh," Drake sighed happily. "Desperation." He looked over his shoulder at the science officer. "What's the internal temperature?"

"In the bridge, thirty-seven degrees. Climbing rapidly."

Drake smiled fiercely, not noticing the perspiration running down his own face.

"Admiral, *our* interior temperature is thirty-three degrees. Also climbing rapidly."

"Yes," Drake agreed. "But we have impulse power. We can leave at any time."

"Why don't we finish him off?" Ariadne asked. "Another torpedo will overload his shields. Then we can leave with a margin of safety."

Drake nodded. He had raised his daughter properly. "Very well. Stand by on torpedo. But hail Kirk for me. I want him to know who's responsible. I want to be the last thing he sees."

"The *Enterprise* is not responding."

For an instant, disappointment flashed across Drake's face. Then he brightened.

"So, he stayed a coward to the end."

"Her shields are fluctuating."

The *Enterprise* seemed to shimmer.

"She's gone into overload," Ariadne said. Her tone was even and colorless.

Drake leaned forward, face now dripping with sweat, fists clenched in expectation.

"Yesss," he breathed. "You know I'm out here, Kirk . . . doing this to you . . ."

Plasma sparks jumped along the *Enterprise*'s nacelles.

Drake licked his lips.

Ariadne kept up her calm commentary. "There go her generators. Emergency batteries coming online. They'll only be good for a few seconds."

The port nacelle strut began to twist.

"Structural integrity field is overcompensating."

The nacelles flared, one after the other.

"Hull breach!"

The engineering hull blossomed into a tiny sun.

"Antimatter release!"

The saucer buckled.

For a breathless moment, the bridge dome rose out of the saucer's center as the outer rim shattered like ice.

"Superheated overpressure . . ."

And then the saucer tore itself apart like a starship made of sand, crushed by an unstoppable wave.

In seconds, all that remained of the *Enterprise* was a river of sparkling, incandescent wreckage, flaring as the plasma reduced it to glowing, disassociated ions.

Drake was exhausted.

He stumbled back to his chair. His uniform was drenched.

It was over.

Kirk was defeated.

Even running the Federation was going to be a letdown after that.

"Navigator," Drake said, "plot a course to take us out of here."

"Uh, Admiral," the science officer said, "we are being hailed."

Drake shrugged. He had been expecting this. "The *Excelsior?"* he asked. Sulu was an annoyance, but he could be dealt with.

"No, sir. It's . . . uh . . . it's Kirk."

Ariadne paled as her father screamed.

His anger was a match for the torrent of plasma they rode.

FORTY-THREE

Kirk stepped forward as Androvar Drake appeared on the *Excelsior*'s main viewscreen.

It was the first time he had ever seen Drake overwhelmed by emotion.

"I saw you die!" Drake said.

"No one died," Kirk told him. His command crew was at his side, along with Teilani. They had been safely transported from the *Enterprise* with her skeleton crew of Chal, minutes before her shields failed, leaving her as a decoy to draw Drake closer. "You only saw the *Enterprise* go out in a blaze of glory. Just the way you wanted."

Someone spoke to Drake on the Klingon bridge. But he stared straight ahead, his eyes feverish. Fixed on Kirk as if nothing else existed for him in the universe.

"Admiral," Kirk said. "I want you to tune your shields to

reflect radiation only. We're going to have to beam you and your crew to the *Excelsior.*"

"You couldn't fool a midshipman with that tactic, Jimbo."

"It's not a tactic. We're monitoring your shield status. They won't last long enough to let you leave the plasma bridge. You wanted to watch me die so much that you hesitated, Drake. The same sin you accused me of. But in your case, it wasn't the right thing to do." Kirk allowed himself the luxury of a smile. *"C'est la guerre."*

Drake sat at rigid attention in his chair. A Klingon chair.

"Every time we've gone head-to-head, I've beaten you, Jimbo. Now it's come down to whose vision of the Federation is going to survive."

Spock stepped up beside Kirk. "He has less than five minutes of shields remaining."

"Drake," Kirk said, "let's continue the debate over here."

"You're the past, I'm the future. Always have been."

Drake imperiously pointed his finger at someone offscreen. Ariadne moved into view, said something into his ear.

Chekov and Uhura both reacted with surprise. "That's Jade," Uhura said.

"The rogue agent," Chekov added.

"She's Drake's daughter," Kirk said, so much becoming clear. "Admiral, please—if not for yourself, then for your crew. For your daughter."

"Set a course for the rendezvous point," Drake said to Ariadne. "We'll deal with the *Excelsior* when we've been reinforced. Full impulse till we're out of the plasma. Then maximum warp."

"Admiral—you can't do that. Full impulse will overload your shields in here."

On the viewscreen, Ariadne turned to look out at Kirk. It was impossible to tell what she was thinking.

Kirk turned to his science officer. "Tell her, Spock. Tell her what readings to look for."

"Check the radiation pressure on your aft shields," Spock

said. "You will see it is out of balance and will not withstand impulse venting."

Ariadne looked at her father.

He shook his head.

"Get us out of here," he said.

Ariadne moved offscreen.

Kirk remembered her words in the Armory. *I'm ready to die for what I believe in.*

"Check the readings, Drake. Let me get you out of there."

"So you can win?"

Kirk knew Drake wasn't going to allow himself to be saved.

"So your daughter—your child—won't die."

A terrible smile twisted across Drake's sweat-covered face. Kirk remembered it from Tycho IV. When they had been surrounded by death. When Drake had believed they would not survive because he had no faith in Captain Garrovick.

"See you in hell, Jimbo." Drake pointed forward. His voice was hoarse but sure. "Take us out."

There was nothing more Kirk could do. He had no choice but to accept the inevitable.

Drake looked directly into the viewscreen. Kirk knew he would be the last thing Drake would see. "Full im—"

The image from the Klingon bridge winked out.

The viewscreen showed the Klingon battle cruiser flare as its shields failed.

It seemed to expand in all directions at once, dissolving in a shower of sparks.

One of them was Drake.

One of them was Drake's child.

Teilani took Kirk's hand. "He believed you, James. About the shields. I saw it in his eyes."

"I know," Kirk said.

"So why could he not accept your offer to save him?"

Kirk stared at the coils and jets of the plasma stream.

There was no trace of Drake's ship.

No trace of the *Enterprise.*

"Once, he was a starship captain," Kirk said. "And starship captains think they're invincible."

"Why, James?"

Kirk smiled. Sadly. Proudly. He had always known the answer to that question, but at this moment, in this place, it meant more to him than it ever had before.

Because it was *the* answer.

"They have to be," he said. "It's their job."

Trailing streamers of fire, the *Excelsior* came about.

She flew for Chal.

FORTY-FOUR

☆

As Chekov stepped onto the *Excelsior*'s bridge, Chal was a jewel on the main viewscreen, so brilliant she cast blue light over the station-keeping crew.

Mr. Scott was debating some fine point about warp balance with the engineer.

Uhura and Janice Rand were whispering together, laughing.

Sulu was in his command chair, sipping tea.

He glanced up at Chekov as Chekov stood beside him, hands behind his back.

"Have you been down there?" Sulu asked.

Chekov shook his head. "Another time, perhaps." The *Excelsior* had to be under way within the hour. A full session of the Federation Council had been called to investigate Drake's actions. Kirk was to be a key witness.

"I hear it's a paradise," Sulu said.

"Eden," Chekov agreed.

They stared at the screen in silence.

Chekov wondered what it was about humans that they spent their lives looking for Edens, knowing it was the one place they could never remain.

After a few long moments, he cleared his throat. "I heard you apologize to the keptin."

Sulu put down his tea cup. So gently it didn't make a sound against its saucer.

"His view of the situation was correct," Sulu said. "I didn't know it at the time. I should have." Sulu grinned for a moment. "He *is* Captain Kirk, after all."

"I vould like to apologize," Chekov said abruptly. "To you."

Sulu looked at Chekov, perplexed.

"For punching you," Chekov quickly explained. "Vhen you saved us from Dark Range. And for arguing with you. Doubting your command decisions. Trying to fight you again vhen—"

Sulu nodded, motioned for Chekov to stop. "I don't need a list, Pavel."

Chekov grimaced. Stopped talking. Rocked back on his heels. "Vell, anyvay. I apologize."

Sulu smiled as if to say the apology wasn't necessary. "I think we all got on each other's nerves this time out."

Chekov glanced back. Mr. Scott and Uhura were coming over, apparently interested to know what Sulu and Chekov were discussing.

"You think by now ve'd be used to each other."

Sulu stared across at the viewscreen. Chekov saw the way he gripped the arms of his chair. The same way Captain Kirk did.

Chekov had tried it once. Knew why Kirk and Sulu did it. So they could feel their ships. Sense the vibrations of the engines. Feel a part of them.

Sulu was born to sit in that chair.

The captain of the *Excelsior* looked around to see his friends gathered at his side. "Maybe when we're all together, we need the captain to keep us from each other's throats," he said.

But Chekov shook his head. "No. I think maybe, ve're just a family. Ve have had our good days. Ve have had our bad ones."

Chekov held out his hand in friendship.

Sulu took it. "But mostly, we've had good ones, haven't we?" he said.

Scott and Uhura agreed.

So did Chekov. "To tell the truth, looking back, they've all been good. And the days ahead vill be even better."

Sulu gave Chekov a skeptical look. "You think we'll all be together again?" He looked out at the viewscreen, past Chal, to the stars. "Out there?"

The stars filled Chekov's eyes and he smiled. "A man can dream, can't he?"

FORTY-FIVE

The suns of Chal were setting.

They cast long shadows on the beach.

Kirk found Teilani there.

She was sitting on a smooth, sea-polished log that was half-buried in the sand. She wore the loose white tunic of Chal, her legs drawn up, arms wrapped around them. Staring out at the deepening red of the sky.

He sat beside her. Wordlessly gave her his gift.

She unwrapped the cloth he had bundled around the thin, rectangular object.

It was a metal plaque.

The plaque.

Kirk had pulled it from the bulkhead by the turbolift, just before he had left the *Enterprise* for the final time.

Just before he had consigned her to the flames and the stars and all eternity.

Teilani ran her fingers across the raised letters.

"U.S.S. Enterprise," she read.

Kirk heard the question in her voice. She didn't know what the plaque meant. He wondered if anyone could truly know, except for those who had served aboard her.

She read the last line on the plaque aloud. "'To boldly go where no man has gone before.'"

"They're going to change that," Kirk said. "On the next one."

Half-built in spacedock. Assigned to Captain Harriman, not Kirk.

The way it should be.

Teilani held the plaque to her heart. He could barely hear her when she spoke. "I'm going to miss you."

"The price we pay," Kirk said gently. "For loving what we cannot keep forever."

Teilani's eyes shone with unshed tears. "Do you love me?"

Kirk kissed her cheek. "Yes," he said.

"Then don't leave."

Kirk held her. He had always known this moment would come. Even when his heart had dared dream of eternal youth, his mind had known that nothing truly lasted forever.

The knowledge of death was the price to be paid for the knowledge of being alive.

"Chal needs you," Kirk said. "There'll be a Federation task force here within the month. They'll work with you. Advise you. Help you do all that you must to make this world your own."

"Where do you belong, James?"

He tapped his finger on the plaque.

"A long time ago, Drake told me to keep this for my grandchildren. A piece of the *Enterprise* to hang over the fireplace."

Kirk stood. He still had far to go.

He touched her hair again. Shining waves. Remembered their silk cascading around him.

"When you have children," he said, "tell them about the *Enterprise.* And her crew. To keep us alive here. Forever young."

She could hold her tears no longer.

They ran from her face to the plaque she held to her heart.

"I promise," she said.

Kirk gave her hand a final squeeze, a final sensation, a final memory to keep in his heart.

And then Kirk let go the dream, turned away, continued his journey.

Alone.

Teilani watched Kirk as he walked away from her. From her life. From her world.

The long shadows of the setting suns made his footsteps in the sand deep and dark, unmistakable.

The stars above began to flicker in the twilight, as if guiding his way.

Teilani watched as Kirk dissolved into glittering light, reclaimed by those stars, until only his footsteps remained.

Though she knew she would never recapture what she had lost this day, she felt the change Kirk had wrought within her. So her tears were tempered with happiness, for she knew a part of him would always be with her on Chal.

As she left the beach, returning to her home, Teilani knew exactly where she would hang the plaque.

And in the years to come, she knew she would sit by the fire, beneath that plaque, to tell the story of the ship called *Enterprise.*

And her crew.

And her captain.

Who would live in her heart, forever.

FORTY-SIX

From his stateroom on the *Excelsior,* Kirk watched the stars streak past him. He never tired of the sight.

Spock and McCoy stood beside him.

He watched their reflections in the viewport.

As always, they were as entranced as he was.

"After the investigations are completed, Starfleet will require a new commander in chief," Spock said.

Kirk couldn't help himself. He laughed.

"I do not think laughter is an appropriate response. You are a logical choice."

Kirk turned to his friends. "Spock, I don't want you even suggesting it."

McCoy pursed his lips. "And why's that? Because it's a job for a younger man?"

"No, Bones—because it's a job for a different man." Kirk patted McCoy's shoulder. "Who knows? Maybe I'll take up with another 'inappropriate' companion and head off to Andromeda."

McCoy frowned, looked at Spock. "Do you suppose he's ever going to let us forget that fight?"

"It was not a fight, Doctor. It was a difference of opinion.

We have had them in the past and will undoubtedly have them in the future."

Kirk raised a cautionary finger. "Ah, but it was a *legitimate* difference of opinion."

Spock raised a skeptical eyebrow. "Hardly, Captain. As Dr. McCoy and I had surmised, your relationship with the young woman did not last."

"Spock, *nothing* lasts. That's what makes everything . . . so precious."

McCoy looked bemused. "I might know an exception to that nothing lasting forever business."

Kirk and Spock waited expectantly.

"Did you know some hotshots at the Academy have programmed your missions into their holographic simulators?"

Kirk didn't react. "I, uh, might have heard something about that. What's your point, Doctor?"

"My point? Dear Lord, Jim—you've been digitized, rerecorded, and holographically enhanced. Cadets will probably be watching you and your adventures for the next hundred years."

Kirk looked back to the stars. "You know, a month ago, before Chal and Teilani, when I didn't know where I was going in what remains of my life, I think I would have resented that kind of attention."

"And now?" Spock asked.

"Now," Kirk said, "I only hope they enjoy those adventures as much as I did."

McCoy nodded sagely. Spock looked confused.

All was as it should be.

Kirk smiled at the sight of the three of them standing together, reflected against the stars. Bound by a friendship that surpassed all the years and all the adventures. Still boldly going long after they had all thought their mission had ended.

No one could have predicted the adventures that had

brought them to this point. No one could predict the adventures that still awaited them.

But whatever the universe had in store for him next, for however long his own journey continued, Kirk knew at last he was ready to face it.

Forever young.

EPILOGUE

☆

Night had fallen, and the stars encompassed all the sky of Veridian III.

Some among them had watched over a child named Kirk, on a farm in Iowa on Earth. Others had watched over a child named Spock, on a mountain villa near the Plains of Gol on Vulcan. Together, they watched over Veridian III tonight.

Spock spoke softly to those stars now.

"I am now, and will always be, your friend."

There was no logic to saying those words aloud.

But it felt *right.*

"Good-bye, Jim."

An era had ended.

It was time for Spock to move on with his own journey.

He glanced down the slope. The honor guard still stood by Kirk's grave, almost imperceptible in the moonless night.

Then Spock's ears heard the faint chirp of a communicator badge. Riker spoke, his words indistinct on the night air.

The starship that was to transport Kirk's remains was overdue. No doubt, Spock concluded, Riker was receiving an update.

Spock's communicator vibrated silently against his wrist.

"Spock here."

It was Riker. His voice betrayed his emotions. "Ambassador, there appears to be some trouble at the salvage site. I'm going to have to ask you to remain here while we beam back to check the situation."

"Of course, Commander," Spock agreed. "What is the nature of the trouble?"

"I'm not sure," Riker replied. "It almost sounds as if they're . . . under attack."

The area around Kirk's grave lit up as Riker and the honor guard were beamed away.

Spock was intrigued.

He glanced up at the stars, calculating the likely position of ships in standard orbits.

A few stars in that ecliptic moved. Streaks of multicolored energy discharged between them.

Starships in orbital battle.

"Fascinating," Spock said.

But except for the moving lights in the sky, the night remained silent and still.

Spock found a place to sit on a nearby rock, the better to preserve his strength. He rearranged his robes, the better to conserve his body heat.

The battle in space still raged above him.

As his eyes adapted to the distant discharges, he could identify the distinctive blue signature of Starfleet phasers.

But the return fire was unidentifiable. He had never seen its like before.

The situation presented an interesting set of problems. In his mind, Spock began to deconstruct them as a series of logical arguments, attempting to identify likely attackers, their motives, tactics, and probable odds of success.

But he was interrupted in his calculations.

The night air thrummed. Something large was approaching through the sky.

Spock rose to his feet. He scanned the dark horizon, trying to identify any occultation of stars that would indicate the presence of a flying craft operating without running lights.

The thrumming increased.

He could see nothing, but his robes began to swirl around him, blown about by some kind of backwash.

Spock raised his hand to shield his eyes from a rising whirlwind of dust.

Directly above him, the stars wavered, and then were blacked out by a silhouette of something he couldn't identify.

A sudden light danced at the edge of his vision.

He looked down the slope toward Kirk's grave.

Amber rays spiked out from between the rocks of the simple cairn.

Above the thrumming and the wind, Spock heard an oddly musical chime.

The light emanating from Kirk's grave brightened, then began to fade. Spock clearly heard the sounds of rocks falling against themselves.

The logic of this situation was inescapable, yet made no sense.

Among the stars, the signs of a space battle had ended.

Above Spock, the watching stars returned and the thrumming backwash vanished as suddenly as if a ship had gone to warp.

Spock drew an emergency light from his belt and made his way down the slope to Kirk's grave.

He played the light across the cairn.

The rocks had *fallen in.*

The grave was empty.

Spock looked to the stars.

"Jim . . .?" he said.

It was not at all logical, but for a moment, a most improbable thought came to him—

Perhaps some journeys were never meant to end.

There were always *possibilities. . . .*